THE ONLY CHILD

THE ONLY CHILD

KAYTE NUNN

W**O**RLDWIDE

TORONTO • NEW YORK • LONDON
AMSTERDAM • PARIS • SYDNEY • HAMBURG
STOCKHOLM • ATHENS • TOKYO • MILAN
MADRID • WARSAW • BUDAPEST • AUCKLAND

WORLDWIDE™

Recycling programs for this product may not exist in your area.

ISBN-13: 978-1-335-00836-7

The Only Child

First published in 2022 by Scarlet, an imprint of Penzler Publishers. This edition published in 2023.

Copyright © 2022 by Kayte Nunn

All rights reserved. No part of this book may be reproduced or transmitted in any form or by any means, electronic or mechanical, including photocopying, recording or by any information storage and retrieval system, without permission in writing from the publisher.

This is a work of fiction. Names, characters, places and incidents are either the product of the author's imagination or are used fictitiously. Any resemblance to actual persons, living or dead, businesses, companies, events or locales is entirely coincidental.

For questions and comments about the quality of this book, please contact us at CustomerService@Harlequin.com.

TM is a trademark of Harlequin Enterprises ULC.

Harlequin Enterprises ULC
22 Adelaide St. West, 41st Floor
Toronto, Ontario M5H 4E3, Canada
www.ReaderService.com

Printed in U.S.A.

PROLOGUE

THE WOMAN CHOOSES the spot deliberately, set against a wall, where nettles grow waist-high in the warmer months. It's softer here, mostly sand, and boggy in spring, but even with snow whitening the ground she can slice her shovel into the earth. It is an effort, but she is strong; they all are, for the work in the laundry and outdoors is hard, and muscles emerge ropy and lean after only a few months. Though she wears gloves now, the skin on her palms is callused and speckled with splinters, further proof of her labors.

She works by the light of a kerosene lamp, shadows chasing her movements, making her seem larger than life. She pushes the shovel into the frozen ground, all her weight behind it, the scrape muffled by the drifts of snow. There is a grim satisfaction, pride even (though that is a sin), in a job well done, the sides of the hole neat, squared off. It is important that it is deep, though it doesn't have to be large, for what is to be buried is little bigger than a bag of sugar.

She is doing God's work, and what greater glory is there than that? Helping these sinful girls, sheltering them, when no one else will. Their families certainly don't want them, not after what they've done, the shame they've brought on themselves and their kin. These girls have sinned in the worst possible way; how could there not be a seed of evil in each of them? It is her responsibility, her *calling*, to rid them of it, just as they are relieved of the results of their sin, their babies given to righteous, *Catholic*, couples.

As she once paid for her sins, so, too, should these girls.

Most are young, afraid, full of remorse so great that they cry into their pillows when they think everyone else is asleep. She's heard them all, felt an answering leap of satisfaction at their distress. Some will come back a second and even a third time, the stain on their souls too deep to be cleansed. These have the mark of the devil himself on them. They are past saving, though she is not supposed to think that. When such evil thoughts arise, she scourges herself in penance. She welcomes the pain, whipping the tender skin of her thighs until she is spent, cleansed, euphoric even.

She nudges the package at her feet. This is the spawn of one of the smallest of them all, one whose belly had grown as round as a prize-winning watermelon. The baby had failed to thrive. There wasn't time for a baptism; nor to register the birth.

It is the bitterest winter, the water pipes to the house have frozen, the shoreline is iced over. With Mother Superior in the city, the island cut off by a blizzard, it has fallen to her to take care of things. She prayed to Mary, her knees bruised by the cold chapel floor, until she received an answer.

She discards her gloves and retrieves a cigarette case from the pocket of her habit. It rattles as she does so for it contains a silver coin. She'd seen her grandmother do that when laying out the dead. She'd taken the quarter—shiny and new—from the cash box in Mother Superior's office, reckoning it wouldn't be missed. She bends, gathering the bundle in her arms in an unwitting parody of a nursing mother, and tucking the case among the folds of linen.

She lowers the package to the bottom of the hole, shovels earth over the top until it is level, jumps up and down three times on the spot to flatten it. More snow is coming, and by the time the sun rises, any evidence of her work will be hidden.

She pauses, crosses herself briefly, picks up the lantern, gloves forgotten, and hurries back to the house.

It is a sorry business.

ONE

Puget Sound, 2013

FRANKIE GRAY HAD been at Fairmile for exactly three weeks when the first body was discovered. Early one rainy day (when wasn't it in the Pacific Northwest?) she headed out with the dog, jogging along the track that led to Huntley's Point. The air smelled of pine and rich, damp undergrowth, and she lifted her face, delighting in the feeling of rain mingling with the sweat on her skin. She didn't care in the slightest that her hair was wet through and would likely be a ball of frizz once it dried. She was in an anticipatory mood (the very best kind) and didn't even mind that the water had snaked its way under her collar, rapidly soaking her back. Her stomach flipped with excitement and nerves as the words *Izzy's coming tomorrow, Izzy's coming tomorrow* sang in time with her footfalls.

Scruff, whose thick coat quickly flattened in the downpour, resisted the pull of the leash, but Frankie ran faster, her thoughts turning to the day ahead, the grimy windows to wash, baseboards that needed priming, elusive plumbers to chase, a room to get ready.

As they approached the marina, Scruff stopped dead in his tracks. "All right, all right." Her voice sharpened in exasperation, though she knew he wasn't to blame.

It had been her idea to come out on such an unpromising morning.

They had reached a bridge, a rickety thing that visitors called quaint, the islanders an accident waiting to happen, with good reason as it turned out. A gaudy display of silk and plastic flowers had been taped to a post. Below them sat a waterlogged pink teddy bear, a mass of handwritten cards, their ink inscriptions smudged beyond legibility by the weather, a collection of spent candles in glass jars, a Mariners baseball cap, and a crudely made cross with the name *Jesse* burned into the wood.

She'd heard about the accident. It happened the day before she arrived, and her mom had been full of the news. A teenage driver who'd had her license barely a month took the corner too fast, ending up in the water. "They think drugs were involved," her mother said, pursing her lips. "What a waste."

"Literally speeding," Frankie deadpanned in response, earning a sharp look from her mom.

She bent down; her eye caught by a small photograph. A University of Washington sweatshirt, long, blonde, straight hair, perfect skin, a pout for the camera. This girl's family would be forever shattered; her mother and father, possibly brothers and sisters too, all facing a gaping hole in their lives.

Scruff was whining, the whites of his eyes showing. "Come on buddy, let's go," Frankie said, breaking into a halting jog. Her right leg still gave the occasional twinge, particularly in rainy weather, and it was a few strides before her gait evened out again.

When she reached the auto shop where she'd left her mom's truck for repairs the day before, she settled the

bill and splashed over to the truck, blinking away the
raindrops that gathered on her eyelashes.

Grateful for her foresight in stashing an old towel
in there (a habit borne more from impromptu ocean
swims than sudden downpours), she stood back to let
the dog scramble in the passenger door and wiped the
rain from her face.

It was less than a fifteen-minute trip back to Fairmile
by road, the last few miles along a dirt track edged with
towering, old-growth Douglas fir and big-leaf maples.
Frankie's wipers worked double time to clear the driving rain. Flicking on the radio, tuned to the local station, she caught the end of a news report, the body of
an elderly woman found in suspicious circumstances.

The words "suspicious circumstances" were something of a cover-all: they could mean suspicious as in
foul play was involved or, less ominously, medically in-
explicable. When she heard the name Pacifica Gardens,
however, her knuckles whitened on the steering wheel.
Ingrid's nursing home. On the other side of the island.

Frankie briefly considered pulling over, making a
call, but common sense told her the likelihood of the
phone being answered was slim; it would be quicker
to drive there. She scanned the road ahead for a place
to turn, then checked the rearview mirror, ignoring the
automatic impulse to reach for lights and sirens. Some
habits died hard.

Instead, she spun the wheel in a tight arc. The tires
squealed in protest and the truck threatened to fishtail
in the wet, but the treads held, and she was traveling
in the opposite direction, managing to stay within a
hair of the speed limit.

As she drew up at the nursing home, she wasn't

surprised to see a cruiser with a six-pointed gold star and the words "Island County Sheriff" in white letters across its doors. She eased into an empty space between two other vehicles, cracked the back window open for the dog, and cut the engine.

Walking toward the building's entrance, she made herself take the long, calming breaths she was supposed to practice more often, doing her best to ignore the tightness in her chest, the thumping of her heart, an accelerated pace that had begun as soon as she heard the news report.

The island didn't have a local TV crew, which was something to be grateful for, though doubtless several from the city would be on their way before too long. A suspicious death would be a lead item on the nightly news unless something considerably more dramatic took its place.

A young woman—a girl really—with stringy blonde hair and pale skin was hunched on a low wall, sheltered from the rain by the building's eaves, pulling hard on a cigarette. She didn't look up as Frankie strode past.

Frankie made it through the front door before she was stopped.

"No visitors today I'm afraid." June, the receptionist, was an abrasively cheerful woman who enjoyed wielding her tiny measure of power with more relish than was strictly necessary. "I'm not supposed to let anyone in." She turned toward the sounds of muffled voices that were coming from the end of the corridor and Frankie strained her ears, hearing the click and electronic whirr of a camera shutter. "Perhaps try again tomorrow…"

"But…?"

June smiled patronizingly. "Ingrid had a good night, and she's perfectly fine."

The tightness in Frankie's chest released, like a rubber band that had been held taut for too long, and for the first time since the radio report she felt able to take a normal breath. It wasn't likely that her grandmother would have been the victim, but her imagination had gone into overdrive nonetheless.

June seemed as if she wanted to say more but was silenced by the arrival of a harried-looking man in an expensively cut dark suit clutching a folder to his chest. His hair was combed back in two slick wings, and Frankie noticed a tiny bead of blood on his chin where a razor had cut too close.

Frankie had made at least a dozen visits to the home in the short time since she'd arrived on the island and was on nodding terms with nearly all the staff, but she had never seen this man before, she was sure of it.

June knew him though, for she straightened, fussing nervously with the papers in front of her. "Good morning, sir."

The man muttered an indistinct greeting, went around the front desk, and leaned toward June, whispering something in her ear.

He paid little attention to Frankie, and she took advantage of their distraction to check the corridor, craning her neck. She saw a tall shape in a doorway, someone wearing hooded Tyvek coveralls.

Anywhere else and the place would have been in lockdown, guards posted to keep visitors out, but this was an island so sleepy that in the off season it was practically comatose, so she doubted whether they'd even heard of such a thing. She'd guess that cops here

dealt with loud parties, acts of vandalism, traffic viola-
tions, domestic disputes. Very occasionally homicide.
Rarely, if ever, murder.

The single-story building huddled in the lee of a
steep hill, with the better rooms looking across lush
lawns that led to the ocean. It was laid out in an elon-
gated H-shape and housed thirty-five residents, all in
varying degrees of mental and physical disability, bodies and minds worn out by long or hard lives, often
both.

Everyone who lived at Pacifica Gardens had their
own room and small private bathroom, equipped with
handrails and shower chairs, though some needed help
using them. Each had a mechanized single bed and a
high-backed easy chair in their rooms, a dresser on
which to display a lifetime's worth of memories and
store their now diminished possessions. The paintwork
was fresh, the carpet (although a bilious, institutional
color that made Frankie think of split pea soup) new,
and the staff were kind, from what Frankie had seen
on her previous visits at least. Still, there was no dis-
guising the smell of antiseptic and boiled cabbage that
pervaded the hallways.

The man opened the door to the back office, and
after a second June turned to follow him, as if she'd
forgotten to tell him something. Frankie seized her
chance, arguing with a conscience that urged her to
go to her grandmother's room. Losing that battle, she
turned in the other direction, to where she'd seen the
shadowy shape. She reached a kitchenette, a little way
along the corridor, unchallenged, and began to make
a coffee. It would be her excuse if someone saw her.

No one took any notice of Frankie as she paused

before the police tape, cup in hand, steam rising from its surface. The familiar, sickly-sweet smell of death crept toward her, and she held her breath as she scanned the scene. Four people crowded the small room, all in protective suits, one with a camera. A figure knelt at an open briefcase on the floor, neatly ordered sample vials in front of her. Swabs. Paperwork. Another figure, squarely built, possibly female, was turned toward the window, murmuring into a phone.

Unlike Ingrid's room, which was dotted with family photos in mismatched frames, this one was sparsely accessorized, the only personal items a crucifix that hung over the dresser and a framed illustration of the Virgin Mary on the wall opposite.

Something—call it a sixth sense developed from years of this kind of work—made the hairs on the back of Frankie's neck prickle when she saw the bed. A rumpled nightgown, the mottled skin and spider-veined legs of a very old person.

What looked to be garden twine fastening the woman's wrists to the iron bedstead. Solid proof that it wasn't accidental.

Pretty young girls found in dark alleys or lonely parks and middle-aged women bashed by abusive partners died violently…but an elderly woman, in a nursing home? Death was hardly an unusual occurrence in such a place, but not like this.

She stood, one hand on her hip, her favorite posture when she wanted to concentrate. Her other hand gripped the coffee cup, which now had a slight tremor on its surface, ripples on a murky pond. The words "What the…?" began to form on her lips and she had to fight the urge to march in and start asking questions.

"We won't be too much longer, Molly," one of the men said.

"Good." The woman's voice was quiet and Frankie had to strain to hear it. She turned, caught Frankie's gaze, and her aquamarine eyes—so bright she might have been wearing colored contacts—signaled irritation that she should be there.

Frankie retreated, feeling like a ghoulish rubbernecker at the scene of a car accident, and hurried in the other direction. September first. That was the date she'd be official. Until then, she had no business getting involved.

TWO

Puget Sound, 2013

"THIS PLACE SHOULD have been locked down." A voice rang out along the corridor, high and clear as a soprano, as Frankie was about to sail past the reception desk for a second time. "Ms. Gray," June called out, stopping her in her tracks. "I thought I'd made it clear that there were to be no visitors."

"Ingrid's desperate for a coffee," Frankie lied. "No one's been in to see to her yet." It was a calculated guess.

"Then don't be too long," June sighed, waving her along. "Or I'll be in even more trouble."

"That's very kind. I appreciate it—and so will Ingrid," Frankie said, saccharine sweet.

A few yards farther along, she stopped outside a door where an old-fashioned ceramic nameplate circled by yellow primroses had been fixed at eye level. She gave two taps with her knuckle as she turned the handle.

"Who's that?"

The voice was shaky, and Frankie's heart contracted at the sight of the old woman with the faded blue eyes and scrappy, cotton-wool hair. Her grandmother was still in bed, elevated on a thick pile of pillows, blankets rucked up around her feet. It was hot, but then nursing homes always were. Steam had begun to rise from Frankie's rain jacket, and she pulled the zip down a fraction. "It's Frankie, Grandma."

"Hello dear."

Frankie smiled. She was having one of her better days.

"Is it visiting time?" Ingrid looked momentarily confused. "I've not even had breakfast yet. At least I don't think so." She cast around the room as if there might be evidence of a meal.

"I was in the area and thought I'd call in. Surprise you." Another white lie. "I've brought you a coffee. Just how you like it."

"No sugar. I'm sweet enough."

They both smiled at the old joke.

"You've changed your hair," Ingrid said.

Frankie put a hand to her head. "It's been raining."

"No, no." Ingrid's eyes briefly clouded. "You've had it cut. It was so beautiful when it was long. Why did you have to go and spoil it? You look like a boy for goodness's sake. You won't get a husband with hair like that." She looked wistful for a moment, the thread of a memory skating away from her.

Frankie suppressed a grin. "I had one of those and it didn't exactly work out. Besides, it's easier this way." Though she had her mom's hazel-flecked eyes and narrow face, Frankie's hair had been short since she was a teenager. Her mom, Diana, was the one with the Lady Godiva locks. Of course, the brown was now threaded with gray, but the style still suited her. It wasn't the first time her grandmother had mistaken her for her mom.

Diana was at Fairmile, probably wondering by now what had happened to Frankie, but hopefully ignorant of the events at Pacifica Gardens. Frankie decided a call could wait; her mother rarely had her cell phone nearby in any case.

"Where's Emma? She hasn't come in to get me dressed yet." Ingrid began to fret.

"Why don't I give you a hand instead?" Frankie placed the cup on a side table and began to fold back the sheet covering her grandmother's legs, revealing two thin sticks, swollen kneecaps, the bluish purple of long-ago scrapes, dark against her pale skin. She leaned forward and clasped Ingrid under the arms, pulling her toward the edge of the bed, and feeling the insubstantial weight of her body as she did so. A woman who had once been a well-respected college professor, a fierce advocate for women's rights, a force of nature, was now so frail. All Ingrid did these days was sit, unable even to read for long, her mind incapable of retaining the information on the page. It just about broke Frankie's heart.

She helped her grandmother to the bathroom and when she was done, lifted her nightgown over her head and threaded her arms through the sleeves of a flowered blouse that she found in the wardrobe. She was reminded of dressing Izzy like this, when she was little, and had to stop herself from counting the number of buttons out loud as she did them up. "Izzy's arriving tomorrow, Grandma," she said, adjusting the collar until it sat straight. "For the whole summer."

"The little girl?"

"She's not so little anymore."

"That's nice, dear." Ingrid's expression was vague again, and Frankie concluded that she didn't really remember her great-granddaughter.

When Ingrid was dressed (elastic-waisted pants and

a pair of shoes with Velcro fasteners completed her outfit), Frankie guided her toward the chair and then handed her a hairbrush. She went to the washstand and found a facecloth, rinsing it in warm water, and began sponging Ingrid's face. Frankie was gentle, for her grandmother's skin was as fine as tissue paper.

When she had finished, she began to make the bed, folding the blanket under the mattress, the movement, of how to tuck a hospital corner, coming to her instinctively from some long-ago summer job. She'd need that skill again, once they had Fairmile up and running.

"Do you know, I'm sure I heard a commotion earlier." Ingrid looked at Frankie, and then bit her lip, as if she'd said too much.

"You did?"

Ingrid nodded, her expression conspiratorial.

"It was probably nothing." Frankie didn't want to alarm her, not until she found out exactly what had happened. "Beautiful." She took the hairbrush from Ingrid. "Your coffee's right there. I'll find out where breakfast is, but I've got to get on, there's still so much to do before Izzy arrives."

Ingrid leaned against the back of the chair, closing her eyes. The simple effort of getting dressed, even with Frankie's help, had exhausted her. "Thank you, dear."

Now that she was reassured that Ingrid was fine— as fine as could be expected—Frankie was in a hurry to leave. As she closed the door, she saw that the water in a vase of flowers on the dresser had turned cloudy, the greenery limp and slimy.

Frankie pushed her way out into the fresh air. It was sweet after the fug of the nursing home; the rain had stopped. She'd almost forgotten how gentle the light was here, even in summer, for she was accustomed to screwing up her eyes against a harsh Australian sun, never leaving the house without a hat and dark sunglasses.

The young woman who had been sitting on the low wall stood up to stub out another cigarette, grinding it with the toe of her shoe. Frankie counted five scattered on the sidewalk in front of her; she wanted to comment on the fact that there was a perfectly good trash can less than three yards away but held her tongue. The woman appeared to be having a particularly bad day, even this early in the morning, and she didn't have the heart to make it worse.

"You're Emma, aren't you?" she asked, having seen her the week before. Frankie's uncanny talent for remembering faces—she'd once had a reputation among her colleagues as a "super-recognizer"—hadn't deserted her. The girl gave a wan smile and looked up with huge, bloodshot eyes. She was younger than Frankie had first thought, could easily still be in school.

She collapsed back against the wall, looking absolutely terrified.

"I'm Ingrid's granddaughter." Frankie sat down beside her, folding one leg underneath her, forcing a relaxed pose. She waited, hearing birdsong and the faint rumble of passing cars from the road.

"I've seen a dead body before, it's as common as you'd imagine in this job, but I never saw anyone tied up like that." Emma sniffed loudly and tucked a strand of hair behind her ear with a shaking hand. Her nails were bitten almost to the quick.

Frankie remembered her first sight of a murder victim. She'd been twenty-one, a rookie in her first year on the force. The man was sprawled in an alleyway, the skin around his mouth purple, his eyes vacant. Her colleague had radioed it in, while she stood rooted to the spot, unable to move or look away.

"It's okay to be upset, that's a perfectly natural re-action, especially under the circumstances," Frankie said, placing a hand on the girl's shoulder. "Is there anyone I can call for you?"

Emma shook her head. "I can't go back in there."

"No one's asking you to."

"June told me to wait. That one of the deputies would want to talk to me…but I don't know what I can tell them."

"You found her?" Frankie asked, her voice soft-ening.

Emma sniffed again, nodded. "She was new. Came last winter. Bernadette, that's what she asked me to call her, none of this 'Sister' business. She was once a nun you see. I didn't even know they retired; I guess I thought they popped off quietly after mass, mak-ing as little fuss as possible." She gave a thin, high laugh, edged with barely contained hysteria. "She was very quiet, spent most of her time with a rosary in her lap. She didn't deserve this." Tears began to roll down the girl's cheeks and she scrubbed at her face angrily. "What kind of man would do such a thing, and to a re-ligious woman, a good woman, especially?" She shook her head. "It's just *wrong*."

Frankie wasn't as certain as Emma that having a deep religious conviction necessarily made one a "good woman," but the fact that the victim had once been a nun piqued her interest. It certainly accounted for the kitschy Virgin Mother portrait. It was interesting that

Emma assumed that a man was responsible, for there would be plenty of women strong enough to overpower an elderly female. "What time did you get here?" she asked.

"My shift starts at six," said Emma. "And I was on time—early actually. It's so light in the mornings that I can't sleep in."

"Do you come in by the front door?"

"Yes. I'm usually the first one here."

"So, what did you do when you arrived?"

"Why are you so interested?" Emma was suddenly suspicious.

"Sorry. I didn't mean to interrogate you. I want to understand how something like this could have happened; to make sure that Ingrid, or any of the other residents for that matter, isn't in any danger."

"We always lock up—there are other doors, at the end of each wing, and one at the back near the kitchens. I had no reason to believe they weren't locked, but I didn't check them all."

"It's okay, you don't need to justify yourself," Frankie said. "Go on."

Emma sniffed loudly again and wiped her nose on the back of her hand. "I did a quick handover with Angela—she was on night duty, and she's always in a rush to get home to her kids at the end of her shift—put my things in my locker and then went into each of the rooms to check on the residents. I'm not required to do that, but I like to when I first arrive. That's when I got to Bernadette's room."

"Was her door open?"

Emma looked uncertain. "I can't remember. I don't think so."

Frankie pressed her fingers to her temples and reminded herself again that she didn't need to get involved. "It's all right, it's probably not important."

"Emma Riley?" There was a crackle of static from a walkie-talkie. A young, uniformed deputy loomed in front of them.

"Yes?" Emma stood up, her movements stiff.

"Would you mind coming with me? We have a few questions."

Emma glanced at Frankie for reassurance.

"And you are?" the deputy asked.

"My grandmother lives here."

"No visitors allowed today I'm afraid."

"So I understand."

As Frankie was leaving, she saw an SUV pull up and a middle-aged man in a red waterproof jacket, tan docksider shoes, and a baseball cap (the preferred island uniform for locals and visitors alike) emerge and walk toward the main entrance with the rolling gait of someone who might spend more time on the water than on land. She briefly caught his expression—anxious, a frown creasing his forehead—and decided that he, too, must have heard the news.

She reached the truck, noticing that it seemed to be leaning to one side. Damn it. One of the tires was flat as a bum note. She bent down and checked. There was no pressure cap on the valve. Cursing the auto shop, she went to the trunk and hauled out the jack and the spare.

THREE

Bend, Oregon, 1949

"WHORE."

The girl's father raised his hand and struck her across the cheek. Spittle flew from the corner of her mouth as she reeled at the force of the blow, her teeth fairly rattled loose in their sockets. Head turned, she saw her mother cowering against the kitchen wall near the back door, half in, half out, as if she didn't know whether to leave or stay. Her mother didn't make a sound, one hand pressed to her mouth in case a word of protest should slip out. Daniel Ryan was the head of the family and no one, not even his son, Sam, who stood almost a head taller than his father, would have questioned anything he did. Not to his face anyway.

It had come to light in the most mundane of ways—Una Ryan had gone to her daughter's room with a new supply of sanitary napkins only to find that the ones she had placed there three months earlier were still untouched. When the girl arrived home from school, she'd gone upstairs and found the package on her bed, the drawer left open.

"Who is he?" her father looked as though he wanted to rip a piece right out of her. The ugly, sinful piece.

The girl ran her tongue over her lip, probing the

tender swelling. "No one." Her voice barely a whisper. She willed herself not to cry.

"Say the bastard's name or I won't answer for the consequences."

Her lips wouldn't form the words.

"Leave her be now, Danny." Una Ryan finally spoke. "I'll talk to her."

Daniel looked from his daughter to his wife as if he didn't like what he saw in either of them, making a noise in his throat that sounded caught between frustration and fury. He stalked from the room, pushing past his wife and slamming the back door behind him.

As soon as he'd left, the girl collapsed onto a chair, her forearms resting on the smooth blue of the Formica table, her body wracked by silent sobs.

"What have you done?" Her mother's words were as cold as the new Frigidaire that hulked in the corner of the kitchen.

"I didn't... I didn't mean for..."

"You were raised to be better than this. *I* raised you to be better than this."

"I'm sorry," she sobbed, loudly this time. "I'm so, so sorry."

"Have you any idea of the shame you've brought on this family?"

The soft sound of her mother crying caused the girl to lift her head.

"Don't you see," her mother said, sniffing and dabbing her handkerchief to her face. "*I've* failed. It was my job to bring you up to be a nice girl, to make someone a good wife someday. To make sure that something like this didn't happen to you."

THE GIRL WAS a pretty sixteen-year-old sophomore at Bend High, a conscientious student, with a thick brown ponytail, cat's-eye glasses, and a straight-A academic record. She loved to read, get ice cream from Goody's, and share popcorn with her friends at the movies.

Bend, Oregon, in 1949 didn't exactly offer much in the way of sophisticated entertainment, but the Tower Theatre on Wall Street transported the townspeople into a glamorous world of adventure, mystery, intrigue, and love. That year the girl wanted to be Hedy Lamarr in *Let's Live a Little*, or Katharine Hepburn in *State of the Union* with Spencer Tracy as her beau.

One clear April afternoon, she arrived at the cinema early, having arranged to meet her friends for the Saturday matinee. The snow had finally melted, the cherry trees were a mass of pink, and bright heads of crocuses had pushed their way up through cracks in the sidewalk. Everywhere there was a feeling of possibility for the new season, a change in the air that made her unaccountably restless.

As the girl lingered in the nearly empty foyer, she noticed an unfamiliar man exiting the projection booth.

"What happened to Jimmy?" she asked. The projectionist had been at the Tower for as long as she could remember. When she was little, he'd always offered her Life Savers; he knew watermelon was her favorite.

"No idea I'm afraid. I only started this week."

She snuck a glance at the stranger, noticing neatly combed, coal-black hair, thickly fringed eyelashes, and a flash of white teeth. He was as handsome as a movie star. She guessed he must be in his late twenties, a far cry from the pimple-faced boys in class, the ones whose Adam's apples bobbed nervously every time they spoke and whose voices still occasionally squeaked when they least expected it.

The next week she deliberately arrived early. She saw the new projectionist again and was rewarded with a smile of recognition, which she returned, lowering her eyes flirtatiously. If her father caught her behaving like this she'd be grounded for the rest of the year, but she couldn't help herself, drawn to the man who gave off the irresistible whiff of Hollywood as surely as if it was cologne.

The week after that, she arrived early again, drenched in her mother's *Je Reviens* (dabbed everywhere you wanted to be kissed, she remembered hearing somewhere), and he offered to show her how he changed a reel, to explain the mysteries of the cine projector.

It was as if they existed outside of the usual rules. Every minute spent in that dim, dusty room seemed to be sprinkled with the magic of celluloid. She didn't tell her friends, not Joan Greenbaum, whom she'd known since first grade and who lived on the next street over, nor her best friend Cindy Olssen, whom she sat next to in English and Math.

Of course, her parents didn't have a clue.

One Saturday, Robert—for that was his name, not Bobby or Bob, but Robert (like Robert Mitchum, he said, not entirely joking)—loosened the collar of his shirt, raked the hair that fell over his forehead, and asked her if she wasn't also too hot. The girl lowered her eyes to her candy-striped shirtdress and agreed that it was quite warm. She'd been aware of the heat rising between them in the confines of the tiny, windowless room. Heat that had as much to do with her growing attraction as it had the weather. They'd kissed before.

Several times. Encounters that left her breathless, trembling, wanting more.

Gazing into his dark blue eyes, she felt as though she might fall right into them. "Can you think of a way we might cool off?" she asked, shocked at her daring. She hooked a finger through the top button of her dress, pulled it undone to reveal the white lace of her underthings, not quite believing what she was doing.

Robert groaned and crossed the short distance between them. He nuzzled her neck, her earlobes, pushed her blouse aside, and kissed her where her collarbones stood out. He tugged at the delicate strap of her new brassiere, tearing it in his haste to undress her. As he buried his face between her breasts, she nearly died with the romance of it all and pressed herself against him, urging him on.

Afterward, it didn't feel so romantic. A soreness, a wetness, and the beginnings of shame that she'd been so easy, that she'd wanted it as much as he had. She prayed he wouldn't tell. No one, not even Cindy, could know.

"I'd better get going. Before anyone misses me." The girl fumbled at her buttons; one had torn off, skittering unnoticed onto the floor.

"You're swell, you know that." It wasn't much as compliments went, but she clung to it anyway. He tucked in his shirttails, buttoned his fly, then came toward her and cupped her face in his hands, his eyes searching hers. He lowered his head and kissed her and once more it felt exactly like a scene from a movie.

They did it again a few days later, and this time it was better.

That summer, while her friends were at the lake,

lounging on the dock that was anchored in the middle of the deep water with the sun soaking into their bare skin, she was experiencing a different kind of pleasure.

THE CHANGE OF season took her by surprise. One day the girl was fanning herself with her pocketbook and wiping the perspiration from the back of her neck, the next, there was a crispness in the air and the leaves were beginning to turn from green to amber and crimson. A week before the start of school, she returned to the Tower, placed her hand on the door to the projection room and was on the point of turning the handle, when a cough behind her caused her to freeze.

"You won't find him there."

It was the manager, a man who didn't generally work Saturdays.

She froze. "I, er…"

"Mr. Mitchell has gone back to Portland."

"Oh." She turned around. "Did he leave an address? A phone number? He… He lent me a book. I should like to return it." It was the first excuse she could think of.

"I believe he was missing his wife and children," he said pointedly.

In that instant the girl knew exactly what she'd been to him. To the man with the movie-star good looks whose last name he'd never bothered to tell her. She felt as soiled as a used handkerchief.

She stumbled out of the theater and along Wall Street, her head down, holding her breath almost the entire walk home. She went around to the back door, praying that her parents would be out, raced up the stairs to her room, and flung herself on her bed, the sobs that she'd been holding in finally let loose.

He'd never said. Never worn a ring.

How stupid she had been to imagine he liked her, that what they'd had was more. More than what, exactly? She hated him in that moment, hated herself harder.

Years later, her stomach would still clench at the smell of buttered popcorn.

FOR THE FIRST few weeks of school, it felt like nothing had changed. She and Cindy and Joan spent recesses huddled on the bleachers, sharing lunch and watching the track team train. Cindy looked on with more enthusiasm than the other two, it had to be said, for she had an unrequited crush on one of the seniors, a long jump record-holder with a shock of white-blonde hair and a confident swagger.

"Want this?" the girl held out her carton of chocolate milk to Cindy. The drink didn't hold its usual appeal.

"You sure?"

"Uh-huh. Go on, take it."

"You feeling okay? You've had chocolate milk for lunch every day since I can't remember when," said Joan.

The girl shrugged. "Perhaps I'm growing out of it."

Cindy gave her a sideways look, but took it anyway, pressing the top of the carton open and tipping her head back to drink from it.

The girl hadn't been feeling like herself for a few months. Then, on Halloween, when she'd tried on her costume from the year before (she always took her little twin sisters around the neighborhood, trawling for candy), it wouldn't zip up. Her mother had reassured her that she was still growing, but the girl knew better. Actually, she'd known for a while. She'd already had to let her skirts out, even the ones that earlier in the year had been cinched with a belt.

One afternoon, taking advantage of an empty house, she examined herself in the long mirror in the hall-way, lifting her blouse and seeing the thickening of her waist, the bluish veins in her breasts. Her period had never been regular, but when she consulted her pocket diary, where she kept a record of such things, she saw that the last time she'd placed a dot next to the date was back at the beginning of May.

For someone who was so smart, how could she have found herself in this position? She knew exactly what happened to other girls who got themselves in trouble. They disappeared, visiting an aunt or a cousin, so their mothers said, but everyone knew that they'd really been sent away for fear of bringing shame on their family.

They almost always came back, some even returned to school, pretending nothing unusual had happened, though whispers swirled around them and most of their classmates knew that they were damaged goods.

Some never returned, and until then she hadn't both-ered to wonder what became of them.

The girl gazed at herself for a long while as the ir-refutable fact of it finally sank in, then lowered her blouse and ran to her bedroom. She lay on the pink flowered bedspread and stared at the ceiling, and imag-ined the faintest movement in her belly, like a fish swimming against the tide.

WHEN HE RETURNED, the girl's father sent the other chil-dren out into the yard. "But it's freezing," one of her sisters protested.

"Get your coats," was all her mother could say, shooting a warning at her son.

Grumbling, they scooted down the steps onto the back porch.

"Who is he?" Her father could hardly stand to look at her.

"No one."

"Unless we're talking about the immaculate conception, I think you'll find it *was* someone," he said, his face flushed.

"Come on, dear," said her mother, blinking red-rimmed eyes. "If you tell us, we can try and work something out. Talk to the boy's parents."

The girl shook her head. "It wasn't…it wasn't a boy."

"Unless you start talking sensibly young lady, there's gonna be all kinds of trouble." Her father stood up and walked over to her, but her mother hovered closer, a protective hand on her daughter's shoulder.

The girl squeezed her eyes tight shut and her whole body began to shake. How could she tell them about Robert? She was all those awful words her father had called her, and more. She'd never dreamed that she would disappoint them like this. She had come first in the Bend Elementary spelling bee three years straight, won the deportment prize, the math award, been the girl whose teachers always said they wished they had a class full of students like her. How could she have given in to such base desires, let her heart rule her head? How could she have been so stupid?

Her cheeks burned, as the silence seemed to stretch on forever.

"She's not going to tell us. And you will not beat it out of her." Her mother's face was set; the lines between her eyebrows and across her forehead had deepened since she'd found out about her daughter's predicament. "We will have to go and see Father Anthony."

The girl opened her eyes. "Whatever for?"

Her mother shook her head. "I thought you were smart, but honestly, I'm beginning to wonder. Father Anthony will know what to do about...about your little problem." Her mother still hadn't referred to the baby her daughter was carrying in any other terms.

"Okay." She was a good girl; she would show them she was. She'd been brought up to be polite, amenable, helpful, respectful. She would do as she was told.

FOUR

Puget Sound, 2013

"Surely not?" Diana sounded less concerned than Frankie would have expected when she told her the news, though her paintbrush hovered, midstroke, over the wall for several seconds.

"Never been more serious I'm afraid." Frankie explained what she'd seen, including the bound hands.

She had found her mother in one of the upstairs bedrooms at Fairmile, at the top of a ladder, her long hair covered by a scarf, and wearing the paint-stained blue overalls and work boots that were her current uniform. Diana's favorite "Yacht Rock" playlist echoed through the empty rooms, The Doobie Brothers crooning "Little Darling." The song telescoped Frankie right back to her childhood, to a wooden house with a wide porch. To her mother painting her bedroom walls the color of sunshine and to her dad coming home from work, shaking his head and smiling at another of his wife's sudden whims. She wished he had lived long enough to see all this.

"Do you think it might have been someone on staff?" Diana began to sweep her brush across the wall again, then paused, thinking. "We don't need to move her, do we?"

Her reaction seemed forced, almost as if she was overplaying it.

Frankie shook her head. "I thought you might ask that. Don't do anything hasty, not until we know more. After all, there aren't exactly many other options."

She and her mom had a couple of snatched long-distance phone calls between Sydney and Seattle six months ago when it had become obvious to Diana that Ingrid's failing memory meant that a move from her house in the city to assisted living had become a matter of some urgency.

Frankie remembered her mother's complaints about how difficult it had been to find somewhere that Ingrid would be happy. Pacifica Gardens was the only facility on the island, and it was a popular place, with a waitlist. "I want to be able to visit her regularly, even if she doesn't always remember me," Diana had said. "I owe her so much."

It seemed an odd way of putting it.

Frankie surveyed the room. "Looking good, Mom." Diana had a knack for seeing the possibilities in the unloveliest of items, drawing out their beauty, or transforming them completely. Frankie sometimes wished she'd inherited the trait.

Built in 1908 by the commodore of the Seattle Yacht Club so that he could watch the sailboat races around the island, Fairmile was a ten-bedroom Georgian-style clapboard mansion set on sixteen acres. It had a wide back porch that overlooked Puget Sound and caught the morning sun. Inside, there were soaring ceilings, generously proportioned rooms, and acres of wood paneling all, from what Frankie had seen from photos taken when her mother bought the house nearly a year ago, in a state of dilapidation so bad that Frankie was surprised the place hadn't been condemned. Gardens—at present a tangle of brambles and weeds—stretched down to the water, where a wooden jetty invited swimming in the summer months. In winter, ice crept out from the shoreline and a heavy snowfall could mean that the house was cut off, sometimes for days on end.

Her mom had got it on the cheap—Fairmile had been vacant for decades, visited only by kids intent on vandalism or making out, scaring themselves and their dates stupid with ghost stories of an abandoned house—but Frankie had no idea how much it was costing to bring it back to life, to realize Diana's goal of reimagining it as a luxury inn.

"Who would *do* such a thing?" Diana shook her head, the idea completely foreign to her, but something about her disbelief didn't quite ring true. Frankie could have sworn that her mom had already heard the news. She dismissed the thought; she was overly suspicious at the best of times.

"What time is Izzy's flight due in?" Diana asked, changing the subject as she descended the ladder and dipped her brush into a jar of turpentine.

Frankie didn't have to look it up; she'd committed the flight details to memory as soon as she had learned them. "Three. I'll leave after lunch. Even with traffic that should be plenty of time. I'm not sure what she'll make of being here though."

"Izzy can help me," said Diana, wiping her brush on a stained rag that hung from her pocket and flashing an optimistic smile.

"I think she'd planned on spending her vacation

surfing at Bondi Beach, not in the rain-soaked Pacific Northwest in a decrepit old house," Frankie teased.

"Hey!" said Diana, frowning. "Less of the decrepit if you don't mind. I'm restoring a grand old dame to her former glory, just you wait. Anyway, she'll be pleased to see you."

"Will she?" Frankie tried not to let herself hope for too much.

LATER THAT AFTERNOON, as Frankie was beginning to worry that Izzy's flight might be locked in a holding pattern, circling Sea-Tac Airport for all eternity, she saw the display flicker and the "landed" notice appear next to the American Airlines arrival from LA. Less than ten minutes later, disembarking passengers began to stream into the arrivals lounge where they were swept up by waiting family and friends, into cars, limos, Ubers, and taxis. She scanned the scene for a girl with dark curly hair, wide-set hazel eyes, and a scattering of freckles across the bridge of her nose, straining to see over the crowd.

"Hey!"

The voice came from somewhere to her left, bringing a sudden welling in Frankie's eyes, a tightness in her throat.

It had been almost five years since she had lived with her daughter. When she'd decided it was best for Izzy to be with her dad, there had seemed to be enough time. Enough time for her to take a job overseas (it was a smart career move, she had justified to herself) for six months and then come back and be a full-time mom again. But six months had turned to a year, then to three, then almost five, before it dawned on her that time was bolting away from her like an unbroken horse.

She'd seen Izzy every summer, flying to LA and last year meeting her partway in Hawaii. Sure, they'd had incredible adventures—gone whitewater rafting in Oregon, hiking in the Cascades, swimming with manta rays on the Big Island of Hawai'i—but a couple weeks once a year wasn't enough. They needed time to just be, to do the everyday mother and daughter stuff, for Frankie to take care of the normal, boring things like dental appointments, signing permission slips, unpacking groceries together, cooking a meal, going for a drive, after-school milkshake treats, arguing about a messy room and curfews... Frankie would *never* tell Izzy, but she and Lucas hadn't exactly planned on becoming parents as soon as they did, and, once upon a time, the idea of being a suburban mom would have had her reaching for the tequila and heading down the highway leaving a cloud of dust in her wake. Now, however, it seemed far more appealing.

Frankie whirled around and at first didn't believe what she was seeing. In place of her cherubic girl was a teenager with the delicate build and poise of a dancer, eyes on a level with hers, hair straightened and shot through with purple streaks, a silver nose ring glinting in the stark airport lighting.

She'd become a completely different person, on the outside at least, in the space of less than a year.

"Izzy?" Frankie had to make a deliberate effort to close her jaw, which had unhinged in surprise.

"Last time I checked, Frankie."

Izzy had stopped calling her "Mom" some time last

year, and Frankie had let it slide, not wanting to rock an already unsteady boat.

"I hardly recognized you. Come here." She opened her arms, stepped forward, and Izzy allowed herself to be hugged. Her smell, at least, was familiar: Pantene shampoo and grape Hubba Bubba. "Wow, look at you. So grown up. I like your hair—is it new?" Frankie pulled back and inspected her daughter's face. Her eyes and voice were the same, but so much else had changed.

"Yeah, I just got it done." Izzy tucked a strand behind one ear self-consciously.

"Good flight?"

She shrugged as if she was unimpressed by the novelty of air travel and rubbed at a smudge of mascara underneath her eye. Suddenly, she didn't look so old, despite the cropped T-shirt and distressed jeans, and Frankie had to swallow hard to dislodge the lump that was blocking her throat.

"Traveling light?" The suitcase at her daughter's side didn't seem capable of holding enough for an eight-week stay.

"Uh-huh."

"Okay then, let's try and beat the traffic."

"Where are we going again? Granny told me her place is called Fairmile, but I didn't exactly get the chance to look at a map before I left." Izzy's stride easily matched her mother's.

"It's less than two hours from here. Orcades Island. The house is on the water. You can swim right off the jetty."

Frankie had spent the morning getting Izzy's room ready, up on the top floor under the eaves. She'd bought flowered sheets and a soft eiderdown for an antique

sleigh bed that Diana had found, adding a side table
and a lamp. She'd even dug out an old comfort toy, a
once-pink sheepskin bear called Coco that had been
Izzy's when she was little. She worried now that it
might all be a bit young for her. "I'm afraid the place
is still a mess. Granny hasn't gotten as far with it as I
expected. When I arrived, the kitchen hadn't even been
installed. She'd been cooking on an old butane stove
for months and had no heating except for an open fire
all winter." Frankie chattered away, hiding the shock of
finding Izzy suddenly so grown up. She'd been looking forward to this moment for months, but now that
it had arrived, she was at a loss to know exactly how
to be with her daughter. Why hadn't she paid more attention when all those smug people warned *blink and
you'll miss it*?

Complicated emotions churned inside Frankie: relief
that Izzy was finally there, grief that she'd missed so
much, anger at herself for being the only one to blame
for that. She felt like she might need to sit down for a
second and get her bearings again.

"You okay?" Izzy regarded her curiously.

"Sure." She reached in her purse for the parking
stub as they approached the truck. A few minutes later,
they joined the line of traffic heading out of the parking deck.

"I still don't understand why you couldn't stay in
Sydney," said Izzy, her cheek pressed to the window, a
tiny pout on her lips. "I really wanted to come and see
you there. You said that this year I could."

"I know, I'm sorry, darling; I wanted you to as well.
Anyway, it's not as far to come here, is it?" Frankie
flicked on the turn signal to move onto the freeway

traffic and did her best to keep her voice bright. "There are some wonderful hikes on the island. We can picnic, swim, hang out. Won't that be fun?" She groaned inwardly at how superficial she sounded.

"Can we go sailing?" Izzy asked.

"We don't have a boat, honey. There's kayaking though."

"Neat," Izzy said flatly as she reached into her backpack for her cell phone and frowned at the screen.

"How's your dad?" Frankie tried again.

"He's okay. Just Lucas, you know," said Izzy, sounding bored now.

Frankie took a small measure of comfort that she wasn't the only parent being called by their first name.

Her ex-husband had reinvented himself as an expert on police procedure, advising the entertainment industry, consulting on cop shows of all things, lending authenticity to detective dramas and crime whodunnits. Frankie guessed that it must pay pretty well, as he had never asked her for a cent in support for Izzy, though she'd offered more than once. As ex-husbands went, she had nothing to complain about. He was a far better parent than her, something she'd reminded herself of whenever she second-guessed her decision to leave Izzy. He'd also never made her feel guilty for taking a job in Australia in the months after their marriage broke down. He hadn't needed to; she'd done that all by herself.

"At least the rain's stopped; I got soaked this morning. It's lovely when the sun comes out." Frankie told herself to shut up, annoyed at having fallen into the trap of gabbling inanely about the weather. She turned on the radio, letting the announcer's burble cover up the fact that her daughter's replies to her occasional questions were monosyllabic at best. There were no further reports of the body at Pacifica Gardens.

After a while, Izzy pulled a pair of headphones from her pocket, pushed them into her ears, and slumped back in her seat, closing her eyes.

Frankie glanced across at her from time to time, seeing the dark sweep of her daughter's eyelashes and her dimpled chin, so like her father's. Izzy was fifteen now; in a few years she'd be gone. A lot was riding on this summer; she wouldn't get another chance. She only hoped she hadn't left it too late.

"We're here," Frankie said in a loud voice as they reached the turn onto the dirt track that led to Fairmile. Tall pines on either side of them made it feel like they were driving through a tunnel.

Izzy opened her eyes and pulled out an earbud. As she pushed up her sleeves, Frankie caught sight of the edge of a tattoo, the petals of a rose peeping out from beneath the fabric. Was it even legal, at her age? She hoped to God there weren't more at the same time as reminding herself that things could be worse.

They pulled up at the house and Frankie tooted the horn to let her mother know they'd arrived.

Izzy unfolded herself from the truck and reached her arms skyward, revealing a large expanse of tanned stomach. She turned in a slow circle, and Frankie saw the house through her eyes: the newly painted white portico, and the three stories of windows—dormer ones at the top of the house, the Sound glinting in the late afternoon light and in the distance Mount Rainier, with its snow-covered dome, floating above the water like an illusion. She choked back a sudden misgiving that it had been a terrible idea to arrange for Izzy to come, noticing the isolation of the place for the first time. She had been so intent on seeing her daughter that she hadn't given much thought as to what a teenager who knew no one on the island might actually do with herself for the long weeks of summer vacation. Much as she wanted to soak up every minute with Izzy, she was aware that if she crowded her, it could have the opposite effect.

"Darling!" The front door opened, and Diana ran out, still in her painting outfit, her arms open wide, Scruff barking a welcome not far behind. "Oh, my goodness, sweet pea, you've grown, even since Easter!" She gathered Izzy in a hug and Frankie looked on, a smile finally curving her mouth at seeing them together. She remembered a long-ago weekend, a clapboard shack on the Oregon coast, toddler Izzy stumbling after her grandmother, not letting her out of her sight for a second. The relationship between them had always been one of mutual adoration.

Izzy broke her grandmother's embrace and greeted the dog, kneeling down and giggling as he covered her face with enthusiastic licks.

The teenager was a child again, for the briefest moment.

Frankie glanced toward the house, seeing the facade turned golden, the dusky tones of a flock of ducks coming into land on the water beyond, and the breeze that stirred the branches of a stand of white birch. Perhaps it would all be okay. Perhaps a summer spent getting the house ready would be a balm for her and would strengthen bonds that had been stretched almost to the breaking point.

"Come on in then, let me show you around," said Diana, leading Izzy up the steps and leaving Frankie to collect the luggage. "How about a refreshment? We should have some soda for you."

"There's lemonade in the fridge, if you like that," said Frankie, following behind. "I picked up some groceries on my way home this morning."

"Thank you, darling, that was thoughtful," Diana said.

"Is this all yours, Granny?" Frankie heard Izzy say.

"Most of it belongs to the bank, and if we don't get the place ready by the beginning of August, we're going to be in a heap of trouble." Diana laughed.

Sometimes Frankie envied her mother's carefree attitude and insistence that everything would turn out just fine; other times she found her loose grasp of reality teeth-grindingly frustrating.

Frankie took Izzy's bag up to her room and then returned down the wide staircase—where Diana had painstakingly stripped back decades of varnish to reveal carved bannisters and timber-paneled walls—and went to the kitchen, finding Izzy sitting at the table with a glass of lemonade. "I thought we might go out for dinner," she said. "Celebrate your first night here. Besides, my cooking's never been up to much."

"Yeah, I remember the hot dogs."

"The charcoal added a certain *texture* I thought," Frankie said with a grin.

Izzy smirked. "We order out a lot at home. The kitchen isn't exactly Sylvie's favorite place either." Sylvie was Lucas's second wife. With her doe eyes, perfect beachy waves, and Pilates-honed figure, she definitely didn't seem the Betty Crocker type. Of course, Frankie had stalked her on Facebook when she and Lucas first got together, gagging audibly at the gushing status updates ("so blessed to be living my best life with this guy" had been one of the worst offenders). Izzy seemed to get on with her well enough, something that Frankie still felt conflicted about.

"It's the local. The Cabbage Shed. In Huntley's Point. They do a pepperoni pizza that's supposed to be pretty good." Frankie checked her watch. "Do you want a shower first? You must be feeling gross after your flight; I know I always do."

Izzy shrugged, something that Frankie was beginning to recognize as her default reaction. "Sure, whatever."

"Your room's the one at the very top," said Diana, taking the empty glass from her granddaughter and placing it in the sink. The dishwashers were due to be installed the following week. "The attic—we thought you might like it up there; give you some private space. There's a bathroom too—you're lucky, we've finished the internal plumbing. Your mom and I were peeing in a bucket until a few days ago." Diana laughed as Izzy screwed up her nose at the idea. "Come on, I'll show you."

The pair went upstairs, trailed by Scruff and leaving Frankie in the kitchen, still marveling at the fact that her daughter was there, in the flesh, and that they were going to be living in the same house together for the first time in far too long. It didn't feel real.

Moments later, there was the sound of footsteps thundering down the stairs and Izzy reappeared, breathless, in the doorway. "Coco!" She held up the sheepskin bear, giving it a little dancing move. "You found him." She sounded puzzled as well as pleased.

"Actually, I kept him," Frankie admitted. "It made you seem a little closer, when I was in Australia." Her mouth twisted in a bittersweet smile. "He used to smell like you."

"But he's at home—at Dad's. I had him on my bed until last year, and then one day he disappeared. I always thought Sylvie tossed him out." Izzy's upper lip curled slightly.

"You had two Cocos, when you were very little." Frankie's expression softened. "We used to swap them over without you knowing, so that they'd both smell the same. In case you lost one."

Izzy's eyes glistened; Frankie didn't imagine it.

FIVE

Bend, Oregon, 1949

"Most unfortunate." Father Anthony perched on the edge of a hard-backed chair, leaning forward, his hands clasped between his knees. He had sucked in a breath as Una Ryan explained, in halting words, why they were there.

The girl hadn't raised her eyes the entire time they had entered the presbytery, fixing on the pattern of the rug as if studying for a geometry test, which to be frank was where she would far rather be.

"And there's no hope of the father...?"

She wanted the ground to swallow her up. Father Anthony had baptized her; had been the priest to officiate at her first communion, her confirmation.

"Unfortunately not." Her mother was firm. The girl hadn't said a word more to her parents about the father. Not for a minute did she consider that it was his problem too, even if she had known how to reach him.

"And how far along?"

"Um. About four months. I think. Perhaps." The girl found it impossible to speak above a whisper.

"Then we must act swiftly. Before her condition becomes obvious. There is a home that we have an arrangement with. In Seattle."

Seattle. The girl knew from geography lessons that it

was more than three hundred miles away. She had never been farther than Portland in her entire sixteen years.

It never occurred to her that it was unfair. That something so quick, so fleeting, could have such catastrophic consequences. That Robert got off scot-free and that her life, her future, was ruined. Though he had promised her it was safe, that he'd take care of things, she should have known better. She was the one to blame; that's what everyone thought. She believed it too.

"What about school? My friends? My classes?"

"I'd say you gave up that privilege, honey," her mother said. "Besides, you can come back; when it's all over. No one—besides us—need know."

"But that'll be too late. I'll have missed so much. I'll never catch up." The girl's voice rippled with regret.

"Perhaps you should have thought of that before…" Her mother stopped, unable to voice what her daughter had done to get herself into this position.

Father Anthony got up and went over to a cluttered desk, opening drawers until he found what he was looking for. "There is, of course, a sizeable fee for such a service." He held out a piece of paper. "The home will, however, waive all costs incurred in the care of your daughter and her baby should she choose to give up the baby to a good Catholic family, A family unable to have a child of their own. A loving family who will give the child the best of everything, including most importantly two married parents."

The girl looked at the letterhead, the word *Fairmile* and underneath *Mother & Baby Home* in black type. Then, she noticed the figures on the piece of paper and swallowed. The total amount was more money than she'd ever seen.

A sense of unreality took hold, as though all of this was happening to someone else, or that it was a bad dream and she'd eventually wake up, incandescent with relief, grateful for her old, dull life.

God didn't seem to be listening to her prayers.

The priest handed the sheet of paper to her mother and returned to his seat. "I'd be happy to hear your confession," he said, addressing the girl.

She gave a tiny shake of her head, couldn't meet his eye.

"We won't take up any more of your time Father," said her mother, folding the paper over and placing it in her handbag. "And we are very grateful for your assistance in this matter."

Her mother had put on her formal voice, the one she usually reserved for answering the telephone. The girl supposed it was to hide her own embarrassment.

Una Ryan got to her feet and stared at her daughter until she did the same.

"Let me know what you decide, and I can make the arrangements. If there is room for her, there is no reason why she cannot go as soon as possible. It's probably best for everyone that way."

"Thank you again Father."

The girl didn't utter a word, followed her mother out of the room, along a corridor that smelled of incense and furniture polish, and into the cold morning air.

"You can't tell them. You can't tell anyone," her mother said.

"Not even Cindy?"

"Absolutely not your friends. Not even your brother or the twins."

"Won't they wonder what's happened, if I suddenly disappear in the middle of school?"

"We'll say that your Aunt Helen is unwell and needs someone to care for her for a few months."

Aunt Helen, her father's older sister, lived in Seattle and had never married, so it was a convenient excuse.

"I worked damn hard to make a perfect life for us and I won't let anything spoil it, do you hear?" Her mother's usually serene face was contorted with what looked to the girl like fury and grief. "I cannot have Marcie Sterling and the other women talking about us, making our family the subject of their petty gossip."

Marcie Sterling was their neighbor, her mother's friend and the district busybody. The girl had always suspected her mother was in competition with her to see who could be the most capable and least flappable housewife.

She nodded dumbly.

"I cannot believe that history is repeating itself." Una spoke under her breath, but her daughter caught the words.

"What do you mean?"

Her mother's eyes narrowed. "You're good at math. Did it never occur to you that your birthday is seven months after our wedding anniversary?"

The girl's mouth formed a circle of shock. "I honestly never thought about it."

"We told everyone you were born early. It helped that you were small."

THE FOLLOWING WEEK, the girl had a ticket to Seattle in her imitation leather purse. She packed a suitcase with her diary, a book, hair- and toothbrushes, and two spare sets of clothes. Her mother lent her a coat that would be large enough to hide her shape in the months to come and had insisted she take her Bible—the white one she'd received for her confirmation from Aunt Helen, her name inscribed on the flyleaf. "It might give you some comfort," she'd said when she handed it to her. The girl took it meekly.

She emptied the pink china piggy bank that sat on her dresser, and tucked the money earned from baby-sitting and birthdays (her aunt was always generous) into her purse. She counted nearly thirty dollars.

The night before she was due to leave, the girl said goodbye to her brothers and sisters, repeating the story that her mother had invented. Her father had refused to speak to her since they had returned from the priest, and had taken to working late, coming home long after dinner had been served, the reek of beer on his breath.

Early the next morning, the girl and her mother walked to the bus stop. Una had booked the first departure of the day, telling her that there would be fewer people around to notice, and she was correct. There were only two other people waiting there, an elderly man wearing a homburg pulled down low on his forehead, and a middle-aged woman with a shawl-collared coat and a sensible brown purse. Beyond a brief curious glance, they took little notice of the girl.

She stood back as the bus approached and as she was about to board, turned suddenly, and hugged her mother fiercely. "I'm sorry." She choked back a sob.

"It's not forever."

"I know."

"You go and take care of Aunt Helen and we'll see you soon." Her mother's voice was loud, though there was no one but the bus driver and the couple to hear her. Gossip could flare at the slightest opportunity, and this was her way of dampening any possible spark.

The girl found an empty seat halfway along the bus, stowed her suitcase on the shelf overhead, and then hunched against the window. As the bus pulled away, a river of silent tears began to flow down her cheeks and onto the glass. She blinked in an attempt to stop them, but her eyes would not stop leaking. It seemed like far too much effort to find a handkerchief. She missed home already, her brother and little sisters— whom she normally barely tolerated—with an intensity that caught in her chest.

The worst of it was that this was her own stupid fault. If she could have gotten out a belt and whipped herself, she would have done so gladly.

The bus rumbled on, stopping in every town it reached, gradually filling up until there was only a handful of spare seats left. Most passengers took one look at her and sat somewhere else.

"Gum?"

She turned to see a stick of Wrigley's thrust toward her, a manicured hand and a clean cuff. She straightened up and saw that the arm—and the gum— belonged to a woman only a few years older than her. Red lipstick, a smile.

"Go on. It won't bite. I always say that something to freshen your breath can take your mind off the worst things."

The girl took the gum and managed a faint smile in return. "Thanks."

"You're welcome, honey."

THE GIRL ARRIVED in Seattle to a scene more chaotic than she'd ever experienced. The ground floor of the large, square, three-story terminal was filled with travelers hauling bags and suitcases, juggling hat boxes, and tugging at the hands of children trailing in their wake. A man rushing to catch a train swept past, jostling her shoulder and continuing on with a shouted word of apology. She felt like a boulder in a swiftly moving stream as people wove their way around her, seemingly oblivious to her presence. Father Anthony had told her that a sister from the home would be there to meet her, and her eyes darted across the cavernous space, searching for a woman in a nun's habit.

It was late afternoon, and the sky outside was already growing dark. What if no one came? Would she have to spend the night on one of the hard benches that lined the hall? And then what? She fingered the ticket stub in her pocket and shivered, though it wasn't cold, and then her stomach fluttered and she couldn't tell if it was from hunger or something else, perhaps the little fish that was swimming in there. Her hand went to her belly but all she could feel was a firm swell where once it had been flat. She scanned the far reaches of the hall for a restroom, something, someone.

"Miss Ryan?"

The girl whirled around to see a short, solid woman in a black habit and white wimple, tortoiseshell spectacles balanced precariously on the end of a stubby little nose. Despite the nun's unpromising expression, relief flooded through the girl. "How did you know it was me?"

The nun raised her eyes to the heavens as if to say that was a dumb question. "I can always tell."

The girl didn't have time to wonder what she meant by that, as the nun picked up her suitcase and began to walk toward the exit. "Come along now, dear," the nun called. "It's a couple miles to the convent, and I don't like to be out after nightfall if I can help it."

The girl had to nearly run to keep up with her, for despite her stature the nun set a fast pace, weaving expertly through the crowds of office workers on their way home.

THE CONVENT OF the Sacred Heart was a large, redbrick building in a quiet side street lined with maple trees wearing the colors of fall: scarlet, russet, and ochre, and the smell of woodsmoke lingered in the air. It reminded the girl of cookouts and s'mores and winter football games, and she felt a pain, like a knife in her side, that her friends would be doing all that without her this year.

Sister Clare—she'd introduced herself as they walked—ushered her inside and showed her to a dormitory where ten narrow beds made up with gray blankets and starched sheets lined each side of the room. She pointed to the bed nearest the door. "There's a washroom down the hall. The dinner bell will be in an hour."

The girl nodded her thanks. After the nun left, she sat down on the edge of the bed and wondered what to do next. The iron springs of the mattress were hard against her bottom even through the blanket, but as a wave of sudden exhaustion washed over her, she kicked off her shoes and swung her legs up, lying back against the pillow.

She was out cold when the dinner bell rang, and it was a moment before she remembered where she was. She lay, listening to the sound of hurrying foot-steps on the stairs, dredging herself up from the deep-seafloor of sleep.

She found the dining room, following the smell of food, but hesitated on the threshold, confronted by a roomful of girls standing at tables of six, their heads bowed and hands in prayer, in complete silence. Sister Clare, standing at a long table on a raised platform at the far end of the room with a dozen other nuns, was too far away to be of any help. A small girl at the table nearest to her looked sideways and caught her eye, gestured to an empty seat. The girl stepped toward it.

After a prayer, dinner was served—thin slices of grayish meat and waterlogged vegetables—by some of the girls. Still no one spoke. The girl, who was used to her brother and sisters play-fighting and teasing one other mercilessly, found her first few mouthfuls hard to swallow. She was hungry though—the little fish was demanding to be fed. She cleaned her plate and ate all the bowl of Jell-O and whipped cream that came af-terward, suppressing the burp that rose from her chest before she'd even put her spoon down.

She began to feel queasy. She tried concentrating on the bowl in front of her, swallowing hard, but the room began to swim, shimmering around the edges. She slammed a hand to her mouth and half-rose from her chair. If she didn't do something quickly, she would throw up her dinner right there on the table and then just about die from the embarrassment of it all.

The girl next to her placed a hand on her arm and rose with her. She guided her out of the room and down a corridor to a bathroom, where the girl emptied the contents of her stomach into the toilet, gasping as she continued to heave.

When she had finished, she felt immediately better, though her legs still shook. She wiped her mouth and washed her hot face in the sink, while the girl who had helped her stared at her feet, saying nothing.

Back in the dining room, she noticed some of the other girls' eyes glance off the rise of her belly. She scanned the room more carefully: none of them appeared to be in the same condition as her. What kind of a place had she come to?

"I could not have believed it if I had not seen it with my own eyes." One of the nuns had risen from her place at the table and begun to read from a large book, telling the story of Gladys Aylward, a missionary in deepest China fighting a one-woman battle against the practice of foot-binding young girls. Despite the gruesome subject—the nun relished the description of yellowed, broken, fetid toes pushing into the soles of their feet—the girl struggled to stay awake as the nun's voice carried across the sea of bent heads. She was about to slide sideways off her chair when she was brought back to reality by the squealing of furniture across the wooden floor. It appeared that the reading had come to an end and the meal was over.

Sister Clare approached. "You'll go up to the dormitory now and be ready to leave after breakfast. We'll take the ferry the rest of the way to Fairmile."

Fairmile. The girl had so many questions, but before she could begin to form even the first one, Sister Clare had joined the other nuns and swept out of the room.

SIX

Puget Sound, 2013

THE CABBAGE SHED was busy for a Tuesday, but the
rain had, for the time being, stopped, and the flush of
sunshine brought locals and tourists alike to sit at picnic tables set out on lawns that stretched down to the
water. Swatting away midges was a small price to pay
to eat at such a pretty spot. Diana waved to a friend
as they found a table, and Frankie went inside to fetch
menus and order drinks.

It was a popular place, with a rustic decor that suited
the island. Essentially an old barn—once used to store
cabbages, hence the name—it now featured a long, polished wood bar, behind which were taps announcing a
mind-boggling array of craft beers.

Frankie was waiting her turn when she noticed
the woman next to her. She was casually dressed in
quick-dry shorts, knee-high (knee-high, really?) hiking socks, and a T-shirt advertising a local trucking
company, her bright copper hair pulled into a loose
ponytail.

"I'm sorry, do I know you?" the woman asked.

Frankie had realized immediately where she'd seen
the woman before—it didn't take a super-recognizer
to figure that out, her luminous eyes would be memo-
rable to anyone but a blind person. She was younger

than Frankie had first assumed, her skin enviably dewy and unlined, but then it was hard to tell someone's age when they were masked up.

"The nursing home," the woman said, as she too made the connection.

"My grandmother lives there." Frankie held out a hand. "Frankie Gray."

The woman did a double take. "As in Frankie Gray, Orcades Island's newest deputy?"

"Not technically until September. I should have introduced myself at the nursing home, but I didn't want to interrupt." The deputy's job was considerably more junior than the one Frankie had previously held in Sydney, but that had been a deliberate choice. She'd once been fiercely ambitious, putting her career above the needs of her daughter, wanting to prove to her ex-husband who was the better cop. She wouldn't do that again.

The woman pumped Frankie's outstretched hand. "Molly Dowd." She was softly spoken, but her smile was wide, and she seemed delighted to run into her and, understandably, a lot more friendly than she had been at the nursing home. "I didn't know you'd arrived already." Her eyes were alight with pleasure, and she seemed more like an earnest wilderness guide than an officer of the law. "Actually, do you mind if I give you a hug? I'm a hugger."

Frankie hadn't been expecting that. "Uh, okay."

Molly enveloped her in an embrace that smelled of fresh air and wildflowers.

"I'm helping my mom out for the summer," Frankie explained once Molly had let her go.

"Well, it's so good to meet you Frankie Gray. I can't wait to work with you."

"Me too," Frankie said, surprised to find herself meaning it. Molly's enthusiasm was contagious.

"Molly?"

Frankie turned to see an older man beckoning from a table to the left.

"I'm sure I'll see you around over the summer," Molly beamed, juggling her drinks and wallet. "It's a pretty small place, as you'll no doubt discover." She looked as if she wanted to say more but turned to leave. "Oh, if there's anything you need to know before you start, I'd be more than happy to help."

"Sure, thanks, Molly. Appreciate it."

"What can I get you?" the girl serving asked.

Frankie recited their order—beer for her, iced tea for her mother, and a Coke for Izzy—then grabbed a handful of menus from the stack on the bar and wedged them under her arm. She paid for the drinks and carried them outside.

"I was telling Izzy that I have a bicycle she could use," said Diana as Frankie approached.

"You do?"

"Although you'll need to get it checked out," her mother replied. "There's a bike store down the street, I think they do repairs. You can take it tomorrow."

Frankie rankled at being ordered around by her mother as though she was a teenager herself, but she let it slide. Besides, it wasn't such a terrible idea, and it would mean that Izzy was at least able to explore on her own without having to rely on one of them to ferry her around all the time.

"I was learning to drive in LA," said Izzy. "Lucas said he'd get me a convertible for my birthday."

Frankie tried not to choke on her drink. Parenting wasn't a competition, she reminded herself, even if she did have more than most to make up for.

"Fish tacos for me," said Diana, putting the menu down. "Izzy?"

"Pizza, thanks. I hear the pepperoni's good."

Frankie smiled. It was an olive branch of sorts.

"Can we get garlic bread?" Izzy asked.

"Don't you think there's enough carbs in the pizza?" The words were out of Frankie's mouth before she could stop them. God, why had she said that? She had meant it as a joke, but judging by the expression on Izzy's face, it had fallen flat.

"I expect you didn't have lunch," said Diana, smoothing over the tension between mother and daughter. "Of course, we can get some garlic bread, sweet pea."

THE NEXT MORNING, Frankie had returned from the trail that skirted the water and was kicking off her sneakers by the time Izzy emerged, bleary eyed and tousle headed.

She had started running as soon as she arrived at Fairmile. It gave some structure to her days and kept her thoughts at a distance, though her fitness was returning more quickly than her peace of mind. It had been less than a year since the accident that had smashed her right leg into several pieces, and technically she shouldn't be running on it, but since when did she ever take much notice of what she was *supposed* to do? Even Scruff had benefitted, shedding a pound or two.

"Sleep well?" she asked, entering the kitchen, her damp socks leaving prints on the stone floor. "Can I make you some waffles? Bacon?" Frankie was trying not to overdo it, but food was love right? If only she knew what Izzy's favorite breakfast was now. Last summer, in Honolulu, she had powered her way through stacks of coconut pancakes each morning, but there was no telling if that was still the case. "Or there's Vegemite if you'd like to try that?" A taste for the viscous, salty paste was something Frankie had acquired while living in Sydney and had eclipsed even her love of PB&J.

Frankie opened the refrigerator and hauled out a carton of milk, hip-checking the door until it closed with a satisfying clunk. God, she'd missed oversized American refrigerators, the ones that dispensed ice and chilled water on demand.

"Thanks, I'll grab some juice for now," said Izzy, running a hand through her hair and not bothering to stifle a yawn. "Maybe some toast." Even sleepy eyed and wearing a T-shirt that reached almost to her knees, she just about stopped Frankie's heart with her beauty. Did every mother feel like this about their children? Did it ever go away?

"I thought we could get that bike looked at later this morning."

"Uh-huh." Izzy moved past her to the refrigerator.

"All right then." Frankie hoped that Izzy might soon become more than monosyllabic. When Izzy was little, she'd been a real Chatty Cathy, full of wonder and questions about the world around her, sometimes to the point of being annoying. Frankie would give anything to have that girl back now. Her once eager-to-please child had been replaced by a girl-woman with a guarded look in her eyes.

Frankie switched on the drip coffee machine—she had suggested her mom order a fancy espresso maker for future guests, but it had yet to arrive—and grabbed her phone.

Molly Dowd. She googled the name, scrolling through the first few hits until she came to one that held her interest. She clicked and waited for the link to open. It was a newspaper article from a couple of years ago. Molly had apparently once been a rising star of the Pierce County Sheriff's Department, honored for helping solve a gruesome double murder in 2010. Frankie scrolled down, coming to a photo that proved beyond doubt that it was the same woman. She pressed her fingers together as the machine gurgled away. So what was Molly doing in a sleepy backwater like Orcades Island?

The door slammed, and Diana bustled in, toting a newspaper and a quart of milk.

Frankie took the offered *Huntley's Point Record* and began to leaf through it, stopping at page seven. There was a postage-stamp-sized grainy black and white photograph showing a middle-aged woman dressed in a nun's habit and white-banded headscarf. The face was unsmiling and jowly behind steel-framed glasses. She looked fierce rather than serene. Judgmental rather than pious. As Frankie scanned the perfunctory report, it became obvious that the journalist had had little chance to pull the story together in time to make the press deadline.

"Doesn't say much. It's almost as though they want the whole thing covered up." Fact of the matter was, the island's economy relied on summer visitors, which was reason enough for someone to lean on the editor, persuade them to bury the story in the middle of the paper, and deliberately keep the details to a minimum.

Diana seemed more interested in locating something from the refrigerator than responding. Frankie felt a needlestick of surprise; her mom usually had an opinion on everything and was more than happy to share it with anyone who would care to listen. It was, however, a fact that almost all her attention was now taken up with getting Fairmile ready to open on time.

"Should we all go and visit with Mom later today?" Diana asked, rummaging through the crisper. "I'd like to check for myself that she's okay."

"GG?" Izzy, who was now standing at the counter buttering a slice of toast, turned to her grandmother, eyes alight. "I haven't seen her in, like, forever."

Frankie hesitated. "I was going to clean out the back bedrooms, and the tilers should have been here by now."

"They called me earlier," Diana said. "Something about a materials delay. Promised they'd be back tomorrow, Thursday at the absolute latest."

Frankie made an exasperated sound and grabbed an apple from the fruit bowl on the table, biting down with a swift crunch.

"I'm almost done in the bridal suite, so we can drive over later today," Diana added. "Why don't you take Izzy to sort out the bicycle this morning?"

"I was already planning on that," Frankie mumbled, coughing as a chunk of apple caught in her throat.

Izzy turned around at the mention of her name, a piece of toast hanging from her mouth.

"Do sit down at the table to eat, please," said Diana,

and for a second Frankie wasn't sure which one of them she was talking to.

"Sorry," they said in unison, both masking a smile.

AFTER IZZY HAD finished her breakfast, Diana directed her to a large shed at the back of the house. It had probably once been a barn or even possibly stables, and Diana had mentioned her plan to eventually turn it into self-contained accommodation, once the rest of the house was finished. For now, however, it was a shambolic structure, with shingles missing from the roof and a door that opened only if you put your weight behind it like you were a lineman going in for a tackle. Diana used it to store all of the old furniture—heavy, dark wooden chests of drawers, scarred dressers, ancient lamp bases with torn shades, dark, dusty oil paintings, and broken bed frames—that had been in the house when she purchased the place, and it was now a higgledy-piggledy mass that threatened to collapse on anyone who entered. Frankie hoped Izzy would be able to retrieve the bike without having to move too much stuff.

She watched as her daughter appeared a few minutes later, wheeling a clapped-out contraption that looked like it was held together solely by rust and good intentions.

"It needs new tires," Frankie said as she rolled the softened rubber between her fingers. "These are definitely cactus."

"Cactus?" asked Izzy.

"Beyond saving." Along with a taste for Vegemite, Frankie had picked up a fondness for Aussie slang.

Izzy said nothing.

"Oh, come on, cheer up. I know it's not exactly flashy—" As they stood and looked at the bike, several large flakes of black paint floated to the ground.

"It was probably made before I was even born," said Izzy, looking at it like something she'd unearthed from a junkyard, which to be fair, she kind of had.

"Well, how about that?" said Frankie. "Retro. It'll be something you can get around on anyway." Privately, she doubted whether a bike mechanic would be able to resurrect it, but she was determined to be optimistic.

"Did I say I wanted to get around?" Izzy muttered under her breath.

SEVEN

Puget Sound, 2013

IT WAS A bright morning and the air was warm, so Frankie wound down the windows, marveling again to herself at the novelty of having her daughter by her side, even if she was spiky as a porcupine and just as unpredictable.

They reached the bike store and as they stood in front of the window, Frankie noticed Izzy's gaze roam the racks of shiny new bicycles, scooters, and skateboards. There was one that held her daughter's attention for longer than others—a mint-green cruiser with a wicker basket on the front and a soft brown leather saddle. It looked exactly like something a California— or Aussie for that matter—girl might ride along the beachfront, her long hair fanning out behind her in the breeze, a surfboard under one arm.

They wheeled the old bike through the door and as Frankie was trying to decide whether to spring for a new one instead, a young man appeared from somewhere in the back of the store, wiping his hands on a cloth. "Can I help you?" he asked.

Frankie pointed to the bike that they had brought with them. "Do you think there's anything you can do to make it roadworthy?"

He looked incredulously at it and then at them but,

on seeing that Frankie was serious, took the bike from Izzy and began to check it over, bending down and muttering to himself as he did so.

Izzy dawdled around the store as they waited, but Frankie could tell that her interest had picked up as soon as the guy helping them had arrived, that she was deliberately playing it cool. Her quick blink and her hands, poised over a leather saddle, had stilled, giving her away. Frankie was used to noticing such tiny tells; it had saved her ass more than once.

"It's never going to be the most radical thing to ride, and one of the wheel rims has buckled, but the rust is only on the surface," he said, straightening up. "New tires, obviously, and a new saddle and I'll have to replace the brake cables…"

"How much?" Frankie got straight to the point.

He named a figure that was about a third of the cost of the peppermint bike that Izzy had been admiring.

"How soon do you think you can get it ready?"

"Come in on Friday afternoon. We should have it done by then."

"Should?"

"We will have it done by then."

"Thank you, er…?"

"Zac." He gave them a lopsided grin. Frankie glanced back and saw that Izzy was grinning at him, had to tamp down a faint flutter of alarm.

They left the bike store and walked back to the truck. "What's that?" Izzy asked, pointing to the memorial that Frankie had passed the previous morning.

"A local girl. Flipped her car into the water and didn't manage to get out in time. Driving too fast most likely."

"Oh, that's awful."

"It can happen all too easily." Frankie refrained from quoting the teenage driver accident stats; there'd be time enough for that another day, and for now she figured she'd made her point. "I'm sorry I couldn't get you a new bike."

"It's okay. I'm only here for eight weeks after all."

"We'll get to do some fun stuff, I promise," said Frankie. "There are some cool places to swim, and we'll go into the city as well... But I also have to help Granny get the house ready. She's put everything she's got into it, and she can't do it all on her own."

"Is that why you came? From Australia I mean? To help Granny?"

"Partly." Frankie hesitated.

"What were the other reasons?"

"Work. Well actually, lack of work. I quit."

"But you love your job in Australia." Izzy blinked at her. "That's what Lucas always says."

"Not so much, as it happens," Frankie said, the corners of her mouth turning down. "Coming here seems like the most sensible idea I've had in ages."

"And is it?"

"It's certainly more peaceful," Frankie said, looking over at the water.

"But you'll go back?" Izzy sounded almost fearful.

"Actually, no. There's something else I didn't get the chance to tell you. Before I left Sydney, I interviewed to be a deputy. I don't think they were exactly beating away applicants, just between you and me."

"Here? On the island?" Izzy halted in her tracks.

"Correct." Frankie didn't add that ever since she'd accepted the offer, she'd been second-guessing herself.

She wasn't sure she was up to the job anymore, even in such a sleepy place as Orcades Island. The trouble was being a cop was all she really knew how to do.

"Wow. Okay." Izzy appeared to be absorbing this new development as they carried on walking.

"I don't start until September, so nothing's going to stop us having the summer together, if that's what you're worrying about," said Frankie, thinking to re-assure her.

"You promise?"

"Absolutely." It seemed an easy enough bargain to strike.

As they reached the other side of the bridge, Frankie recognized the person coming toward them. The deputy. Molly Dowd. In uniform this time, forest-green pants and a short-sleeved shirt, a star on her breast pocket. No long socks, at least none that were visible.

"Hello again."

"Small towns, huh?" said Molly, as cheerful as when they'd previously met. She didn't hug Frankie this time: perhaps it was the uniform that made her more cir-cumspect.

"Is this your daughter?"

"Izzy."

"Hey."

"The resemblance is strong with this one."

She said it in a dorky voice that made Frankie think of Yoda and caused her to let out a snort of laughter. Fact of the matter was, Frankie had never imagined she and Izzy shared more than their annoyingly frizzy hair and eye color, but it was nice that someone else saw it differently. "Any leads?" She'd always been incapable of switching off. "On the nursing home case I mean."

Izzy had wandered a few steps away, absorbed in something on her phone.

Molly hesitated. "I shouldn't discuss an ongoing investigation but well, under the circumstances I guess it's okay to share…"

Frankie thought again of the bony wrists tied to the bed frame. "What have you got so far?" She drew closer, her hands resting lightly on her hips. "Cause of death?"

"We're still waiting on a toxicology report, but it wouldn't surprise me if she'd been drugged: there are no signs of a struggle. Also, something rather odd. There were leaves, in a vase, just not the usual thing you'd expect in a bouquet. None of the staff recollect having seen them there the day before."

Frankie looked expectantly at Molly.

"*Urtica dioica.* Stinging nettles."

She winced.

"They're common to the island, but who would put such a thing in a person's room? And according to the logbooks, she didn't have any visitors in the week leading up to her death."

"No family?"

"She was a ninety-year-old nun. Single her whole life. Stands to reason she wouldn't have any relations left."

"Good point. CCTV?" Frankie asked.

"One camera at the front that captures the parking lot. No cars arriving or leaving until the start of the day shift."

"In the rooms?"

"No call for it apparently—this is a quiet town, nothing like it has ever happened here before, not as far as I'm aware anyhow." Molly fixed her with an earnest expression. "I'd hate for you to get the wrong idea about the island. It's really a wonderful place. Truly. You're going to love it here."

Orcades Island was sixty-five square miles, give or take, with a population just shy of a thousand (it swelled to four times that in the height of summer). Frankie didn't need Molly to tell her that a homicide— on the entire island, not merely in the nursing home— was likely a once-in-a-decade event. She held up a hand. "I already do," she reassured her. "And I've seen far worse."

Molly looked relieved, as though Frankie might have judged the island on this single, bizarre crime.

"Any sign of forced entry?"

Molly shook her head. "The locks are a four-digit code. It's reset every month."

"Good."

"But one of the side doors was left unlocked— whether that was deliberate or an oversight remains to be seen. There's also CCTV from the gas station farther along the road, but we've not had the resources to examine it yet."

"One of the other residents then?"

"Unlikely. You've seen them; they're all pretty harmless. But we will be questioning them. Sensitively, mind." Molly paused. "There's another odd thing though: Ms. Evans used to work on the island, when she was much younger, in the early nineteen forties and fifties I believe, although she returned to live at Pacifica Gardens only recently."

"So where did she work?"

"Fairmile."

Frankie stilled. "But that's where…"

"I know," said Molly.

"I thought it had been derelict for years."

"It has. But you will, of course, be aware that it was once a home for unwed mothers. After the Second World War until the nineteen seventies, I think. Run by the Catholic Church."

"Of course," Frankie lied, wondering why her mother had failed to mention this. "But I'm not really aware of the full details."

"It was once a landmark house, by all accounts. It'll be just wonderful to see it brought back to life," Molly said, the enthusiasm returning to her voice again. "Your mom's doing such a great job, if what Jed at the lumberyard says is anything to go by."

"Did they find any fingerprints?" Frankie asked, focused on the crime.

"Nothing usable."

"Unusual fibers?"

"From a pink robe."

Frankie would bet that half the female residents of Pacifica Gardens would have a pink or blue robe of some kind. Ingrid's was rose pink, for heaven's sake. "But you must have *some* idea?" Frankie stopped herself. "Sorry, that was rude of me." It didn't come easily not to be in the thick of an investigation, not to be the one calling the shots.

Molly didn't seem bothered. "Either way, it doesn't appear to be random. We believe Ms. Evans was specifically targeted, so you needn't worry about your grandmother, or the safety of anyone else there, if that's what's concerning you."

"Suspects, at this stage?"

Molly hesitated. "Two former members of staff were

dismissed a little more than a month ago. Regina Halversen. Last known address is in West Seattle. And Alan Bloom. We're still working on an address for him. Apparently, they were both implicated in alleged ill treatment of the patients, neglect really, and there was some talk that they were stealing from them, though it was never proven."

"What would they have against the victim specifically?"

Molly shrugged. "We think Ms. Evans might have been the one who complained about them."

It seemed hardly reason to commit murder, but Frankie had known of people killed for less.

"What's Sergeant Sandberg's opinion?" Frankie had been interviewed over the phone and had yet to meet the incumbent sergeant in person, thinking to keep a low profile until she started her new job.

Molly shifted from one foot to the other. "He's on vacation—a fishing trip up in the Cascades." She shot Frankie an apologetic look and something told her this wasn't an unusual occurrence. "Unreachable. But don't worry, we're expecting a team from the mainland to help us out. It'll all be just fine." She was back to being peppy.

"I'm sure you've got it under control," Frankie said, biting back her own thoughts on how to conduct the investigation.

"Anyway," Molly changed the subject, perhaps realizing she'd said enough, "there's a trivia night at The Cabbage Shed tomorrow, if you like that sort of thing. Do stop by if you're free. We're one short and could really use the help." She smiled broadly. "I know what it's like to be new to a place too."

Molly was positively midwestern in her niceness, but a small, suspicious part of Frankie wondered if she was using the invitation as an excuse to find out more about her. Still, it couldn't do any harm to go along; in fact, it could work both ways. "That's a kind offer. I'll try and make it."

"Seven-thirty, room at the back."

It was only when Molly had gone that Frankie realized what had been bugging her about the scene in the nun's room. The crucifix on the wall.

It had been upside down.

EIGHT

Puget Sound, 2013

DIANA WAS IN the garden sawing at an overgrown rose-
bush with a large kitchen knife when Frankie and Izzy
returned to Fairmile. "Can't find the pruning shears
anywhere," she said, stopping to wipe a strand of hair
from her face. "These poor things haven't been cared
for in years. I'm not sure they're even salvageable."

"Oh Granny, you've cut yourself."

A smear of blood decorated her cheek.

"Blasted thorns. Here—" she held out a bunch of
flowers to Frankie, "take these inside, carefully mind,
and wrap them in some paper. I thought Mom might
like them."

"They'll brighten up her room. What time are you
thinking of going?"

"Whenever you're ready, darling. After lunch?"

"That okay with you Izzy?" Frankie asked.

"It's not like I have anything better to do."

Frankie had decided that ignoring such comments
was the best approach and went into the kitchen in
search of a first aid kit. Diana followed and Frankie
watched as her mother washed her hands, seeing the
diluted blood swirling down the drain.

"Band-Aids are in the cupboard above the refrigerator." Diana had dried off her palm, but blood had

already begun to well up from the cut again. "Luckily it's not deep," she added, dabbing at it.

"I ran into one of the island deputies again, the same one I saw at The Cabbage Shed last night," said Frankie. "Turns out she was an investigator in the murder of a couple of girls in the city—in Renton I think— a few years ago." The fact that it was almost always girls was no surprise to Frankie.

She hauled down an old tin box and rummaged for something to cover the cut. "She said that Bernadette Evans—the former nun from the nursing home—used to work at Fairmile, years ago. When it was a mother-and-baby home apparently." Frankie turned her head, watching for her mother's reaction.

"So, we should expect a visit from your future colleagues at some point?" Diana's expression had faltered for a fraction of a second, something that you'd miss unless you were paying close attention, which Frankie was. "Though I don't know what they'd hope to find— the place was empty for so long. And it was decades ago," she added, dismissing the connection.

Frankie peeled the wrapper off a dusty Band-Aid, motioning for Diana to hold out her injured hand. "How come you didn't mention it before?" Frankie carefully applied the Band-Aid, making sure she covered the cut completely. "There you are. Now don't go getting it wet or it'll come right off," she said, and for a moment it was as though their mother-daughter role had been reversed.

"Mention what?" Diana asked, distracted.

"About it being used as a home for pregnant girls."

"I don't suppose I thought it was important. It was a long time ago. Besides, I'd rather focus on the fact that it was an Admiral's former home—that's a far better story to tell prospective guests, don't you agree?" she said brightly.

Frankie couldn't help feeling that she was being given the brush-off.

"OF COURSE, they've been in to ask us questions. Not that I could tell them much, other than the fact that I didn't see anything, or anyone. At least not as far as I can remember." Diana, Frankie, and Izzy had arrived at Pacifica Gardens to find Ingrid more animated than on Frankie's previous visit, dressed in a soft lavender blouse and tan slacks and with an excited light in her faded eyes. Her hair was, for a change, styled in the kind of uniform rows of tight curls that were rarely seen in nature, and Frankie remembered her mother saying that a stylist came in once a week. "I didn't mention that Angela sometimes falls asleep at night when she's supposed to be on duty. Poor dear works three jobs and she's always so tired. You can't begrudge her a nap now and then, can you?"

"But Grandma, the deputies might want to know that," Frankie said. "It could be important."

"Oh, do you really think so, dear?"

Diana was arranging the flowers they'd brought in a crystal vase that sat on the chest of drawers. They were all crowded into the small room, Frankie and Izzy sitting on the bed, with Ingrid in her chair.

"Well, if she'd been awake, she might have been able to identify whoever it was that broke in. But I don't think it's that important," said Frankie, not wanting to upset her, "though I'll be sure to pass it on just in case."

"She could have been killed herself," said Izzy, who had heard the story from Ingrid when they first arrived.

"Oh, don't be so melodramatic young lady. Who did you say you were again?" Ingrid asked.

Izzy smirked.

"This is Izzy," Frankie reminded her grandmother as she got up to open a window. "Your great-granddaughter; she's come to stay for the summer. From Los Angeles."

"I never did like that place," said Ingrid, looking like she was sucking on a lemon. "Too many cars, not enough road for them all."

Izzy laughed and Frankie was relieved that neither the comment nor the fact that her great-grandmother didn't recognize her seemed to bother her. She placed a sympathetic hand on Izzy's, a small thrill sparking through her when her daughter briefly squeezed it back.

"Julie told me that they've increased security," said Diana. "More cameras are being installed outside; I saw the workmen as we came in."

Frankie wanted to say wasn't that a bit like shutting the stable door after the horse had bolted but held her tongue. After her comment at dinner the night before, she was trying her hardest not to offend either her mother or her daughter. It felt like walking on eggshells, but for all their sakes she wanted them to get along this summer. To have the chance to make some good memories together, to compensate for all the lost time, if that were possible.

Diana finished arranging the flowers and stood back, appraising them.

"There's something of yours over there," said Ingrid. "You left it last time." She indicated a small bookcase with a trembling hand.

Diana went over to it and picked up an object. Frankie

hadn't noticed it when they had walked in; it was almost the same color as the book it had been resting on. A wooden-handled knife. Useful for pruning. And cutting twine.

"I wondered what I'd done with that. How careless of me." Diana placed the knife in her purse and Frankie caught an odd look on her mother's face.

"Who did you say this girl is?" Ingrid asked again. "She's quite pretty, but what's she got in her nose for heaven's sake?"

Frankie saw Izzy's mouth twitch again at Ingrid's words. "It's a ring GG," she said.

"Well I never." Ingrid folded her hands together and Frankie could tell she didn't approve.

"It looks lovely, doesn't it Grandma?" Frankie said, daring her to say otherwise. "Perhaps you should get one?"

She was rewarded for her teasing with a bark of laughter.

They stayed for another half an hour or so, until Ingrid began to tire, and it was time to leave.

They were no more than a few minutes down the road when Frankie glanced back to check on Izzy. Her daughter had fallen asleep in the back of the car, her head pressed against the strap of her seatbelt. Frankie's heart contracted as she saw Izzy's softened face, the echo of her little girl still there. The realization of how much she'd missed almost winded her. She'd thought her decision to extend her stay in Australia the best one given the circumstances, but now it seemed like the biggest mistake she'd ever made.

NINE

Puget Sound, 2013

THERE WERE STILL a couple rooms that Diana hadn't touched—including one that must have been used as a study or an office at some point, for the walls were lined with built-in shelves, with a tall double-door cupboard pushed into one corner. Frankie had popped her head inside the room not long after she first arrived, seeing towering piles of books almost completely obscuring the floor and barricading the windows and decided it was something to tackle another day.

Bernadette Evans had once worked at Fairmile. Why did she think there might be a connection? The upside-down crucifix was unsettling. If there was the slimmest chance that some record of the former nun's time at Fairmile might have been left behind, the study would be the obvious place to look.

The next morning, sneezing as she dislodged the layers of grime that had been allowed to accumulate, Frankie began to sift through the things left undisturbed seemingly for decades. Dust motes swirled like pollen, but at least the sun was now streaming through the flung-open windows. She soon managed to make enough space for her and Izzy to work—Frankie had resorted to bribery to get her to help, promising they'd go somewhere more exciting in the afternoon.

They lined up the piles of books in the hallway, wiping the leather and board covers with rags to get the worst of the dust off. "Most of these will have to go to the thrift store," Frankie said, turning one over in her hands.

"Do you really think anyone will want them?" Izzy asked.

"I don't know what else we can do with them," Frankie replied, adding a Psalter to a stack of Bibles and lobbing a handful of misshapen candle stubs into an empty box.

"Can I have this?" Izzy held up a tarnished crucifix.

Frankie shrugged. "I don't see why not. Check with Granny to be sure—technically everything here is hers."

"Ooh look at these." Izzy had reached the tall cupboard, and sneezed as she brought out a long, black garment, followed by a yellowed cloth that might have once been white.

"What?"

Izzy held what looked like a dress against her, the sleeves falling past her wrists. "Smells like Sunday school." She wrinkled her nose.

"Incense probably," Frankie said, coming closer. "It could be a habit. And this—" she took the cloth from her daughter. "Is probably a wimple."

"A what?"

"A nun's headdress."

Frankie lugged another pile of books out to the corridor, but nearly dropped them when a low clanging noise sounded from inside the room.

She returned to find Izzy dressed in the nun's habit and holding a pair of handbells, looking delighted at the sound they made.

"Actually, they might come in useful, Julie Andrews," Frankie said. She blinked in surprise at how anonymous the costume made her daughter look—and how ageless. She could have been anything from fourteen to forty. Of course, the nose ring was an incongruity. She expected that, even today, the Church frowned upon piercings.

"To wake the guests up you mean?" Izzy pranced about the room, swishing the long skirts of the habit.

"They might help to hurry along the ones who don't check out on time," said Frankie with a grin. It made her happier than she could have imagined seeing the playful side of her daughter reemerge.

"Are we nearly done here?" Izzy asked, taking off the habit and collapsing into an easy chair, coughing at the cloud of dust that bloomed from the upholstery.

Frankie looked at her watch. They'd only been working for a little over an hour. "Why don't you go and grab a soda for us both?" she suggested.

At least they'd cleared the bookshelves on one wall, but there didn't seem to be anything here that would give a clue about the house's previous inhabitants. Perhaps it had been too much to hope for. Frankie sat back on her heels, considering her next move.

At one end of the room was another bookcase, now almost empty. There was always a chance that something could have fallen down in back of it. She stood up and got her weight behind it, giving it a hefty shove, noticing as she did so that it had been obscuring a cupboard door, built into the wall. She pushed the bookcase out of the way and grabbed the door handle, swearing as it came off in her hand. Casting about, she saw a letter opener on the windowsill and reached for it.

Bending down, she pushed the wider end of the opener along the edge of the door, using it as a lever. At first the opener bent, but then there was the sound of cracking paint, and the door inched open, swinging on its hinges with a rusty squeal.

Frankie felt a small thrill pulse through her at the sight of ledgers, stacks of them, bound in bottle green and deep red. She pulled one from the top and opened it, turning mottled yellowing pages covered in thin, spidery script. Columns, dates, figures…notes for deliveries, laundry services…an account book.

She put that aside and pulled out another. This was more promising. It contained lists of names, though she had to squint to read the writing: Eleanor D., Kathleen M., Nora S., Emily J., Anne C., Teresa O'G., Mary Patricia C… Nothing that could identify them. Oddly, each line had two sets of Christian names. Perhaps they'd all been given alternate names, to further shield their identity. There was also a column for their age. Frankie drew in a breath. Most were between seventeen and twenty-five, but some were as young as thirteen. *Thirteen.* The list went on for hundreds of pages. These must have been the girls who came to the home. There were so many of them. Had they arrived alone? Dragged there by embarrassed parents? Come willingly, relieved of their burden? Been so desperate that their only option was to be banished to such an isolated place. Brought here to hide their shameful secret.

Frankie knew a little about what it was like to give up your child, but to have no hope of ever seeing them again, to have very little say in the matter…that was something else entirely.

Turning to the front of the ledger, she saw the years

1940–55 inscribed on the front page, below it another list of around a dozen names, nuns who must have worked there. Sister Marie-Therese, Sister Agatha, Sister Cecelia, Sister Clare… Her heart sped up as she ran her eyes down the list, her breathing shallow.

She came to the bottom of the page and let out a frustrated sigh.

There was no Sister Bernadette listed.

FRANKIE, IZZY, and Diana were having lunch when the sound of a vehicle coming up the long drive caused them all to look up from their sandwiches—peanut butter for Izzy, salami and tomato for Diana, and Vegemite with cheese for Frankie. "Deputy's car," said Diana.

"How do you know that's what it is? Could be anyone."

"I just do," she said mysteriously.

Frankie rose from the table and went to the door, where she stood under the portico as two uniformed officers pulled up and got out of their cruiser. Scruff, who had been lying on his bed near the door, didn't even bother to raise his head. "Some guard dog you are," murmured Frankie as she saw Molly coming up the path, wearing a smile fit to split a melon.

"Frankie, hello again. Meet my partner, Deputy Scott Jennings. He'll be heading back to the city once you start work."

An awkward young man with white-blonde hair and a film of sweat on his upper lip held out a damp hand for Frankie to shake. "Good to meet you, ma'am." He could conceivably have started shaving only last week, but his voice was deep and his handshake firm. Frankie had actually met him once before, when he approached

Emma in the nursing home parking lot, but he gave no indication of recognizing her and she didn't remind him of the fact.

"You, too, Scott," she said, ushering them into the breakfast room. She directed them toward one of the two long, rectangular tables that filled the space. Diana wanted her guests to mingle with one another, and so had ordered the tables, made on the island from reclaimed wood, specifically for that purpose.

"Molly! It's been so long," Diana beamed. "I used to teach her cousins," she explained. "Molly would sometimes come and pick them up from school. I've known her since she was a teenager."

Frankie's parents had moved to the island from the city nearly two decades ago, after Frankie had left for college. They'd come in search of peace and quiet, for though Orcades Island had a busy summer season, the rest of the year vacation homes were shuttered, and the lodging inns closed for several months. Frankie's dad had died suddenly, not long after the move, but Diana had chosen to remain on the island, taking a job teaching art part-time at the small elementary school.

"What a lovely surprise to get your phone call."

That's how her mom had known who was coming.

"Very nice to see you again, Mrs. Pearson."

"Diana, please. This is my granddaughter, Isabella," she said, introducing Izzy, who looked up briefly from her phone and acknowledged the visitors.

"We've met before. Hey, Izzy," Molly replied.

"Hey."

"Have a seat," Diana said, before turning toward the open double doors that led to the kitchen. "Now this is about the nun. The one from the nursing home. That's right, yes?"

"We understand Ms. Evans worked here, though it was a number of years ago." Deputy Jennings consulted his notebook. "From May 1942 until the end of 1953, after which time she returned to Seattle, where she lived until she came to Pacifica Gardens."

"She may well have done, though I would have no idea of the specifics I'm afraid. And I can't quite see what her connection to Fairmile might have to do with anything that happened to her recently," said Diana.

"We're exploring every angle," Molly said. "Apparently, she had become rather unmanageable at her previous nursing home," she continued. "And Pacifica Gardens is one of only a handful of facilities in the state that specializes in treating such cases, though they take very few. Most of the residents, such as Ingrid—" she smiled warmly at them, "are easier to care for."

"And how exactly do they treat these difficult residents?" Frankie asked, her words coming out more forcefully than she had intended. "Sedation?"

"Ms. Evans's—Sister Agatha as I believe she was formerly known—treatment was in line with current protocols," said Deputy Jennings, checking his notebook again.

"Though the amount of sedative noted in the toxicology report *was* on the high side," Molly added.

Frankie started. *Agatha*, not Bernadette. Agatha had been one of the names at the front of the ledger she'd been looking at, she'd swear to it.

"That poor woman," Diana said when she returned with the drinks, mugs chinking as she placed them on the table. Frankie studied her. Something in her mother's tone struck her as slightly off, though she couldn't pinpoint why. That Diana was stressed by the enormity of getting the house ready was the most likely explanation.

"Coffee, darling?" Diana asked, pushing a mug in her direction.

"But the *specific* nature of it…?" Frankie wanted to say *ritualistic*, given the placement of the crucifix and the bizarre arrangement of weeds, but was mindful of Izzy in the room. "Izzy, would you mind fetching the cookie jar?" she asked.

"Is why we are exploring every angle," said Molly, her eyes shifting to Izzy, who had got reluctantly to her feet.

"It's a long shot, but was there anything, any documentation in the house when you bought it?" Molly asked as Izzy returned with a plate of oatmeal cookies. "Anything left behind? I realize it was empty for several decades."

"Furniture, the odd painting, old books, moth-eaten rugs, cutlery, garbage really…" Diana replied, taking a sip of her coffee. "What I couldn't get rid of I put in the barn. Perhaps the historical society would be a better bet? They might have some of the house's old records, that is if the nuns didn't take them with them."

As Molly made a note, Frankie wondered why her mother hadn't mentioned the study, the one she'd been clearing out this morning. She, too, kept quiet, for she didn't want the ledgers taken away before she'd had a chance to reexamine them.

The two deputies exchanged a glance, checking with each other that they were finished with their questions, and drained their mugs. "If there's anything else you remember, anything at all…" Molly held out a card. "My number's there."

"Yes, of course," said Diana. "And lovely to see you again my dear."

"You too Mrs.—Diana. And Frankie? Quiz night? You haven't forgotten?"

Frankie *had* completely forgotten. "Of course. If that's okay with you, Izzy? We're here to spend as much time as we can with each other," she explained. She stood up, stretching her leg, which prickled with pins and needles. "Iz, would you mind showing them out?" She didn't say anything more to Molly, figuring that she might not appreciate Jennings learning that they'd already spoken privately about the case.

As she heard the door open and then shut and the sound of an engine revving, Frankie turned to her mother. "What about the study?" She hadn't yet told her mother about the ledgers.

"Oh, there's nothing but stacks of old Bibles in there. Wait, do you think we should call them back and let them know about those?" She picked up the card.

Frankie shook her head. "I'm halfway through sorting through the stuff. Why don't I finish and then if I find anything useful, we can contact them then? If that's the case, we can tell them we only just discovered it." Which was partly true.

TEN

Fairmile, 1949

THE GIRL SNIFFED the sharply scented air as they turned off the main road and onto a winding track shadowed by towering pines that almost entirely blocked out the light. The house came into view, revealing itself as they rounded a bend in the track. It was set in a clearing, with the shoreline beyond. A snow-capped mountain—Mount Rainier she'd discovered, overhearing a conversation on the ferry—hovered in the distance like a mirage.

She imagined Fairmile must have once been a grand mansion; it had a wide front porch that ran the length of the sprawling first floor and a row of dormer windows on the third floor. A wooden jetty pierced the black water like a needle, an orange and white life preserver hitched to a post at the end. To the left were two large boatsheds painted in a weathered shade of crimson so faded it appeared almost pink in the gray morning light.

Perhaps it had been a place where parties would have been held, tennis matches and croquet tournaments; where children launched themselves from the jetty, squealing as they splashed into the freezing water, or took out sailboats and canoes. Where the women would have worn white all summer long, perhaps accessorized with a jaunty sailor's cap, and the men loose, pale cotton pants, boaters, and regatta-striped jackets... She let her imagination run free for a moment.

Now, the clapboard was dingy and broken in places, the porch scoured and splintered by rain, the roof missing shingles. The yard was scrubby, the grass yellow and thin, the tennis court overgrown, its net saggy and full of holes, though she could see a well-tended vegetable patch to one side, a sizeable woodpile, and beyond that another, smaller building with a cross atop the roof that was unmistakably a chapel.

It was in the middle of nowhere. An ideal place to shut away girls who got themselves in trouble, to quarantine them, as though illegitimate pregnancy was a nasty disease you could catch if you weren't careful, or to pretend they didn't exist at all.

As they got out of the car, she saw two girls sweeping the front porch. Both were obviously pregnant, their bellies stretching the dull fabric of their dresses. The girl didn't know why but the mere sight of them, in a similar predicament to her, eased the knot in her stomach.

"Jean, would you show our new arrival to her room please? She'll be sharing with Sara."

The girl called Jean—her cheeks dimpling as she smiled fleetingly—put her broom to one side and took the suitcase from Sister Clare. "You'll be on the top floor, in one of the attic rooms," she said, her lilting accent labelling her as a girl from the South—Tennessee or Kentucky perhaps.

"Where are we?" the girl whispered as she followed Jean up a wide, curving staircase.

"Fairmile." Jean turned to her, a puzzled look on her face.

"But *where* is this?"

"Oh, I see what you mean. Orcades Island, in Puget Sound."

The girl vaguely remembered the Washington coastline from a second-grade coloring exercise, and she'd certainly heard of Puget Sound, but she didn't recall Orcades Island. "Is Fairmile the only house here?" They had come straight from where the ferry docked, and they'd not passed a single dwelling on the fifteen-minute drive.

"No, silly. There are plenty more houses all around the island. Now, here we are." She opened a door to a small room with a sloping ceiling containing two single beds. "Little One—that's Sara—sleeps here as well. She's new too."

"Little One?"

"You'll soon see. You're lucky they had space for you both. Two other girls went home last week."

The girl didn't ask whether they had taken their babies with them.

Jean pointed toward a small dresser. "The top drawer's yours. Bathroom's down the hall on the left," she said, leaving her to unpack.

The girl hadn't brought much with her—a couple changes of clothes, skirts that her mother had let out as far as the waistbands would allow, and an old sweater of her father's that would stretch over her stomach as she grew bigger—and so she quickly arranged them, closing the suitcase and sliding it under the bed. She went to the window, which looked out over the dark expanse of water, seeing nothing but the distant shapes of other islands. She might as well have come to another country, it felt so far from home and all that was familiar. One thing was certain, no one who knew her, or her family, would ever find her here.

That was exactly what her mother had wanted.

She sat down on the bed, unsure what to do next. Was there going to be anything to keep her occupied while she waited until her baby was born? The two girls she'd seen had been sweeping, so she guessed that they would be expected to help keep the house clean. She fretted about missing class. She'd only been able to bring one textbook—math—with her and that wouldn't be nearly enough to stop her from falling behind.

The door opened again, and another nun appeared. A slight woman, whose habit stopped a few inches short of the ground, revealing sensible brown shoes and thick ankles in worsted hose. Her plain face, with pale skin and eyebrows so fair they were almost nonexistent, was stern. "Miss Ryan? I'm Mother Mary Frances. Mother Superior." Her lips parted in a smile, but the girl could tell it was fake. Her eyes were like chips of glacier ice. "Follow me downstairs now." Mother Mary Frances didn't wait to see if the girl was behind her and so she had to scramble to catch the door before it swung shut again.

The nun led her into a small room on the ground floor. Bookshelves lined three of the walls, there was a large desk, and a low-set square-paned window that looked out onto the vegetable patch. Before she took the seat that Mother Mary Frances indicated, she caught a brief glimpse of three girls armed with hoes and a shovel, raking the ground in a lackluster fashion. She swallowed a grin as she saw another nun, tall and mannish in her hands protected by heavy-duty gloves, splitting wood with an ax, looking like an avenging bat. It seemed incongruous somehow, to see a nun with an ax, but the girl supposed someone had to do the job.

"I expect you're wondering what will happen now that you're here?"

The girl nodded as the nun shuffled some papers in front of her.

"Father Anthony of Saint Patrick's sent through the request, and it says here that you're five months along. Is that correct?"

She nodded again.

"Very well. You will be seen by our midwife every week to make sure that you and the baby are healthy. When it comes time for your confinement, there is a birthing ward here, although if it looks like there might be complications, you will be taken to the hospital on the mainland. There is also a doctor, on the other side of the island, but only if we can't manage ourselves."

"And the baby?"

"Never doubt that you have committed a mortal sin." Mother Mary Frances's face softened a fraction. "But God offers forgiveness to those who repent. If you truly love the baby, you will give it up. We have so many fine married couples who are unable to have children of their own. You will be doing a wonderful thing by giving the baby the best chance for a good life."

The girl wasn't stupid. Her mother had made it clear that once she'd taken care of her "little problem" she would be able to return to school. There was no place for a baby in that picture.

"All our girls are expected to take a turn in the yard, the kitchen, and the laundry. We aim to be as self-sufficient as possible at Fairmile, for we have no wish to be a burden. You have been assigned to the laundry for the next month and will begin there tomorrow. It's where all of the new girls start, while they are strong enough for the heavy work. Don't worry," the nun said, seeing the girl's expression. "You'll pick it up." She went on to explain mealtimes, activities such as knitting and needlework—"You can make a layette if you like. Many of the girls enjoy that." The girl hated needlework almost as much as she despised knitting, but the thought that she might be able to make something to give to her baby, however poorly done, was more of a comfort than she expected. "You can choose the wool, and we have quite a selection of fabric."

It would probably be the only choice she was allowed to make.

"Now, we give all our girls a new name while they are here. Discretion." Mother Mary Frances tapped her nose and then opened a ledger, ran her pen down a ruled page. She paused for a moment, then scratched something with her fountain pen. "Brigid," she said.

The girl had never been fond of her given name but now she hated the name Brigid even more.

SHE MET SARA that evening as they all—twenty girls and five nuns—gathered for dinner. Mother Mary Frances introduced Brigid to each girl in turn. She was forced to think of herself as Brigid now, though she was slow to respond when called, believing the nuns were referring to someone else.

It would take a while to learn all of the girls' names, but she saw straightaway why Sara had earned the nickname "Little One." Sara was tiny, slight and fair-haired

with a lisp and enormous liquid eyes that reminded
the girl of Hershey's syrup. Her swollen belly stuck
out almost obscenely from her small frame, stretching the knit of her sweater. It soon became clear that
the other girls looked after her in a way that seemed
almost motherly. Brigid saw one girl pass her an extra
slice of bread and margarine from the pile in the middle of the table, another refill her glass after she gulped
down her water, yet another stroke her hair as though
she was a cherished little sister.

"She's *thirteen*," the girl next to her whispered once
they had sat down and begun eating. "Poor thing.
Hasn't cried a single tear since she's been here."

A year older than her own sisters. The thought
chilled her. Brigid wondered what must have happened (well apart from the obvious) for Sara to end up
at Fairmile but had already realized that it was a question you didn't ask.

Her meal was in front of her, as was a large lozenge-
shaped pill, cradled in the bowl of her spoon. She eye-
balled it and waited to see what the other girls would
do.

Each of them popped the pill in their mouths, took
a sip of water, and swallowed.

"Vitamins," said the girl sitting across the table from
her. "To help the babies grow big and strong."

Brigid followed suit, then forked up a piece of meat
from the stew on her plate to hide the bitter taste. Next
to the stew was a small pile of wilted greens. She took
a mouthful, expecting spinach, but the taste was different, tangy.

"Nettles," said the girl beside her, noticing her confused expression. "If you've misbehaved, Sister Ag-

atha makes you go and pick them. If you're not careful they'll sting like you've been swarmed by a whole pile of fire ants. I think she likes that. But they're okay once they're cooked."

Brigid forced herself to keep chewing, saying nothing in reply.

She listened to the quiet hum of conversation—unlike the convent in the city, it seemed that the girls here were allowed to talk at mealtimes. She was reassured to discover that some of the other girls seemed much like her—normal, kind, funny, smart girls—and she felt somehow less alone, less of a complete idiot for getting herself into the worst kind of trouble.

"Sister Agatha's definitely the meanest," said a tall, dark-haired girl called Sally, speaking softly so that the nuns, sitting at their own table at the other end of the room, wouldn't hear. "If she can find a reason to punish you, she will. Once she made Marianne—" Sally pointed to a freckle-faced girl sitting farther along the table, "balance a book on her head for more than an hour. And she was *dying* to use the bathroom. All because she said Marianne cheeked her. Which *of course* she hadn't. Marianne's the straightest girl here. I don't think she's ever put a fingernail out of line, let alone said something she shouldn't."

"Got it." Brigid took another bite of the stew. It was better than it looked, but that wasn't saying much. "Anything else I need to know? What happens, when, you know…"

"When the baby comes?"

Sally placed her knife and fork together on her plate and folded her hands serenely in her lap, unintentionally cradling her belly. "I haven't been here that long myself."

"It's in God's hands," said another girl sitting opposite.

Brigid did her best to hide her irritation at the ridiculous piety.

After dinner, the girls were allowed to gather in a common room, furnished with a couple couches and several armchairs, and warmed by a log fire. Brigid followed some of them there, seeing the others bring out sewing, needlework, or knitting. There was a basket of wool in shades of white, cream, and yellow, and folded squares of fine cotton lawn. "You can start with a washcloth or a wrap," said Jean, seeing her confusion. "All you have to do is hem it."

"Why would I want to do that?"

"Don't you want to make something nice for the baby?" Jean asked, then added, in a whisper, "That they can have from you."

"I'd not really given it much thought," said Brigid, remembering the nun's earlier suggestion. "But, yes, I suppose so."

"It's not as hard as it looks," said Sara. "I'll show you how." She lowered herself onto a seat next to Brigid, threaded a needle, and handed it to her with a piece of muslin. "If you roll the edge of the fabric over, you can stop it from fraying." Brigid watched as Sara made tiny, neat stitches in her own piece of fabric, her fingers flying.

"Where did you learn to do that?" Brigid asked.

"My mother was a seamstress. She practically put a needle in my hand before I could walk." Sara looked wistful, but then her expression shuttered.

ELEVEN

Puget Sound, 2013

IZZY AND DIANA were curled up in front of a movie when
Frankie went to leave, a bag of M&M's between them,
with a Coke for Izzy and a tumbler of whiskey for her
mom. Frankie clocked the alcohol, surprised. Diana
rarely drank spirits. "What are you watching?"

"Sleepless in Seattle," said Diana.

"You're kidding, right?"

"It's so uncool, it's cool," said Izzy, pouring a handful of candies into her mouth. "Besides, it's local." Her
words were garbled as she crunched down.

"I guess it is." Frankie felt a tiny sting of jealousy
on seeing her mother and daughter so much at ease in
each other's company. She and Izzy had gone swimming after the deputies had left, watching dragonflies
flit above the water and chatting idly about nothing
very much. Away from her phone, Izzy had been more
talkative, and Frankie hoped that they'd made the glimmer of a breakthrough.

"I'll head off then, get some fresh air on my way,"
Frankie said.

"Where are you going again?"

"Quiz night."

"Oh yes," said Diana, distracted. "I remember now."

Frankie pulled on her sneakers and decided to go out

along the track that wound beside the water and led to Huntley's Point, hoping a walk there might calm her mind. She'd had no opportunity to revisit the ledger, making the decision to swim with Izzy rather than return to the study, but she'd been unable to stop thinking about who might have wanted to kill Sister Agatha/Bernadette, and why, turning the problem over and over in her head, each time coming up with a wilder theory.

Had the woman been loved, respected, feared, or hated? Perhaps all these things and more. What could a nun have done to make someone do such a thing to her, or was it random—someone with a vendetta against the Catholic Church? No, Frankie had a feeling it was personal; no one would leave such a pointed calling card—the stinging nettles—unless it meant something.

As she skirted the boatsheds, she carefully avoided the trench that the plumbers had dug a few weeks before, which was now half-full of muddy rainwater. She would call them again in the morning to find out exactly when they might be thinking of coming back to finish the work. She couldn't remember what it was they were supposed to be doing there; Diana had organized it.

The long, slow dusk had stilled the air and there was no sound except the gentle chirrup of cicadas. As she walked, Frankie felt a little of the day's tension fall from her shoulders. There was solace in her soft footfalls, the thick, almost bouncy bed of pine needles, and the feeling of disappearing down a shadowed path.

As she reached The Cabbage Shed, she saw a group of people about to enter. "Frankie! You're just in time." Molly hailed her. "The quiz starts in ten minutes."

Five pairs of curious eyes swiveled toward her. Damn. It didn't look as though there'd be an opportunity to speak to Molly on her own, to voice the questions that had been uppermost in her mind on her walk there.

Molly made a quick round of introductions among the people she was with, though Frankie strained to catch all their names. "The new deputy, huh?" one of them asked.

"Not officially, not until September," she replied. "Until then I'm on vacation."

"Nice."

They swept into the bar and a drink was thrust in her hand before the group moved to a large table underneath a window.

"We're the Hopeless Causes," said a man with a ruddy complexion who she thought was called David. "We almost always come last." He took a long drink from his beer and grinned amiably at her. "So, what's your talent?"

"I'm sorry?"

"What are you good at? Literature? Science? Art? No, let me guess, geography."

Frankie scooted along the bench seat, her back to the wall, giving her a good view of the room. Old habits, again. "A little of everything?" she offered.

"Excellent."

The rest of the team joined them, and Molly squeezed in next to her. "Pleased you could make it," she said, whispering in Frankie's ear. "We need all the help we can get."

"I wouldn't be too sure that I'll make much of a difference," Frankie replied.

"Ah, it's all a bit of fun. Helps bring the crowds in

too. That's my brother, Joe." Molly indicated a rangy, dark-haired man wearing faded Levi's and a T-shirt that stretched pleasingly across his shoulders. He emerged from behind the bar with a sheaf of papers in his hand and a pencil behind one ear. "I know," she laughed, seeing Frankie's expression. "We're nothing like each other. He takes after our dad. I got the Scandinavian genes on Mom's side; he got the Russian ones."

"Really? Dowd is a Russian surname?"

"Dudnickov originally. Anyway, he makes up the questions. His bar; his quiz."

"Fair enough."

Joe Dowd. It was a solid, honest, unpretentious name and it appeared to suit him. Frankie watched him surreptitiously as he moved about the bar with an easy, unhurried grace. His chest stretched The Cabbage Shed logo on his shirt and, combined with a five o'clock shadow and cheekbones you could sharpen a knife on, meant that he was, objectively speaking, a stone-cold fox.

Definitely not her type.

Who was she kidding?

There was a call for hush and Joe began to speak, reading out the rules in a rich, melodious baritone that carried over the hum of the bar. Warm voice, hot body… Frankie tried not to stare but failed miserably. She inadvertently caught his eye, saw a spark of curiosity there, a lazy smile that flipped her stomach like a pancake, and she quickly looked away.

The quiz progressed and Frankie discovered that Molly had been telling the truth, though it wasn't that the Hopeless Causes were particularly lacking in general knowledge. The questions were esoteric at best, bizarre at worst, and it seemed as though half the fun of the exercise was in bantering with Joe, who, it had to be said, gave as good as he got. "Which four South American countries are currently not on fire?" he asked, a grin playing on his lips as the crowd collectively groaned.

"Call that a question?" someone yelled over the hubbub.

"I see we've a quizmaster for next week," said Joe, pointing into the crowd. "Consider yourself nominated, Roger."

The comment was met with cheers of approval as the crowd grew rowdier and more beers were called for. Frankie finished her drink only to find another take its place and experienced the unusual sensation of her cheeks aching. It had been a long time since she'd been able to switch off completely.

Finally, after five rounds of questions, another team—Les Quizerables—was declared the winner by half a point, and the group around their table began to drift away. "Half of them are orchardists or vignerons," Molly explained. "Apples, cherries, grapes. Their day often starts before dawn. Another?" She raised an eyebrow and her glass simultaneously.

"I shouldn't." Frankie glanced at her watch and saw with surprise that nearly three hours had disappeared.

"I can drop you home," said Molly. "You really don't want to be walking down that road in the dark; the craters are god-awful. I've had enough anyway," she added, swallowing the dregs of her beer and getting to her feet.

Frankie was quick to agree, not least because her leg now ached fiercely. She also wanted to seize the chance to talk to Molly on her own.

They left the pub with a farewell to Joe—again, that slow smile that radiated warmth and promised something even more interesting—and the few remaining Hopeless Causes, David having extracted a promise from her to join them again the following week.

"Have there been any developments?" Frankie asked once they were in the privacy of the car.

"We've had half a dozen officers drafted in from the city, all guys. None of them seem to be interested in my opinion." Molly pulled into the street and looked uncharacteristically despondent. "Besides, they'd all rather be on the Snoqualmie case. The homicide of an old woman—even a former nun—isn't exactly as compelling as finding a serial killer."

In the past two years, the bodies of three young women had been found in the national forest twenty-eight miles east of Seattle, the last one only a month ago. Frankie had heard about it from as far away as Sydney. "*I'm* interested," said Frankie. "What have you got?"

"Okay. As I suspected, the cause of death was an overdose of barbiturates…"

"Accidental?"

"Given the way her wrists were bound, I'd argue against that."

"Someone on the inside?"

"We're interviewing Regina Halversen later this week. She has a new job at a daycare center in West Seattle, in charge of the three-year-olds room."

"And the other former staffer? Alan Bloom?"

"We're still trying to locate him. But his ex-coworkers certainly didn't have anything nice to say. According to them, he was always mouthing off, telling them he was gonna be rich one day, the usual crap-talk. One of them suggested Bloom might have been stealing medications and selling them on the black market. Obviously when Ms. Evans made her complaint, his sources of income—both legitimate and otherwise, if that's to be believed—dried up pretty quickly. There's also an arrest on record—a decade or so ago he was named in an extortion case, but he was never convicted. The guys from Seattle seem to think that once we find Alan, the case'll wrap up pretty quickly."

Frankie absorbed this information. "And you don't?"

"I'm not so sure it's that straightforward. And there's another odd thing."

"Oh yeah?"

Molly shifted in her seat. "She had scars. On the front of her thighs. They were old, but it looked like she was once whipped. Many, many times."

Frankie shuddered at the thought.

"They found a device, in her toiletry bag of all places."

"What?"

"A scourge I discovered it's called. A small leather whip with braided ends."

"Kinky."

"Yeah, well, apparently it used to be a thing: highly religious men and women believing that bodily desire was evil and that it must be controlled. Self-flagellation. Not uncommon at all." Molly's voice had become a whisper, her expression one of distaste.

TWELVE

Puget Sound, 2013

THEY TURNED DOWN the long, pitch-dark drive and Molly eased off the accelerator, watching out for potholes in the asphalt. The pine trees that flanked the road made the night seem darker than it had at The Cabbage Shed.

"Here we are," she said, her tone lightening. They pulled up outside Fairmile, where a light shone from the portico, and she killed the engine. "It's good of you to help your mom for the summer."

Frankie appreciated the fact that Molly hadn't asked her too much about her past, for she wasn't sure she was ready to explain it to anyone. Even her mother had got the abridged, heavily edited version of Frankie's former life in Sydney, what exactly had led to her stepping out onto a busy street and forgetting to check for traffic. You could wallow in your poor decisions, making yourself utterly miserable and achieving nothing, or you could suck it up, vow not to repeat them, and move on. At least that's what she kept telling herself.

"Kinda strange to be living with your mom when you're nearly forty." Frankie gave a humorless laugh. "I'll get my own place eventually."

"Not at all. I get it: family is important. It's part of the reason I came back to the island too."

"Thanks for the lift. And the invitation. I had fun tonight."

"I should be thanking you."

"What for?"

"We would have lost by so much more without you."

A bubble of laughter escaped Frankie's lips as she went to open the door. "I doubt it."

She crept into the house, not wanting to wake her mom or daughter, but heard the burble of the TV coming from the den. She opened the door to see the two of them pretty much where she'd left them, though Izzy's head now rested against a pillow at an awkward angle, a blanket pulled up to her chin. Her eyes were closed, her mouth slightly open.

"She's surely not comfortable like that," Frankie whispered.

Diana eased herself off the couch and gestured that they should leave Izzy where she was. Clicking the remote to turn the screen off, she followed Frankie into the kitchen, stumbling over the steps that led into the room. She only just caught herself from falling.

"You okay, Mom?"

"I was worried about you," said Diana, ignoring her. "You've been gone for hours. Was starting to think I might have to call the sheriff's department." She slurred slightly and Frankie wondered exactly how much whiskey her mom had downed. "Sorry," she replied, stifling a groan: she wasn't used to answering to anyone but herself.

"You could have wrecked an ankle down a rabbit hole and been lying there in the dark…anything."

Frankie gritted her teeth. "I didn't expect to be gone

nearly so long. It didn't occur to me that you might worry. I'm used to looking out for myself."

"I know. So?" Diana asked. "Did you have a good time?"

"Mom!" She flicked to exasperation. "I can't believe I have to answer that question."

"Frances Louise, would it kill you not to be so damn secretive?"

Frankie sighed dramatically. "Yes. I met some nice people."

"I'm still your mother, you know. I care."

Frankie felt instantly remorseful and moved to hug her mom. "Don't think I don't appreciate it, even if sometimes it seems like the opposite."

Frankie went upstairs but couldn't sleep, the names Regina Halversen and Alan Bloom giving her no peace. She knew this feeling—the first threads of an investigation just waiting to be pulled on until it all unraveled. It was what she did, what she was good at, and it was impossible for her to resist.

Finally, she fumbled for her phone and began to search. She found half a dozen Alan Blooms living in the state. Two were in their sixties, one was a businessman, judging by his photos on LinkedIn, one a medical practitioner, and one was a chef. Only one looked like he could have possibly been employed in elder care: the final Alan Bloom was thirty-two, liked hunting (if a check-in at Dave's Sports three weeks prior was anything to go by), House of Fun Slot Machines and Las Vegas casinos, drove a silver SUV, his favorite movie was *Fast & Furious*, he had 152 friends, and was self-employed, at least according to Facebook. His last post was some six days ago, a rant about fishing quotas.

She moved on, finding twenty daycare centers in West Seattle, and made a careful note of the name and number of each. When she finally fell asleep, she still hadn't decided what she was going to do with the information.

EARLY THE NEXT MORNING, the house echoed with the sound of soft rock, booming male voices, off-key whistling, clanking, and hammering as a team of workmen began stripping paint, laying pipes, and tearing wallpaper from the remaining rooms. Frankie made herself a coffee and escaped to the dock. She drew up a chair and dialed the first number on her list, even as she was telling herself not to.

"Hello, is Regina available please?" she asked when the call had connected.

When the person replied that they had no one there of that name, she apologized for the wrong number and moved to the next one on the list.

She hit paydirt at number eleven, GoodStart Early Learning, but hung up as the woman on the end of the line went to transfer her. Telling herself she wouldn't be getting in Molly's way, not really, Frankie gulped the remainder of her drink and hurried back to the house for her purse and keys. She went upstairs and looked in on Izzy, thinking she might like to come with her, but her daughter was sprawled across her bed and showed no sign of moving even when she tapped her gently on the shoulder.

It would take at least two hours to make the round trip into the city, and God only knew she had more pressing tasks to attend to, but she wanted to see Regina Halversen and Alan Bloom for herself, to determine if either was the kind of person capable of sedating and tying up a defenseless old woman.

GOODSTART WAS A cheerful-looking building painted in primary colors, with giant cutouts of zoo animals on the outside walls. As Frankie approached, she could see toddlers crawling over play equipment and sand-pits, and a group of older kids wearing sun hats drinking out of plastic sippy cups. Introducing herself to one of the women supervising, she asked for the director, pretending that she had recently moved to the area and was considering enrolling her daughter in the fall, that she was turning three. "Regina's over there." The woman pointed to a crouching figure with long fair pigtails and orange overalls at the far end of the play area. "She's in charge of the Butterflies—the threes and fours—you're welcome to speak with her now."

Smiling her thanks, Frankie made her way over, slightly alarmed at the lack of security about the place, at the fact that she was able to walk in with no one asking to check her identity or sign her in. As she drew closer, she watched Regina patiently resolve an argument between two toddlers squabbling over pos-session of a toy dump truck, while extracting a wipe from a packet on the ground and cleaning up both of their goopy noses.

Frankie waited until she had finished and then coughed to alert Regina to her presence.

"Oh, so sorry, I didn't notice you there." Regina got to her feet. "May I help you?"

Frankie gave her the same story she'd given the first woman and Regina launched into an explanation of the routines and care ratios of the center, all while keeping a watchful eye on the kids in her care.

"And how long have you been in charge of the Butterflies?" Frankie asked.

"Actually, not particularly long, a month or so. But I love it here." She smiled happily. "And your daughter will too," she promised.

"Oh," said Frankie. "I'm sure she will." She pretended to survey the scene. "Can I ask where you worked before?"

The sunny expression left Regina's face for a moment. "It wasn't a daycare center. I decided it was time to come back to my first love—the under-fives." She beamed again and Frankie was left in no doubt that Regina Halversen would no more smother an old woman than she would a fly.

Next, she went to Dave's Sports. Her certainty wavered as she reached it—the place was enormous, at least three thousand square feet, give or take. She should have realized—the city was surrounded by water and had a reputation as a magnet for lovers of the great outdoors. The chances of someone remembering Alan Bloom's visit weren't high.

The store was divided into sections for clothing, hunting equipment, fishing gear, boating accessories... She located the fishing department and pretended to browse, waiting for an assistant to spot her.

It wasn't long before she was approached by a husky guy with a full beard, checked shirt, and trousers that featured a boggling array of pockets.

"Know what you're after?" he asked.

"Actually, I could do with some help." Frankie said

that she was shopping for a gift for her brother. "This is his favorite store in fact. He comes here all the time."

The assistant pointed out a few items and Frankie pretended to consider them. "I don't want to get him something he's already bought."

"No problem. If he's a regular customer, we'll have a record of his recent purchases."

"Oh, that would be wonderful," Frankie said. "His name is Alan. Alan Bloom."

She followed the store assistant to the counter, tried not to look at her watch while he served another customer, and then waited as he searched the computer, telling herself she was simply making inquiries, helping out an understaffed sheriff's department.

"Ah, here we go." He paused. "There are two Alan Blooms—which is your brother? Huh, whaddya know, they both live in Lake City. Is he the one on Northeast One-Hundred-Fifteenth Street, or Goodwin Way?"

Before Frankie could answer, the assistant, ever helpful, continued. "Wait. He must be the one on One-Fifteenth—number 16898—I can see he was here on the weekend."

"Yes, yes, that's him."

"Well, he bought a new rod—*nice*—two reels, lures, and a hat. Looks like he's planning on going fishing."

"Oh, yeah, he loves to fish," she agreed, casting her eyes around the store. "I might get him some socks actually," she added, her eyes snagging on a display.

"Good choice."

"I'll take a look," she said. "And thank you so much for your help."

She browsed the socks for as short a time as was reasonable before picking a pair of knee-length ones for no other reason than that they reminded her of Molly. She took them to the counter, where a different assistant was now working.

As she walked out of the shop, she shook her head at how easy it had been to get Alan Bloom's address.

Some half hour later, Frankie knocked on the door of 16898 115th Street. It was a low-set house that had probably seen its best days sometime in the 1970s, with little done to maintain it since then. The gutters had rusted through and the trim around the aluminium window frames was flaking, the timber beneath swollen and warped. Weeds grew in profusion in the front yard, obscuring the path. Frankie parked across the street and waited. There were no vehicles under the carport, and the curtains were drawn. No sign of anyone being home, but she went and knocked on the front door anyway, a story about being a rep for an electrical company ready to go.

When there was no answer to repeated knocks, she edged around the side of the house and peered through a window, where a crack in the curtains offered a dim view of a living area. It was untidy, but not badly so. She could make out a dark brown couch and a few scattered cushions, with cans of beer and a collection of pizza boxes on a coffee table.

No sign of anyone home. So why did she feel as if someone was watching her?

THIRTEEN

Puget Sound, 2013

HAVING NO LUCK in locating Alan Bloom and with time running out, Frankie returned to the island. As soon as she got to Fairmile, she went to the study. She asked Izzy if she wanted to help clear out the rest of the books there, but when met with a lack of enthusiasm, decided to leave her to her own devices for a while. "We'll go into Huntley's Point and pick up your bike later," she promised.

She went straight to the cupboard containing the ledgers and pulled out the one that covered the 1940s and '50s. Lowering herself to the floor, she opened the cover. At the start of each year, the record-keeper had noted the names of the staff—all nuns, beginning with Mother Mary Frances, the Mother Superior at the time, and then listed beneath, the names of the other nuns, around half a dozen of them, some of the names reappearing year after year. Turning the pages, she came to 1942, seeing the name that she hadn't paid much attention to when she first found the ledger: Sister Agatha.

That year, it appeared that fifty or so young women had given birth. Her finger traced down the list, seeing another list of names mostly one, sometimes two: Amelia Rose, Charles William, Stephen, Catherine, Patrick John, and a series of weights that roughly matched those of a newborn. The names the women had given their sons and daughters. There was another column of dates, anything from six weeks to a year after their dates of birth, with either the note "Adopted" or, very, very occasionally, "Returned." She read on, through the list of babies born each year of the decade.

Frankie fumbled with the ledger as she worked out that all but three of the babies born to girls at Fairmile in that decade had been adopted. That was nearly five hundred babies given up. Fairmile was a home for unwed mothers, but even so, that seemed a horrifying statistic. Had all the girls been willing to give their babies away so readily? Somehow, she didn't think so. It had been one of the hardest things she'd ever done to leave Izzy with Lucas, and she'd been able to spend ten years with her before that, *and* knew she'd still see her regularly.

She reached for the other books in the cupboard. There were more account ledgers, with notations for linen and sundries, butcher's and grocer's bills, and monies received "for upkeep."

The last thing she came to, wedged at the very back, turned out to be an album of photographs. The prints had been fixed to the pages with little triangular pockets at each corner, and showed black and white images of girls, the majority taken from behind, as if the photographer didn't want anyone to be able to identify them.

The dates began in the 1940s and went right through to the late 1970s. A few were captioned, but only with first names—Julie, Jane, Carole, Sylvia… Most were not.

She saw the front portico, and there was another one

taken at the back of the house, on the verandah, show-ing three women sitting in iron beds. It was taken from a distance and their faces were indistinct.

There was a picture of a row of infants in their cots, blankets tucked so tightly that they looked like insect cocoons. Toddlers playing outside on a tricycle and a swing. A young woman's face at a window that Frankie recognized as being where the kitchen was now. A solemn-faced pair of nuns, bodies hidden behind shape-less black habits, hair scraped under wimples: almost everything feminine about them hidden from sight.

Then she found one, showing three girls sitting on a couch, what appeared to be knitting and sewing on their laps. She slipped it out of the album and turned it over. The names Sara Ollenberger, Brigid Ryan, and Sally Shanahan were written in light pencil, together with the year, 1949. The first evidence of surnames that she'd been able to find; a slip-up perhaps?

One of the girls couldn't have been more than twelve years old. The huge mound of her stomach obscene on someone so young.

Frankie studied the photo. There was something fa-miliar about one of the girls, but she couldn't place it. It flickered at the edges of her memory but remained frustratingly out of reach—usually she knew immedi-ately if she'd seen someone before, and precisely where and when. The third girl must have moved at the exact moment the shutter clicked, her face out of focus.

Frankie took the photo from the album, placing it to one side before continuing on, in the hope that a memory would surface, and she'd be able to make the connection.

In the final few pages, she came across a grouping

of nuns taken outside the front of the house. Three rows. Either some of them were shorter than the others, or they'd found a bench on which to stand the back row. Underneath, in the same spidery writing as in the records ledger, their names, the year 1951. Frankie matched the names with the faces. She found Sister Agatha, a tall, spare woman at the end of the middle row, cat's-eye glasses obscuring her gaze. It showed a younger person than the photograph used by the newspaper, but it was definitely the same woman.

She ran a finger over the image, as if by touching it she might absorb some clue as to what had happened at Fairmile all those years ago, but of course it was futile. She slipped this photo from the album and set it next to the one of the three girls.

"Coffee?" Diana called from the hallway.

"Please." Frankie was glad for the break and after shuffling a few more books into a pile, followed her mother into the kitchen.

"Look what I found," she said, accepting the mug Diana was holding out with one hand and passing her the photo of the group of nuns with the other. "There's a whole album."

"Yes, well I don't think we want to focus on that aspect of the house's history, do we?" Diana glanced at the photo. "Hardly the kind of thing prospective guests want to think about."

"Aren't you even the slightest bit interested?" Frankie asked.

"Okay, show me again." Diana relented, motioning to her.

Frankie held out the photo. "There—" she pointed to

Sister Agatha. "That's her, the nun from Pacifica Gardens."

"Looks like a right sourpuss," said Diana, her eyes resting briefly on the picture.

"What kind of a life would it be?"

"Oh, I don't know…never having to worry about a roof over your head, or where your next meal is coming from," Diana said dismissively.

"I must say I can't think of anything worse," said Frankie, surprised by her mother's tone. "Bound by rules, never allowed to have any fun. Not to mention never having, well, you know…"

"They have a different idea of fun, perhaps," said Diana, her face set. "But yeah, I can't imagine it myself. Denying yourself so much…"

Frankie remembered Molly's words about the scourge. "Having a warped idea of pleasure and pain."

ONCE SHE HAD finished sorting through the remaining books in the study, Frankie persuaded Izzy to help her take them to the secondhand bookstore in Huntley's Point. "I'm not sure if they'll want them all, but I can hardly toss them in the recycling. We'll call in and see if your bike is ready too," she said.

They were both sweating by the time they had unloaded the books from the back of the truck. The bookstore owner had taken everything except the Bibles and Psalters, of which there were several boxes. "See if the local church has any interest in those perhaps?" she'd suggested.

"Ice cream?" Frankie asked Izzy as they left.

"Sure." Izzy brushed her hair out of her eye and Frankie caught sight of the tattoo again, a budding rose inked in deep red, with the word *sacrifice* in curling script beneath it.

"When did you get that?" she asked, deliberately keeping the judgment from her voice.

"A few months ago."

"And was Dad okay with it?"

"You mean you don't approve?" Izzy asked, a challenge in her eyes.

"I never said that."

"You didn't have to."

"Look…" Frankie began.

"You don't get to say what I do with or to my body. Besides, I'm sixteen."

"Not until next month," Frankie reminded her. "And I thought you had to be eighteen before tattooing was legal?"

Izzy shrugged.

"But you're right; it's not my place to criticize, I get that. I was simply wondering what it meant." She aimed for conciliation.

"I doubt you'd understand."

Frankie stopped and looked at her daughter. "Try me."

They arrived at the counter. "I'll have salted caramel," said Izzy, ignoring her. "Thanks," she added, a little more sweetly.

Frankie let the matter drop. "One scoop or two?"

After they had been served, they walked to the bike store in silence, both concentrating on their ice creams, which threatened to melt in the sun unless they gave them their full attention.

As they reached the door, Frankie remembered she had planned to call in to the library. She glanced at her watch; it was almost closing time. "Izzy would you mind checking on your bike? There's something I need to do. I'll meet you at the store in about ten minutes, okay?"

"Sure."

Frankie finished the last of her ice cream and hurried across the street to the library.

"Okay if I go into the back room?" Frankie asked the man dozing behind the counter. Her mother had mentioned that the local historical society used it for displays.

He grunted his agreement, barely raising his head, and she walked quickly toward the far end of the room, seeing glass cases, tattered flags, sepia-toned photographs, old lace, rusted farm tools, and the like. She scanned the photos, which seemed to be predominantly of the main street in various eras, before stopping in front of one of Fairmile. It showed a number of women in elegant tea dresses and wide-brimmed hats lounging on the back lawn. An idyllic scene.

"Find what you were looking for?" The man had stirred himself and appeared in the doorway. "It's nearly time to lock up." He glanced pointedly at his watch while simultaneously raising a set of bushy eyebrows.

"I'm interested in Fairmile," she said, pointing to the photo. "From when it was a mother-and-baby home?"

"That's all we've got here, I'm afraid. Your best bet will probably be to go into the city, the Seattle Central Library."

It had been too much to hope for that there'd be something on the island. "Okay, thank you," Frankie replied. "I'll definitely do that."

When Frankie returned to the bike store, the sign had been flipped to shut and as she pushed the door, it only served to confirm that fact. She scanned left and right, searching for Izzy, feeling a tiny flicker of panic in not being able to locate her.

There was an alley along one side of the store and Frankie half-walked, half-ran down it, slowing as she heard the sound of laughter, both high and low in pitch.

Izzy and the boy from the store—Zac—were standing over the bike, heads together. Frankie coughed and they startled, as if caught doing something they shouldn't.

"I couldn't find you," she said.

"Sorry," said Izzy, looking anything but. "Zac was showing me how to tighten the brakes."

"They were pretty rusty," he said. "I've cleaned them up and replaced the calipers and cables, but they might come loose again."

"Thank you, Zac. It looks great." In fact, it was little short of miraculous: the repainted frame and mudguards gave the claptrap old machine a much smarter appearance.

"I put on a new saddle too," he said. "Should make it a bit more comfortable. You can have this helmet." He held out a black dome with straps hanging from it to Izzy. "It's old stock, but best to be safe, especially if you're going to be riding on trails."

Frankie saw Izzy and Zac exchange a smile and she wondered if it had been the right thing to do to leave her daughter on her own with him. *Stop*, she told herself. Izzy was fifteen not five, and perfectly capable of looking after herself. That was the thing though. Having not been around for Izzy, or any other teenager, for the past few years, Frankie had very little idea where precisely the boundaries should be drawn.

She cast back to her own teenage years, reminding herself that she'd gotten up to plenty that her own mother hadn't been aware of and survived unscathed.

"The tires are suitable for gravel and dirt, as well as asphalt," he said. "There are some nice trails through the forest if you know where you're going."

"Thanks," said Frankie. "It looks great. Doesn't it Izzy?"

"Yeah, thanks." Izzy gave him a shy grin.

He tipped his head in acknowledgement. "Stop by anytime."

After settling the bill, they left via the alley and returned to the truck, Izzy wheeling the bike alongside her. "Actually…" Izzy said as they got to the bridge. "I wouldn't mind riding back to Fairmile. It won't be dark for ages, and I know the way. There's really not much traffic—not compared to LA anyway."

Frankie couldn't think of a reason to object, took a deep breath. "Just come straight home, yeah?"

"Of course. Besides, I've got my phone if I need to call." Izzy patted the pocket of her denim cutoffs.

Frankie waved her daughter off down the street, reminding herself to take the slow, deep breaths that would loosen the tightness in her chest. Had her mother found it this hard to maintain the balance between giving her independence and making sure she didn't run wild? How did you do it without being worried every second? She'd seen too much in the course of her job to be so naive as to think that the world was a safe place, especially for women. She pushed away her doubts, rolled down the windows, and drove back to Fairmile, temporarily soothed by the fresh scent of the forest and the silvery glimpses of water beyond.

Frankie hadn't even pulled up outside the house when Diana came running toward her. "Where's Izzy?" she asked, resting a hand on the edge of the car as Frankie came to an abrupt halt.

"Cycling home. What's up?" Frankie registered the worried look on her mother's face.

"Good. She doesn't need to see this. Come with me."

Mystified, Frankie followed her mother around to the back of the chapel, near the tennis court, where several of the plumbing crew were at the ditch they'd previously dug. A couple of shovels lay scattered on the ground and the excavator they'd been using to deepen the trench was at the far end.

"Bones." Diana's voice, normally calm and measured, wobbled on the word. "They've come across some bones. They were putting in new pipes to go to the boathouses and found them…" She trailed off.

"What kind of bones? Like a family pet?" Even as she asked the question, Frankie knew her mother wouldn't be quite so concerned over a buried cat or dog.

"I don't think so."

FOURTEEN

Fairmile, 1949

"Dammit," said Brigid under her breath, wrestling the waterlogged clothes with a pair of long-handled wooden tongs. She was trying to avoid the scalding water in the copper washing pot; after a week of working in the laundry, the skin on her hands was raw from the harsh soap that the nuns provided, and she sported several burn marks on the tender skin of her forearms.

"You will *not* swear in this house."

Brigid dropped the tongs, startled by the voice that boomed at her through the steam. She had thought it was just her and three of the other girls there.

Sister Agatha—the nun she'd seen at the woodpile— glowered at her. "Do you hear me, girl?" The warning she'd been given was true: the nun's voice had a streak of meanness in it a mile wide.

"Yes, Sister." Brigid wiped a strand of sweaty hair from her forehead.

"Get on with it then. We do not tolerate slacking at Fairmile."

Sara was at the other end of the room, rubbing the stained linen on a ridged wooden board and pretending not to listen. Across from her, Sally wrung the water from the clean sheets between the rollers of a mangle.

Brigid wondered how she might retrieve the tongs, which were now floating in the hot, cloudy water.

When Brigid was sure that Sister Agatha had gone, she straightened up, feeling the ache in her back and arms. She did her best not to think of her friends who would be in algebra or history right now. Even home ec—measuring out flour and baking soda, creaming butter and sugar with a wooden spoon, or composing a menu for a theoretical dinner party—was preferable to this. She couldn't believe that she'd once complained about having to knead dough for dinner rolls. The fact that the laundry was steamy and warm was the only good thing to be said about it.

The next part of the process was the most dangerous. When the clothes had been soaked for long enough, and the water cooled only slightly, she had to drag the sheets (which weighed a ton) onto the drainer and rinse them in cold water. The linoleum on the floor inevitably became wet and slippery underfoot. "I'm sure I'm getting chilblains," she complained, flexing her sore fingers. No one took any notice; each of the girls was absorbed in her own job.

Catherine, a girl who'd been there for more than a month but had never graduated beyond the laundry for reasons that no one had explained, had the responsibility of starching the nun's wimples. It was her job to mix the white powder with a little water to make a paste, stir in boiling water, and then steep the fabric in the mixture.

It was a far less arduous task, but one that came with a punishment if not done correctly. Brigid had already seen Sister Agatha lose her temper at Catherine, striking her on the shoulder for not adding enough starch to the mixture. She had also witnessed the sly pinches that the nun inflicted on some of the girls without warning as she glided past them in the hallway. Though it had shocked and then enraged her the first time the nun did it to her, it had since become a point of pride that she never made a sound or flinched at the pain. Of course, Sister Agatha never uttered a nasty word or committed a spiteful act when any of the other nuns were within earshot.

Brigid was still peering into the washing tub when out of the corner of her eye she saw Catherine double over, one hand clutching her side, her eyes bulging. "Are you okay?" she asked, though it was clear Catherine was not. She wiped her wet hands on her apron and hurried to her side.

"It's nothing, really. I'm fine." Catherine spoke through gritted teeth.

She obviously wasn't.

"I get these pains sometimes."

"Is the baby coming?" Brigid's eyes were wide. She knew this would eventually happen to them all but being confronted by it made it suddenly real.

"It's too early. I'm not due for months yet."

"It's simply your body stretching." Sister Teresa, a nun to whom Brigid hadn't yet spoken directly, swept into the room. "Nevertheless, I think you should go and lie down for the rest of the afternoon," she said, placing a hand on Catherine's forehead. "It's far too hot in here if you're feeling unwell." She, at least, seemed kind.

"But the starching…" Catherine protested.

"Can be done by one of the other girls I'm sure," Sister Teresa said, calmly escorting her from the room.

"What do you think?" Brigid asked, peering into the tub of starch that Catherine had begun to prepare.

"Add a bit more, just to be safe," Sally suggested, coming over to take a look.

"Okay." Brigid tipped extra starch powder into the tub, where it clumped and refused to dissolve. She tried pressing the gelatinous clumps against the sides, but they dodged her spoon, sliding frustratingly out of reach. In the end, Brigid gave up and tossed the waiting wimples in. "I know I'm gonna mess this up," she muttered to herself, wishing she still cared. She remembered Catherine watching the big clock that hung from the laundry wall, checking until the big hand reached the half hour, so she sat back and did the same, perching on a stool and leaning back against the wall. She closed her eyes briefly, giving herself up to the swooning feeling of exhaustion, promising herself that she'd rest for no more than a few minutes.

When Brigid came to her senses, Sara was shaking her arm, and she blinked blearily at her. "The starch," Sara said. "How long has it been?"

"Right, yeah, okay. Give me a second." Brigid yawned and struggled to her feet, ignoring the soreness in her back. She looked into the tub and groaned. The wimples were a congealed mass floating on top of the water, which, she now discovered, was the consistency of Jell-O.

"We can try adding some more hot water," said Sally, coming toward her carrying a heavy kettle, wisps of steam escaping from its spout.

Brigid stood back as Sally hefted the kettle to the side of the tub and began to pour. Sally was stronger than she looked. Boiling water spat up toward them, but she barely flinched. When Sally had filled the tub almost to the brim, she put the kettle down and handed Brigid a pair of tongs. "Try and stir it. See if that helps."

It didn't.

AFTER DINNER THAT EVENING—noodles in a gloopy sauce that was supposed to be cheese but only reminded Brigid of the starchy mess she'd made—she and some of the other girls were helping to clear away the dishes when Sister Agatha bore down on them. "I should like to see the girls who worked in the laundry today."

Brigid noticed the set of her jaw and the pinched mouth, eyes glittering behind her spectacles, and her stomach did a backflip. She was pretty sure it wasn't the baby. Wary glances flew between the girls.

"Of course, Sister," said Catherine. "Would you like us to come now, or finish here first?"

"See me in the office in ten minutes."

The girls didn't speak as they finished clearing the dishes and then walked along the hallway. Catherine gave the door a nervous tap and they filed in, one by one when commanded to do so.

Sister Agatha was apparently absorbed in a document that sat before her and it was some minutes before she acknowledged them. She was playing mind games, exactly like one of Brigid's former teachers had done, making them wait until she was ready, letting their sense of unease fester. The nun wanted them to understand that she was the one with all the power here, not that they needed reminding for a second.

"The wimples," Sister Agatha said eventually, looking at them over the spectacles perched on the end of her beaky nose. "A catastrophe, wouldn't you say?" Her voice was as cold as the stones that ringed the Fairmile shoreline, and she sat back, making a steeple of her fingers, waiting for one of them to speak.

Brigid opened her mouth to take the blame, but before she could, Sally spoke up.

"I'm very sorry, Sister Agatha. That was my fault. I don't know how it happened. I should have been paying better attention."

Brigid blinked. It had been *her* fault, not Sally's. She looked sideways, but Sally stared firmly ahead. Brigid was about to own up when Sister Agatha sucked in a breath, her lips thinning to show yellowed teeth. Slowly, she reached for a silver case on the desk, flipped it open, and retrieved a cigarette.

"I would have expected more from you, Sally. You've been here long enough to know better."

She lit the cigarette, inhaled deeply, and regarded them with disdain.

The girls fastened their gaze to their feet and Brigid tried to swallow the lump of guilt that had lodged in her throat. She wanted to speak up, to take responsibility, but couldn't begin to form the words, silenced by the thought of the possible consequences.

"Very well. Tomorrow morning, you shall forfeit breakfast and spend two hours on your knees in the chapel, Sally. Use the time for contemplation of your sins." Sister Agatha blew out a stream of smoke and returned her attention to the paperwork in front of her. "Do not be late."

They left the room, Sally walking so fast that Brigid had no chance to ask her why on earth she'd shouldered the blame for a mistake that she'd had nothing to do with, no chance to thank her friend for doing so.

BRIGID HAD NOT been inside the chapel, but instead of going to the dining room for breakfast the next morning—though her stomach was crying out for food—she slipped out of the back door and hurried toward it. If Sally was going to have to kneel on the rough floor, she would at least be there alongside her. It was the only way she could think of making up for her mistake, compounded by not speaking up when she had the chance.

The air in the chapel was frigid and she winced as the door creaked when she opened it. It reeked of incense and Brigid wrinkled her nose at the smell, transported straight back to her first communion, the itchy white lace dress she'd been made to wear, the worry that she might get the words she had memorized in the wrong order, the shame when she had stumbled over them.

Sally was at the front, facing the altar, on her knees. Brigid didn't see the nun, at least not at first. It wasn't until Sister Agatha spoke, her voice echoing off the vaulted ceiling, that Brigid noticed the shadows in a corner take the shape of a person.

"What do you think you are doing here?"

"I—I was the one responsible for the mix up with the starch," Brigid stammered, knowing that she should have owned up the day before.

The nun held her hand up, silencing her. "Sally will take the punishment."

Sally gave no sign of having noticed them, staring directly ahead, at a portrait of the Virgin Mary.

"But…"

"Silence!"

Brigid turned to leave. She'd tried.

"However, there is no reason why you shouldn't join her."

As Brigid lowered herself next to Sally, she noticed that the other girl was kneeling on a small pile of green leaves and that tears squeezed from the corners of her eyes. Brigid felt her stomach twist so hard she almost cried out. The pain wasn't the baby growing inside her, but guilt that another girl was taking her punishment.

After they'd been there for what felt like forever, but couldn't have been more than a few minutes, Brigid heard the door close softly. She dared to crane her neck to look behind her. The chapel was lighter now, a soft glow coming from the long, stained-glass windows and casting beams of colored light on the pews that were arranged in strict lines facing the altar. As she twisted, her back flared in complaint, and her whole body began to tremble. The cold coming up through the stone floor had snaked its way into her bones, making her jittery, as if someone was pulling the strings on a marionette.

"She's gone." Brigid still felt the need to whisper. Sally, who surely must have heard, continued to stare straight ahead. By now, Brigid's teeth had begun to chatter so loudly they felt like they might fall out of her head, and she blew on her fingers to try and warm them. "We'll freeze to death here if we're not careful."

No response.

"Why did you say it was you when it wasn't?"

Sally gave the slightest shrug. "Someone had to; why shouldn't it be me?" she whispered.

As Brigid reached for her hand and squeezed it, it struck her that ever since she'd found out that she was pregnant, all she'd done was fight against the unfairness of it all, repeating the words, "Why me?" over and over in her head. It had never occurred to her to think the opposite—why shouldn't it be her?

Sally spoke again, so softly that Brigid had to shuffle closer to hear.

"Oh Jesus Christ!" Brigid cried, as her knees met the leaves. Stinging nettles? No wonder Sally was crying; the pain must be unbearable. She'd thought Sister Agatha merely cruel, but in fact she was a downright sadist.

FIFTEEN

Puget Sound, 2013

"WE NEED TO clear the area. Immediately." Frankie directed the workmen who were standing around the pit, looking alternately horrified and fascinated, their faces drained beneath summer construction tans. "Have you got anything to cover it with?" Light rain had begun to spot the ground and as she looked up, she saw that the sky had darkened to the color of a bruise. "Plastic sheeting, ideally."

"I'll go and check in the van," said one of them, looking glad for something to do and scooting off toward the driveway.

"I've called the sheriff's department," said Diana. "They said they'd send someone over as soon as they could, but they've been called out to a crash on Jinks Road."

Frankie nodded and walked over toward the far end of the trench, her hands resting on her hips. It was about two feet deep, and she could make out the faint glimmer of a pale dome that could be a skull at the bottom. It didn't look very big. Tiny, in fact. So small it could fit in the palm of her hand.

There was no sign of fur or hair.

She couldn't take the risk that it wasn't human.

Who-or whatever it was had been there for quite

some time: there was no obvious clothing or textiles, which could have rotted away. Unless, of course, the body had been buried naked. She couldn't imagine how anyone would do that, if it was human, but that of course didn't make it impossible. She knelt down and put her fingers to the edge of the trench, rubbed the soil between them. It was grainy. Bones could stay preserved for a long time in sandy soil. The rain began to fall harder now, and the plumber returned with a roll of thick blue plastic. Frankie watched as he unfurled it the length of the trench.

"We were about to finish up," said one, scratching his head. "Then we saw it. A few minutes earlier and we would have cut through the whole thing, scooped it up and crushed it." He cast a rueful look at the excavator that sat, inactive now, on the other side of the trench. "Oh," he said, digging into his pocket. "We found this." He handed her a small, flat rectangular box, pressing it into her hand as if he was giving her a tip.

Frankie held it up, wiped away a smear of mud from the surface. The box was metal, but underneath the tarnish she could make out an image of a swan, inlaid in a whiteish material. "There's a clasp on the side," she said, pressing it with her finger. To her surprise it popped open. A coin and a few flakes of tobacco fell into her hand. "A quarter?"

"It was right there with the bones."

Frankie took a closer look at the coin, trying to determine the date. "1949." She vaguely remembered an old tradition of burying a body with some money for the afterlife, a payment to the man who ferried souls across the River Styx. Would someone have been that superstitious? "It's possible the skeleton has been there that long, or nearly that long, at least. I'd say it was deliberately placed there," she said, almost to herself.

"You guys might as well get going for the day," said Diana to the plumbers. "There's not much more that you can do. I'll let you know as soon as we know anything. I'd appreciate it if you kept this to yourselves—it's not what we need right before we're about to welcome guests here."

"Okay then, Mrs. Pearson."

Frankie didn't hold out much faith that they wouldn't mention it to their wives or their girlfriends or their fishing buddies, and that before long not a single islander would be in ignorance of the fact. She only hoped that the news wouldn't spread to visitors or to the mainland too quickly.

The men ambled off, clearly reluctant to leave, one of them casting a backward glance toward the trench. Frankie and Diana stood for a moment as the rain spattered down. "No sense in waiting out here Mom, there's nothing more we can do right now. Come on, let's go inside."

As they turned back toward the house, Frankie stepped around a patch of tall plants growing beside the path. "Mind the nettles," said her mother, pulling on Frankie's arm to move her out of the way. "Mighty painful if they touch your skin."

When they reached the house, Frankie went to a front window, looking out for the deputies' car and for Izzy.

She estimated that it was about a twenty-minute cycle from Huntley's Point to the house, and it had now been a little over half an hour since she had arrived home. As the rain blurred the dark shapes of the pines, she began to worry where Izzy could have gotten to. Had her daughter been overconfident about knowing the way home? There weren't many places to take a wrong turn, but even so…

"Did you sync Izzy's phone to yours?" Diana asked, coming into the room and reading her thoughts. "You can do that, can't you?"

"It didn't occur to me." Should she have known to do that, as a mom? Of course she should.

Frankie saw a sheriff's car at the end of the drive, and she moved away from the window, going to the front door. As she sheltered under the portico, the vehicle drew up beside the truck.

"Hello again." Molly walked toward them, her smile dimmer than on previous occasions.

Diana appeared in the doorway, behind Frankie.

"Mrs. Pearson."

Another person got out of the other side of the car, and Frankie immediately recognized her daughter's slim build and dark hair. "Izzy! What happened?"

"Found her a couple of miles back," Molly said. "Without any lights, or a helmet."

Izzy wore a distinctly sulky expression.

"Oh God, I'm sorry. That's my fault," Frankie apologized. "We weren't expecting the storm." She didn't mention that Izzy had a perfectly good helmet but had obviously chosen not to wear it.

"Didn't want her to risk an accident, and I was heading this way in any case. I understand there's been a discovery…"

"Thank you," said Frankie, ushering her toward the back of the house. "Skeletal remains. Possibly human." She wasn't going to jump to conclusions, despite the evidence. "Might have been there for quite some time. Potentially archaeological."

Molly approached the trench and bent down. She lifted one edge of the plastic sheeting, pulling a flashlight that was clipped to her belt and shining it into the space. After a careful inspection, she replaced the plastic and stood up. "I'd say you're right on the money." She motioned to Frankie that they should move inside.

"We're obviously going to need to investigate," Molly said, before radioing back to the station. "It's a job for a forensic archaeologist. There's one based in the city. Max Hansen. We'll do our best to get him out here as soon as possible, but with the weekend, it might not be until Monday. In the meantime, I'll cordon the area off with tape and you will need to make sure the site is undisturbed."

"There are some old wooden boards in the barn," Diana suggested.

"Good idea, we don't want any animals getting into the area. I'll send someone out to put up a tent, but it might not be until the morning. We'll do our best to keep this quiet, for your sake as much as the rest of the island."

The Orcades economy traded on its reputation as a safe, clean, and beautiful place to visit, drawing people from as far away as the eastern states, even internationally. The suspicious death of the nun was bad enough, without adding the possible remains of a newborn buried in an unmarked, shallow grave.

"There was something else," Frankie said, showing Molly the cigarette case. "With the bones. A coin too. The plumbers had already pulled it out," she apologized, flicking open the catch.

Molly pulled out a plastic evidence bag and indicated that Frankie should drop it in. "It's highly unlikely we'll get anything useful in terms of fingerprints or DNA, not after all this time," said Molly. She glanced up at the sky. "Not to mention the rain."

"Why don't we get the boards?" Frankie suggested. "And I'll give you a hand with the tape."

"Appreciate that."

As they walked toward the barn, Frankie thought about how to drop her visit to Regina Halversen into the conversation, though there was really no way of mentioning it casually without giving herself away. "How are things going on the Bernadette Evans case?" she asked.

"Tests so far are inconclusive—there was a fair amount of contamination at the site. Fragments that match the DNA of several residents and current staff were found on materials in the room—a water glass, a Bible...but that's not unusual."

"Nothing on CODIS?" The national index system was the best way of finding a DNA match from its database of samples.

Molly shook her head. "Anyway, there's no more to be gained by not releasing the body."

"How about the ex-employees—Halversen and Bloom? Any luck with them?"

"Halversen's in the clear, and Bloom's coming in tomorrow. His alibi is shaky—claims he was away on a fishing trip, by himself, on the night in question—but there's nothing to place him at the scene." She sighed. "The city cops were reassigned yesterday. A pair of hikers uncovered a body on the weekend, not far from where the others were found, so that's become top priority." The state had a reputation of attracting serial killers: Ted Bundy, Gary Ridgway—the Green River killer—now there was another in Snoqualmie…

Molly sounded uncharacteristically pissed at the lack of support.

"Would you mind if I sat in tomorrow? Behind the glass?" Frankie asked. "I wouldn't be in your way." She really shouldn't be getting involved, but that had never stopped her before.

"Matter of fact, I'd appreciate another opinion. He's due in at noon."

"I'll be there."

A fishing trip, Frankie mused. Wasn't Sergeant Sandberg away on a fishing trip, out of contact? She shrugged; it was probably a common pastime in this part of the world, no different than her Sydney colleagues going on a surfing safari in the Mentawais.

When Molly had driven away, Frankie returned to the house, finding Diana slicing tomatoes for dinner. "It'll mean a delay of God knows how long," she said, focused on their planned opening.

"Mom that was probably once a person, an innocent child," Frankie replied. "They deserve at least to be treated better in death than they were in life."

"Oh, I know, I'm stressing about the opening. I'm sorry."

"That poor, poor little baby." It had to be a baby, from the size of what she'd seen. Doubtless connected somehow to the time Fairmile was a mother and baby home. "Didn't stand a chance." Frankie's skin prickled. "Where's Izzy?"

"I sent her upstairs to change, she was soaked through. She's so much like you," said Diana with a faint frown.

"I remember your favorite phrase almost as soon as you learned to talk was 'I do it myself.' Fiercely independent."

"Foolhardy if you ask me. What was she thinking, riding without a helmet? These roads are so narrow, a car or a truck coming the other way could have wiped her out in a split second." Frankie's mood flipped from anger to concern and then back to anger again.

"Best to let this one lie," said Diana. "Or I can talk to her if you like?"

"She's my daughter," said Frankie.

She found Izzy in her room, wrapped in a towel and stretched out on the bed. She appeared to be watching a makeup video.

"Put your phone down for a minute, could you please, Iz?"

Izzy dropped her cellphone and glared at her mother.

"I'm not going to give you the third degree, if that's what you're thinking, but if you're brought home by a deputy again…" She let the threat hang in the air. Now was not the time to bring up the fact that having her daughter in trouble with the local law enforcement wouldn't do Frankie any favors. "Listen, I'd like you to share your phone location with me." She held up a hand as Izzy began to protest.

"It's not to check up on you. I'll only use it if I absolutely have to. It's in case something happens…".

Izzy shrugged and picked up her phone. "Whatever. I could *literally* not care less."

Frankie took that to mean Izzy would do as she asked. "And Granny could do with a hand in the kitchen if you wouldn't mind getting dressed."

"What was it like?" Izzy asked, putting her phone down again.

"What was what like?"

"Did you, like, see a lot of bad stuff in your last job?" Frankie nodded.

Izzy nodded. "Is that why you left? And came here?"

Frankie was soaked through from the rain herself, but leaned against the doorway, taking a moment before answering. "Partly. But I missed you. I missed Granny and GG. I'd been away too long." She couldn't tell her daughter about the last case she'd been working on. How badly she'd screwed up. The face that still appeared in her mind's eye when she was least expecting it, and which had culminated in a stupid, careless accident that left her with a busted-up leg, and which could have been so much worse. "Anyway, I need a shower. Do you think you might go and help Granny? She's making hamburgers."

BY THE TIME Frankie had cleaned up, she could smell dinner cooking. Toweling her hair dry, she pulled on a pair of shorts and a T-shirt. She shoved her feet into a well-worn pair of Ugg slippers, for the stone floors were cool, even in summer, and they had yet to furnish the place with rugs. A few weeks of home cooking, rather than fast food wolfed down at irregular intervals, had added a few much-needed pounds to her too-skinny frame, and regular exercise and fresh air had erased the pallor from her skin. Sometimes she didn't recognize the healthy, clear-eyed, tanned woman staring back at her in the mirror. The pain in her leg still woke her in the early hours every now and then, but she could run for at least forty minutes now, and she didn't have to remind herself to *just breathe*. Well not quite as often.

"Shall I set the table?" she asked, reaching the kitchen where Diana and Izzy were standing side by side, one grilling onion, the other adding cheese to the burger patties.

"Sure, honey," said her mom, focused on the stove. "I'm worried what might happen if word spreads," she added, turning to Frankie.

"Let's hope it doesn't come to that, hey?"

"Do you think it's from when Fairmile was a birth home?" Izzy asked. Frankie had shown her some of the old photos in the album, talked to her about what had happened to the girls who came there.

"Highly likely I'd say," Frankie replied. In the shower, she'd been mulling over the death of Bernadette Evans and the discovery of the tiny skeleton. She couldn't shake the thought that there might be a connection, however tenuous. "We'll deal with it, whatever happens," she added, her voice firm.

Diana reached for a wine bottle next to the stove top, offering it to Frankie, who declined, before pouring herself a glass, filling it almost to the brim.

SIXTEEN

Puget Sound, 2013

THE NEXT MORNING, Frankie and Izzy drove across the island to Pacifica Gardens. "The last time you saw GG she was pretty alert, even if she didn't remember who you were," Frankie warned. "But that's not always the case. Her illness can affect not only memory, sometimes it changes a person's morality or judgment. Someone with dementia can say some pretty out there things, things that they don't really mean. I don't want you to get too upset if she doesn't respond as you might expect."

When they arrived, Ingrid was up and dressed, parked in a chair in the sunroom that looked out across to the water. Frankie embraced her grandmother and she and Izzy pulled up a seat next to her. "How are you?" Frankie asked, as Izzy took her great-grandmother's hand.

Ingrid nodded but didn't speak. Frankie had done a deep dive into the disease when Ingrid was first diagnosed, discovering that as the disease progressed, sufferers eventually lost the ability to converse altogether. She tried not to think too much about what might happen then, whether there would be anything left of her grandmother's personality at all.

She glanced around the room. There was one other resident there, a woman of a similar age to her grandmother, but looking far sprightlier, chatting to a staff member. There was something about the set of her jaw that set off the electric buzz of a half-forgotten memory, but Frankie couldn't place it. A balding, middle-aged man sat with her and by the similarity in their features—the deep-set eyes and strong nose—Frankie guessed he must be her son. She recognized him: he'd been hurrying across the parking lot the day that Sister Agatha/Bernadette Evans's body had been found. Maybe it was the fact that the pair looked so alike that caused her to think she'd seen the woman before.

"Can I get you a glass of water, GG?" Izzy asked.

"That'd be nice, dear."

Frankie was relieved to hear Ingrid speak, though she wasn't exactly sure her grandmother knew who Izzy was. "I'll go, darling," she said to Izzy, getting to her feet. There was an urn of hot water, tea-making paraphernalia, and several pitchers of ice water on a table at the back of the room. She poured a glass and turned, nearly bumping into the man who had appeared next to her.

"Whoops, sorry," he said, taking a step backward and holding up his hands.

"No, it was my fault. I should have been paying attention. That's your mom?" she asked, indicating the woman he'd been sitting with.

"It is." He swelled with pride as he spoke.

"How long has she been a resident here?"

"A little under a year. In fact, we only reunited six months or so before that." One of his eyelids gave a slight twitch as he spoke.

"Oh?" Frankie's curiosity was piqued.

"Rosalie is my birth mother. I was adopted as a baby."

Frankie blinked. She had mixed feelings about people who told you their entire life story on first meeting (she didn't even know this man's name for heaven's sake), but part of her was fascinated by those who overshared, mostly because she wondered how they felt able to spill everything—from a medical diagnosis to a dark family secret—to someone they'd only just met. It must be very freeing, to have no fear of being judged.

"How did you manage to find her?" She wanted to hear the full story now.

"It wasn't easy. Records always used to be sealed—an adopted child wasn't allowed to know their birth parents' details—we were even given new birth certificates. Can you believe that?" He was suddenly indignant, and his eye began to twitch again. "It's different now; there are a number of reunion registries. If you want your adopted parent or child to get in touch you leave your details. Turns out Rosalie had hers on file for years, but I only recently learned that I was adopted. My adoptive parents never had the courage to tell me."

"That must have been a big shock. How was it?" she asked.

"How was what?" His mouth was set in a grim line.

"Finding your mother after so long."

The man's eyes welled up and he fumbled in his pocket, bringing out a crumpled white handkerchief and using it to blow his nose loudly.

"I didn't mean to upset you. I'm sorry."

"No, no; it's okay. I still get emotional about it, that's all." He shoved the handkerchief back in his pocket.

"Is Rosalie from the island?"

He shook his head. "The city. But she had me here. At an unwed mother's home."

There could only have only been one such place. "Fairmile."

"How do you know?" He blinked at her, taken aback.

"It's a long story."

"Ironic that she's ended up back on Orcades Island, huh? But it is the best facility in the county."

"So you brought her here then?"

He nodded. "I couldn't bear for her to be stuck in a concrete jungle overlooking a freeway, which is where she was when I found her. I've been sailing from the island for years—I've got a place in Crane Bay—so it seemed like the perfect solution. Funny, I've always been drawn to the island, and now I know why."

"I heard there's quite a wait-list," said Frankie, thinking of how difficult it had been for her mother to get a spot for Ingrid.

His gaze slid over Frankie's shoulder to where his mother was sitting. "I'd do anything for her."

"Does she have other children? You have siblings?"

"No, I was her only child," he said as the corners of his mouth turned down. "I thought at first that she didn't want me, and that was why she gave me away, but it turns out she never stopped looking for me." He glanced toward Izzy and Ingrid. "She and your grandmother are great friends, so that's been a wonderful bonus for her."

Frankie hadn't been aware of that.

"She told me they've known each other since they were girls."

Frankie turned, distracted by her grandmother waving a hand and asking for water, before returning her attention to the man and holding out her hand. "I'm Frankie."

"Liam Gardener," he said, taking her hand. "But she insists on calling me Marty. That was the name on my adoption papers, the one she gave me."

"Nice to meet you Liam." Frankie made a quick calculation based on the fine lines that fanned out from the outside edges of the man's eyes, the deeper wrinkles that cut across his brow, the hair loss. "You were born when? The nineteen fifties?"

"Nineteen forty-nine actually."

"What's Rosalie's surname?"

"Shanahan." His eyes narrowed. "You a journalist or something? Nah, you're far too pretty. But you sure ask a lot of questions."

Frankie ignored the comment about her looks—it felt distinctly creepy; he was more than twenty years older than her. She knew then where she'd seen the name—and the woman, albeit a much younger version—before. Sally Shanahan. Rosalie… Sally… She was distracted by another call from Ingrid. "Can I talk to you some more before I leave? I might have something of interest for you."

Liam nodded, looking puzzled, and Frankie hurried back. "Sorry, Grandma, here you are," she said. She held up the glass to help Ingrid drink from it and told herself that there had been nothing odd in the way Liam's gaze kept sliding between her grandmother and Izzy as they spoke.

"Thank you, dear." Ingrid smiled at her after she'd taken a sip, but there was a vacant expression on her face.

"Grandma?" Frankie asked, looking toward Rosalie. "Do you know that woman over there?"

"What's that, dear?" Ingrid craned her neck in the direction that Frankie had indicated. "Never seen her before in my life." She returned her unfocused gaze back to the window "Are you sure GG?" Izzy asked. "She's smiling at you."

Frankie had been lied to by some convincing criminals in her fifteen years as a cop: despite her grandmother's memory being unreliable, she'd lay bets that Ingrid wasn't telling the truth.

Two women at the same nursing home: Sister Agatha and Rosalie, both with a connection to Fairmile at a similar time, one of them now dead, likely murdered. Two old friends, one of whom claimed not to know the other. The knowledge made Frankie decidedly uneasy.

Before they left, Frankie stopped to say goodbye to Liam, who was by his mother's side again.

"Liam, would you have a moment for a quick word?" She swiveled her eyes toward the door.

"I never gave him away," Rosalie interrupted, her voice insistent. "He was taken. No one asked me; no one told me where they took the babies." Sudden fury had twisted her gentle features.

"I know, Mom, I know," he soothed. "No one thinks you did." He turned his attention back to Frankie. "Won't be a moment."

Frankie couldn't help but notice that Rosalie was gripping Liam's wrist so tightly it would almost certainly leave a mark.

"This might sound bizarre," Frankie whispered a few minutes later as they stood by the door, even though she doubted that the two women would be able to hear her from so far away. "But I'm actually living at Fairmile for the summer. My mother owns it—I'm helping her remodel it as a guesthouse. Anyway," she continued, "I've been clearing the place out, and I came across some old material from when it was a home. There are photographs, including one I think might be of Rosalie. Should I bring it in for her? Or do you think it would be too upsetting?"

He glanced back at his mother and then at Frankie, appearing to consider the question. "Why don't you let me see it first? The last thing I want to do is upset her, but I'd really like to take a look at it."

"Okay." Frankie pulled out her phone and made a note of his number. "I'll be in touch."

As she was about to leave, she asked a final question. "Rosalie might have known Bernadette—Sister Agatha—from that time?" Frankie spoke quietly, so as not to alert anyone who might overhear them.

"She's certainly never mentioned it." Liam's voice was firm, but Frankie saw a flicker of something pass briefly across his face, and she wasn't sure she believed a word of his denial either.

"He's late, dammit. I knew it."

Molly was more agitated than Frankie had ever seen her when she arrived at the sheriff's offices right at noon, having dropped Izzy back at Fairmile.

"I told the Seattle guys that they oughta bring him in then and there, but oh no, they said he assured them he'd get the ferry over and be happy to answer any questions related to his employment at Pacifica."

"You think they scared him off?"

"Of course I do."

Frankie looked at her watch. It was now nearly ten past. "Give it another twenty minutes, and if he's still a no-show, tell the boys in the city to pay him another visit."

SEVENTEEN

Puget Sound, 2013

"It's DEFINITELY A NEWBORN—the fontanels weren't fused. Based on the size of the bones and the skull, likely even premature." Max Hansen, a tall, stooped man with thinning sandy hair and half-moon, wire-rimmed spectacles, emerged from the tent as the sun was beginning to retreat behind the trees and cast long shadows over the chapel.

He'd arrived early on Monday morning, and he and his team worked through the day, only taking a break when Diana brought out a tray of sandwiches and coffee. Someone had also called in a specialist radar imaging company from the city, and so three men and one woman were using remotes to direct small, wheeled boxes up and down the area behind the chapel. "The soil's sandy, so if there's anything to find there's a good chance we will," one of them said.

Frankie wasn't at all reassured by this.

She was, however, relieved that it hadn't been necessary to bring in cadaver dogs; the sight of the highly trained canines at a crime scene never failed to unnerve her. "Do you think it could be an unofficial...?" Frankie asked her mom. She didn't want to utter the word "graveyard." They both knew that would be a disaster for Fairmile, that it would attract the attention of the world's media, not merely the local stations.

"We'll find out soon enough," Diana said, a tense expression tightening her lips and making her look older than normal. She was taking a lot on with the remodeling of Fairmile and the launch of a new business, and the stress of it all was beginning to show.

Neither of them had been able to do much that day. They'd both spent far too many hours standing at the window that looked out over the chapel as well as making regular trips out to see what was going on under the guise of offering refreshments.

Izzy had set off for town in the late morning, telling (not asking, Frankie noted) her mother that she had arranged to meet Zac for a bike ride and taking a backpack stuffed with snacks with her. "Just keep your cellphone on, okay?" Frankie called after her, realizing as she said it that if they were going on a trail ride, she might well end up out of range anyway. Her daughter was almost sixteen, she reminded herself, resisting the urge to run after her and tell her to be careful. Frankie had met Zac twice now, and he seemed like the kind of nice, respectful boy she would want her daughter to hang out with, so she shouldn't waste her energy worrying. But then who said a mother's fears were ever logical?

"We'll transport the remains to the ME's office downtown," said Max, breaking into her thoughts.

"ME?" Diana asked.

"Medical Examiner." He stood, although his shoulders still remained hunched over. He was a man forced to bend to look at things closely on a daily basis. "We can probably extract DNA from the bones, but that's about it."

"Is there any trauma?" Frankie asked.

Max shook his head. "Nothing obvious."

"How long…?" Diana asked.

"We should get preliminary results in week or two," he replied.

"No, I meant, how long do you think it's been there?"

"Hard to tell. Any fibers that the body might have been dressed or wrapped in have long since rotted away. I'm pretty convinced it's not recent."

"Well, that's something at least," said Diana.

"Worth putting on the DOE Network?" Frankie asked, referring to the international organization that helped track missing persons.

"I suppose, but it's a long shot. It'll be added to NamUs too."

"What's that?" Diana asked.

"The National Missing and Unidentified Persons System." He stripped off his protective gloves. "They're both relatively new agencies."

"Given the history of this place, it's more than likely no one will be looking," said Frankie, unsure if that was good or bad.

"Poor little thing," said Diana.

One of the radar operators came up to them. "We'll be making a full report, but from what we can tell, there aren't any others there."

"Oh, thank goodness," said Diana, her face clearing. "That would have been too upsetting."

"Not to mention having to dig up the entire backyard." Max regarded them soberly.

"One's bad enough." Frankie's words were carried away on the breeze as she turned toward the tent.

An unmarked grave. Buried like rubbish. Someone had wanted it kept secret, unrecorded.

She glanced at her watch. Nearly five p.m. Izzy had been gone all day. She told herself that wasn't late enough to worry, not yet.

The search teams began to pack up and Frankie went inside. Despite the relief that no more remains had been discovered, she couldn't seem to wind down from the anxiety that had ratcheted upward inch by inch as the day progressed. She threw on a pair of running shorts and her sneakers and headed out again along the path toward Huntley's Point.

She'd reached The Cabbage Shed, three miles away, before she allowed herself to stop and catch her breath. She was stretching out a tender calf muscle when Joe emerged, a metal keg resting on one shoulder, a dish towel over the other.

"Frankie!"

"Hey." She took in the unshaven jaw, the flexed bicep, the frayed neckline of his white T-shirt, even the ketchup stain on the front. A grin curved her lips. There was something about the set of his shoulders that sent a dart of pleasure straight to her solar plexus, a simple reaction that was one part appreciation, nine parts desire.

He set the keg down next to several others and for a second they stood there, eyes locked.

No one had looked at her like that for the longest time.

"You thirsty?" he asked eventually.

Frankie swallowed, newly aware of her dry throat. "I

came out without my purse." She made a face. "Could you stand me a glass of water?"

"I can do better than that. Come on in. We're close to opening in any case."

Frankie followed him inside, grateful for the cool, dim interior, and pulled up a seat at the bar, surreptitiously wiping the sweat from her face with the sleeve of her T-shirt.

"What's your poison?" he asked, spreading his arm to indicate the length of the bottles arrayed behind the bar.

"Vodka and poor life choices?" She was only half joking.

He barked in amusement, and she felt the almost forgotten sensation of lust curl deep in her belly. It felt good to make someone laugh, especially when that someone was an attractive man.

No. It was a terrible idea. Another example of a poor life choice. "A beer will be fine. I've still got to get back, though I might walk instead of run."

"Sure thing." He poured a glass of something hazy and golden and slid it toward her.

She swallowed half of it in a few gulps and then put the glass down, playing with the condensation on its smooth surface. A slow, twangy country song played over the sound system, making her feel its longing. Joe was busy behind the bar, checking on ice, lemons, inspecting glasses, polishing those that didn't meet with his approval, and she took the opportunity to study him unobserved. He was completely at ease, relaxed in a way she'd never been able to manage, and it was a pleasure simply to watch him move around the confined space.

Dishes clattered in the kitchen, and she could hear someone whistling along to the music, but she and Joe were alone in the cavernous bar in a way that felt intimate. "My sister tells me you just got here. From Australia, right?" he asked.

She nodded. "It was time for a change of scene. Actually, it's really good to be here." It was true, despite the events of the past few days. She took another draught of her beer, relishing the crisp coolness. "Spend some family time, you know. Catching up."

"That's right, your daughter's visiting for the summer."

She gave him a surprised look.

"Molly mentioned it." He neatened the rows of glasses on the shelf above the counter. "The locals have got to talk about something." He flashed her a semi-apologetic look.

"You have kids?" she asked, aware that she was fishing.

"A son. He's at college in Portland; that's where his mom lives too." He grinned. He'd known why she was asking.

"And you've been here all your life?"

"I was an island kid, but after I finished college I got itchy feet. Traveled for a year that turned into a decade...spent some time in Australia, as it happens. Queensland mostly. Gorgeous beaches. Turtles. Dolphins." His face took on a faraway expression.

"So, what brought you back?"

"That's the million-dollar question. This island gets its hooks into you I guess...almost everyone comes home at some point or other." He sighed. "Anyway, it seemed like the answer at the time."

"And was it?"

He surveyed the bar. "I can think of plenty worse places to be."

"Amen to that." She paused. "Hey, do you remember Fairmile from when you were a kid?"

"A little. We kept away, which wasn't hard—it's not like you can stumble over it by accident."

"No, I guess not. Were there any stories about it?"

"A few. It was abandoned by the time I was a teenager; the nuns had gone. Some of my buddies thought it was fun to graffiti the walls, smoke a little weed by the water there. Pretty harmless stuff."

Frankie drained the last of her drink.

"Another?" he offered.

"No, thanks. I'd better head off. Izzy will be home soon, and I want to spend some time with her—that's what this summer is all about. Though I'm not sure she sees it that way."

"Teenagers, huh? Law unto themselves."

"Yup." She stood up to leave. "Thanks for the beer; I'll settle up next time I see you."

"On the house." He waved her away. "Actually, I remember when I was a really little kid seeing them arrive on the ferry every now and then. The nuns I mean. They had these huge white headdresses that flapped in the wind. Like the angels on the top of a Christmas tree. Sometimes they had a girl or two with them; I asked my mom once why the girls were so fat; it wasn't until I was older that I figured out they were pregnant."

Frankie thanked Joe again, thinking how attractive he looked when he crinkled up his eyes as he smiled, the warmth that radiated from them. It had been so long since a man had made her feel something merely by looking at her, causing her skin to tingle without a single touch.

Still didn't make it a good idea though.

She left The Cabbage Shed, gave her calf another quick massage, and then headed back along the track that led to Fairmile. She was almost home when something that Joe had said came back to her. How he remembered seeing the nuns on the ferry.

The girls weren't brought to the island by their parents; the nuns must have gone into the city to collect them.

EIGHTEEN

Puget Sound, 2013

IZZY WAS HOME by the time Frankie returned, zoned out on the couch and nursing a soda. Her face had freckled in the sun and her shoulders were pink, but Frankie managed to stop herself from dispensing advice about sunscreen, happy that her daughter was safely home.

"I can't move," Izzy groaned, putting a hand to her forehead in a melodramatic gesture. "We cycled for *hours*. Must have gone around the whole island. My legs are *cooked*."

"But you had a nice time?" Frankie asked.

"It was okay. Zac's cool."

Heaven forbid Izzy should sound *too* enthusiastic about anything.

Frankie was full of more questions: had it been just the two of them, where had they gone, and so on, but she left them unasked. She could remember how annoying it had been when her mom wanted to know every detail of her life at that age.

"I thought we could go into the city tomorrow?" she suggested. "Would you like that? See the sights? Get some lunch together?"

Alerted by a beep from her phone, Izzy grunted in a way that was neither a yes or a no and picked it up, instantly absorbed by her screen. Frankie left her to it.

She was tired herself, the result of being on edge all day about what the investigators might find as much as the effort of her run.

She went up to the second floor, taking each step one by one and feeling every day of her thirty-nine years. She found Diana coming out of the soon-to-be bridal suite, wiping her paintbrush on a rag. "Everything okay?"

"Fine, Mom. I needed to blow off some steam, that's all."

"Sure, honey." Diana sounded distracted, probably still worried about the tiny skeleton and its potential impact on the reopening of Fairmile. There wasn't much that Frankie could say to ease her fears. "Don't overdo it, hey?"

"No, Mom, I won't. I might grab a shower before dinner. That's if you don't need me to do anything?"

"Izzy can help me. If she ever moves again."

They both laughed at that, and Frankie was struck how normal it was to share a harmless joke about her daughter with her mother. Normal was good, she reminded herself.

Over an early dinner, Frankie mentioned again that she was thinking of going into the city. "I thought you might like to see the sights, Iz," she added, resting her knife and fork on her plate. "But I also want to check out the Seattle library records, see what I can find out about the history of Fairmile. What do you say? Feel like a ferry ride?"

"Will there be time to shop?" Izzy asked, looking slightly more animated than she had since her return from her bike ride.

"Think your legs will be up to it?" Frankie teased.

Izzy smiled in reply and Frankie was almost breathless at the transformation in her daughter, her peachy skin flushed from being outdoors, the way her eyes reflected the golden light of dusk streaming through the window.

"Do we *have* to go to a boring library though?"

"Tell you what." Frankie perched on the edge of the couch. "Why don't we see the sights in the morning, have some lunch, and then you can cut loose for a few hours by yourself?"

"Deal."

After dinner, Frankie combed the ledgers again, focusing this time on the book that covered 1949 to 50. She counted the names, figuring out that there were 106 babies born to girls there in those two years, including two sets of twins. So many girls in trouble, all sent to a single small island. Her mind fairly boggled; it must have been the same across the country, especially in tucked-away places where the girls wouldn't be recognized.

"OH MY GOD. LOOK!" Izzy pointed excitedly to a shiny black and white creature slipping past them as the ferry ploughed its way across the water.

They were on their way into the city.

"Orcas! Aren't they amazing?" Laughter bubbled from her. "I've never seen anything like it. I mean, we get dolphins at home, but these…"

Frankie grinned, both at the orcas and her daughter, pleased to see that there was still a sliver of her little girl there, the one she remembered from before, the one with pigtails and an isn't-the-world-astonishing expression in her eyes.

The pair weren't the only ones enchanted by the creatures, and it seemed as though half of the ferry's passengers had come out onto the deck to take a look. A mother picked up her toddler from a stroller, holding her up to see them. Phones and cameras were held high as people did their best to capture the sight. Izzy got her camera out too—a smart-looking Nikon—from her backpack and adjusted the focus. After a while, she looked back at Frankie. "What? I taught myself from YouTube videos."

Frankie was unable to put into words how it felt to see her daughter so absorbed, to be proficient at something that she had learned on her own, that Frankie had no clue about.

"The geeks shall inherit the earth." Izzy grinned and then returned to the viewfinder.

Frankie was reminded of traveling on a similar ferry, on Sydney Harbour, on a summer's day like this one, the water sparkling and a breeze carrying the scent of salt and frangipani blossom. She felt a stab of regret; she probably wouldn't ever go back.

Later, after they'd wandered through Pike Place market and taken the elevator to the top of the Space Needle—"It's pretty cool," Izzy admitted grudgingly—they found a restaurant on Pioneer Square and ordered lemonades and grilled salami and mozzarella sandwiches with fries that Izzy declared one of the best things she'd ever eaten. They perched side by side on stools at the window and watched the parade of passersby.

"Why did you stay so long in Australia?" Izzy asked, playing with the striped paper straw in her drink.

"What?"

"You were gone so long. For *years*. And why couldn't I have come too?"

"Oh, honey, I didn't mean to." Frankie's throat constricted. "And it wasn't the kind of job where I could have a child as well." Frankie turned to face her daughter. "Irregular hours, sometimes weeks undercover. You had your dad, honey. And Sylvie. That was a more stable place for you to grow up. And we saw each other over the holidays, didn't we?" It had been the hardest decision, a choice between a career and motherhood. Men did it all the time, she had reasoned when she accepted the job, why shouldn't she? Besides, the role of mother hadn't come easily to her, whereas Lucas seemed to know how to be a father right away. He had the easy confidence that he was doing the right thing, whereas she was permanently terrified of getting it wrong. He was far better suited to be the primary carer.

She had been unable to eat, read, or concentrate on a movie the entire, endless flight that carried her halfway across the world, but after a few months, the ache subsided to a dull pain. Izzy was still the first person she thought of when she woke up and the last before she went to sleep. She had called, written letters and cards, sent gifts, determined that her daughter would not forget her, but it had taken her far too long to realize that it was a poor substitute for actually *being* with her day in, day out.

Poor Rosalie—Sally—how must she have felt to have given away her son as a tiny baby, to never hear of him again. Did she think of him for the rest of her life, worry about him? Light a candle on his birthday every year? Wonder if someone, somewhere had baked a cake, wrapped a gift? According to Liam, she must have. Imagine not knowing what had happened to your child, whether they had grown up in a loving home, whether they were happy, healthy, whether they had gone on to have a family of their own. Not knowing if you had grandchildren…would it eat away at you little by little, destroy you slowly from the inside? Even if you did find each other again, there were so many lost years that could never be regained…

She saw the pain on Izzy's face as the cynical teenager's facade dropped. "Oh, darling, I'm sorry," Frankie leaned across and hugged her daughter. Frankie hoped Izzy was beginning to understand, although she wasn't sure that her daughter was ready to completely forgive her yet.

"But you're not going back?" Izzy's voice was small. "You have a job here now, right? But not till after the summer."

"Absolutely," she said firmly. Checking up on Sister Agatha's past and helping Molly out didn't really count. Their conversation was halted by the arrival of an ice-cream sundae with two long-handled spoons, and the pinging of Izzy's phone. "I'm sorry if you're missing your friends back home," Frankie said after a spoonful of chocolate sauce and vanilla ice cream.

"What?" Izzy looked up. "Oh. No, it's just Zac. He wants to know if I can go to a party tonight. Can I?"

All traces of hurt were gone, and Frankie smiled at how nice it must be to live in the moment. She raised her eyebrows, teasing.

"It's not like *that*." Izzy took a spoonful of dessert.

"Okay, honey, if you say so."

"So can I?" she mumbled.

"Find out the details and we can talk about it,"

Frankie replied, checking her watch. "When we're done here, I need to hustle to the library."

"Mind if I check out the stores?"

"Uh-huh. Do you need any money?"

"It's fine," Izzy shrugged. "Lucas gave me some, and I have money from dog-walking too."

"Don't get lost."

Izzy rolled her eyes and Frankie held up her hands. "Okay, okay, I'll stop with the overprotective mom act."

NINETEEN

Puget Sound, 2013

SEATTLE CENTRAL LIBRARY was hard to miss: the flashy glass cube took up an entire city block, and featured diamond-shaped steel bracing that made it look as though it had been captured by a fishing net. Frankie found the entrance on Fourth Avenue, walked across a wooden floor covered with raised lettering to the escalators and then up to the genealogy collection on the ninth level. The previous afternoon, she'd called and made an appointment with a researcher and so announced herself to the man at the desk.

A few minutes later, a young woman, with finely braided hair secured in a ponytail in such a way that made Frankie think briefly of Sister Agatha's scourge, beckoned her into a side room. "I've found a few things that might be of interest, Ms. Gray. Fairmile House on Orcades Island?" She checked a form and Frankie nodded.

"We've got five decades of the Seattle Genealogical Society Bulletins," she said. "I've found several mentions of Fairmile."

"Actually, I was particularly interested in its use as a mother and baby home, especially in the nineteen forties and fifties," Frankie said.

The woman hesitated and her face faltered. "The

Catholic Church would have most of those records I believe."

"I hadn't realized." Frankie kicked herself for having gotten her hopes up.

"They're pretty reluctant to release that kind of information, unfortunately."

If the Catholic Church had information to hide, then even a search warrant or subpoena wouldn't be of much use.

The woman flipped her braids to one side. "We're in the process of digitizing our collections, but as you can imagine, there's a ton of material to get through. You might want to check the local history collection. I think there's something on mother and baby homes in the state. There could be a mention of Fairmile there."

"Thank you." Frankie found a vacant computer terminal and began to search the collection, highlighting several books that looked as though they might contain useful information. After a short wait for them to be brought up from the stacks, she had amassed a small pile that she began to leaf through.

She read of several homes, including those run by independent charities and the Catholic Church. One recently published book contained first-person accounts by women whose babies had been all but snatched from them within hours of giving birth. She caught her breath as she read of the callous way the girls had been treated, how it had caused them anguish for the rest of their lives, even affecting some of them physically, making them chronically ill. Many of the homes made the girls go by different names while they were there, ostensibly for their own protection, but to Frankie it felt like they were further stripped of their identity. She'd been right about the dual lists of names that she'd found in the ledger.

Until that moment, she had, like many she supposed, more sympathy for the children who had been adopted, the sense of loss they often felt, and hadn't considered how shameful and devastating it must have been for the birth mothers of those children. Even though she'd seen the figures from the Fairmile ledgers, she was shocked by the numbers involved. According to one of the books, between 1945 and 1973 some one and a half million babies were adopted in the US. That meant there had been one and a half million girls (give or take)—mothers—most of whom had no choice but to give away their babies.

Her pulse sped up when she discovered that all the Catholic homes in Washington State had been centrally administered from a Seattle nunnery, The Convent of the Sacred Heart. She searched for the address and discovered that it was a few blocks from the library. Acting on a hunch, she gathered her things, returned the books, and flew out of the building. She was halfway to the convent when she forced herself to slow down and figure out exactly what she hoped to achieve by showing up without an appointment.

"MAY I HELP YOU?"

"My name's Frankie Gray and I'm a freelance writer." Frankie smiled, winningly she hoped, at the serene-faced nun who answered the door. "I'm researching an article on local adoption and wondered if someone might be available for a comment? Something along the lines of the Catholic Church's proud tradition of helping young women and families?" It was laying it on thick, but the nun seemed to consider the request seriously.

"We're not involved in the adoption process these days. What publication did you say you were from?"

Frankie hadn't. "The, er… *The Orcades Times*," she invented. "And I'm looking at adoption in the 1950s."

The nun regarded her suspiciously now. "There's only one Sister who will remember that time. I'll have to see if she's available. Usually, we would ask for an interview request in writing."

"I'm sorry," Frankie apologized. "I would have called ahead, but I'm only in the city today and thought I would take a chance." She smiled again, hoping to soften the woman's resolve.

"Wait here."

The nun who eventually appeared in front of Frankie was one of the frailest women she'd ever met. She might have once been tall, but now she was bent over like a hairpin, her pale skin in soft folds gathered around her face and her habit dragging along the floor as she walked. She extended a bony hand and as Frankie took it, she looked into a pair of cloudy blue eyes, the whites threaded with tiny, snaking blood vessels. "I'm Sister Jude," she said. "Come."

Frankie followed her shuffling steps toward a small room furnished with several soft armchairs in muted colors, and a low table on which sat a large Bible and a number of religious pamphlets.

"You have questions about adoptions?" Sister Jude asked once they had both taken a seat.

Frankie got straight to the point. "I'm specifically interested in Fairmile." As she said the words, she noticed Sister Jude's eyes shift upward, as if she was remembering something. Most people would have missed it, but not Frankie.

"Fairmile?"

"On Orcades Island. I understand it was once a mother and baby home and was administered by this convent."

"That is correct." The nun folded her hands, her expression implacable, waiting for Frankie to continue.

She took a punt. "I am sure you have heard about the recent incident at Pacifica Gardens. On Orcades Island."

Again, the tiny flicker of her eyes.

"A tragedy. Sister Agatha left the order quite some time ago. The last I heard, she was working for an outreach program in the city. Helping victims of domestic abuse."

That explained her change of name.

"May I ask why?"

"Her reasons were her own. Perhaps she felt she could do more good out in the world. It was, in the end, between her and the Lord."

Frankie didn't believe that explanation for a minute. "A lost sheep perhaps?" She had to work to keep the sarcasm out of her voice.

"Hardly. Besides, I am not here to indulge in idle gossip, Ms. Gray."

"You used to work at Fairmile. Perhaps Sister Agatha was a colleague?" It was an informed guess, for Frankie remembered seeing one of the photographs captioned with the name of a Sister Jude.

The nun looked startled, but quickly regained her serene composure. "Indeed. For a number of years. I was a sister-midwife. There's no greater joy than bringing a new soul safely into the world."

"Would you have any idea who might have wished her ill?" Frankie wasn't going to be side-tracked. "The former Sister Agatha?"

"Our community is deeply saddened but as I said, she left the order quite some time ago and we were not personally in touch. We continue to pray for her soul." Sister Jude made it clear that the subject was closed. "Now, I understood you were here to discuss adoption? Are you, in fact, an adoptee yourself? We receive a number of such visits, even now, after all this time."

"No, no. Not at all." Frankie shook her head. "But in fact, my mother has recently bought Fairmile, and I am naturally curious as to its history."

The nun reclasped her hands, a subtle fidget. "What a coincidence." Her tone told Frankie that in fact she considered it to be far from that. "A journalist you said?"

Frankie ignored the question. "There is still a lot of work to be done. Rewiring, new plumbing, yard work… right now it feels as though the whole place is being dug up." She watched to see if the nun would react.

"I can imagine." Sister Jude's voice was flat but, there was an unmistakeable twitch of her eyelid. "There really isn't much that I can tell you that you probably don't already know. Fairmile was a sanctuary for unwed mothers and their babies for more than forty years. We helped girls who found themselves in trouble and were able to bless many good Catholic families with the child they so sorely desired."

"Win win," said Frankie grimly, thinking of the accounts she had just read in the library. A bell chimed from somewhere within the convent and Sister Jude got shakily to her feet, teetering for a second as she gained her balance. "I am afraid I have no more time to offer Ms. Gray."

Reluctantly, Frankie left the convent, sure of only one thing: Sister Jude knew more about what had gone on at Fairmile than she was prepared to divulge.

FRANKIE WAITED FOR her daughter near the ferry terminal as commuters knocking off for the day swarmed around her. She checked her phone for the fifth time, but there was still no message. Izzy was ten minutes late and the ferry was due to leave in another ten. She tried calling, but Izzy's phone went straight to voicemail. She checked the location of Izzy's phone, but all it told her was that it was switched off.

Frankie was as jumpy as a frog on a tin roof, unable to shake a feeling that something bad was about to happen. No need to worry, she told herself. Izzy had likely gotten carried away and forgotten the time. She scanned the crowds, taking deep breaths ("in through the nose, out through the mouth") to fight a rising sense of anxiety.

TWENTY

Fairmile, 1949

"UNBUTTON YOUR BLOUSE and pull down your skirt."

Brigid lay back on the examination bench, watching as Sister Jude, a nun who looked not much older than Brigid herself, took out a metal horn. Brigid flinched at the coldness as the nun placed it on her stomach and leaned over to rest her ear on the other end. Sister Jude kept it there for a minute and then straightened up. "Baby sounds just fine." She whipped out a tape and measured the distance from Brigid's belly button to her pubis. "And growing nicely." Sister Jude consulted a chart. "You're twenty-two weeks now, is that right?"

Brigid nodded.

"Think of the good you can do," said the nun, changing the subject. "To atone for your sins."

Brigid braced herself for the coming lecture. The message was the same—only the form of the words was slightly different—every time she saw Sister Jude.

"There is a good Christian family out there that cannot have a child, that longs for a child. A couple who will make the most wonderful parents. You will be giving them the gift of life, a precious baby." Her eyes hardened. "We have a number of couples on our list—doctors, bankers, accountants—who will be able to give the baby everything he or she needs."

"Do I even have a say in the matter?" Brigid instinctively cupped her belly.

"You will most likely have other children." Sister Jude reached forward on her desk and picked up a cigarette. "Forget this and get on with the rest of your life. You can go back to school, go to college even, if you're smart enough. There's plenty of time for you to be a proper mother. When you're married. Or to go out and do good in the world: there are other choices." Sister Jude tapped the cigarette and put it to her lips.

The nun-midwife talked to her constantly about giving up the baby. She always referred to it as "the baby," not "her baby." She pretended that she was sympathetic, but Brigid wasn't fooled. Not a jot. She might have been a little kinder than Sister Agatha, but they were both on the same side.

A tear slid from her eye, and Brigid brushed it away angrily, furious that her body was betraying her. She was trying not to care, but it was impossible. Since the first flutter of a kick inside her, she'd felt a rush of protectiveness that surprised her with its ferocity. She understood now why people said they would die for their children.

"You're not able to be responsible for another human being right now. Think about it: How will you earn money and look after him or her? Let alone pay back what it has cost your parents to keep you here." Sister Jude exhaled a stream of smoke, making Brigid's eyes water.

In the few weeks that Brigid had been at Fairmile, she'd thought of little else but how she could keep her baby. Sister Jude—and the other nuns—made it clear that there was very little chance of it. Her parents, too, would never take her back if there was an infant there. Her mother would literally die of shame; she had told her so herself.

"The baby will be called a bastard—do you really want that?" Sister Jude went on.

Brigid had read *The Caucasian Chalk Circle* in English class the year before, and she knew that if it came to a tug-of-war, a real mother would let go in order to save her child. It would be so selfish of her to keep her baby, not to want the best for them. But then surely, a baby's rightful place was with its mother? Who else could care for it, love it, as much as she?

"Why don't you make a list?" Sister Jude regarded her through narrowed eyes. "Think of everything a family—a mother *and* a father—can give a baby, and then what you can give him or her. It might help you see things more clearly."

Later, Brigid surprised herself and did as the nun suggested, drawing a line down a blank page with two headings either side of it: "Give the baby up" and "Keep her" (she had a feeling she was carrying a girl, though she couldn't have said why). The first column was easy: money, security, legitimacy, food, clothing, a college education… She was sure there were more.

On the other there was a single word: love.

It didn't seem enough.

TIME AT FAIRMILE passed quickly, as Brigid fell into the house's routine, summoned for meals and housework by a series of bells that punctuated the day. She was moved on from the laundry after the starch catastrophe and was assigned to the cleaning roster with two other girls, Lilian and Kathleen. "You'll do less harm there," said Sister Agatha.

After their chores were done, the girls were permitted to go outside, wrapped up against the increasingly cold weather. They weren't, however, allowed past the far gate and certainly not into Huntley's Point, the island's small town, even if they had the stamina to walk that far. There were few visitors; they were too isolated for most of the girls' parents to make the trip. Once, Kathleen went out for the afternoon with her father who had arrived on foot, having walked from the ferry on the other side of the island. He brought a tin of caramels, though Kathleen only offered them around the one time. Sally gave her piece to Brigid. "They make my teeth hurt," she explained. She might be giving it up out of kindness—who didn't like caramel?—but Brigid took the candy, nevertheless.

Brigid hadn't seen anyone else apart from the other girls and the nuns, although an occasional deliveryman came to drop off supplies of food and the few other things that were needed. "An atomic bomb could have gone off somewhere and we wouldn't know about it," she complained one day to Sally and Catherine as they skimmed stones at the water's edge.

"Is that so bad?" Catherine replied.

"Of course it is!" Brigid tossed a pebble, watching it skip across the surface of the Sound. "Two, three, four, five…that's the best yet… Don't you want to know what's happening in the rest of the country? We're completely cut off here."

"I hadn't really thought about it," Sally admitted.

"The nuns won't even let us look at a newspaper. I haven't seen a movie or read a book for weeks." Brigid complained. "And anything could happen to us here and no one would know."

"What about our parents? They'd find out, surely?" Catherine asked.

Brigid scoffed. "They really don't want to hear from us. Not until this is all over and our little problems have disappeared."

"My mother is like that, but my father is trying, though he doesn't say much. I really disappointed them." Sally's words ended on a sob.

The wind gusted off the water, sending distant sailboats scudding and pressing the girls' sweaters against their growing stomachs.

"When are you due?" Brigid asked Sally.

"Beginning of January." Sally bent down to pick up another stone. "I kinda like the idea of him or her being born into a new decade. The nineteen fifties. It has a nice ring about it, don't you think? A fresh start."

Brigid shrugged, skimming another stone.

"I'm stuck here until March," Catherine complained. "It feels like forever."

"I hope it'll have a good life. That he or she is happy and treated well," said Sally. "That they go to a nice family. That's all you can wish for, right? Health and happiness."

"And what will you do? After, I mean?"

A shadow passed over Sally's face. "Go home I suppose. How about you?" she asked. "You seem like you wanna *be* someone. Like you've got plans."

"What do you mean, like the First Lady?" Brigid laughed, giving them a regal wave.

"No, dummy."

"Or the President? Or the first person in space?"

They all fell about at the ridiculous suggestions, their giggles ringing out across the water. Then Brigid sobered. She was no more likely to become the first female president of the United States or person in space than she was to be allowed to keep the baby who was growing inside her. She wondered if it had fingernails yet. Eyelashes? Would it have her features? Her chestnut hair?

"Wouldn't it be something to be a movie star? Like Joan Fontaine or Lauren Bacall?" Sally asked, wistfully.

"I love the name Lauren," said Brigid.

Catherine gazed into the distance, biting her lip. It was an unspoken rule: the girls never talked about their real names.

"I'd kinda like to be a teacher," Brigid added, kicking at the stones with the toe of her shoe, "as impossible as that seems."

"I was gonna be a championship figure skater when I was ten," Catherine said, glancing down at her belly. "Guess that's no longer an option." Another giggle bubbled from her lips and Brigid joined in. It was nice to have something to laugh about. She liked to think that she, Catherine, and Sally would have been friends if they had met in normal times.

A fallen maple leaf floated past, its burnt orange color reminding Brigid of her sisters' hair, and how they hated to have it brushed, crying at the knots in it. She swallowed a lump in her throat and let another stone fly, flinging it across the water. It was getting harder and harder to imagine returning to her old life. "I'd like to be the kind of person other people look up to, admire. Somebody who matters," she said.

"Look at this." Sara and Brigid were lying on their beds, having finished their chores for the day. Brigid put down the book she was reading. Sara had lifted her sweater and was contemplating the enormous dome of her belly. The rest of her body was so tiny that it looked obscene, and Brigid was filled with sudden fury that this should have been allowed to happen to her. She was a *child*.

Suddenly, there was a ripple across its pale, veined surface, a sharp point of an elbow or a knee or possibly a rear end moving underneath her skin, shifting from one side of her body to the other. Sara began to chuckle. "It's so weird," she snorted, "I just know I'm having a boy."

"Not a whale?" Brigid asked, swallowing her anger for the sake of her friend.

"Could be," said Sara, wiping the tears from her cheeks. Her belly began to jerk. "Holy cow, I think he's got hiccups now."

When it came to what to expect of giving birth, they were offered scant information. Sister Jude made no mention of it, harping on instead about the importance of giving up the babies for adoption, implying that they wasn't really theirs in the first place.

None of them had any idea what they were in for.

That night, screams tore the nighttime silence, waking Brigid, along with everyone else in the house. She crept out of bed and poked her head around the door, peering into the gloom. In the distance she saw the figures of two nuns—one of whom appeared to be Sister Jude, though it was hard to tell one from another from behind—scurrying along the hallway, headed for the farthest door, where Kathleen and Sally slept.

"Who is it?" Sara appeared at Brigid's side, straining to see.

"Maybe Sally, though she's months away still."

A light bobbed along the hallway as another nun hurried toward the door and the two girls withdrew into the shadows.

"That sound would curdle milk," said Sara as they huddled in their beds again, covering their ears at the awful noise. "I'm going to pray for her." She closed her eyes and began murmuring under her breath. Brigid caught something about the "poor banished children of Eve" but didn't join in.

"Can it be that bad?" Brigid asked during a lull. She looked over at Sara, seeing the whites of her eyes reflected in the moonlight coming through the window. "I'm sure it's not like that for everyone," she said, as much to reassure herself as Sara.

"What if she splits in half, like a melon? What if the baby can't come out at all? I've heard that sometimes it can get stuck." Sara's voice shook, and she sounded exactly like the frightened little girl that she was.

Brigid went over to her, and Sara shifted over until there was room for both of them to lie side by side. "She'll be okay. They know what they're doing."

The screams turned to guttural groans and the two of them jumped.

"It sounds like a creature from the depths of the ocean," Sara whispered.

Neither of them got any further sleep.

BY THE TIME the sun was up, the girls had washed and dressed and made their beds as they'd been taught to. They left their room as one of the nuns swept past with an armful of bloodied sheets. "Did you see that?" Sara whispered, her eyes round as wagon wheels.

Brigid could only nod.

Downstairs, a hubbub of excited chatter filled the dining room. "Did you hear?" one of the older girls, Marianne, asked Brigid as she pulled out her chair.

"You mean the noise?"

"Everyone heard that," Marianne rolled her eyes to the ceiling. "No, Sally had twins. A boy and a girl. They've taken them to the nursery. Even Sister Jude didn't know there were two babies."

"Are they okay?"

"I think so. You know what the nuns are like, especially Sister Agatha. It'd kill them to tell us too much."

Brigid took an unenthusiastic mouthful of her breakfast. "Are we allowed to go and see her?"

The nuns filed into the dining room and the girls fell silent.

"You will no doubt all be aware of last night's disturbance," said Sister Agatha, standing in front of them and effortlessly commanding the attention of everyone in the room. "Sally is not to receive visitors; she must be allowed to rest. In case that's not clear enough, no one shall enter the room at the eastern end of the second floor."

Sister Agatha joined the other nuns at the table and the subdued hum of conversation began again. Brigid swallowed her questions with her porridge.

TWENTY-ONE

Puget Sound, 2013

FRANKIE HAD FELT like this in the weeks before she left Sydney. Panicking over the slightest delay, dreams where she was always too late, her mind freefalling in an avalanche of irrational fears that she could neither outpace nor out-reason. No matter how much she told herself she was overreacting, she couldn't seem to shake it. She'd got as far as the Macquarie Street offices of a high-priced psychologist but had fled after half an hour. She'd found the breathing exercises in a magazine placed in the waiting room—"Thirteen ways to prevent a panic attack"—so the appointment hadn't been a total waste of time.

Finally, over the heads of the crowd, she spotted Izzy coming toward her and let out a shuddering breath. "Hey," she said, steadying herself as Izzy reached her, doing her best to appear relaxed. "Success?"

"Yeah, there are some pretty good stores. Better than LA." Izzy moved a wad of gum from one side of her mouth to the other, oblivious to her mother's concern. "Sorry I'm late—completely lost track of the time. And my phone ran out of battery."

"Let's hurry then, or we'll miss the ferry."

"Did you find what you wanted?" Izzy asked once they'd boarded.

"Partly. I was trying to find out about Fairmile, the time when it was a mother and baby home." Frankie paused, looking out at the water. "Those poor girls… contraception was almost impossible to come by then, and of course getting an abortion was expensive and dangerous. Not to mention illegal. They were treated like pariahs, shunted off to have their babies in secret…and it was almost impossible for them to keep the babies once they had them. They were offered no support at all. It was practically criminal."

She was aware she might be preaching, but it felt important for Izzy to know how things used to be for girls who got in trouble, how they were shamed, not so very long ago.

Twilight greeted them as they drove off the ferry, the outline of the pines stark against a sky painted gold and rose, mist rising from the water, seabirds coming home to roost. After the bustle of the city, it was soothing to return to the peace of the island.

"So, can I go to the party?"

"What?" Frankie had forgotten all about it.

"Zac says he'll come and pick me up and drop me home."

"And where exactly is this party?"

"Um, I'm not sure. The other side of the island I think, nothing big, a friend of his is having some people over."

"So, which is it, a party or a casual gathering?"

"Sheesh. Lucas never gives me this much grief."

"I'll bet."

Izzy scowled and Frankie relented. "Be home before midnight."

Izzy went to protest but saw the look on her mother's face and appeared to think better of it. "For sure."

They reached the house and Izzy flew inside, stopping to give a quick wave to her grandmother, who was lounging on a chair at the end of the dock with Scruff at her feet, a glass of wine in one hand, a bottle and a spare glass on a small table beside her.

"Everything okay, Mom?" Frankie asked when she reached her, pulling up a chair and pouring herself a glass.

"I'm not exactly certain."

"What?" She had Frankie's full attention now.

"My car. There was plenty of gas in it when I pulled up yesterday, but when I got in it this morning, the gauge was showing empty, and it literally wouldn't start. I had to call a friend and get them to bring some over."

"God, Mom. I hope you're not losing it," Frankie joked.

"Frances Louise. I am not senile yet. And that is not at all funny."

"It was a joke." Frankie looked at her with concern. "But do you really think someone came all the way out here and drained it without us noticing? Even if that were possible, and I highly doubt it is, why?"

"I have no idea, but it's got me rattled. Oh, I know—" Diana held up a hand as Frankie was about to speak. "It's probably kids messing around."

"Maybe." Frankie wasn't entirely convinced.

"There was a note. Left under the wipers."

"A note? What did it say?"

Diana reached into the pocket of her cardigan and held out a square of paper. It had a colored pattern on one side, plain on the other.

"Stop digging." Frankie was disbelieving. The

words were blocky, in capital letters, as if someone was trying to disguise their handwriting. "Are you kidding me?" Someone had found out about the skeleton and was trying to wind them up, that was the most likely explanation.

Diana made a dismissive sound in the back of her throat. "Like I said, probably kids having a joke at our expense. Anyway, how about you guys? A successful trip?"

"I'm not sure yet." Frankie gazed out at the water. "Mom, I think we should show this to Molly."

"She's got more than enough on her plate right now. Oh, and by the way, you might be interested to hear that the funeral for the nun, Bernadette Evans—Sister Agatha as she once was—is next week." Diana seemed to almost relish the news.

"That soon? Don't they still have tests to run?"

Diana set her glass on the arm of her chair and picked at a fleck of paint on her skin. "Apparently not. The medical examiner has released the body. Inconclusive evidence."

Frankie had been scanning the local news sites for clues, but aside from a flurry of initial reports, there had been no more coverage of the incident. It hadn't made the national papers (she'd checked online); sources had been focussed instead on a shooting spree in Santa Monica the same day. The suspicious death of a former nun didn't merit a mention. "What time?"

"You're not thinking of going?" She gave her daughter a sideways glance.

"It might be interesting to see who turns up," Frankie replied. *Of course* she was going. "Any information on the bones?"

Diana shook her head. "They've taken everything away and the plumbers are back on the job."

"Let's hope they don't find anything else," she said, stifling a shiver as a cool breeze gusted in off the water. "For all our sakes."

FRANKIE AND IZZY had been home less than half an hour when there was the sound of a car approaching, followed by the honk of a horn. "Izzy," she called in the direction of the house. "Zac's here."

"Coming," came a distant shout.

Frankie raised a hand as the boy opened the car door, and she went over to meet him. "She'll be right out," she said. "She's got a curfew. And there's to be no alcohol; she's not even sixteen."

"Yes, ma'am, and I'll make sure she gets home on time."

"Appreciate that." Frankie couldn't help herself. She wanted to be the cool mom, but it didn't come naturally. At least Izzy hadn't overheard her. She turned to see her daughter tripping out of the house, wearing a short denim skirt, a T-shirt that barely covered her midriff, and a slick of cherry lip gloss.

"Have a nice time, darling." She gave herself a virtual high five for not commenting on Izzy's skimpy outfit. Look how well she was doing!

"For sure." Izzy flashed her a dazzling smile.

"Love you." From anyone else it would have been a throwaway line, but Frankie's throat closed over as she uttered the words—it had been so long since she'd been able to say them in person. She held her breath, but there was no reply from her daughter. It had been too much to hope for.

Frankie watched as they drove off, leaving exhaust fumes and dust in their wake, then returned to the dock. "I don't feel much like eating," she said to Diana, disappointment a lump in her chest. "Izzy and I had a big, greasy lunch in the city earlier. I think I'll take a walk."

"You're the only person I know around here who takes a walk when they could drive."

"Don't make that sound like a criticism, Mom." Frankie's tone was light, but the warning was there.

"I wasn't."

"Almost everyone walks in Sydney at least some of the time, you know." It was true. Living in the inner city, she hadn't needed a car.

"Sure thing, honey." Her mom's voice was mild. "There's food in the refrigerator if you change your mind when you get back. I'm going to hit the sack early." Diana moved toward her and placed a hand against her cheek. "She'll be okay."

"It's not easy."

"Ain't that the truth."

FRANKIE TOOK THE path that wound along the water's edge, mulling over the day's events.

When she found herself at Huntley's Point, outside The Cabbage Shed, she went inside, half hoping to run into Molly, fully hoping to see Joe.

She was in luck. Her new friend was at the bar, swapping a joke with her brother and nursing an end-of-day beer. Molly was wearing those crazy socks again, a lime-green pair this time, and her hair was in two long braids. The combined effect made her look like a cross between a Girl Guide and Britney Spears and for a moment Frankie felt strangely protective of her.

"Hey!" Joe's face lit up as he greeted her and Frankie took a second to appreciate the feeling of being seen, the sensation of an attractive man's eyes meeting hers.

"Frankie, so good to see you," Molly beamed as she drew up a stool beside her.

"I heard about the funeral plans," Frankie said in an undertone.

"News travels, huh?" Molly leaned in.

"There are some things I should let you know," Frankie said. "I found some ledgers, in a cupboard at Fairmile. From when it was a mother and baby home. I've had a good look through them and I don't know how much use they'll be to the investigation, but there are photographs…"

"Have you got them now?"

Frankie shook her head. They were being copied, but Molly didn't need to know that. "I'll bring them in right away. Tomorrow, I promise."

"Good. What else is there?"

"Diana said that her car was drained of gas overnight, and that someone left a note."

Molly's eyes turned to flint as Frankie told her what it had said.

"She reckons it's local kids doing stuff for kicks… but I thought I should mention it."

"Have her come to the station tomorrow as well, and she can make a formal statement. Bring the note too. We don't stand for any kind of intimidation on this island."

"I'll do my best to persuade her. Hey, did Alan Bloom ever show up?"

"Nope. We're working on it." Molly was uncharacteristically short.

They ceased their conversation as Joe placed a glass in front of Frankie. "You look like you've got a thirst."

"Parched." She heard a hint of a double entendre in his remark and batted it right back, teasing him as lust curled in her belly in response to his nearness. "But I've come to the right place."

"Indeed you have."

There was no opportunity for more banter as Molly was met by some of the team from the quiz night, and they moved to a table. "Join us," she insisted.

"Sure." Frankie had only intended on staying for one drink, but before she knew it, they were four rounds down and she was enjoying the conversation and the buzz from the beer. Someone had ordered a plate of fries, jalapeño poppers, and onion rings for the table and she realized she was hungry after all. The bar filled up, a band began to play, and people got up to dance. Joe appeared in front of her, held out a hand, and she was about to protest, but gave in to the small voice in her head saying she was a total fool if she turned him down, and followed him onto the floor.

Frankie hadn't danced, not like this, for years, but they moved well together, his body echoing hers. He held her lightly, easily, and she felt the heat where his hand rested on her back flaming a path directly to her solar plexus. It took all of her will not to pull him more tightly to her.

The band took a rest, they broke apart, and Joe went back to the bar, serving a stream of thirsty customers. Their group ordered more beers and Molly began to talk about a hike some of them were planning the following weekend. Frankie's gaze roamed the room, taking in the knot of guys playing pool in one corner pretending not to watch the women at a table across from them; the couples out on a date night, holding hands and offering each other bites from their plates; the young bartenders in a seemingly effortless dance of glasses and liquid and ice, the whirr of a blender mixing cocktails above the roar of conversation. It was a welcoming place, full of life and energy, and she found herself really enjoying being there.

At closing time, Molly and her friends hugged her goodbye. "Are you sure you don't want a ride?" one of the guys from the team asked. "I'm dropping Molly home, and it's not too far out of my way."

Frankie insisted she'd prefer to walk, though the truth was probably a little more complicated. "No, really," she said. "I'm good." She held on to her drink, lingering over the last few sips, before carrying it up to the bar.

She locked eyes with Joe.

"Close up for us, Eddie," he called to one of the bartenders as he tossed a towel behind the counter.

"Right, boss."

"Shall we?" he asked, coming around to meet her.

Frankie nodded, and she felt the warmth of Joe's hand on her back again as they left the bar. She'd had a few beers (more than a few actually), enough to silence the sensible voice in her head that would no doubt tell her this was a bad idea, but she was still very much in control.

Outside, a chorus of frogs began to croak, a sound that for no reason made her laugh and she lifted her head to see a sky spangled with stars.

"Beautiful night." Joe's voice was husky. She leaned against him, resting her head briefly on his shoulder.

Joe took his time driving to Fairmile; the way was poorly lit and there were potholes to trap the unwary. When they arrived at the house, he cut the engine and they sat in silence for a moment, listening to the sounds of the night.

Frankie could feel the thrum of her pulse, the tension in the air.

She wasn't sure who moved first, but all at once they fell on each other, hands, mouths, an awkward tangle of limbs, shirts lifted, buttons torn open, breath ragged. Necking like a pair of horny teenagers.

A light went on in an upstairs window. "Is that you Izzy?"

Her mother's voice.

They froze, pulled apart, and Frankie began to tuck her shirt back in the waistband of her pants, shaking her head ruefully and trying not to giggle. "Living with mom, huh?" she whispered.

Joe chuckled.

"Another time perhaps."

"You bet."

"Thanks for the ride home." She leaned in and kissed him again, then opened the passenger door before she could change her mind. A big part of her wanted to stay with him, to go somewhere else, somewhere without a prying mother, but for now common sense held the greater sway.

"Hey, Mom," she called as she ascended the stairs.

"I thought you'd come home hours ago. I was listening out for Izzy."

Frankie looked at her watch. Half-past midnight. "She's not back yet?"

"I haven't heard a car."

"I'll check her room." Frankie continued up the stairs and eased Izzy's door open a fraction. Chaos met her: discarded clothes, shopping bags, makeup, a mind-boggling array of cleansers and spot zappers, an unmade bed...which was unoccupied. She opened the door wider and stepped into the room. A packet on the nightstand caught her eye and she flipped it over. Contraceptive pills. Half-empty. Her little girl. She swallowed, then closed the door and went back down the stairs. "I'll wait up Mom, you go back to sleep. No sense both of us staying awake. I'm sure she won't be long."

A murmur of assent from her mother's room.

The shock of finding her daughter still out had sobered Frankie, but she went down to the kitchen and made a cup of tea anyway. She sat at the table, dialed Izzy's number and waited, her pulse revving to an all too familiar accelerated thud.

TWENTY-TWO

Puget Sound, 2013

"LEAVE A MESSAGE and I might get back to you."

There was a beep and Frankie hung up. She'd called Izzy's number three times now. Each half hour. Sent four texts of increasing terseness. The last one had been simply a series of question marks. It was now two a.m.

She was on the point of dialing the Orcades Sheriff department when she heard the rumble of an engine as it jolted over the rutted road to the house. Relief and anger washed over her in equal amounts as she saw the headlights sweep through the trees.

She didn't, however, recognize the car.

Standing by the front door with the porch light on, she watched as Izzy emerged, hair wild, her T-shirt askew.

Her daughter was home. Safe.

And in a whole heap of trouble.

Frankie waited until the driver had disappeared, and Izzy was close. Frankie opened her mouth to speak but Izzy held up a hand and got in first. "I know I'm way past curfew. Zac's car broke down and we had to wait for someone to come and get us."

"And you couldn't call and let me know? I've been going out of my mind. I had *no* idea where you were."

"You haven't known where I am for years."

"Stop right there Isabella Gray." Frankie felt the knot in her stomach clench even harder.

"What? I explained. It wasn't my fault."

"We'll talk about it in the morning. But I don't want you hanging out with that boy anymore, not if this is what happens."

Izzy pushed past her, and Frankie caught the flash of an eye roll, inhaled the unmistakeable smell of pot on her daughter's clothes.

"NOT EVEN AN APOLOGY." Frankie seethed to her mother as she fired up the coffee machine the next morning. "I don't think anyone ever taught her the words, 'I'm sorry.'" She had been up for hours, taking out her frustration on the weeds that choked the rear of the house, slashing and carting the vegetation to a huge pile behind the barn. Even though she was wearing elbow-length gardening gloves, she'd been unable to avoid being stung by the knee-high nettles, which aggravated her already sour mood.

"They're narcissists, teenagers. It's all about them," said her mother patiently. "You were exactly the same at that age; no thought for anyone else, or that I might be worried when you came home late. And you did, on more than one occasion, in case you'd forgotten."

Frankie let out a long sigh. Her anger dropped from boiling point to a gentle simmer. She reckoned a cup of good coffee and some time out would take it off the heat completely. Perhaps she *had* overreacted.

"About that note," she said. "Molly suggested you call in to the sheriff's office and she can file a report."

"We'll see," said Diana vaguely.

It was a still, warm morning and as she looked out

of the window, Frankie could see the water, dark and glassy. She carried her coffee out to the jetty, settled herself in a chair, and took the first sip from her mug, savoring the rich aroma and cheering herself up with the memory of Joe's silky mouth, his body pressing against hers. She watched a pair of ducks take to the air and pictured a long-ago summer afternoon at an outdoor swimming pool, toddler Izzy stepping confidently straight into the deep end, unaware that she was walking into water that would not support her. The spilt-second as Frankie registered what was happening, leapt from the steps, and in one swift movement dove into the water and pulled her from the depths. People nearby stopped and stared at the swiftness of her action, as if they couldn't quite believe what they'd witnessed. The instinct to protect your own, even if it wasn't always successful or appreciated, was hard-wired.

Izzy flopped down on the chair beside her, Scruff curling himself at her feet. "Hey."

"Izzy."

"I'm sorry I was late." Izzy was contrite.

"Did you have any idea how concerned I would be?"

Izzy shrugged, lobbed a pebble into the water. "Lucas never notices."

"Never notices?" Frankie's mouth hung open. "What, he just goes to bed? Doesn't care what time you come home?"

"Pretty much."

"Iz, I saw the packet of pills. In your room. I wasn't spying; they were right there." She took a breath. "I'm glad that you're being careful…"

"They're for my skin," said Izzy, looking embarrassed.

"Okay, if you say so." Frankie tried not to let her anger flare again. "But listen to me: young girls are vulnerable. You might think you're invincible, but you're not."

"You worry too much." Izzy threw another stone into the water, throwing it farther this time.

"Maybe I do," Frankie admitted. "When I was growing up, there was a girl in the grade below me who went missing. I've never forgotten it. She had gone to take out the trash one night and didn't come in again. She was found, a week later, on a deserted stretch of railway line." Frankie didn't add that the girl had been strangled with a nylon cord; that she had been sexually assaulted. "My mom wouldn't let me go outside on my own for months, even after they'd caught the guy who did it. A soldier from the nearby army base. She wasn't even safe at the end of her drive."

"But this *is* a safe place."

"Nowhere is ever completely safe honey. And the fact is that mothers worry, about their daughters far more than their sons. I wish that wasn't the case, but it is."

"Well, whatever, I'm fine."

"Did you hear anything I just said?"

"I said I was sorry, okay? Jeez, get off my case. Stop being weird." Izzy got to her feet and tramped back to the house, leaving Frankie wondering what she'd done to upset her. Izzy's moods were more volatile than a toddler's sometimes.

THE DAY OF the funeral, Frankie showered and then put on the only dress she owned, linen, in a pale lavender color that contrasted with her dark hair. It made her feel uncharacteristically girlish, but she could hardly show up in her usual cutoffs and muscle tee.

Diana shuddered when Frankie suggested she might come too. "Last funeral I went to was your father's; they're not for me."

Frankie remembered that day. She'd been away at college, had taken the call before breakfast, hearing her mother's broken voice telling her that her dad had suffered a fatal heart attack. He'd been fifty-one, an age that now seemed to her to be far too young.

"Besides, I never even met the woman."

Something about her tone made Frankie pause for a second. "Neither did I, Mom." She left Diana to finish the painting.

The tiny church on the edge of Huntley's Point was surrounded by well-tended gardens, blooming with roses in all shades of pink. Frankie parked a few yards from the entrance, and as she walked toward it heard the faint strains of a piano, the high notes of "Ave Maria."

Inside, it was cool and dim, the only light coming from a few narrow windows that cast long beams across the wooden pews. Incense filled the air, making Frankie wrinkle her nose. Flowers—leftover from a wedding perhaps—filled a pedestal stand to the left of the altar. There were only three other people in the church, all of whom had their backs to Frankie. One sat in a wheelchair that had been pulled up alongside the end of a pew, head covered and bowed in prayer.

The coffin was at the front of the church, polished mahogany with brass handles, a spray of white blooms arranged in the shape of a cross atop it. Frankie supposed that Bernadette/Sister Agatha's funeral service was being held here and not at the convent in the city because she'd left the order. She wasn't sure whether to be surprised or not that there were so few mourners. She'd have thought that the former nun would have made some younger friends, acquaintances even, in her outreach work.

Frankie sank down on a pew toward the back of the church, already regretting her decision to come. It wasn't the fact of the funeral itself, for she'd attended her fair share of such things in the line of duty, more a sense that she had no real reason to be there. It was too late to leave now; the priest had arrived at the altar, emerging from a side door and ascending to the pulpit. As he cleared his throat and began to speak, Frankie had the feeling that someone was watching from behind her. She reached for her purse and got out a mirror to check the back of the church, but the space was so shadowy there was no way of telling.

Frankie lingered after the service, waiting behind as the other mourners filed out. She started as she recognized the person in the wheelchair, tiny and hunched over. Sister Jude, pushed along by a much younger nun, wearing more modern garb. She caught the old nun's eye as she was wheeled past her.

Frankie followed them out, momentarily distracted by a silver SUV pulling out of the lot in a tearing hurry, scattering gravel in its wake. Someone had been in a rush to leave.

She turned her attention to the young woman in charge of the wheelchair, seeing her lean over, listen to something Sister Jude said, then put the brake on and head toward a parked car.

"Sister Jude." Frankie greeted the nun. "How are you?"

"It is good that Sister Agatha has gone to her eternal reward."

"It must be a comfort to have faith," she replied, as sincerely as she could manage.

Sister Jude's eyes darted from Frankie to the church gate, checking on the whereabouts of the other nun. She reached for Frankie's arm. "Things happened—at Fairmile. It wasn't right. I should have spoken up at the time, but you must understand, I had been taught to respect my elders, to do as Mother Superior instructed."

Her words were whipped away by the breeze and Frankie wasn't sure she caught them all. "What exactly was it that happened?"

Sister Jude fixed her with an unblinking stare. "We were supposed to help these girls. Keep their babies healthy too."

It felt as though Sister Jude was looking for absolution, though Frankie was the last person who could grant her that.

"Poor Sally."

"Sally?" It took a moment for the name to register. "Sally?" she asked. It was a common name, especially in older generations. There had to have been more than one Sally at Fairmile over the decades, several among the hundreds of girls who gave birth there.

"When was this?" she pressed.

"The coldest winter. Everything froze, even the water pipes."

The young nun came hurrying back along the path, a blanket under one arm. Sister Jude erupted in a throaty cough, her body convulsing as her eyes signaled to

Frankie to keep quiet. "Cigarettes. Should've given up years ago," she gasped. "Too late for me now."

"Come along then, we'd better get you back." The younger nun had reached them and began to fuss, tucking the blanket around Sister Jude's legs. "She's easily tired," she said to Frankie.

Frankie raised a hand in farewell as Sister Jude was wheeled away. Whose secrets had she been keeping for all those years? Her own, or someone else's? She walked back to her truck, seeing something fluttering under the windshield wiper. A ticket? No. She knew almost straight away what it was.

She had to read the note twice, not believing what she was seeing at first. The words *"You have been warned. Mind your own business, or you'll find out what it's like to lose someone."* were written in spiky ballpoint on a sheet of colored paper.

She remembered the car pulling out of the lot earlier. A silver SUV. Alan Bloom drove an SUV, she'd seen it on his Facebook profile. Trouble was, there were hundreds of silver SUVs on the island.

TWENTY-THREE

Puget Sound, 2013

A FEW DAYS LATER, wrestling with an oversize shopping cart with a mind of its own, Frankie was in the dry goods aisle of the big-box supermarket on the mainland, trying to decide if her mom wanted to offer guests more than three kinds of cereal, when her phone buzzed. She fished it out of her purse and checked the screen.

Joe.

Asking her if she was free that evening.

She was, but she hesitated to reply. Saying yes would take things to a level she wasn't sure she was ready for. He didn't deserve to be strung along. It was a small island, and he *was* Molly's brother, something she should probably have thought about more carefully before letting him drive her home. She replaced her phone and continued shopping.

After Frankie had packed her purchases into the back of the truck, she drove across town, heading for the convent. If she could see Sister Jude one more time, she might be able to tease out the story of that winter at Fairmile. She was sure the nun had wanted to say more after the funeral.

Frankie was in luck—Sister Jude was sitting at a table in the gardens of the convent, her knotted hands clutched around a cotton handkerchief. Distant patches of blue—the ever-present Sound—were visible from where they sat, bees droned in the nearby flowerbeds, and the traffic was a faint hum.

"I really don't have anything more to tell you," she whispered, her eyes darting about as if she was afraid of being overheard.

"The roses smell so beautiful this time of year," said Frankie pleasantly. Someone at the convent had green fingers, for the lawn was thick and lush, the bushes heavy-headed and bountiful. She took a seat opposite the elderly nun and inhaled, reminded of her grand-mother, who wore a similar scent. "I live at Fairmile now, with my mother, Diana."

Sister Jude looked at her sharply. "I'm old, not senile."

"My grandmother Ingrid has not been so fortunate. Some days she doesn't even know her own daughter." She watched the nun's face for a sign of recognition.

"She's at Pacifica Gardens now, is friends with a woman called Rosalie. Or Sally Shanahan as she was probably once known. You remember her, don't you?"

"There were so many girls…" said Sister Jude, ap-parently focused on a bee, its back legs laden with pol-len, emerging from an unfurled bloom.

"She had a baby boy, a son, Marty."

"She had a little girl too," said Sister Jude wistfully. Frankie sat back and waited for more.

"Twins. She had twins." The nun's eyes began to water, aggravated no doubt by the bright sunlight, and she dabbed at them with her handkerchief.

"A daughter? What was her name?" Frankie asked.

"Jenny."

"What happened to Jenny, Sister Jude? You remem-ber, don't you?"

Frankie let the silence stretch. She thought of Rosalie—Sally. A mother who never got to be a mother. How infinitely sad that that was. She looked back at Sister Jude. The nun was slumped over, like a doll that had lost its stuffing. For a brief moment, she feared the worst had happened. But then there was a slight rise in her chest, and Frankie realized that she'd merely fallen asleep. Or perhaps it was a ploy to avoid more of her questions.

IT WAS LATE by the time Frankie returned to Fairmile, and she roped in Izzy to help her transfer the groceries—everything from sacks of flour and apples to toilet paper and frozen bagels—to the kitchen, finding a place for everything in the pantry, refrigerators, and the storage cupboard that had been built in one of the hallways.

Diana had made pasta for dinner and Frankie pulled out a bottle of red from the case she'd bought. It was only as she glugged the purple-red liquid into two glasses that she remembered Joe's text. She reached for her phone but put it down again when she discovered it was out of charge. She placed a glass at her mother's side, picked up her own, and went through to the adjoining dining room. "How was your day?" she asked Izzy, who was setting out forks and bowls for three.

"Fine I guess." Izzy sounded bored.

"I'm sorry there's not much to do here. Perhaps tomorrow we can spend some time together? Do something fun."

Izzy rolled her eyes.

"Come on, Iz. What's really going on?" Frankie tried directness.

Izzy placed the last fork down, fiddling with it. "All my friends at home are having a great summer, going to the beach, hanging out together. I've got no one here."

"Do you want to go back to your dad's?" Frankie prayed that she didn't.

Izzy hesitated. "It's not that."

"Well, what is it then?"

"Zac's having a party on the weekend. But I know after what happened before that you won't let me go."

Frankie considered it. "I'm sorry for what I said about not wanting you to hang out with Zac; I can see that I wasn't exactly being fair. You're nearly sixteen and I have to trust you. If the party's on the island and I can pick you up at a decent hour, then perhaps it'll be okay."

"Don't worry; it won't even get started until late, so there's really no point. It doesn't matter," Izzy sighed.

FRANKIE LAY AWAKE that night thinking about Sister Jude's words. Liam certainly wasn't aware he had a sister. Had she been adopted too? She debated whether it was her place to tell him, and by the time she eventually fell asleep, she had made her decision. If she was in his shoes, she'd want to know. He'd given her his number when she'd told him about the photos, and she texted him as soon as she woke up, arranging to meet him for coffee in Huntley's Point.

TWENTY-FOUR

Puget Sound, 2013

THE BLUEBIRD CAFÉ was crowded when Frankie pulled up. She was preoccupied by a rattle that was coming from her truck and debating whether to call in at the auto shop after her meeting. She had spotted a silver SUV parked a little way down the street, and paused for a moment, turning to scan the sidewalks, only moving on after the gentle beep of a horn hurried her up. It was ridiculous to think that it might be Bloom's car—there were probably a hundred similar cars on the island.

Liam was already inside, waiting for her at a table tucked away toward the rear of the café, partly hidden behind a laminated menu.

"The muffins are good," Frankie said, sitting down opposite him. "Especially if they're berry."

"Blueberry I'm guessing," he said, looking around the cozy room, which was decorated in purplish blue and white, with matching gingham cushions, and a complicated-looking weaving made from wheat ears on the wall. The local businesses in Huntley's Point encouraged a down-home atmosphere—as well as The Cabbage Shed and the café, there was an old-fashioned malt shop, a couple cute boutiques selling nautical knickknacks, and a gas station where they would come out and pump your gas for you. Frankie had noticed that locals greeted everyone with a howdy or a hey, always with a wide smile. At first, she'd imagined it was a deliberate tactic to sweeten the visitors, but she was less cynical about it now. Either that, or she'd simply gotten used to it.

A waitress came and took their order—two coffees and two berry muffins.

"Thanks for meeting me."

"You said you had some information about Rosalie, and her time at Fairmile."

Liam seemed pleasant enough, but Frankie sensed an undercurrent of anxiety. She watched as he twisted his water glass in circles, first one way, then the next.

"I had a copy made for you," she said, bringing out the black and white photograph of the three girls. Frankie had examined the image carefully. One of the girls pictured had the same slight frame and generous mouth that Rosalie did.

He stared at it blankly for a moment and Frankie wondered if she'd made a mistake in showing it to him. "You think one of them is Rosalie?" he asked.

"I'm certain of it," said Frankie, telling him about the writing on the back of the original. "There, that's her." She pointed to the girl on the right, then offered him the print. "Keep it. Wait for the right moment to show her."

He held it for a while, studying it carefully, then put it down on the table.

"I also went to visit a convent, in the city, the other day," Frankie continued, recounting her conversation with Sister Jude. "She might be old, but her mind is clear. She definitely said that Sally—Rosalie—had another child, a daughter that she called Jenny. If she's to be believed, then you have a sister. A twin."

Frankie was alerted by his reaction, a micro pause, as if he needed to choose his words carefully. If she had to hazard a guess, she would have said he wasn't as surprised by this as he should be, despite what he'd told her before.

"A twin sister? Are you sure? But Rosalie's never mentioned anything about a having had a daughter. Did the nun say what happened to her? To Jenny?" He took one of the paper napkins from a holder on the table and began pleating it between his fingers.

She shook her head. "That was all the information she gave me."

The waitress approached and they paused their conversation while she poured their coffees and delivered two large muffins, still warm from the oven, to the table.

"I could ask Rosalie," Liam said, cutting his muffin into careful quarters. "But I don't want to risk upsetting her." His eye twitched. "I always wondered what it would be like to have a brother or sister."

"Me too," said Frankie, though in truth she quite liked being an only child. Less competition. "Were they good people?" she asked. "Your adoptive parents?"

He scoffed, a harsh sound that caused a couple at a nearby table to look up in surprise. "I didn't exactly get the Hallmark version. None of the nice families wanted a boy with a club foot."

"I'm sorry." That might explain the rolling gait she'd noticed in the parking lot of the nursing home.

"Why? It's nothing to do with you."

"I'm sorry for bringing it up; it's clearly a painful topic." Frankie glanced toward the front of the café and saw Joe in the doorway, holding a takeaway cup. Their eyes met and then, with a faint smile in her direction, he turned to leave. Damn. She'd completely forgotten his message. He must think she wasn't interested. She turned her attention back to Liam.

"Ever since I was a kid, all I wanted was a sibling. Someone to look up to or who might look up to me. But a twin? The other half of me? It seems doubly cruel not to have known that." There was a bitter edge to his words. "After all this time. How would you feel, in my shoes?"

"Cheated, I suppose." She looked at him with a little more sympathy, then pulled the ledger from her purse. She hadn't got around to turning it in to Molly yet. "Strangely, I can't find a record of Jenny's birth, but this was at Fairmile." She opened it to the page she'd marked. "Look, here." She pointed to the line where the name Sally S. was written in a spidery script, traced her finger along to the name Martin James, the date, 17 December 1949, and a weight.

"Five pounds, three ounces."

"Tiny."

"I always thought my birthday was the 11th of December. Turns out even that wasn't true."

"What do you mean?"

"The date on my birth certificate is the 11th, not the 17th."

"It might have taken them a while to register the birth…or perhaps it was a slip of the pen…a one and a seven are easy enough to mix up."

"Possibly." He drained his coffee mug and lowered his eyes to the photograph, as if there might be an answer there. "Say, I don't suppose you'd like to go sailing one afternoon? Bring your daughter too? I have a sweet little ketch."

He looked so earnest, so hopeful, that Frankie almost agreed; only the tiny suspicion that he might be hitting on her held her back. "Thanks, but I've kind of got a lot on my plate at the moment—helping Mom with the house and spending time with Izzy." She gave him a look that suggested she was overwhelmed. "You know how it is."

"Sure, of course, don't even worry about it, just a thought."

She winced as she saw his face, the humiliation she'd hoped to avoid inflicting on him and, underneath that, barely concealed rage. "I hoped I was helping. By telling you what I found I mean, but I'm not sure I have."

"Yeah, well perhaps some things should be left well alone." Liam rose, tossing a few dollars on the table.

As he exited the café, she saw that he had fashioned a tiny crane from the napkin he'd been fussing with, leaving it on top of the photograph.

Frankie sighed, fearful that she'd done more harm than good, and picked up her phone. There was a message from Molly.

I'm drowning in paperwork. Up for a hike? There's one place I still want to search. Meet me at eight tomorrow at Pacifica Gardens? It was followed by three emojis: a magnifying glass, a pine tree, and, unaccountably, a snake.

Sure thing, she typed back.

Frankie gathered her purse and went to leave, picking up the photograph. As she studied it again, looking at the closeness of Sally and the other girls, a realization struck her.

TWENTY-FIVE

Fairmile, 1949

BRIGID TUCKED A broom under her arm and tiptoed up the stairs. She was supposed to be sweeping the hallway, and so the broom was in case anyone stopped and asked what she was doing. She passed Sister Jude on the second floor, but the nun seemed to barely notice her, muttering to herself as she juggled an armful of rubber-teated glass baby bottles and a pile of diapers.

As Brigid crept closer to Kathleen and Sally's room, pretending to sweep, she listened for any noises coming from within. Up here, away from the bustle of the first floor, it was quiet. So quiet that she could hear her heart thumping. She rested the broom against the wall and turned the door handle, aware that if she was caught, she'd face a punishment likely far worse than kneeling in the freezing chapel. By going directly against Sister Agatha's wishes she could be thrown out, sent back to Bend, and then what would her parents do? She reminded herself of Sally's kindness to her and steeled herself to ease open the door.

The room was dim, the drapes drawn against the light. Sally lay in the narrow bed farthest from the door, the covers pulled up to her chin. She looked to be asleep but opened her eyes as Brigid closed the door softly behind her.

"How are you?" Brigid whispered.

"My baby?" Her voice was hoarse, probably from all the screaming.

"You had twins. Didn't they tell you?"

Sally's mouth dropped open. "Are you sure? Twins?" She said the word as if it were a marvel.

Brigid nodded. "Was it awful?" she asked.

Tears welled in Sally's eyes and Brigid rushed to her side.

"I want my mother," Sally sobbed. "It wasn't supposed to be like this."

"It's okay, it's okay." Brigid took her hand. "You're a mother yourself now, how about that? You had a boy and a girl. They're in the nursery downstairs." She hid her shock that the nuns had not even told her, had not let Sally see her own babies.

"Can you…?" Sally's voice cracked. "Can you go and see them? I want to know they're okay. That they've got all their fingers and toes." She attempted to smile but it felt short.

"Of course," Brigid promised, though she had no idea how she was going to manage to sneak into a nursery doubtless watched round the clock by the nuns. "You get some rest now, huh? Everyone is thinking of you; they all care."

Sally seemed comforted by this and closed her eyes again, drifting back to sleep. Brigid saw how pale she looked, the dark circles under her eyes evident even in the dim light.

She jumped as she went out into the hallway, not expecting to see Sara lurking in the shadows. "Holy cow!" she whispered, clapping her hand to her chest. "You scared the life outta me."

"We aren't supposed to go in there," Sara hissed.

"Did you know they didn't even tell her she'd given birth to twins? Let alone allow her to see her own babies." Brigid could feel the heat rising in her cheeks. "It's downright *cruel*."

THAT EVENING, after dinner, Brigid saw Sister Jude hurry up the stairs, and guessed that she was headed to the nursery. As the other girls began to make their way to the sitting room for more tedious knitting, she waited until the nuns had disappeared. "Sara," she called.

"Yes?"

"I don't feel too good. I think I'll go upstairs and lie down. Can you let Sister Agatha know, if she asks?"

"Sure. I'll come up later and check on you if you like."

"No need." Brigid waved her away. "I'll be fine if I rest."

Brigid climbed the stairs to the first floor, looked down to make sure that no one could see her, and continued along the hallway until she reached the final door, the one where the nursery was. She tapped lightly on the door and went in.

"Brigid." The nun sat in an easy chair, a blanket-wrapped baby tucked under her arm, a bottle in the other. Behind her was a row of cots, empty except for one, which contained a tiny mound, a bonnet-covered head.

"I'm sorry Sister Jude. I'm not feeling too well. I've been getting a burning feeling in my chest."

"Honestly girl, don't you think I've got better things to do?" Sister Jude cooed down at the baby she was holding, in a soft tone quite different than her usual abrupt one. "It sounds like nothing more than a case of indigestion. Quite common in late pregnancy you know."

"Oh," said Brigid, pretending ignorance. "I didn't." She drew closer. "Is that…?"

"This is the boy. The girl is over there."

"He's beautiful," Brigid breathed, taking in the tiny face with its cap of curly dark hair. His rosebud pink lips were now fastened around the teat of a bottle. "Like a newborn lamb," she whispered.

"They came early, but praise be, not too early. The little girl isn't as strong as her brother though." Sister Jude sighed and adjusted the bundle on her lap. "They're too small to go anywhere for a few weeks."

Sally would be relieved, though Brigid didn't dare to say that out loud. "What will happen to them?" she asked.

The nun made a clucking sound, as though she were regretful about something. "It will be harder to find a family for the boy."

"Why?"

The nun pulled the blanket covering him aside. The baby's tiny foot was misshapen, turned in on itself at an unnatural angle.

"He'll grow out of that, won't he?" Brigid asked hopefully, though in truth she had no idea.

"Unlikely. But he is a child of God nonetheless, and the Lord will provide."

Brigid took advantage of Sister Jude's good mood and moved closer to the cot, peering inside. The little girl was tiny, much smaller than her brother, and her skin had a sickly yellow tinge. It looked like she was struggling to breathe.

"Come away now," said Sister Jude, looking up from feeding. "Go and fetch yourself a glass of milk. That should help ease your pains."

"Yes, Sister." Caught up in the sight of the tiny newborns, Brigid had almost forgotten her excuse for coming into the nursery. She tore herself away and climbed the stairs to the second floor. Instead of going to lie down, she continued along to the end of the hallway and went into Sally's room.

"You look better," Brigid said.

Sally was sitting up in bed, sipping from a glass of water. She'd combed her hair and swept it off her face with a barrette. She looked almost her normal self again. "Did you get to see them? Did you?" Her eyes locked on Brigid's.

"Oh, Sal. They're absolutely perfect," Brigid replied, coming to sit beside her. "The boy is bonny and healthy and they've both got the most gorgeous curly dark hair and the longest eyelashes, just like yours."

Sally leaned back on the pillows, letting out a sigh. "And the little girl?"

"She's…she's…" Brigid didn't want to upset her friend, chose her words carefully. "She's smaller than her brother. But I'm sure she'll catch up to him in no time. Sister Jude is taking really good care of them both."

"I wish I could see them." There was an ocean of longing in her voice. "To hold them, even for a minute."

"Have you asked?"

"Of course." She lay back against the pillows.

"And?"

"They said perhaps. When they're stronger. When I've recovered." Sally sighed. "I think they're stalling.

Sister Agatha even said it might be easier if I didn't see them. That I'll be able to get on with my life again if I don't get attached."

"It's so damn unfair."

Sally nodded and a tear rolled down her cheek.

"Don't be sad. At least you get to give them a name. Have you thought about that? How about movie stars: Lauren and Gary, or Clark and Ingrid?"

"That's crazy!"

Brigid was pleased to have made her friend smile, and for a brief moment they were two carefree teenagers again.

Sally shook her head. "Martin James, after my grandfather. And Jennifer Denise. Denise was my grandmother's name. But I haven't had the chance to tell anyone, tell them that's what I want them to be called."

"They're lovely names," said Brigid.

"But when the nuns take them away, their new parents might want to call them something different," Sally fretted.

"Doesn't matter. They'll always have the ones you— their birth mother—gave them. I'm sure they have to put those on the birth certificate." Brigid wasn't sure, not at all, but she said it anyway.

"I hope you're right."

Brigid leaned forward and hugged Sally impulsively. "I'm sorry that I got to see them and you didn't, it doesn't seem at all fair." The nuns were supposed to be doing the work of the Lord, but sometimes it felt like it was driven by the devil himself.

"Nothing about this is fair," said Sally, sudden rage flashing in her eyes.

BEFORE BED THAT NIGHT, Brigid begged a couple of sheets of notepaper and an envelope from Sara and wrote to her mother. She thought hard about what to say; it was important to get what she was about to ask exactly right, to strike the balance of contrition and boldness. Ever since leaving the nursery and seeing the two little babies, a plan had been taking shape in her mind. The more she considered it, the more she believed she had come up with the perfect solution to her problem. In fact, she was astonished it hadn't occurred to her before. It would mean that she could finish high school, go to college even, and still get to see her child every day, to watch him or her grow up, to be a part of their lives, even though he or she would never know precisely who she was to them.

"Dear Mother," she wrote, being careful not to blot the page and to write as neatly as she knew. After a few sentences telling her how well she had settled in at Fairmile—and painting a rosier picture of the nuns than was strictly true—she began to plead her case. "It has occurred to me that instead of being forced to give up my baby, that you might be of a mind to raise this child as though it is your own." She paused, flexing her fingers. "Of course, I will do everything I can to help, and I'll get a part-time job to pay for things. It would mean that I can finish high school, and maybe even go to college, but not lose my baby." She signed off, feeling strange about using her real name, then added a PS. "Please, I beg you to consider this, for your grandson or-daughter's sake, if not for mine."

The next morning, Brigid gave Mother Mary Frances money for a stamp and handed over the precious letter, crossing her fingers that her mother would agree to her request. She made a silent promise to the baby growing inside her—kicking more than a Rockette now—that she would do everything she could to try and keep her, and to be the good girl her parents had raised her to be, no matter what.

TWENTY-SIX

Puget Sound, 2013

MOLLY WASN'T ALONE when Frankie pulled up at the nursing home parking lot early the next morning. Scott was there too, dressed head-to-toe in khaki hiking gear, complete with a CamelBak, a hiker's pole, and chunky lace-up boots.

Both Scott and Molly were sporting knee-high socks, leading Frankie to conclude it must be more of a practical choice than a fashion statement. Perhaps she should have worn the ones she'd bought at the sporting goods store in Seattle.

Scott was chewing on an energy bar, chugging it down with a takeout coffee, and looked like he was about to go on an adventure race, not up and down a hill a few times.

Frankie had brought a bottle of water, bug spray, her mom's gardening gloves, and an apple, but that was about the sum of her preparation.

"I do geocaching in my spare time," Scott said, explaining the getup.

"Cool."

"Got you one too," said Molly, handing her a paper cup. "We could start at the top of the slope there—" she indicated a thickly forested hill behind the nursing home, "and work our way back. It's pretty dense and we'll need to make sure we don't lose each other, but the only way is down."

"Anything to watch out for?"

"Garter snakes." Molly grinned. "Harmless."

The three of them threaded their way up a rough path that led to the top of the hill. "It's an old mountain biking trail," said Scott. "But it's hardly used anymore. As you can see." He kicked at a clump of leaves. "It's the only means of approaching Pacifica Gardens if you want to be sure to be undetected."

The going was steep, and Frankie slipped on her bad leg, the tread on her running shoes failing to gain purchase on the loose pine needles that carpeted the way. If she was going to live here permanently, then she might have to pay another visit to Dave's Sports and kit herself out with some decent hiking boots. "You okay?" Molly asked, stopping for a moment.

"All good," Frankie reassured her, getting to her feet and shaking out a twinge of pain.

By the time they reached the top, where there was a small clearing, her legs were scraped, and her throat was dry from the dust that they had raised as they walked. She stopped to catch her breath, inhaling the smell of pine resin and reaching for her water bottle.

"You should get yourself some socks like mine," said Molly, eyeing the scratches on Frankie's legs. "I can tell you like them."

Frankie caught the mischievous look on her face. "Never say never."

"Not a bad view," said Scott as he reached them.

They could see all the way down to the water's edge and out across the Sound, the irregular shapes of islands dotting the water. "It looks so peaceful from here," Frankie replied, seeing the roof of the nursing home way below them. "As if nothing violent could ever happen."

"I love these islands," said Molly. "I came back because I missed them so much."

"But your career..." said Frankie.

Molly raised an eyebrow.

"I Googled you..." Frankie admitted. "The *Seattle Times* called you 'a rising star of the Pierce County force.'"

Molly looked back at the view. "There's more to life than work. Balance—isn't that what everyone is always on about?"

"I'm a slow learner," Frankie admitted. "But I'm trying my best."

They went to the far edge of the lookout and separated, leaving about five yards between each of them. Taking careful, unhurried steps, they began to push their way through the undergrowth between the pine trees, watching for anything out of the ordinary. It was shadowy beneath the canopy, the murky green light and the silence making it feel eerie. It was only Scott calling out at intervals that reminded Frankie she wasn't alone out there.

She stopped as she came across the remains of a picnic, a mess of old beer cans, sandwich wrappers, and chip bags. Using a stick, she lifted a piece of dirty cellophane, uncovering more cans. The paint on them was faded to the point of being indecipherable, and she continued on. They had been there far longer than a few weeks.

The three of them regrouped when they reached the bottom of the hill. Molly had bagged and labeled an old blanket. "I doubt it's anything, but you never know," she said, placing it in the trunk of her car.

They trudged up the hill twice more, Scott retrieving a hubcap and an umbrella, its spokes bent, but not rusted.

Frankie was beginning to feel light-headed. Though she was fitter from her few weeks on the island, she was no match for the others, who both seemed to barely notice the effort of climbing up and down the hill. "Here," said Scott, tossing her an energy bar.

"Thanks," she said with a smile, tearing open the wrapper with her teeth.

"One more sweep," Molly promised.

On the final trip down the hill, Frankie heard a disturbance in the branches overhead. Two birds fighting over the same territory, most likely. She gazed upward, noticing how the sunlight filtered through the branches. Then, a little to her left, a flash of bright blue. At first, she thought it a bird's wing. She took a few steps closer and squinted. It was a rubber glove, spiked on a branch just out of reach. Then, on the forest floor, its twin. She called out to Molly and Scott, not wanting to risk moving and losing sight of it. "I've got something," she said.

She waited, hearing the two of them snapping branches as they made their way toward her.

"There—" she indicated the glove resting on the pine needles. Next to it was a cigarette butt.

Scott got out a camera and began to take photographs. Molly waited until he had finished, then bent to pick up the glove on the ground, bagging it carefully, and then doing the same with the cigarette butt. "We're in luck," she said, straightening. "The glove's latex. If it's not been here too long, there's a chance we might get a print from the inside."

"Though it's probably one of the nurses' castoffs," said Scott. "Place like this, they would go through a few thousand pairs in a year. Stands to reason some would end up as litter."

"All the way up here?" Molly didn't look convinced.

"How about the other one?" Frankie used her stick to point toward the glove that dangled beyond the length of even Molly's hiking pole.

"Give me a boost, can you Scotty?" Frankie asked.

"I'll steady you," said Molly.

Working together, they got within inches of the glove and Frankie made a final heroic effort, stretching and hooking it off the branch.

"I'd say we'll call that a day." Molly bagged the glove and added it to the collection of items that they'd found. "I'll get these to the lab for analysis on Monday, but I'm not holding my breath that they'll lead to anything. At best, they might help build a case."

"At least we'll know we've done all we can," said Scott.

"Any news on the skeletal remains? The newborn?" Frankie asked.

Molly shook her head. "There's not a lot to go on—carbon dating isn't that accurate in such cases. I doubt we'll ever really know, apart from the fact that he or she was almost certainly born at Fairmile when it was a mother and baby home, and then something happened for the body to be placed there, and not in a cemetery."

Frankie waved Molly and Scott goodbye and went to her truck.

"For Christ's sake." There, fluttering on the windshield was a note. The same paper as the previous two times. "Are you freaking kidding me?" she muttered, giving it a cursory glance.

Back off.

"Everything okay?" Molly called from across the parking lot.

"Have a look at this," Frankie replied, when Molly reached her.

"Scott," she shouted after scanning it. "Bring us another bag, will you? This is the second one, right?"

"Actually, it's the third," Frankie admitted.

As Scott was sealing up the note, Frankie caught sight of her rear tire. Flat as a pancake.

Swearing loudly, she bent down to investigate. She ran her hands over the rubber, seeing straightaway what the problem was. Someone had slashed the tire wall, a cut about six inches long.

TWENTY-SEVEN

Puget Sound, 2013

I⊤ WAS PAST noon by the time Frankie made it back to Fairmile, having had to replace the slashed tire with the spare. As she drove through Huntley's Point, she kept her eyes open for a silver SUV, but for once there hadn't been a single one to be seen.

She found Diana putting the finishing touches to the bedrooms. "Doesn't it look good?" she asked, showing Frankie the results. "Izzy helped—she's got a knack of knowing where to put things. She's worked really hard."

"I'm impressed," said Frankie. "She must get her artistic flair from you."

"She's been helping me sort out a website too—get her to show you some of the photos she's taken, they're really good."

"I'm glad she's finding something to do," said Frankie. "Hopefully it'll keep her out of any more trouble."

"Come on now, give her a break. If you don't ease up, you'll never get to know her again."

"I'm working on it." Frankie sighed. "By the way, there was another note on the truck this morning. I was out at Pacifica Gardens."

"I didn't know you'd gone to see Mom?"

"Actually, I hadn't."

"Well, what did it say?"

Frankie repeated the message.

"Back off what?" Diana asked.

Frankie shifted uncomfortably from one foot to the other. "I might have been helping Molly out…"

"Frances Louise Gray. Really? I thought you didn't start your job for another two months? Anyway, what were you doing out at Pacifica again? Didn't the cops from the city search the entire place?"

"You sound like you want it all to go away," said Frankie.

Her mother bit her lip.

"I kind of volunteered to help check the forest behind the home again," Frankie admitted as her mother shot a look at her. "What? She needed the help."

"I don't like this, Frankie. Anyway, who could have a grudge against you? Against us?"

"It could just be kids, as you first suggested. Or it could be a former employee. The one I think I mentioned was sacked a couple of months ago, but he'd have to be pretty stupid to be still hanging around there. Or it could be one of nuns from the convent, unhappy about us digging up the grounds at Fairmile— but *really, nuns*?" She shook her head. "That doesn't seem likely."

"I agree, it does sound a little far-fetched," Diana agreed. "But be careful, okay?"

"Yeah, Mom, always," Frankie reassured her. Diana didn't know the half of it.

"And maybe stay out of things that aren't any of your business. You don't have to get involved until September, right?"

Frankie snorted and her mother rolled her eyes.

"I'd say it's a little late for that."

"I'M TURNING IN," said Diana, a few hours after dinner. "Got a book to finish. See you both in the morning."

"Night, Mom." Frankie glanced at her watch.

"Night, Granny."

Scruff barely raised his head.

The night was still warm, and an idea occurred to Frankie. "Feel like a moonlight dip?" she asked Izzy, who was lounging on the couch, absorbed in something on her phone.

Izzy looked at her mother as if she didn't recognize her. "Ookay," she said slowly. "I think."

"You haven't lived until you've swum by moonlight," Frankie promised her. "Go and get your bathing suit on."

Less than five minutes later, they were downstairs again, towels under their arms. "Race you!" said Frankie with a laugh, heading for the back door. Izzy followed close behind her, and they ran along the path that led to the jetty. The boards held the faintest whisper of the day's warmth. Frankie trod on a sharp stone, swore, and then tried not to giggle. She felt suddenly little older than her daughter.

Tossing her towel on one of the chairs, she curled her toes over the end of the jetty. "Ready?" she asked, glancing around to see Izzy hanging back.

"You go first," she said.

"Uh-uh." Frankie shook her head. "We'll do it together." She reached for Izzy's hand, guided her to the edge, and stared at the black water below. "Dive shallowly," she warned. "You don't want to hit the bottom."

Frankie saw the look of anticipation on Izzy's face. All those opportunities she'd missed in the past five

years, the memories they could have made together…
"On three," she said. "One…two…three…"

She felt Izzy push off in the same instant that she did, their hands separating as they hit the water.

Moments later they surfaced, spluttering and shrieking. Only Diana would have heard them and, even then, the house was a fair distance from the water, not to mention that her mother slept like the dead. "Jesus, it's freezing!" Izzy gasped.

"You sound like a soft California girl," Frankie teased, flipping water at her.

Izzy responded by sinking under the water, her hair spreading out like a mermaid's, before emerging and stroking rapidly away from the jetty with a strong, confident freestyle.

"Don't go too far," Frankie called out, but Izzy had already disappeared into the gloom.

"Hey!" she said, unable to suppress a note of panic. "Iz! Come back."

She waited, treading water, listening for the sound of her daughter's strokes, but there was nothing, only the slap of wavelets against the dock some way behind her.

Frankie's breathing quickened, her chest tightening. Stay calm, she told herself, Izzy will soon return.

Time slowed.

Frankie stared into the darkness, straining to see movement, the splash of an arm slicing through the water. All she could hear was the thump of her heart in her chest, blood pounding against her eardrums, echoing in her skull…then she felt a sharp tug on her leg, pulling her down. She screamed as her head went under the water, bubbles rising all around her.

"Mom…?" Izzy spluttered as Frankie bobbed to the surface. "Are you okay? I was only teasing."

Frankie gasped for breath, choking on a mouthful of water she'd swallowed. Panic began to bloom again and her chest felt like a vice had clamped on it.

"Hold on," Izzy said, reaching under her arms and dragging her back to the jetty. She curled her mother's fingers around the cold metal rung of the ladder, placing her own on top of them.

Frankie tightened her grip and began to haul herself upward. "I'm fine. Really," she insisted, but her voice was shaky.

It was only when they were both standing on the jetty, shivering under their towels, that Frankie began to speak, her teeth chattering with shock as much as the cold. "You scared me. I thought… I thought I'd lost you." *And without Izzy, she had nothing.* The realization socked her in the stomach, winding her, and she had to hold on to the life preserver fastened to the railing to steady herself.

"I'm sorry. I didn't know you'd react like that." Izzy took a step toward her mother and wrapped her arms around her. Under the cool clamminess, Frankie felt the warmth rising from her skin.

"I couldn't see you. Anywhere. Everything was black." Frankie's shaking slowed to an occasional shudder as Izzy held her, shushed her gently. "And then something grabbed me…"

"I'm sorry I did that, Mom. It was a stupid joke." *Mom. Her daughter had called her Mom.*

"I'm the one who should be apologizing to you," Frankie said.

Izzy tightened her arms around her mother, and they

stood like that for a while as the breeze ruffled the surface of the water.

When Frankie had stopped shivering, she broke away and sank onto one of the chairs. Izzy perched on the other, taking hold of her mother's hand. "It's okay. Isn't that what you told me? 'It'll be okay, and it won't be forever.'"

Frankie remembered those words. "Five years *was* too long though, wasn't it? I can't make up for that."

"We're here now."

"Yes, we are."

The silence stretched between them until Frankie shifted her gaze from the black water and met her daughter's eyes. "I'm never going missing from your life again like that," she said, leaning forward and tucking a strand of hair behind Izzy's ear. "You're gonna get so sick of me."

"Promise?" her daughter held out a pinky.

TWENTY-EIGHT

Puget Sound, 2013

WHEN FRANKIE ARRIVED at Pacifica Gardens, she found
Ingrid and Rosalie in the recreation room, sitting across
from each other doing a jigsaw. Both of them wore
thick-lensed glasses and were bent over the puzzle,
absorbed in their task. Frankie almost didn't want to
disturb them. There was an easy dance in their actions
that told her these women were comfortable in each
other's company. She discredited Ingrid's earlier insistence that they didn't know each other. Her grandmother may be losing her memory, but it was obvious
that these two women had been friends for a long time.

Ingrid had been one of those capable young war
widows, a shortage of suitable men being the reason
she never remarried, raising a child on her own, according to Diana. Working two jobs, studying at night,
until she became a college professor, a rare thing for
a woman at that time, particularly a single mother.
Frankie had never met her grandfather. Diana had told
her that he had died not long after the war, had served
in the Pacific. Ingrid hardly ever talked about him,
except to mention his movie-star good looks and his
love of Tootsie Rolls. They seemed strange things to
remember from a marriage, even a brief one.

Frankie's phone began to buzz, and she stepped out

of the recreation room, seeing a text from Molly consisting of three emojis: a pointed finger, a red flower, and a phone handset.

She rang her back immediately.

"Guess what?"

Frankie heard the barely concealed excitement in her voice.

"We were able to get a partial fingerprint. From the glove you found."

"And a match?" Frankie cut straight to the chase.

"Yep."

Frankie held her breath and waited for Molly to elaborate.

"Alan Bloom."

"So, he threw a pair of gloves out the back." Frankie sighed. It didn't prove anything.

"A long way out the back," Molly reminded her.

"Any luck tracking him down?"

"Nope. No joy from the city cops. There's an alert out for him, but they've got more pressing things to do than spend too much time looking. It's like he disappeared off the face of the earth."

"People with something to hide have a way of doing that. Still, it's a good result."

"You know as well as I do we're going to need plenty more than a discarded glove to get a conviction. I'll fill you in on the finer details later if you like—at The Cabbage Shed?"

"Sounds good. And I'm sure Sergeant Sandberg will be pleased. When's he due back by the way? I should probably call in and introduce myself."

"He's been delayed. *Apparently.*" Frankie could hear Molly's growing frustration. "His wife's father lives in

California, and he's had to take personal leave. Went there straight from his vacation."

When Frankie returned to the rec room, Izzy's dark head was huddled with Rosalie's, concentrating on the puzzle.

Ingrid appeared to have gotten bored with the activity and was sitting a little way away. Frankie moved closer until she was standing behind her grandmother and put a gentle hand on her shoulder. She hadn't mentioned her suspicions to her mom, had wanted to wait until she had the chance to see her grandmother first.

"Brigid?" She spoke clearly, directing her voice toward her grandmother's ear. There were two names she could have used: Brigid or Sara. She'd decided to go with Brigid, for no other reason than it sounded similar to Ingrid.

"What's that? No, they're not playing bridge, it's a jigsaw." Ingrid's voice shook slightly, and Frankie was pretty sure her grandmother had heard her perfectly well.

"Sorry, my mistake." She bent down and kissed Ingrid on the cheek, feeling guilty for shocking her grandmother, even if she had been correct in the flash of insight when she looked at the photograph again, that Ingrid Abrahams and Brigid Ryan were one and the same person.

As she pulled up a seat, she caught her grandmother's eye. The look on her face was as bland and unruffled as the water beyond the rec room windows; only the tap-tap-tap of her fingernails against the table an indication that she was even the slightest bit agitated.

Frankie reached into her purse and pulled out the photo she'd shown Liam. "Grandma? Have a look at this."

Ingrid reached for her glasses, which were on a gold chain around her neck.

"Do you recognize anyone?" Frankie asked.

The photo fluttered in the old woman's shaky grip. "I… No, I don't think so. Where did you say you found it?"

"In the study, at the house."

"Which house?"

"Diana's."

"Diana's house? In Tacoma?"

"No, Grandma. She bought a new house, remember. On the island. She's turning it into a guest house."

"Where is it?"

"Here on the island." Frankie kept her patience, though it was wearing thin. "It's called Fairmile. It's a beautiful old house, or it will be once we're finished. Mom told you all this didn't she?"

Ingrid began to shake her head from side to side. "No…no… No." She moaned, a soft, utterly heart-breaking sound.

One of the nurses came up to them. "Perhaps she's had enough for now. Shall we get you back to your room, Ingrid?"

Frankie watched, feeling guilty that in her insistence on getting to the truth she'd upset her grandmother. When would she ever learn to leave things alone?

After witnessing her grandmother's reaction, she decided against showing the photo to Rosalie. For now, anyway.

WHEN THEY HAD returned to Fairmile, Frankie went straight to find Diana as Izzy disappeared up to her room.

"Everything okay? You look a little hot and bothered."

"I'm fine, Mom. But see this?" she asked, holding out the photo. "The girl on the right is Grandma's friend Rosalie from the nursing home—I'm almost certain of it."

"You're the expert, but there's no doubt there's a resemblance," said Diana, inspecting it carefully.

"There's something else." Frankie swallowed, hoping she wasn't making a huge mistake. "The girl on the left is, I believe, Grandma. She must have been about sixteen at the time. Which means…" She recalled her grandmother's insistence that she marry Lucas when she had found out she was pregnant with Izzy. Now she understood why.

"Mom?"

"Honestly Frankie, can we talk about this another time? I've got enough to think about getting this place ready. The landscapers canceled on me this afternoon—the main guy called in sick. Says he'll be off for at least a week. Where am I going to get someone else at such short notice?" The pitch of her voice rose with each sentence until she was practically shrieking at Frankie.

Frankie pressed her fingertips to her temple. It sounded very much like she was avoiding the issue. "Okay, all right." She couldn't work out why her mom was overreacting. Surely it wasn't that shameful a family secret, not these days. "I need to cool off." She went to her room and pulled on a bathing suit, wrapped a towel around her waist, and headed back down to the dock.

Dropping her towel on the warm boards, she made

a graceful swan dive into the water. Her head cleared instantly, and she gasped as she came up for air. She treaded water for a minute and then kicked lazily on her back, thinking about her conversations with her mother and grandmother.

Usually, the water soothed her, but not today. There was so much she didn't know, had never thought to ask before now. It felt like they both were keeping secrets from her.

TWENTY-NINE

Fairmile, 1949

THE WEATHER TURNED COLDER, and the girls were forced to wrap up as best they could, layering sweaters and pulling on scarves and mittens, even when they were inside. The wind howled off the Sound, blowing underneath the ill-fitting doors and finding its way through the gaps in the window frames. Somebody—girls who had long ago left Fairmile most likely—had made draft stoppers in the form of knitted snakes and they pressed them against the doors, but the gusts were so violent that they often blew halfway across the room. In the mornings, Brigid and Sara woke to a find that thin sheets of ice had formed on the inside of their window, and it became harder and harder to climb out of the covers.

Sally was allowed to rest in bed for a week, and then she joined the others, put to work cleaning alongside Brigid and Sara, though she still seemed weak.

"Have they let you see them yet?" Brigid asked as they cleaned the door handles on the first floor, wrinkling their noses at the pungent smell of the polish.

Sally beamed. "Late last night; but Sister Jude said not to tell the other nuns, that they wouldn't approve. She says I can come every night after lights out, as long as I'm quiet."

"How are they doing?"

"Marty has the chubbiest cheeks and is so handsome. But Jenny—" her voice faltered. "Jenny isn't so well. Sister Jude thinks she might have a touch of jaundice. She even suggested I try breastfeeding her. But when I did, nothing would come." She looked despondent, then brightened. "It was wonderful to hold her, to feel her skin against mine. Brig, I can't even describe how that feels." Sally cast her eyes down, her cloth suspended in midair. "But I've failed her already. I can't even do the most basic thing."

"Don't be ridiculous. None of this is your fault, do you hear that? It's not like they even gave you a proper chance at it." Brigid surprised herself with her vehemence. In the few months she'd been at Fairmile, it had become increasingly apparent how unfairly they were all treated. Yes, they had gotten themselves in trouble, and yes, perhaps they should have been more careful, not given in to the urging of their boyfriends, their own desires. But why weren't the boys being punished? How was it that the men and the boys got off scot-free, without any interruption to their lives, their dreams and plans? She burned with the injustice of it all.

The chiming of the doorbell interrupted their conversation, and they both looked at each other and then the door. Few visitors ever called at Fairmile.

"I'll answer it." Sister Agatha swept past them.

"She must be expecting someone," Brigid whispered. "She's usually in the chapel at this time."

Sally picked up the can of polish and moved into the dining room. "I've got other things to worry about."

Brigid stayed, giving the round handle far more attention than it warranted, all the while keeping watch on the front door a few yards away and hoping to catch a glimpse of the visitor.

She was expecting it to be a new girl, but Sister Agatha stepped back to admit a somber-looking man with round wire-framed spectacles and a shabby black jacket. He carried a bag that Brigid immediately recognized as one similar to that used by her family doctor in Bend.

As the nun ushered him past Brigid and up the stairs, she caught a sour whiff of alcohol—the same smell that her father sometimes carried after a night playing cards.

Of course. Sally's tiny daughter, Jenny. She must have gotten sicker.

Brigid cast around for her friend, thankful that she hadn't seen the doctor's arrival, for it would have surely sent her into a spin. She decided not to mention it.

That evening, Brigid complained again of stomach pains, foregoing her evening meal to make a convincing point. Her untouched plate was enough to make Mother Mary Frances stop by her table and ask why.

"It hurts," said Brigid, doubling over in false agony.

"Very well, go and see Sister Jude after dinner. She should be finished in the nursery by then."

"Yes, Mother, thank you." Brigid winced in pain again and let out a groan.

"Perhaps I should go with her?" Sara suggested. "In case…" Sara was one of the nun's favorites, and rarely drew attention to herself.

"All right, go now, both of you."

Brigid left the dining room, making sure to hunch over and clutch her side, leaning on Sara's arm. She caught sight of a couple of the other girls' worried faces and wished she was able to reassure them that it was all a ruse.

When they reached the nursery, they could hear the high-pitched bleat of a newborn. They crept in, surprised to find no sign of Sister Jude.

Sara went to the cot closest to the window and picked up the little boy, rocking him in her arms. "Hush now, hush now," she crooned.

"You seem to know exactly what to do," said Brigid, astonished.

"I have two sisters. My mother made me help take care of them when they were little." Sara continued to rock and pat, and the baby quieted, his sobs subsiding into gentle hiccups.

There was no sound from Jennifer's cot, and as Brigid went over, she could see that the baby's face was a dark yellowish color, her lips purple-blue. "She doesn't look well at all," Brigid murmured. "Even I can tell that."

"Exactly what do you two think you're doing here?" Sister Jude's voice boomed across the room.

They'd both been so absorbed in the babies that they hadn't heard her come in. Brigid could smell the slightly sweet aroma of the cigarettes some of the nuns smoked and her stomach roiled for real this time. "We were looking for you," she said, swallowing against her nausea. "I had pains again; much worse this time."

"Probably round ligament pains, I'm sure that's all they are." Sister Jude sighed heavily. "All right, take a seat and I'll examine you in a minute." The nun's expression told Brigid that she didn't completely believe her. "And you Sara, of all the girls, should know better than to interfere when you've all expressly been told not to."

"He was crying." Sara cast her eyes to the ground and looked as though she was afraid of being beaten.

"Honestly, girl. Babies cry. You don't have to pick them up all the time."

"Yes, Sister Jude. I'm sorry."

"Put him down now, and then go back downstairs and join the others."

Sara reluctantly placed a now sleeping Martin back in his cot, tucked the blankets securely around him, and left the room.

"Now Brigid. Where precisely is this pain?"

Brigid was about to lift her blouse when the door opened, and Sally burst into the room.

"Someone said they saw the doctor here this afternoon," she said, gasping for breath. "Is that true?"

Annoyance flared momentarily in Sister Jude's eyes, quickly replaced by a more pious expression. "The little girl—"

"Jenny," said Sally.

"Yes. You know that she isn't doing so good. Dr. Banks says that she has jaundice—her liver isn't working as well as it should be. And she is still having difficulty feeding."

Sally seemed to crumple, but then squared her shoulders and went over to her daughter. "Let me stay." She stroked the baby's cheek, tears welling up in her eyes.

Sister Jude shook her head and if Brigid hadn't known better, she might have said there were tears in the nun's eyes. "It will be too upsetting in the long run; you know it will."

"But I'm her mother." Sally faltered on the word.

Were they even trying to help? Brigid wanted to yell at the nun. She'd thought that Sister Jude at least partly seemed to understand their feelings.

"Don't worry yourself, dear," said Sister Jude, going

to Sally and patting her shoulder. "We've got it all under control here. You go and finish your dinner. Run along now."

Sally seemed as though she wanted to protest again but backed down in the face of the nun's unyielding expression. She took a last, lingering look at her daughter and left the room.

THERE WERE NO calendars at Fairmile, none that Brigid had seen anyway, and one week seemed to blur into the next. However, on Sundays all of the girls were required to attend chapel, unless they were unwell. Brigid couldn't see the point, but figured she'd used her excuse of stomach pains a little too often recently to get out of the service.

"Will you pray for them?" Sally asked as they walked the short distance from the house.

"Of course," Brigid said, taking her friend's hand.

"Jenny especially."

"She's in God's hands," said Sara, joining them.

"Oh stop that ridiculous nonsense." Brigid finally lost her temper. "She should be in the hospital. Any other baby in her condition would be. I don't understand why the doctor can't see that."

Offended, Sara walked away from them, catching up with a girl a few yards in front. She turned to look at them once, but Brigid ignored her, refusing to back down.

The sermon was no different than the ones Brigid had heard in previous weeks. All had an emphasis on sin and resurrection in one shape or form. Today's lecture told the story of Jesus and the fallen woman, and it was all Brigid could do not to yawn her way through the entire thing. She'd been sleeping badly, convinced that she could hear a baby crying somewhere in the house, but whenever she woke there was silence. Only the cold in the chapel kept her awake—they could see their breath, hanging like clouds in the frigid air. That and a sharp poke in the ribs from Sally, who sat next to her, when her head began to loll.

The girls weren't required to work on Sundays, and so after chapel they were left to do as they pleased. Some girls read, some knitted or sewed, a few went for walks in the grounds if it wasn't too cold—always in pairs or small groups, for those were the rules— and others gathered around a light music program on the radio.

Brigid used the time to study. She was determined not to get left behind when she eventually did go home, and so she diligently worked her way through her math textbook, struggling by herself to figure out the problems that she hadn't yet covered in class. After about thirty minutes, she flung the book down with a defeated sigh. "I wish I could call Joan or Cindy. How am I supposed to do this on my own?"

"What's that?" Sara glanced up from her perfect needlepoint.

"It doesn't matter."

Brigid got out her diary instead, saw that Christmas was the following week. A few days earlier, Sister Agatha had gone to the edge of the woods with an ax and returned, wearing a sour expression but dragging a small pine tree behind her. Sister Clare had decorated it with popcorn garlands and a few colored glass baubles, but aside from that there was little else festive about the place. Brigid's mother had sent a parcel, which lay with those for some of the other girls at the foot of the tree. Tears pricked her eyes when she saw the looped cursive writing, and she hoped it might contain a reply to her letter. She'd had to stop herself from looking at it every time she passed; it only served to make her feel more cut off from her family.

CHRISTMAS EVE WAS much like any other day at the house. No one came to visit, and although the nuns (even Sister Agatha) were more cheerful than usual—they were about to celebrate the birth of Jesus after all, a high point in their calendar—most of the girls were subdued, reminded of their families and all that they were missing. They were all expected to attend the evening chapel service before dinner and, as they left the house, it began to snow, the first of the season. The bellies of the clouds were heavy with it. Despite herself, Brigid was entranced by the softly falling flakes that tingled her nose and cheeks. Some of the other girls—Marianne and Sara among them—began to dance, twirling around and giggling in delight like little kids. "It's so pretty," said Jean, gazing in wonder at the flakes she'd caught on her mittens. "I ain't never seen snow before." They looked so incongruous with their round bellies, like an ungainly elephant ballet, that Brigid's spirits lifted momentarily.

"Come along now girls, or you'll all freeze to death." For once, Sister Agatha's voice had lost its razor edge of spite.

SHE WOKE EARLY on Christmas morning. Sara was still asleep, gently snoring, as Brigid eased herself out of bed and went over to the window. Their room looked out to the water, with the chapel to her right. Dawn had crept over the clouded horizon and the light was pearly, the rising sun painting the sky with pink and gray. Brigid was surprised to see a bobbing light approaching from the water. She shivered and pulled her robe close, watching as a boat moored at the end of the jetty. It might have been a fishing or cargo vessel. A dark figure leapt from the deck and began to unload boxes—crates most likely. Brigid had seen similar shapes in the kitchen, packed with cabbages, squash, and apples, as well as empty ones left there. She hadn't made the connection before—she'd assumed everything came by truck.

This boat didn't stop for the holidays then. Did it come every day? Or only a few times a week? Or less often than that? She tucked the question away, resolving to keep an eye on the times the crates were left at the jetty, and when they disappeared. She had the perfect vantage point from which to observe the comings and goings there.

"MITTENS, HOW NICE." Brigid unfolded the gaudy paper and tried to be grateful. There was a card with drawings from her little sisters that made her smile, and a letter from her brother, telling her about football games lost and won and the car he was saving for. Her mother must have forced him to write to her, for Brigid doubted he would have done so of his own accord.

Nearly all of the other girls had received small gifts—books, stationery, candy—everyone except Sara, who watched the others, a smile fixed on her face as if it bothered her not a bit. Brigid wasn't fooled; she wished she had a gift for her, but there was nowhere she could have bought anything. Still, she should have tried, perhaps made something, however humble.

Brigid saved the letter from her mother for last, her hands trembling as she unfolded it. This should contain the reply to her request. At first, it looked as though her mother had agreed: "My dearest daughter, we miss you terribly and cannot wait until you are able to return. I hope you are staying healthy and getting plenty of fresh air…" Fresh air? Didn't her mother realize it was the middle of winter? "I received your letter, and please be assured that I have given it a great deal of thought. However…" Brigid's vision blurred as she read the words that told her that her parents would never agree to her solution. Words that said her mother had her hands full with the twins, and that she could not take on any more responsibility, that, hard as it was, Brigid had to face up to the consequences of her actions. "The best course for all concerned would be if you were to give the baby up to a nice Christian family, one who can afford it every comfort," she wrote. And, finally, brutally, "No man is going to want you with another's baby on your hip."

Brigid blinked back the tears that threatened to spill over and stumbled up the stairs to her room.

Sara, seeing her distress, followed soon after.

"Nothing's ever as bad as you think it is," Sara soothed, coming to sit beside her. "And if it is, it will someday be better."

"What would you know? You're just a kid." Brigid spat back, not caring that she was being unfair. Disappointment sat like a stone in her gut, making her mean and unkind.

"I've seen plenty enough to know," said Sara calmly.

"There's no hope. No hope at all anymore," she cried, burying her head in her thin pillow.

The sound of Brigid's sobs was drowned out by the wail of a much louder voice. She stopped at the noise and sat up.

Sara went out into the hall and peered down the stairs. "I'm pretty sure it's Sally," she said, returning to the room.

The noise had increased in volume now that the door was open. It sounded like the howl of an animal, thin, high, cutting so cleanly through Brigid that she had to cover her ears. Something must have happened to Sally's baby girl.

THIRTY

Puget Sound, 2013

Music was booming from the rear deck of The Cabbage Shed when Frankie arrived, and as she closed the door of her truck she got a feeling as though she was being watched. It was happening all too often now, and she'd always trusted her instincts. She scanned the cars parked in the lot but when she couldn't see anything out of the ordinary, headed inside.

Earlier, Molly sent her a text featuring a beer glass and a dancing girl. Frankie had replied with a thumbs up, resolving to get more creative with her emojis in future.

She had dressed carefully (after dithering about what to wear, and she never dithered), conscious that she might be seen, that it might be appreciated. It was a new feeling, and she still didn't know what to think about it. She eventually decided on a shirt the color of a blue jay's wing that she'd bought on impulse at the airport before leaving Sydney and had even ironed it—earning a raised eyebrow from Diana. She'd also unearthed her makeup bag and applied blush, mascara, even lip gloss, but as she parked the truck it felt like too much, and she rubbed at her mouth self-consciously.

She pushed through the crowd toward the bar, thinking to get a drink, while keeping an eye out for Molly.

She was anxious about seeing Joe—he muscled his way into her thoughts with more frequency than she cared to admit. It was embarrassingly late to bring up his text about a date, and every time it crossed her mind, she'd been unable to imagine what she might actually say to him.

She didn't notice him at first, but then he appeared from a door at the back and the smile on his face was wide and uncomplicated, the kind you give to people you really like. It warmed her to look at him. She grinned back at him like a goof and gave him a foolish little wave. Perhaps he hadn't minded that she'd never returned his message, or perhaps it hadn't been that important to him. She hoped it was the former.

Molly materialized next to her, and Frankie cringed inwardly that she might have noticed her inexpert flirting. "I've got a table over there," she yelled over the noise and indicated a spot to Frankie's left. "It's a bit quieter too." One of the bartenders took their order, and they eased their way over to the table, beers held high to avoid being jostled.

They sat down and Molly raised her glass in a toast. "To never giving up."

"Amen." Frankie took a long draught of her beer. "What's the latest?"

"We've found Bloom."

"You have?"

"Ratted on by a neighbor who was sick of the cars that kept turning up at his place in the early hours. Seems like he thought the fuss had died down and he came home, took up where he'd left off."

"Left off?"

"Dealing. The Seattle cops found pills, coke, weed…"

"Anything to link him to Pacifica?"

"Not yet, although it seems likely he was stealing medication. The cops found some old pill bottles with labels showing the names of Pacifica residents in the backyard shed, so he's got some questions to answer in that regard. But we still can't prove that he was on the premises that night—the gloves could have been thrown out anytime in the weeks before then, when he was employed there. I'm not sure he's the one behind the notes either. I doubt he'd want to risk being seen on the island."

"Bugger." Frankie leaned back and listened to the band. The crowd out on the deck seemed to think they were pretty good, hollering their appreciation and stomping on the floor with their boot heels when they took a break. She glanced over to the bar, saw that Joe was flat out taking orders and serving drinks. "I went to the city a couple weeks ago," she said, returning her attention to Molly. "I stopped by the convent, the one that administered Fairmile when it was a mother and baby home. I met with a Sister Jude. Said I was a journalist researching adoption."

Molly gave her a sharp look and Frankie wondered if she had overstepped the mark. "She was very tight-lipped then."

Molly nodded. "I know, we interviewed her too." She was making her point that she had been doing her job.

Frankie continued. "Then I saw her again at the funeral and she said something strange. I think she felt she could talk, without the likelihood of anyone overhearing."

"Go on."

"She said something happened at Fairmile. That it wasn't right. She couldn't tell me the year, but said it was the coldest winter of the century. I checked—that was most likely nineteen forty-nine to fifty. Months of snow and freezing conditions. She also mentioned a girl called Sally."

"What's that got to do with Bernadette Evans?"

"I'm not sure yet. I think it's connected to the tiny skeleton that the plumbers uncovered. And I might have found two women who were once at Fairmile, in the late nineteen forties or early fifties."

"They'd be...what? In their eighties, nineties?" Molly pursed her lips. "Still alive?"

"Uh-huh. And they're both at Pacifica Gardens. One is friends with my grandmother, Ingrid. Her son—who she gave birth to at Fairmile—was adopted, but he's recently found her." She hesitated. The implications of what she was about to reveal could be devastating for her family, but the truth would come out sooner or later. "I think Ingrid and Sally—or Rosalie, which is her real name—met at Fairmile when they were girls."

"Your grandmother? She was at Fairmile?" Molly's jaw hung open. "Wow. You don't think they...?"

Frankie shrugged. "Unlikely, but even so..."

"That color looks good on you, Frankie." Joe appeared in front of them, a dish towel casually thrown over one shoulder, a bowl of sweet potato wedges in his hands. "Hey Molly," he said, putting the bowl down and reaching in to kiss his sister on the cheek. After that, it seemed only natural that he kiss Frankie too. She caught a faint aroma of salt, lemons, something musky. Her cheek burned where his lips had grazed it and she wondered if Molly had noticed. There was every chance she had—a good detective always saw the things that others didn't, the half-hidden stuff, and Molly had certainly proved her mettle in the short time Frankie had known her.

Joe pulled up a chair, and as he smiled at Frankie her mouth went dry. "You're not cold?" he asked, concerned.

She had wrapped her hands around her elbows to stop her fingers from sleepwalking toward his. "No, not at all." She laughed, feeling suddenly awkward.

"There's some blankets in the back if you are. We keep them for folks sitting outside. It can get cool when the breeze comes off the water."

"Really, I'm fine, but I do appreciate your concern." They grinned foolishly at each other until Frankie thought Molly might really begin to realize something was going on between them. What *was* going on, exactly?

The band started up again, the lead singer belting out a tune. Joe got to his feet. "No rest for the wicked," he said with a half grin. "Catch you later, sis. Bye, Frankie."

She and Molly listened to the music for a while, ordered another beer, and chatted about nothing in particular, but then Molly stood up, pleading an early start in the morning, and Frankie couldn't think of a reason to stay. She told herself that she'd be an idiot to repeat her previous behavior, no matter how appealing it might be in the moment. That was a path strewn with pitfalls. She returned their empty bottles to the bar, giving a carefree (who was she fooling?) wave to Joe as she left. He was serving a customer but gave her a small acknowledging nod.

It was foggy by the time Frankie arrived home, and as she watched it hover over the newly laid turf like a carpet of snow, she thought of the bitter cold, the ice storm that had halted the ferries, cut off supplies to the islands of Puget Sound for three weeks in January 1950. Anything could have happened and no one on the mainland would have been any the wiser.

THIRTY-ONE

Puget Sound, 2013

DIANA WAS SITTING at one of the dining tables surrounded by files and paper. "The office is nearly finished Mom," said Frankie. "I'll have it ready for you by the end of tomorrow." Seeing a pile of stapled forms, she asked, "Did you advertise for housekeeping staff?"

"Already taken care of," Diana replied, sounding satisfied. "Four local women who've been cleaning houses on the island forever."

"Great. Sounds like you'll be in good hands."

"All that's left to do is move this into the office, finish off the landscaping, get the signage installed, and launch the website." Diana pushed her glasses up on her nose and raised her head from the sea of paperwork. "Apart from the boathouses of course, but they were always going to come later, regardless of the plumbing delays." The area where the skeleton had been found was still cordoned off, though it was hidden from view of the house. They'd heard nothing since the tiny bones had been taken away by the forensics team. Frankie didn't doubt that most of the residents of the island knew of the grim discovery by now, but at least no one had directly asked her about it.

"Maybe it was all too long ago," Diana mused, clearly thinking along the same lines as Frankie.

"Someone must know, even now," Frankie insisted. She had decided not to force the issue of the photograph she'd shown Diana of Ingrid at Fairmile. It didn't come easily, but she wanted her mom to tell her in her own time. Either that, or she'd ask Ingrid about it, though that course of action would require a gentle approach.

"Oh, and I sent Izzy's images over to the marketing agency yesterday," said Diana, focusing on the present again. "They're going to get back to me by the end of the week with a brochure design. We'll find our feet in the fall, be ready for Thanksgiving and Christmas, and take bookings for spring weddings."

"Sounds like a good plan." Frankie flipped over a sheet of paper, seeing a timeline in her mother's careful handwriting. "Where is she? Izzy, I mean. She wasn't up when I left this morning."

"Still asleep."

"It's nearly noon."

"She's a teenager."

"Even so."

"Pick your battles, dear," her mother said serenely.

Irritated, Frankie went upstairs to find Izzy was awake and lying on her bed, her laptop open and Scruff beside her. "I'm doing some editing on the shots I took the other week. I thought I'd make a video that Granny can put on the website. Take a look if you like."

Izzy's tone was casual, but it was obvious that it mattered to her. Frankie sat beside her on the bed as Izzy scooted over to make room. Together, they leaned back on the pillows and Frankie waited as Izzy pressed a few keys and adjusted the size of the screen.

The video ran for around thirty seconds: "Any longer than that and people get bored," Izzy explained.

She'd added soothing music as the images faded in and out, showing the house, the jetty, the dark waters of the Sound, a bird's-eye view of the island taken from the lookout. It finished on a photo of Frankie and Diana leaning against the portico, aprons on and sleeves rolled up, smiling as if ready to welcome guests. Frankie had forgotten that Izzy had taken it. "I'm not finished yet, but you get the idea," said Izzy.

"It's incredible," said Frankie proudly. "Your grand-mother's going to love it."

"And you?"

"Me? Of course I love it too." Frankie dropped a kiss on Izzy's forehead. She couldn't remember the last time she'd done that. "My clever daughter." Izzy smiled and Frankie was reminded of her sunny, generous little girl again. "Do you feel like doing something together this afternoon? We could go into Huntley's Point, get some ice cream?" she asked, sitting up. "Have a swim?"

Izzy frowned at the screen. "Actually, Zac asked if I wanted to hang out with him later. It is okay if I see him now, right?"

"Sure. Let your grandmother know if you'll be back for dinner, okay?"

"Okay."

Izzy set off on her bike after lunch. Frankie put the final touches to the study while Diana went outside to su-pervise the planting of an orchard. "Apples grow so well here," she said. "I've chosen all the heirloom varieties."

Planting trees was such a sign of faith in the future; it was a good feeling to imagine Frankie would hope-fully still be there in a few years' time when they had matured. "I'm going across to see Grandma," Frankie said, coming out to check on the progress. She was conscious of the time she'd missed while she had been living overseas, and that the dementia was taking Ingrid away from them little by little.

"Okay," said Diana, a shovel in one hand and a sapling in the other. "Give her a kiss from me. I'll try and get over to visit soon."

When Frankie went back inside to collect her purse, noticing a newly arranged vase of flowers on the dining room table. She picked up the paring knife next to it, fingering the blade thoughtfully.

INGRID WAS IN her room when Frankie arrived. She was sitting in her easy chair, which faced the window, a large-print novel in her lap. "Hello, my dear." She lifted her face in pleasure.

"How are you, Grandma?"

"Perfectly well, thank you, Frances."

It was a good day.

"Would you like me to read to you?" Frankie motioned toward the book.

"Oh no, I don't think so. I can't keep the characters straight in my head for more than five minutes. I've read the same page over and over for the last hour." She said this with humor, but a touch of regret colored her words.

"May I?" Frankie picked up the book, saw that it was a recent bestseller. "I'm not surprised. I couldn't follow this one either." She smiled as she raised a dry chuckle from her grandmother.

"Tell me, how is that other girl? The young one who looks just like you?"

"Izzy?"

"Yes, her."

Frankie went to brush off the inquiry with a superficial remark but stopped herself. "Actually, I'm finding her a little tricky to understand." She told Ingrid about Izzy's mercurial moods, her dismissive tone, her occasional, redemptive sweetness. "I can't get a handle on her."

"She's got a good strong backbone; don't worry so much." She patted Frankie's hand, her eyes losing focus as she seemed to drift off somewhere else. Frankie remembered that Ingrid had once been a teacher, then a college professor. She must have seen thousands of young people finding their way in the world. It was a comfort to hear her words.

"Grandma, may I ask you something?"

"What is it, dear?"

"Can you tell me about what life was like when you were a girl? I don't think I even know where you grew up; was it in Seattle?"

"No, not Seattle. Bend, Oregon." A cloud momentarily crossed the old woman's face. "But I left there a very long time ago."

"And your parents? Brothers and sisters?"

Ingrid shook her head. "I don't…"

"It's okay if you don't want to talk about it."

"I…got on a bus and came to Seattle. I was sixteen. I'd never traveled so far in my life."

"And you were pregnant," Frankie said softly.

Ingrid started and for a moment Frankie feared she'd been too blunt, but then Ingrid reached into a drawer and pulled out a piece of paper, handing it to Frankie.

It was a black and white photo that showed a young woman—no more than a girl really—a baby cradled in her arms. It was unmistakeably Ingrid.

"That's Mom—Diana?"

Ingrid nodded.

"At Fairmile?" Frankie had recognized the entrance behind her in the picture.

"Yes."

They sat for a moment in silence.

"But granddad...?" Frankie was unable to stop herself from asking.

"I wasn't married." Ingrid blinked. "Does that shock you, dear?"

Frankie, who had figured out the truth some time ago, put a reassuring hand on her grandmother's arm. "No, Grandma, it doesn't. It makes me sad for you; that's all. It must have been very difficult in those days. I can't begin to imagine."

"They made us give up the babies. Said it was God's will. That was a load of bullshit." Her eyes blazed.

Now Frankie *was* shocked; she'd never heard Ingrid use such a word.

"I lost some of the best friends I'd ever had—Sara— one night she simply disappeared, and her little baby too. I couldn't even try and find her afterward: none of us were allowed to use our real names. We had no choice but to give our babies away, even if we desperately wanted to keep them. We didn't have a hope in hell, there was no one to turn to."

Frankie reached for her grandmother's hand. "I'm so sorry."

"They told us we were selfish if we even asked about keeping them, said we'd have to pay them back for our board and food. Well, who could afford to do that? Hardly anyone, I don't mind telling you. My parents certainly didn't want to know. Their own grandchild..."

"So, what happened?" She shifted closer as Ingrid began to explain.

THIRTY-TWO

Fairmile, 1949

IT DIDN'T TAKE long for the news that Sally's little girl, Jenny, had passed on to circulate among the girls. In a small measure of sympathy, Sister Mary Frances allowed a few of them to visit Sally later that afternoon.

They found her lying on her bed, staring at the ceiling.

"I don't think she even knows we're here," Sara whispered.

"You've still got Marty," another girl said.

Brigid fumed at the tactlessness of the remark. She squeezed Sally's hand and leaned down, muttering the words, "I'm sorry, I'm so sorry," in her ear.

Sally failed to respond; she was far away.

"She hasn't spoken since it happened," said Sara after they'd realized there was little comfort to offer and retreated to their room.

"I've never seen anyone look so dreadful," said Brigid. "It was like she'd completely checked out."

"What do you think will happen now?"

They didn't have to wait long. Sally's father arrived to take her home two days later. The girls gathered to wish her goodbye, but she didn't appear to hear them.

Brigid remembered a word from English class.

Catatonic.

That's what Sally was.

No one mentioned that her baby son, Marty, wasn't going with her, though they were all thinking it.

ONE DAY, about a week after Sally had gone, despite the snow and freezing rain that had turned the paths to and from the house into an ice rink, Brigid and Sara went out into the cold. "I swear if I don't leave these walls soon, I'll go mad," said Brigid as she pulled on her new mittens. Her back ached and her feet were so swollen that it was an effort to force them into her boots, but she couldn't wait to be free of the house. Sister Agatha's sly pinches had increased in frequency the larger Brigid's stomach grew and there was a heaviness indoors that seemed to press down on her shoulders like a lead weight.

The snow made the landscape look like the cake served at her cousin's wedding a few years ago: hard, crunchy icing and underneath, soft, luscious fruitcake. They had each been given the tiniest sliver, no more than a mouthful really, but she'd never eaten anything so exquisite. Now, she let a mouthful of snow melt on her tongue, just as she had done with the sugar, imagined its sweetness, the taste of happier times.

They walked across the lawn, the soles of their boots breaking through the layers of ice and snow, and Brigid glanced toward the boatsheds and the jetty, seeing the crates piled there. There had been no sign of the boatman since the week before.

She grabbed Sara's elbow as she stumbled over a fallen branch. Their heavy bellies had shifted them off balance, and it was sometimes hard to remember to be more careful. This was the worst part of being pregnant, the aches and the indigestion and the pulling at her ribs as though the baby itself was wrenching them apart to make more space. Brigid had stopped looking at herself in the bathroom mirror, hating the markings that had appeared on her face, the dark line down her belly, the stretchmarks that striped her sides. She felt old and ungainly and fat. Where had her strong, athletic body gone? The legs that had carried her up the hockey field and the arms that cut through the water of the swimming pool? She'd never be the same again.

"Not much longer, huh?" Much as she couldn't wait to meet her baby, she didn't think she'd ever want to be pregnant again, not for the rest of her life.

"It feels like I've been here forever," Sara replied.

"Same."

"How did it happen?" Sara asked tentatively. "For you I mean? Did you love him—the father?"

Brigid stopped in her tracks, surprised by the question. A few of the girls had talked about what had happened, boyfriends who told them they were being careful, that they wouldn't get pregnant, that they'd stand by them if they did, that they loved them. Boyfriends who'd turned out to be faithless, each and every one.

She and Sara had never shared their stories.

"I was an idiot, that's what." Bitterness laced Brigid's voice; the memory was no longer a good one. "Carried away by foolish ideas of romance and thinking I was getting away with something, that I had a wonderful secret." She told Sara the whole sorry story, finishing with her discovery that Robert was married, that he already had a family of his own.

Sara wrapped an arm around Brigid's thickened

waist, the much younger girl comforting the older one. "My uncle—" she began, speaking so quietly that Brigid had to strain to hear. "My uncle lived with us. Ten people in a two-story row house. He had a room upstairs and he taught me how to play chess after school and before my father came home. It was nice to be singled out, you know? He made me feel special. Then, well, he…" Sara bit her lip.

"It's okay, you don't have to say any more." Brigid hugged her back. "It's not your fault, do you understand that?"

Sara shrugged. "I guess."

She halted and turned Sara to face her, gripping her friend by the shoulders. "I mean it. He took advantage of you. For heaven's sake, you're only thirteen. That's wrong. Illegal, too, I believe." It was easy to be outraged on someone else's behalf, much harder to stay angry at her own situation.

"Okay." Sara gave her a tremulous smile.

"Good. And when this is all over, I want you to go back to school and work as hard as you possibly can, because one day you are going to *be* someone." Brigid was talking to herself as much as Sara. "Then nobody can make you do anything you don't want to."

"Sister Clare said I might be able to go to a place in the city. A convent with other girls, orphans, and suchlike." Sara sounded hopeful.

"I stayed there on my way here. It's nice."

Brigid saw something like joy light up the little girl's face and she thought of her own sisters, wished she could see them again. She sniffed, from the cold and the now-familiar ache of homesickness.

"Sara… Brigid…" The voice calling their names floated across the snowy lawns. "Come inside now."

Sister Agatha.

They turned toward the house, hurrying as fast as their waddling bodies and the heavy snow would allow.

"Come in at once."

The nun stood at the door, waving them in.

"Sorry, Sister. We only wanted to get some fresh air." Sara apologized for them both, her cheeks pinked by the cold and the effort of running. She bent over, trying to catch her breath.

"You stupid girls. It's far too cold to be outside, and you shouldn't be exerting yourselves like that. It's bad for baby. You're not to blame, Sara, but Brigid, you should know better."

"Sorry, Sister Agatha." Brigid did her best to sound contrite, but it had been worth it to escape the house, even for a few minutes.

"Make sure it does not happen again. Or I shall be forced to punish you."

It was clear she relished the prospect.

The girls slid past her, peeling off their gloves and stocking caps as they went to the mudroom. Brigid put her hat and mittens on a drying shelf, shoving along several pairs of gardening gloves to make room for them.

She sank onto a narrow bench, her numb fingers slowly unbuttoning her coat. Sara sat next to her, and they both bent over awkwardly to remove their boots.

"Oof!" Sara's belly was so large that, try as she might, she couldn't reach the laces.

"Here, let me undo yours and then you can do mine," Brigid suggested, lowering herself awkwardly to her knees to help her friend. The ridiculousness of the situation struck her afresh, and she began to giggle, not sure if it was with hysteria or humor. Last year, she'd been running track, training almost every afternoon, reveling as the cold wind rushed through her hair, sprinting until she felt she would collapse with exhaustion. Now look at her. Barely able to tie her own shoelaces.

"What's so funny?" Sara asked.

"Honestly, I don't know," said Brigid, when she'd calmed down. "But if I don't laugh, I might cry."

A WEEK OR so later, the weather turned even colder. The girls awoke to a vicious wind that whipped the waters of the Sound until its surface resembled egg whites, sending waves to break almost as high as the boatsheds and freezing in places until the shoreline was a slushy mess of water and debris. "Do you think they'll be swept away?" asked Sara, as they stood at the window watching the scene. "What about the jetty?"

"I'd say it's weathered its fair share of storms," Brigid reassured her. "It'll likely be standing long after we've gone."

Snow began to fall again, lightly at first, but as the day wore on it began to come down more heavily. The spiky shapes of the Douglas fir trees were softened by a layer of white, and the air was muffled. The girls listened to the reports of the blizzard on the local radio station, while the nuns hurried to tuck blankets under the doors to stop the flurries from entering the house.

The storm continued though the day and into the next week and supplies of food began to run low, for the house was now cut off by both land and water.

Meals began to focus heavily on potato, with meager

helpings of canned green beans and very little meat. There was no fruit to speak of, for the usually plentiful apple supply had been eaten, and the woodpile, once stacked above the girls' heads, was now at knee-height.

Brigid was left with plenty of time to stew over her mother's letter, rereading it in case she had misinterpreted the words somehow. But it was there, clear as day. Her baby was not welcome at home, and if Brigid wanted to keep it, she was on her own.

"They can't *force* you to give your baby up, can they?" she asked Marianne one day as they sat together sewing. Brigid had managed to hem several cloths of triple-folded muslin for diapers and was now working on basting the trim of a receiving blanket, but the layette for her baby was pitifully sparse. She let her stitching fall in her lap.

"They can make it very difficult," Marianne replied.

Brigid nodded, thinking back to the list Sister Jude had suggested she make. Still, some stubborn part of her refused to give up on the idea. She told herself she was smart enough to figure out a way if she really thought about it. Late at night, before she went to sleep, and at odd times in the day, she had begun to talk to her baby as it squirmed and wriggled inside her. The poor thing was cramped for space now, for it was nearly time, a matter of weeks until it was due. She would sing softly to it, snatches of lullabies that she remembered from her own childhood, promising to be a good mother, that she would try so hard never to lose her temper and would tell her baby how much she loved it every single day. The promises became a life raft.

"Do you know of anyone who has? Kept their baby I mean?"

"They don't tell us, do they? Least of all something like that. All they talk about is how grateful the families are who can't have children, the gift you've given them. Like it cancels out your own sin in getting pregnant when you're unmarried." Marianne scoffed.

"But they can't give them away unless we say so, right? Don't we have to sign something, adoption papers? They can't just take our babies from us."

"What choice do we have though? It costs money to raise a child."

"I know, but…" Brigid stopped. She couldn't finish the sentence.

FAIRMILE HAD BEEN cut off for nearly ten days when the thaw came. The sky lightened and the mercury in the thermometer by the front door rose by nearly twenty degrees. Rain arrived, washing away most of the snow, leaving great shiny puddles on the paths and lawns.

"We might yet have a silver thaw," Sister Jude warned as she examined Brigid one morning, tutting over her swollen ankles.

"A what?"

"All that water'll turn to ice if it we get another cold spell."

One morning before dawn, Brigid watched from her bedroom window as the boatman left crates piled high on the jetty, and a delivery from the town butcher reached them. Later, as she saw Sister Agatha and Mother Mary Frances, a pair of giant bats, one tall, one short, flapping their way across the mushy lawns to retrieve them, she began to formulate a plan. It wasn't a foolproof one, but it was the best she could come up with and she figured she had to give it a shot.

Two new girls arrived, escorted by a nun from the convent in Seattle. "They look as scared as I was," said Brigid to Sara after being introduced to them.

The nun—Sister Rosa—stayed overnight, and Sara was called to go and speak to her.

"What did she want?" Brigid asked, when Sara returned.

"She was really nice," said Sara. "She told me all about Sacred Heart, and what the other girls there are like and what a wonderful place it is."

"See? It's all going to work out."

"But what about my baby? I'll be abandoning it."

Brigid placed a hand on her shoulder. "You've heard what the nuns say. Your baby will have the most wonderful, loving family."

"You really think so?" Sara's eyes were shining at the possibility of a future for herself.

"That's what they promise us," Brigid said, keeping her doubts to herself.

THIRTY-THREE

Puget Sound, 2013

"WHEN WERE YOU going to tell me, Mom?" Frankie had driven back to Fairmile, arriving to find her mother still in the yard, on her knees, smears of mud decorating her cheeks. "Don't you think I deserved to know?"

"Know what?"

"You know exactly what I mean. About Ingrid. And Fairmile."

"First of all, don't take that tone with me. And secondly, help me. I seem to have seized up." She held her arms out to Frankie.

"I think the least you can do is give me is an explanation." Frankie hauled her mother to her feet.

"Can I clean up first?" Diana asked as she straightened herself, rubbing the small of her back with one hand. "Then I'll tell you whatever it is you want to know."

They reached the back door and Diana kicked off her work boots, heading toward the kitchen as Frankie followed a few steps behind.

"It's complicated, but I suppose that is a big part of the reason I bought the house," Diana said, scrubbing at her hands with a nail brush. "Besides the fact that it's a beautiful building, of course. I wanted to make something good from a place that had seen such sorrow and distress."

"Is that all?"

"Where we come from matters; it's important to remember that. To own the house where I was born, despite the circumstances, is quite something." Diana said. "And there was an element of hoping for closure. For Mom. She hasn't seen the new Fairmile yet—I want to make it perfect first. I hope it will help her make peace with that part of her history."

Frankie couldn't see how it would help, but then she was hardly an expert on resolving trauma. "You don't think she has? Made peace I mean?"

"Not completely. That generation were so good about burying their emotions and getting on with things."

They weren't the only ones.

"But our history can be found in our present, just like Fairmile is here."

Frankie wasn't entirely sure what she was getting at. "When did you find out?" she asked.

"She told me when I was eighteen. Said I deserved to hear the truth."

"Did it change anything for you?"

"I was pretty upset at first. Didn't speak to her for a few days. But then I got to thinking how strong a person she was to have done what she did."

"So why did no one ever tell me?"

"It was her story to tell, not mine."

"How long had you known that Sister Agatha was at Pacifica Gardens?"

Diana glanced away and, in that moment, everything clicked into place. Frankie opened her mouth to speak but found herself lost for words. Her throat seemed to have completely closed. There were too many little signs that, when taken all together, seemed to add up: the paring knife, the nettles in the nun's room and that grew at Fairmile, Diana drinking more than usual, Ingrid's history, Diana's reticence to discuss the case when normally she'd have been fascinated by it, her relief when the funeral was allowed to go ahead…

What kind of monster suspected their own mother of such a thing, even allowed herself to think it possible? Stumbling to the door, she ran outside and down toward the dock, convinced she'd finally lost her mind.

Frankie was wearing sandals but that didn't stop her from running along the path that led to Huntley's Point. She sprinted, her feet flying over the pine needles, barely noticing the branches that tore at her T-shirt, the brambles that scratched her legs, or the tree roots that threatened to trip her up. It was as if she were in a trance, her mind separated from her body.

She'd been in this state once before, unable to bring order to her whirling thoughts.

The first time, it had happened after hours spent reviewing security footage from cameras in the vicinity of a Balmain warehouse, footage she should have checked days earlier. She rubbed her eyes, blinked, and had only just seen it out of the corner of her eye. A gas station camera, blurry, but unmistakeable vision of a little girl in a light-colored sweatshirt. What made her pause was the fact that the girl appeared to be wearing only one shoe. A grubby-looking sneaker.

The date and time-stamped footage showed it to be the day before they had raided the warehouse.

FRANKIE WAS OUT of breath by the time she arrived at The Cabbage Shed, and bent double, gasping and dazed, wondering what to do next.

"Frankie?"

She looked up as Joe came into view.

"I saw you from the window. Is everything okay?"

Frankie hesitated. Now was not the time or the place, and she didn't know him anywhere near well enough to dump all of her fears on him. She struggled to get her breathing under control, to still the shaking of her legs.

"Is it Izzy? Your mom?"

She shook her head. "No, no, they're—" She gasped. "Fine."

"Your grandmother?"

"Uh-uh."

"Well, what then? Pardon me for pointing out the obvious, but you're not exactly dressed for jogging."

Frankie gave a snort of surprised laughter, hopping from one foot to another. "It's a stress reaction. If I'm feeling overwhelmed, I have to get out and sprint as fast as I can. Get out of my own head."

"Ohh-kay." He drew out the syllables as though he wasn't sure whether to believe her or not. "Stay right where you are, and I'll fetch you a drink."

When Joe returned, she took slow sips from the glass of water he offered, allowing her breathing to return to something approaching a normal rhythm. "Sorry," she said. "I didn't mean to give you a shock."

"Don't worry." He looked as if he wanted to say more, but she cut him off.

"Have you seen Molly recently?"

"Not since Tuesday, but then that's not unusual. She mentioned something about being slammed with over-time. Blew off trivia last night because of it."

Trivia. The Hopeless Causes. She'd been so caught

up with things at Fairmile that it had completely slipped her mind.

Joe glanced back toward the doorway, watching as a large group of people pushed their way in and the sound of a saxophone floated toward them. "I'm a barman down," he said apologetically.

"Of course."

His eyes searched hers.

"Really, I'm fine." She handed the glass back. "Thank you."

As he turned to leave, she caught a bleak expression flash across his face and kicked herself for not getting back to him as soon as he had messaged her. It was little consolation that they were probably both better off not getting involved.

Frankie limped slowly back the way she'd come, not caring that night had fallen. The moon was full and would give her enough light to find her way home.

Home. She didn't know what to say to her mother, couldn't begin to formulate the words. She had plenty of experience getting suspects to tell her the truth, to reveal their secrets no matter how much they resisted, but interrogating a family member? She didn't have the stomach for it.

Her phone buzzed but she ignored it, too disturbed to be able to focus on anything else.

The house was in darkness by the time she arrived home and her mother's car was missing from the driveway. Frankie pushed open the front door (they almost never locked it) to find an anxious Scruff who was very pleased to see her. She went to the kitchen, going to a cupboard to fetch some kibble as the dog whined and wove frantically between her legs.

It wasn't until he'd been fed—scoffing down his dinner as though he hadn't eaten for days—that she checked her phone. Five missed calls. From Izzy. There was a blinking message notification. She pressed the number to retrieve the message, heading to the refrigerator. The sound was garbled, and she strained to hear it. Then there was Izzy's voice, asking for water, saying she felt unwell. Then more garbled words, what sounded like Izzy was saying *pain*, but she wasn't totally sure. Frankie heard a sound like water slapping against something. Then the message abruptly cut off. She played it back again. Still couldn't make out the words.

She checked her watch. Nearly nine. She'd taken longer to walk home than she realized.

She raced up the stairs toward Izzy's bedroom, but it was empty, the drapes closed, a faint hint of perfume hanging in the stuffy air. Her backpack was missing; she usually took it with her whenever she went out. She dialed her daughter's number, returning to the kitchen as she waited for it to connect.

No answer. She thought for a moment, then sent a text, asking if everything was okay and could she please call?

Frankie set the phone down. Waited a second. Then picked it up again. Sent another message.

Izzy? Sweetheart, please just let me know where you are. She checked the locating app, but there was no clue as to where Izzy might be; it hadn't updated since the morning, when she was at Fairmile.

It was only once Frankie had put her phone down that she saw the note, half-hidden underneath a jug of flowers.

THIRTY-FOUR

Fairmile, 1950

IN FEBRUARY, temperatures plunged once more. Going outside was a risk as everything was now covered in a layer of ice, exactly as Sister Jude had predicted. The girls who were near to giving birth were kept indoors, Brigid and Sara among them. "God forbid any of you fall and hurt the babies," said Mother Mary Frances.

"They wouldn't care if we injured *ourselves*," Marianne grumbled.

Brigid was about to agree with her when a stabbing pain in her side meant that she had to sit down suddenly, knocked sideways by the sensation. It was like the worst kind of monthly cramp.

"Braxton-Hicks," said Sister Jude when Brigid went to see her. "Go to the kitchens and fetch a hot water bottle if you think that'll help." She looked back at her notes. "But it probably won't. You'll just have to ride it out."

"Braxton-Hicks?" Brigid had no idea what Sister Jude was talking about.

"Practice pains."

It didn't feel like her body was practicing anything.

All that afternoon and into the evening, Brigid battled the spasms that winded her without warning. They only lasted a few seconds, but while they did, it was

like a vice clamped around her middle. She was petri-
fied of what was to come. Women *died* in childbirth.
She didn't dare go back to Sister Jude again; the nun
would only send her away. When the pain didn't ease
up, she began to worry that she was truly in labor,
though she really had no idea. No one had told them
anything of any use.

The pains continued all through the night, leaving
Brigid gasping for breath. She did her best to stay quiet
but must have woken Sara in the early hours.

"I'm going to fetch one of the nuns," Sara whispered.

Brigid was about to tell her not to bother when she
felt a warm gush between her legs. Had she wet herself? Shame burned in her throat.

In the dim light, she saw Sara crawl out of bed and
cinch the belt of her dressing gown high over her belly.

"Hurry," Brigid urged, changing her mind. She shuffled along the bed to where she could reach her own
dressing gown, draped over the end of a chair there,
and tried to mop up the spreading wetness on the bed.
She'd be punished for sure. She moved awkwardly for
her belly was as big as a barrage balloon, and she had
to stop as another wave of pain gripped her. When it
subsided, all she wanted was her mother. Why wasn't
her mother here? She needed her *now*.

Sara was gone so long that Brigid had almost forgotten she'd left in search of help. She was all alone, making guttural groans that would have embarrassed her at
any other time. If anyone heard her, they might think
it a cow in distress. The image fleetingly cheered her.

Eventually, the door opened.

"What is all this nonsense?"

Sister Agatha. Of all the nuns, why her?

The nun towered over her like a vengeful ghost. Brigid closed her eyes as a wave of fear and pain washed over her again.

"Sister Jude has been detained in the city by the weather, and Dr. Banks can't reach us, so I'm here to look after you."

Brigid gritted her teeth in the face of another contraction. They were coming so fast now that she couldn't catch her breath between each cramping wave.

She saw a flicker of sympathy cross the nun's normally sour face, but she didn't have the ability to do anything except focus on the feeling of a red-hot knife ripping through her. She screamed until her throat was raw.

"Do stop carrying on, or I shall have to restrain you," said Sister Agatha, fumbling for the light. "Sara, fetch me some water, and plenty of cloths. Warm water, if at all possible." The word "please" never passed her lips when talking to the girls.

"Yes, Sister."

Brigid heard the door open and close again, and the sound of footsteps hurrying along the hall. "Is there…?" She swallowed, gathering courage. "Is there anything you can give me? For the pain?"

Sister Agatha looked at her as though she'd requested a Coke and fries or perhaps a box of powdered-sugar doughnuts. "This is your penance, girl." She clicked her teeth dismissively. "I suppose we can find an aspirin if you really think you need it."

Brigid nodded. She was pathetically grateful for anything.

"But first I must examine you." Brigid felt the chill

as the covers were lifted and her legs were roughly pushed apart. Sister Agatha had brought a flashlight with her, and Brigid could feel the faint heat it emitted on her tenderest parts.

The nun sighed to herself and replaced the covers. "I am going to have to shave you; a pity there is not equipment for an enema."

Brigid blanched. She hadn't heard of either thing being necessary. It felt like such an indignity.

Sara returned, carrying a bowl of water, linen folded under one arm. "Here you are, Sister," she said, placing them on the nightstand.

"Keep watch while I fetch the razor from Sister Jude's surgery." Sister Agatha left the room with a swish of her habit and the girls were on their own again.

Sara came to her, grasped her hand and squeezed it, her eyes wide and frightened.

Brigid didn't know how long the nun was gone, for she rode the contractions as though she was a small boat on a great swollen ocean. Somewhere in the distance she heard the sound of a cow bellowing again. It was a few minutes before she realized it was she who was making all the noise. She squeezed her eyes shut and willed it all to be over.

Time seemed to stretch and compress until she had no idea how long she lay there. In the lulls between the pain, she listened as the wind rattled the glass in the window frames, heard the hoot of an owl, and caught her breath until the next wave hit.

Sister Agatha returned, her sleeves rolled past her elbows and Brigid was grateful to see the corded muscles of her forearms, for those arms that split wood would at least be of use in pulling this baby out of her.

The nun lifted the covers and Brigid cried out as another contraction ripped through her, bucking and straining. "If you don't stay put, I'll have to lash you to the frame," Sister Agatha scolded, angling the beam of her flashlight.

"You try keeping still," Brigid replied, gritting her teeth.

"If that is how it is going to be." The nun brought out two long strips of fabric, which she proceeded to use to tie Brigid's wrists to the iron bed frame. Brigid was too stunned to resist.

"All right girl, you're nearly there. When you feel the urge, I want you to push like you've never done before, do you hear me? Do you hear me?"

Brigid's eyes had nearly rolled back in their sockets and her legs, spread-eagled now, had begun to shake. "I don't think I can do this. I'm sorry." She began to sob, beaten down by it all. "I can't take any more. I want my mother."

"Yes, you can, Brigid. Yes, you can. You are strong enough to do this."

The nun's fierce tone cut through the fog that had descended over her, and Brigid did as she was told, pushing until she had nothing left.

LATER, LONG AFTER the sun had risen, Brigid slept, the deep sleep of absolute exhaustion. When she woke, it was to find Sara beside her, offering a cup of water and a sandwich on a plate. "Baloney. Best I could manage."

"Where is she?" Brigid's eyes searched the room for her baby. The little girl with the thatch of black hair, born in the early hours. She pushed herself up in bed and winced at the unexpected pain in her wrists, noticed red marks from where she'd been bound to the bed, felt again the indignity of it.

"She's with Sister Teresa. In the nursery. She's beautiful, Brigid." Sara's eyes filled with tears.

"Isn't she?" Brigid allowed herself to dwell on the memory of the sweet, scrunched up face, the eyes so much like her father's, the dark, impossibly thick eyelashes, the starfish hands that curled around her pinky. Fingernails like the tiny shells that she'd found washed up on the beach at Coos Bay the summer before. She'd fallen utterly, irrevocably in love with her daughter the second she saw her, greasy and bloodied, screaming at the outrage of coming into the world.

"You were so brave. I even heard Sister Agatha say so."

"I can't believe that." Brigid struggled to sit. She felt split in two, as though an ax had cut her half open, her stomach doughy where once it had been tight and full, but adrenalin still fizzed in her veins. She couldn't believe she'd done something so hard.

At first, she'd been disappointed, for she had wished for a boy, a boy who wouldn't ever have to go through what she had done, but then it hadn't mattered. Her daughter was perfect, and she could have walked on clouds, the hours of terror and agony almost forgotten. But now she was scared, for the world was now irrevocably changed. What she had longed for and now dreaded having to give away was wrapped in a blanket in the nursery. Living, breathing. Separate from her. Depending on her.

"What's the date?" Brigid asked.

"February ninth. Thursday."

"I thought so, but I wanted to be sure."

"Why?"

"What kind of mother doesn't remember the date of her child's birth?"

"Of course."

"When can I see her?"

"Soon, I'm sure. But you need to rest now. And eat. Get your strength back."

"I still don't know what to call her. I want to give her a name." Brigid took a bite of sandwich, suddenly ravenous. Her arm brushed against her breast, and she winced. She felt the other one. They were both swollen, hard as rocks.

"Can you ask Sister Agatha if I can feed her? Please?"

"I… I'll try."

As Sara made the promise, the door opened and Sister Agatha swept through it, in her arms a tiny, wrapped bundle that was making an ungodly racket out of all proportion to her size. "She won't take a bottle at all," Sister Agatha said, scowling in disgust. "And she's got a fine pair of lungs on her." She handed the baby to Brigid, who hastily crammed the remainder of the sandwich in her mouth and took her, instinctively angling her head toward her breast. "Thank you, Sister," Brigid said, after swallowing her mouthful of food.

"Don't thank me." The nun turned away as Brigid fumbled with the buttons of her nightgown and pressed her daughter's mouth toward her nipple.

After that, the nuns brought the baby to Brigid on a strict four-hour schedule, and she was free to gaze in wonder as her daughter suckled lustily, her screams now silenced, to lock eyes with her and tumble helplessly into their depths. Any lingering space in her heart that had been occupied by Robert, that no-good, yellow-bellied lowlife, was gone, flooded by love for her baby daughter. The little girl was all hers, nothing to do with anyone else.

When Sister Jude returned from the city, she came to examine Brigid, bringing cabbage leaves and a camera.

"Cabbage?" Brigid was mystified.

"Place them on your breasts. It'll soothe them. Believe me, I know what I'm talking about."

Brigid was so sore she was prepared to try anything, however outlandish it seemed.

"But before you do, let me take a photograph."

Brigid was still too exhausted from the birth to question it. She attempted to tidy her hair, tucking it behind her ears and looking toward the lens of the Box Brownie. The baby slept in her arms, not even flinching as the shutter clicked, though the unexpectedness of it made Brigid blink.

Later, after Sister Jude had gone, she rubbed the cabbage leaf between her fingers. Was the nun really telling the truth? She guessed there was no harm in trying.

LATE ONE AFTERNOON, while Brigid fed her daughter, Sister Jude settled in for a chat. "I understand you're a bright girl, that you were top of your class. What a shame it would be for you not to at least finish high school." Her expression was kindly, but Brigid knew that her intentions certainly weren't.

"Who says I won't?" Brigid jerked her head up with such suddenness that the baby's mouth slipped, and she let out a wail of protest at being deprived of her dinner.

"Now dear, that simply won't be possible if you are taking care of a baby now, will it?"

"Maybe my mother can help." Brigid helped the baby latch back on and stuck out her chin stubbornly.

"We know that's not possible."

"How do you know?" Were they reading her mail? Of course they were. Nothing was private in this damn place.

"Could you bear to hear your daughter called a bastard, for the other kids in the playground to whisper about her behind her back?" Sister Jude said softly. "Do you really want your child to suffer with the stigma of illegitimacy? What kind of mother would wish that?"

Brigid refused to let herself think about it. "I'd like to telephone *my* mother. To tell her about the baby."

"The charge would have to be added to your bill; long-distance is expensive. You can use the phone later this afternoon if you like, once you've finished feeding." Perhaps realizing that she wasn't getting anywhere, Sister Jude stood and left Brigid to it.

BRIGID HELD HER breath as the operator connected the call. She'd chosen a time when it was likely only her mother would be home, after her father would have gone to work and her brothers and sisters caught the bus to school, but perhaps her mother was already out getting groceries or having coffee with a friend? Now that she'd worked herself up to break the news, she couldn't bear to wait a minute longer.

She was on the point of hanging up, when she heard the click and then her mother's formal voice on the line, the one she saved especially for answering the phone.

"Mother?"

"Oh!" Brigid could picture her mother's hand flying to her mouth. "Is that you, dear?"

"I had a little girl. She came earlier than I expected. She's so tiny. But beautiful. I still don't know what to call her, but you should see her…" Brigid's words tumbled out in a rush as she told her mother all about her new baby daughter.

She'd been speaking for more than a minute before she realized that her mother hadn't said a thing in response.

"Mother? Are you still there?"

A beat of silence.

"Yes, dear. I'm glad you're both okay." Her mother sounded strangely remote, and it wasn't merely the echoing effect of the long-distance phone call. "But I can't stay long on the line."

"She's your granddaughter."

"Don't say that. I can't, I simply can't…" Her mother stopped speaking, leaving the sentence unfinished.

Brigid stuffed her hand in her mouth to silence the sob that threatened to rise up and overwhelm her.

She reached for the receiver hook on the telephone and disconnected the line.

THIRTY-FIVE

Puget Sound, 2013

HER MOTHER'S WRITING.

"At a friend's place, don't wait up."

Frankie rang Diana, but there was no answer from her either. She left a message asking her to please call, then grabbed her keys. She was at the front door before she had time to think about where she was going.

She drove over the bridge, seeing a group of teens in the gathering dusk, hanging out by the temporary memorial. One of them, a skinny girl wearing cutoffs and a dark tee, was rearranging the silk flowers that had been left there. On impulse, Frankie braked hard and pulled over. The kids looked up as she screeched to a halt and got out of her truck.

"Any of you seen a girl, about this tall—" she held her hand up to her forehead, "purple streaks in her hair?"

They exchanged glances, shook their heads. "'Fraid not," said the skinny girl, showing metal braces on her teeth as she spoke. "Benny, you know anything?"

A boy with a tattoo of a Celtic knot on his thin bicep shook his head at Frankie blankly.

"Anywhere kids go around here?"

"You could try the football field." One of the other girls spoke up. "There's an old tire swing. Sometimes kids hang out there, if they've nothing better to do."

"Where would I find that?"

The football field was on the outskirts of Huntley's Point, and only a few minutes' drive away. Frankie parked on the perimeter, straining to see any sign of a swing amid the growing gloom. The place looked deserted, but she began to jog across the field, aiming for the far side where there was a cluster of tall trees. Sure enough, when she reached it, there were a couple of old tires hanging from the branches. But no kids. No Izzy.

Cursing, she ran back to her truck, turning back in the direction of the main street.

This time, she parked in front of the bike store. She peered in the window, hammered on the door, rattling the "closed" sign against the glass. When there was no answer, she went around the back, but there was no sign of anyone.

She hadn't a clue how to get hold of Zac (Should she have gotten his number? Did mothers even do that?), nor where he might live.

The sheriff's office was on the next block, and she sprinted the few yards to the front door. Molly was behind the counter, a cup of black coffee and a splayed novel with a white swan on the cover beside her. Ready for the night shift.

"Frankie!" She beamed. Then she saw Frankie's expression. "Is everything okay?"

"It's Izzy," she gasped. "I haven't seen her since this morning. I can't get hold of her. She left this—" Frankie held out her phone and replayed Izzy's message, feeling her heart thud along with her daughter's words.

"Okay, let's take things one step at a time," Molly

said, her voice calm and measured. "Is she in the habit of taking off? Disappearing like this?"

"She's only been with us a few weeks." Frankie paused, newly aware of how little she knew about her daughter. "But she's a good girl. There's no way she would disappear for this long without letting us know."

"I see." She got out a pad of forms and began to fill the top sheet in. "Her full name?" Frankie was impressed with Molly's formality as she carefully noted Frankie's answers in rounded script, relieved that she was taking things seriously.

"Has she made any friends on the island?"

"No. Wait, yes. There's a boy from the bike store, Zac. I'm afraid I don't know his last name. There's a chance she could be with him."

"Zac Bergen."

"You know him, know where he lives? Oh, thank God."

"I'll make inquiries of his family as a priority," Molly assured her. "Do you have a recent photograph?"

Frankie reached for her phone and showed her a picture she'd taken two days earlier. Izzy had one hand up to her forehead and was squinting into the sun, but it was a reasonable likeness. "It's the best I've got. I'll send it to you," she said, tapping at her phone.

"Good."

"Her bicycle's gone."

"I know the one. Blue, with a brown saddle, right?" Molly made another note. "Was there any reason for her to go off without telling you? Any disagreements, an argument? You know what teenagers are like, sometimes they overreact to things."

"Not recently." Frankie paused.

"Any more notes left for you?" Molly asked.

Frankie shook her head. Oh God, the notes. Was Izzy's disappearance somehow connected? Until then, she'd half clung on to the hope that Izzy was off somewhere with Zac, that she was nothing more than late getting home.

Molly checked something on her computer and then picked up the phone next to her. "Mrs. Bergen? Molly Dowd here from the Orcades Sheriff Department… I'm trying to locate a friend of Zac's…" She had a brief conversation and then hung up. "She says she's not seen her son today, and he's not answering his phone."

Frankie's stomach twisted painfully. Had he and Izzy gone off somewhere together, and something happened to them both? She'd have a few choice words to say that boy when she caught up with him; he was all out of second chances, that was for sure.

"Okay. The best thing you can do now is go home and wait," Molly said. "We'll put a notice out here and on the mainland. And call us if you hear from her. I'm sure she's fine, but best to be safe. Try not to worry," she reassured her, shuffling the papers together and closing the folder. "I'll be here all night, and I'll send Scott out in the car as soon as he comes on shift." She checked her watch. "He's due in half an hour."

When Frankie left the office, she couldn't make herself go home. Instead, she drove to The Cabbage Shed, at the other end of town, and went inside. Joe looked up as soon as she entered. "Hey," he said, with a smile that turned to a look of concern as he saw the expression on her face. "Everything okay?"

"No," she replied, struggling to keep her emotions in

check, the lump in her throat from choking her. "Izzy's missing."

He muttered a few words to the bartender next to him and came over to meet her, engulfing her in a hug. Frankie softened into him for an instant, but then pulled away.

"Perhaps she got lost—she doesn't know the island that well," Joe offered. "How long has she been out?"

"Since about noon." Frankie shook her head. "She wouldn't just go off somewhere on her own…" She stopped herself. "Unless it was to take photos."

"Come on then."

"Where are we going?"

"You'll see in a minute."

Frankie followed him out of the bar, calling her mom on the way and leaving a message when there was still no answer.

They went to her truck, and he climbed in the passenger's seat, directing her toward the road that led to the state park in the center of the island. Before long it became a winding dirt track, full of switchbacks and hairpin bends. The air was thick with bugs, many of which splattered against the windshield. "I'm not sure she would have biked all the way up here," said Frankie, doubtfully.

"She could have hitched a ride."

Frankie concentrated on the road ahead of her, wincing as the tires slid on a patch of gravel as she navigated a savagely tight bend. Below them was a sheer drop, the valley dense with pines. The sun would soon set, making the trail even more treacherous.

At the top of the hill was a wider stretch of gravel, marked by a sign for a lookout. She pulled over and they got out of the car. The place was deserted. "Sometimes people come up here," he said, casting about for any signs of recent visitation. "To park, picnic, check out the views. Or take photos."

Frankie recognized some of the scenes from the video Izzy had made. "Well, she's not here now." She concentrated on filling her lungs, in and out, in and out, as evenly as she could manage. "Sorry, that was harsher than it was meant to be."

He was right, even at dusk the views were spectacular, stretching all the way to the mountains, a series of dark, wooded islands, expanses of beaten pewter sea in between. She slapped at a mosquito, smearing blood on her arm. Joe had taken a few steps, his attention caught by a long white cord on the ground. He bent down and picked it up, bringing it toward her. "Someone's lost their earphones," he said, handing them to her.

"Apple. They could be anyone's." Frankie fought the desire to believe that they belonged to her daughter.

"But Izzy had a pair, right?"

"How did you know?"

"I saw her with them when you came in for dinner a few weeks ago."

"You noticed that?" Frankie felt a sudden chill.

He dug his hands in the pockets of his jeans. "I noticed all of you."

Frankie's phone, which was in her pocket, began to ring and she grappled for it, hope rising that it might be Izzy.

She checked the screen. Lucas. His timing was uncanny. "Hello?" she answered.

"How're you doing Frankie?" came the voice on the other end. "I've been trying Izzy for the last couple of days, wanted to check in with her, but she's not answering. How's it all going up there?"

"Er…" Frankie wasn't sure how to reply. She didn't want to admit that Izzy was right now nowhere to be found; Lucas would see it as proof of her incompetence as a mother, but then if Izzy did get in touch with him… Hell, her daughter could conceivably be on her way back to California for all she knew. "She's not here at the moment. In fact, I'm not actually sure where she is; I haven't been able to reach her either. She was with us this morning, but she's been gone all afternoon."

"Did she say where she was headed?"

"I just said we don't know where she is." Frankie did her best to keep her voice level.

"Did you have a fight?"

He always did know how to get to the heart of things. "Not recently," she admitted.

There was a short bark of laughter from the other end. "Welcome to my world, Frankie."

"What, she argues with you too?"

"Why do you think I was so keen for her to come and spend the summer with you? Izzy…she's lovely, delightful mostly, but sometimes we simply can't figure her out at all."

Frankie let out a breath. Perhaps she wasn't the worst parent in the world.

"Let me know if she gets in touch, will you?" she asked.

"Okay."

"And…"

"What?"

"I suppose there's a slight chance she's on her way back to LA."

Lucas chuckled again. "I'm sure it's not that bad."

"Izzy's father," she explained to Joe after she'd hung up.

"There's no sign of her here, and it's getting dark," he said. "Why don't we call into the sheriff's office and see what Molly's been able to find out?"

"Are you sure you don't need to get back to The Cabbage Shed?"

"The boss is pretty easy-going." He shot her a lazy grin that flipped her stomach in spite of herself.

"Great. And thanks, Joe. I'm glad I'm not on my own up here."

"You're never on your own, Frankie. Not on Orcades Island. Locals look out for each other."

It was a small comfort that he considered her a local, though in truth she was definitely more of a blow-in.

They drew up outside the sheriff's office and found Molly.

"I've been over to Zac's folks' place. Zac had just got home—he'd been out with his buddies, said he hasn't seen Izzy all day."

Frankie's chest tightened.

"He said that Izzy mentioned a new guy she'd met. Someone older. She was boasting that he had a flashy house and a boat. That they were going to explore the islands together. He did add that he thought she might have been exaggerating, to make him jealous."

Frankie had been worried enough about Izzy going off with Zac, but this was a million times worse. "Did you get a name?" she asked, trying to breathe, telling herself not to panic, not yet. "Of this guy?"

"Sorry, she didn't tell him." Molly shook her head.

"A boat?" She remembered the slosh of water in the background of Izzy's message.

"Uh-huh."

"Pretty much everyone round here has one of some description," said Joe. "Been sailing since I was a kid myself."

Frankie raised her eyebrows.

"*Duchess.* And before you say anything, I didn't name her."

"Okay."

"She's moored in the marina."

"Then what are we waiting for?"

"You do know how many islands there are out there?" he said.

THIRTY-SIX

Puget Sound, 2013

"I'LL SEARCH EVERY single boat, every single island if I have to." Frankie couldn't let go of the feeling that Izzy was in trouble somewhere out there; she'd never forgive herself if she waited until morning.

They chugged out of the marina on a rising tide, Joe having first grabbed sailing jackets and a couple burgers from The Cabbage Shed. "We gotta eat," he said, handing a box to Frankie. She'd missed lunch, and although she wasn't especially hungry, took it from him, grateful for his foresight.

Frankie had felt her heart leap then crash as she saw Izzy's bike resting against a pole at the approach to the marina's jetty. "See," she said. "She's definitely gone out on the water with someone."

"Could be." Joe rubbed his jaw, thinking. "But that doesn't necessarily mean she's in trouble. Kids…you know, they like to push the boundaries; have no idea what it's like for their parents."

"I get what you're saying, but I think there's more to it than that in this case. Call it a mother's intuition." Frankie lifted her chin stubbornly.

The night was calm, with enough of a breeze to make the going steady, and if it had been at any other time, it could have been romantic, standing beside Joe at the helm, the sails filling with wind and the sky pin-pricked by a million stars.

Frankie thought she'd hidden the fact that she was shivering, but Joe motioned to her to take the wheel as he went down below. "Steer her straight," he said, calling back to her over his shoulder. "Toward the island up ahead."

Frankie did as he asked, and he reappeared after a few minutes, a blanket under one arm, and a thermos in his hand. "Coffee," he said. "We're gonna need it."

Frankie wrapped the blanket around herself and watched as Joe expertly handled the boat. "Keep watch for any lights—they might have gotten a campfire going, so if we spot that, we're in luck." He handed her a pair of binoculars and she began to scour the shoreline.

After about half an hour, they'd circumnavigated the island. "It's only the first one," he said evenly when they'd failed to spot anything. "Plenty more out there."

He adjusted the sails and altered their course. "There's one place we used to go years ago. Not many people, even locals, know about it. It's a little tricky to reach."

"What makes you think she might be there?"

"Honestly, I've no idea, other than it's the kind of place someone might take a person they were trying to impress."

"Why's that?"

"You'll see."

They plowed across the dark water, staring into the darkness.

"So why'd you leave?" Joe asked, startling her out of her thoughts.

She thought about lying, fobbing him off with a

throwaway line about family, change of scene…something banal. "Sydney?"

"C'mon," he said, noting her hesitation. "I'm a bartender. Makes me a good listener, if nothing else."

She took her time to find the right words. "I failed," she said eventually. "I should have kept a little boy safe, and I didn't." She lapsed into silence again.

"What happened?" Joe asked, his voice soft.

"Elijah Brown. Two weeks shy of his fifth birthday. Disappeared from his foster family's front yard early one morning in March 2012. I was part of the investigation team. Once we'd ruled out the immediate family—and there were a few shady characters there—we widened the search. The question of child trafficking was raised almost from the beginning, though it's not *that* common in countries such as Australia." The wind was making Frankie's eyes water, and she wiped them with the back of her hand. "There was a tip-off that they were looking for fair-skinned kids with light hair. Boys in particular." Her stomach roiled as she thought about what such sick people did with the kids they took.

"Christ, where do you start with something like that?"

"The local cops appealed for witnesses, set up a reenactment with a dummy dressed in the same green T-shirt that Eli was last seen wearing, posters, news reports, appeals for witnesses, everything…to begin with they thought he would have been smuggled out of the country at the first opportunity, most likely to Southeast Asia."

"And then?" He seemed to realize there was more to the story.

"They brought three of us in to work on it, all victim identification experts. After six weeks, we had nothing to show for it but gritty eyes, a room full of paperwork, and dead ends. Then there was a report of a child matching Eli's description seen peering out of a warehouse window in Balmain—that's an inner suburb of Sydney. Of course, there had been other sightings, but this was different."

Joe shifted the tiller, his attention snagged by the looming shape of an outcrop of rocks to starboard.

"Eli had two different color eyes—one blue and one hazel. The witness was close enough to see this, but she insisted it was a girl. Even so, she reported it because she remembered seeing Eli's photo on the news."

"Go on." Joe squinted into the distance.

"We raided the warehouse. Of course it was too late. But they'd left in such a hurry that a pair of shorts and a dirty pink-and-white sneaker were left behind. They were exactly the size that would be worn by a five-year-old."

"And?"

"But—and here's the thing—they were pink. Girls' clothes. We realized that whoever had snatched Eli had been dressing him up as a girl, had let his hair grow in an attempt to disguise him."

"I still don't understand why all of this is your fault?" Joe looked curiously at her.

Frankie took a deep breath. "Another, earlier, report had come in, a few weeks before, of a child crying in a service station near the warehouse. This was before we knew that it might be a location of concern though. I was the one assigned the report, and didn't follow up, other than taking a statement from the witness, because they had insisted it was a girl."

"But surely there would have been dozens of such sightings."

"Hundreds actually."

"And you were looking for a boy."

"Nevertheless…" Frankie felt the familiar recriminations surface. "I compounded my error by failing to review all of the security footage from the vicinity of the warehouse. There was just so much of it."

"And only so many hours in a day, yeah?" Joe offered.

"I guess, but it was one of those cases that get under your skin, you know? And it was my fault. I was the one to tell his parents that we got so close but that we had lost him again." It probably explained why she was out here now on a wild-goose chase after a missing teenager who was likely to be simply letting off steam. Nevertheless, she refused to ignore her instincts, especially when it came to missing kids, and especially when it came to her daughter. "After that, I stopped believing that I could do the job. I had a breakdown I suppose. Concentration was shot, couldn't focus, could barely get myself out of bed in the morning. I was signed off on stress leave."

There was silence as Joe concentrated on navigating the boat.

"You've gotta forgive yourself, Frankie. Believe me. You're only human," he said eventually.

"And then, one morning I dragged myself out for a run and a car came out of nowhere. It knocked me to the ground and sped off. One minute I was hauling my ass up Ocean Street and the next I was hooked up to an

IV with my left leg pinned in four places. I still don't know why I stepped into the road not looking where I was going, but it was a pretty effective way to trigger a major life review." Her voice was flat. "While I was recovering in hospital, I made the decision to come home. I just couldn't be there any longer."

"Hell of a wake-up call," said Joe, his eyes fixed on the horizon.

"Whoa!" she cried as she looked up to see a sheer wall of rock rearing dead ahead. Despite the gloom, she could make out a narrow gap, a lighter patch of sky in the seam between the rock and the water. "You weren't kidding about it being tricky," she breathed, as Joe kicked the motor into life and eased the boat through a narrow passage between two cliffs. "I can practically reach out and touch it," she said, trying not to wince as the sides came perilously close to grating on the jagged rock.

Joe seemed not to hear her as he focused on guiding the boat through the gap. Even he looked relieved as they emerged into a horseshoe-shaped lagoon.

"Tell me we don't have to return that way?" Frankie asked.

He ignored her and Frankie felt a tiny flicker of unease, suddenly aware that she was out in the middle of nowhere with a man that she really knew very little about. "That's where we're headed," he said, pointing to a narrow beach at the far end. She blinked hard, straining to see. Did she imagine it, or was there a faint glow of light?

THIRTY-SEVEN

Fairmile, 1950

IT WAS A small square of photographic paper. Brigid pinched it carefully between her fingertips, not wanting to mark the print. She almost didn't recognize herself, the fierce gaze at the camera that seemed to show someone ready to take on the world, her daughter cradled in her arms.

"I made two copies," said Sister Jude. "I thought you might like it. To remember her by. I wrote your name and the date on the back."

"That's very kind of you." She hadn't expected this from the nun, and she would treasure it. The first photograph of her daughter, though the angle was such that you couldn't really see her face. The fact that it might be the only one she would ever have was left unsaid, and when Sister Jude had gone, Brigid vowed that she'd make sure there were many more photographs of her daughter, *years'* worth in fact.

She'd tried to forget the disastrous phone call with her mother, thinking instead of what she might do, where she could possibly go, knowing that she could never return home. She would miss them, her family, the twins especially, but her love of her daughter trumped everything. She told herself that perhaps after a few years, her mother and father might relent, that they might come to accept her and her daughter back into the fold. In the meantime, she'd show them. She'd make it on her own, despite their lack of support.

Before she left Bend, she'd copied her aunt's address into her diary, knowing that she was on her way to Seattle. She'd never been to the house before, but she'd already memorized the street name and number. When her aunt had come to visit them two years earlier, she'd talked of her redbrick town house in a tree-lined street in Capitol Hill, of the parks and lakes, theaters and museums that she patronized. It had seemed the height of sophistication to Brigid, for whom Bend often felt dull and uneventful.

Once again, she wrote a letter. This time, to her Aunt Helen, begging for her assistance. Brigid imagined a future where she would offer them a roof over their heads, perhaps even help her study. She suggested that she could help in the house, act as a companion if her aunt should require it, do the marketing, the cleaning, anything really, until she was able to stand on her own two feet. It seemed like a fair suggestion; she could only hope her aunt would be less concerned by what her friends and neighbors would think than her parents were.

TWO WEEKS AFTER Brigid's baby was born, Sara went into labor. Brigid saw her not long after breakfast, leaning on the arm of Sister Clare. She called out "good luck" and crossed her fingers that the girl would be okay. Her own experience was far too fresh; the violence of it still vivid in her dreams, causing her to thrash with a such ferocity that her blankets often ended up on the floor and she woke, gasping and chilled to the bone. Sara was so young, and so small; it didn't seem right that she should have to go through such a thing.

Brigid waited. And waited. And waited.

Darkness drew in, the drapes were closed, dinner was served, and then it was time for lights out. Though she was exhausted, Brigid couldn't sleep for worrying about her roommate. She tried to distract herself with her math textbook, but her eyes slid across the rows of numbers and she was unable to work out even the simplest calculations. Giving birth seemed to have turned her brain to mush.

Eventually, she gave up and lay awake, listening for a sign that might tell her something, anything, but all she could hear was the wind as it soughed in the trees. At nearly midnight, Sister Clare came in with her baby, who was stirring, her mouth searching for a nipple.

"Is there any news?" she asked.

The nun handed the baby to Brigid and shook her head. "These things take time dear, as you well know." Sister Clare sat at the end of her bed and checked her wristwatch. The baby was allowed fifteen minutes on each breast and no more, but to Brigid it always went too fast.

"But how is she?"

"As well as can be expected."

That told her absolutely nothing.

Later, Brigid must have slept, for when she woke the sun—the first she'd seen of it in more than a week—was streaming through a gap in the drapes and Sister Teresa was at her side with the baby again. "You can bring her back to the nursery when you're finished," the nun said, seeming distracted.

Brigid blinked. "Oh, okay." Usually, the nuns brought

the baby to her and then whisked her away again. She hadn't even been allowed to bathe her, to change a diaper. The only thing she was allowed to do for her daughter was feed her.

Sister Teresa left the room, forgetting to close the door and clearly in a hurry to be somewhere else.

As Brigid huddled beneath the covers and fed her daughter—not watching the clock for once—and gazed down at her, she felt her heart swell with tenderness for the tiny being, and a blaze of pride that she'd made such a perfect thing.

She heard the faint sounds of the house coming to life at the beginning of the day. The metallic clang of pots, the chink of china, an occasional snippet of conversation all floated toward her. At one point, she heard quick footsteps scurry along the hallway outside her room, but she didn't call out, for fear it was a nun and not one of the girls.

When her daughter had finished feeding and brought up several satisfying burps, Brigid reluctantly gathered herself to return her to the nursery. She put the baby on the bed, wedging her between two pillows, while she dressed hastily and ran a brush through her hair. She was starving, but breakfast would have to wait.

Brigid was nearly at the nursery when she saw two nuns ahead of her. Sister Agatha and Sister Jude. She slowed, for they hadn't noticed her approach, and appeared to be deep in conversation.

"I say we should fetch Doctor Banks immediately," she heard Sister Jude hiss.

Sister Agatha held up a hand. "The baby's life is to be saved before the mother's; you know that."

The other nun shook her head. "There is still time to save both. We have to at least try."

"She has the seed of a sinner within her."

Brigid hesitated in a shadowed corner, shocked by what she had heard.

"She is as much a child of God as her infant is." Sister Jude had raised her voice now. "And she has done nothing to deserve this."

"You are more deluded than I imagined. That girl has the devil himself within her."

"What absolute nonsense. Do not imagine that I shall not report this to Mother Mary Frances when she returns."

"She left me in charge. Now go back and do your job—save the baby at all costs."

Brigid felt her own newborn squirm in her arms. As she'd been listening to the nuns argue, she'd accidentally squeezed her too tight. As the baby opened her mouth to howl in protest, Brigid slipped her little finger in her daughter's mouth and let her suck on it. She couldn't let the nuns find her eavesdropping. She crept back in the direction she'd come, her heart pounding. Poor, sweet Sara. She could not believe that even Sister Agatha could be so heartless.

Back in her room, Brigid placed the baby on the bed, for she was shaking so badly she feared dropping her. She'd never felt more useless: there was absolutely nothing she could do to help her friend.

THIRTY-EIGHT

Puget Sound, 2013

THERE WAS NO one at the secret beach after all; the lights had been nothing but fireflies. Frankie and Joe searched a dozen more islands until the sun came up, at one point hailing a passing sailor to ask if they'd seen anyone matching Izzy's description. "I'm sorry, but I think we should let the coast guard continue the search," Joe said, turning the boat for home. Though they'd been able to sail for the majority of the time, the wind had now died down and the water was flat and still. "We're almost out of fuel." While they had been out on the water, Molly had radioed them with the news that she'd arranged for an official search to begin at first light.

Lucas had also left her two messages, saying Izzy hadn't turned up there and asking for Frankie to call him as soon as she had any information.

Now, Frankie sat in the kitchen at Fairmile with her mom, her eyes red-rimmed, hair stiff with salt, and nursed a coffee. She had perhaps wrongly imagined danger while out with Joe, but the feeling of foreboding that had come over her wouldn't let up. As she took in Diana's anxious expression, she kicked herself for even having had the whisper of doubt about her too. It simply wasn't in her mother's nature. Diana might be occasionally infuriating, often hard to understand, but there was no way she was a cold-blooded killer. Though could she be an accomplice?

Frankie's fears and suspicions skittered around in her mind until she could hardly think straight. She took a deep draught from her mug, anxious for the caffeine to take effect. "Izzy could be anywhere. Anything could have happened to her."

"She's not a bad kid, you know."

"That's exactly why I'm worried."

Diana went to the stovetop. "Could you stand to eat? I can scramble some eggs," she offered.

Frankie raked her scalp with her fingers. "Thanks, but I'm not hungry."

"Let's try not to imagine the worst," said Diana, turning and placing a hand on her shoulder.

"The *worst*?" Frankie's voice rose, and before she knew it, she was shouting. "The *worst*? Do you have any idea what the worst could be?"

"Of course I do, but there's no sense in torturing ourselves. Let's try and keep calm and think. Why don't you go and get your head down, even for a couple hours," Diana suggested. Frankie went to protest, but her mother interrupted her. "You're no use to anyone without some sleep. I promise I'll wake you the second we hear anything."

Frankie trudged upstairs, stripped off her damp clothes, and stood under a scalding shower. Something had been nagging at her ever since she'd heard Izzy's message, but she was too tired and too wired to think straight.

IT FELT LIKE a betrayal, but exhaustion got the upper hand and Frankie slept. By the time she woke up, it was early evening and raining again. For a little while, as she lay listening to it patter on the roof, she forgot the reason she was in bed at that time of day. Then it hit her. Her stomach dropped, like she was in an elevator shaft, and the memory of the night at sea, the fruitless search, the uneasy feeling she'd had out on the boat with Joe, came rushing back. She sat up, momentarily dizzy, and reached for her phone.

No missed calls. A message from Molly, sent at lunchtime, saying they were searching the island. Another from Lucas, asking if Izzy had returned. She listened to them both and then tried Izzy's number again. It went straight to her voicemail, telling Frankie that the battery was likely now dead.

When she reached the kitchen, there was a note from her mom on the table.

Gone to see Ingrid. Everyone out looking for Izzy.

Everyone? Frankie wondered whom exactly that meant. And why wouldn't her mom be looking, why go and see Ingrid now? It immediately made her suspicious again.

She rang Molly, who suggested she meet her at the sheriff's office in town. "I can fill you in on where we're at," she promised.

Not knowing how long she might be gone, Frankie grabbed a jacket and a water bottle, then shoved her feet into a pair of sneakers. Scruff whined to be allowed to come with her, probably thinking there would be a walk in it. She was about to leave him behind, but then relented and scooped him up, heading for her truck.

"Almost the entire island is looking," said Molly,

when Frankie burst through the office door. "The farmers, the orchardists, the winemakers. Half the town closed early to join the search."

Frankie blinked in surprise. They would do that? Drop everything for a missing girl?

"Joe rounded everyone up and he's let us use The Cabbage Shed as the HQ. He's even offering dinner for those who are able to keep searching tonight, if she still hasn't been found."

Frankie choked back a lump in her throat. She couldn't believe that people—many of whom she'd never met—could be so generous. She felt a pang of guilt that she could have had even the most fleeting doubt about Joe—he was also doing so much to help. Trouble was, she was suspicious of almost everyone; it was one of the pitfalls of her job.

"Diana's well-liked in the town, but we'd do this no matter who it was. We look after our own," Molly said. "There's a group searching the national park— Joe said you found some earphones there, that they might belong to her."

Frankie nodded.

"We've had reinforcements from the city, and they've been going door-to-door. They only arrived a couple hours ago though, and there's a fair amount of ground to cover. I'm headed out again myself," she added. "To the far west of the island. There aren't many homes there, and they're all pretty isolated, but I'm going to check every one of them."

"I'd like to ride along, if you'll let me?"

Molly considered the request.

"Please. I need to do *something*."

"Okay. Let's go then."

The rain had begun to spatter again, rattling like nails in a tin as it hit the hood of the cruiser. Frankie opened the passenger door to let Scruff hop into the footwell beside her as Molly took the wheel. The rain thickened as they drove, but Molly kept her foot pressed firmly on the accelerator.

"Where exactly are we headed?" Frankie asked after a while. Dusk had begun to fall, and they'd turned onto a dirt track, but she hadn't seen any road signs for several minutes. Water washed small rocks and mud across the road and the truck skidded. Molly slowed a fraction, the wipers swishing double-time as they struggled to clear the windshield.

"Crane Bay. There's only a dozen or so houses there, most of them vacation homes."

Crane. She'd thought Izzy was saying the word pain, but it could just as easily have been crane. Adrenaline began to fizz in her stomach, and she felt light-headed from lack of food.

"You okay?" Molly asked. "Your face is whiter than a marshmallow in a snowstorm."

Frankie failed to raise a smile. "I don't think I've eaten today."

"There's a candy bar in the glove compartment," she said, taking one hand off the wheel and reaching across to pop it open. "Oh Henry! Only the best."

"Thanks." Frankie tore at the yellow wrapper and wolfed it down in three bites. In a few moments she was feeling slightly better, her blood sugar returning to normal.

It was completely dark now and a sea fog had rolled in, swallowing the road in front of them. Then, a turn sign loomed out of the blankness, and Scruff whimpered as Molly swung the vehicle sharply left. Frankie stroked his head, trying to reassure him.

The first house they came to was a single-story wooden shack with a rocking chair on the front porch. Lights glowed at the windows.

Molly pulled over and they both got out of the cruiser, leaving the dog in the car.

They dashed toward the house, getting soaked in the few seconds it took to reach the porch. Molly knocked firmly, calling out a loud hello. "Will they even hear us over the rain?" Frankie shouted.

Molly shrugged. "Let's at least give them a chance."

After a moment, the porch light went on, bathing them in a warm glow. A voice called out from behind the door. "Who the hell is it at this time of night?" They didn't sound pleased at being disturbed.

"Sheriff's department," said Molly. "We're looking for a missing girl. Tall, with purple streaks in her hair, fair skin, a nose ring." She pulled a print of the photo Frankie had given her from a pocket on the inside of her coat and held it up to the glass panel in the door. "Have you seen her?"

There was a moment's hesitation and then the door opened and an elderly man in overalls stood in front of them. He squinted at the photo. "Nup."

"Have you seen any kids hanging around here? Anything unusual?"

"Nup." He shut the door and the porch light went out, thrusting them back into darkness.

"Okay, thanks," Frankie called out. *For nothing*, she added under her breath as they ran back to the cruiser.

A few yards farther on they came to a gate, beyond which stretched a long unlit driveway. Molly cut the engine and Frankie got out. As she came closer, she saw that it was padlocked. Owned by someone from the city most likely, like Molly had said.

Ignoring the irritation that they couldn't get access, she dashed back to the car, and they set off again.

They stopped at seven more houses on the road that wound around the bay. Most were situated down seemingly endless driveways, and they had to travel the length of them before being able to see if anyone was home. A couple were shuttered, but most were occupied. It was a Saturday, and plenty of owners came for weekends in the summer. Some of the people who answered the door were more friendly than the first person they'd called on, but none of them had seen anyone matching Izzy's description, nor anything out of the ordinary that evening.

Molly bypassed a side road and Frankie asked why they weren't searching down there.

"It leads to Joe's place, and he's at The Cabbage Shed, so there's no sense in checking there."

"Right. Of course."

By the time they had been to every house in Crane Bay, Frankie's sneakers were squelching water and the rain was running in rivulets down her face. She'd stopped being angry with Izzy hours earlier, now she was just scared. The more time went by without hearing from her, the more the worry grew, clawing at her chest until she could hardly breathe.

"That's all of them," said Molly after they'd been to the last house. The vehicle's radio crackled, and Molly checked in with Scott. "They're calling it a night. It's too dangerous to go on searching the park in the dark," she said, though Frankie had heard every word of the short exchange. "I'm sorry. We'll try again in the morning."

Another night with Izzy missing. Even a layman knew that the first seventy-two hours in a missing person's case were crucial.

"Stop!" Frankie called as they were about to pass the locked gate again. "I want to check, for my own peace of mind."

Molly stomped on the brakes and the cruiser slid to a halt, slewing halfway across the track. Molly regained control and pulled over, not far from the gate.

"Come on, Scruff," Frankie said, as the dog whimpered. He yipped his approval as she opened the passenger door for him to join her. Lifting him over the gate and letting him scramble to the mud on the other side, she placed a foot on the middle bar and swung her leg over, being careful not to slip on the wet metal. She couldn't risk another injury, not now. Molly followed close behind, grunting as she hauled herself up.

The dog had run ahead of them, and Frankie struggled to catch up, stumbling as she picked her way along the uneven path in the dark.

"Fresh tracks," said Molly, pointing her flashlight to a set of tire marks in the mud.

Then, they rounded a bend and came upon the house. It was a grand mansion, almost as impressive as Fairmile. There was a silver SUV parked in the driveway and Frankie felt suddenly nauseated.

A faint light glowed from a first-floor window, but downstairs it was dark.

They reached the front door and Frankie pressed a brass bell button, hearing a chime coming from somewhere deep within the house. She knelt down and picked up Scruff, who had begun to whine, crooning to him. "Calm down, boy," she whispered, stroking his fur.

They waited. And waited.

There was no answer. "The light could be on a timer," said Molly. "To make people think someone is home."

"All the way out here, past a locked gate?" Frankie asked.

"Some people don't take any chances. There's an alarm too." She pointed to a small square box fixed to the wall a foot or so from the front door.

Molly turned to leave, but Frankie put a hand on her sleeve.

Her gut—and Scruff's anxiety—told her not to give up just yet. As Frankie strained to listen to the sounds around them, she heard water slapping against wood, the metallic tinkle of a boat at anchor.

Then, she heard the clunk of a bolt being pulled back, and the door creaked open.

THIRTY-NINE

Fairmile, 1950

BRIGID TRIED EVERYTHING to find out what happened to Sara and her baby. She asked Sister Jude, who murmured something about her having gone away; she even summoned the courage to ask Sister Agatha, but all she got was a frown and a dismissive reply that it was none of her business. Girls disappeared all the time, leaving for home once they'd had their babies, but generally with some warning, and they were usually allowed to say goodbye.

The girls speculated among themselves, and much like a game of Telephone, Sara's story changed out of all proportion to the probable truth.

Marianne said that she heard that the devil himself had possessed her and that the nuns were forced to tie her down, that her baby had been born with two heads. Emily, one of the new girls, said that Sara's parents had come to fetch her and her baby in the dead of night.

Brigid missed the calm presence of her roommate more than she could have imagined possible, but exactly how she might get away from Fairmile now began to consume her waking thoughts. Her two closest allies—Sally and Sara—had disappeared, and she had received no reply from her aunt.

One morning, after feeding her baby, she was summoned to see Mother Mary Frances.

She knocked on the office door and entered as she heard the voice from within.

"Hello, my dear, do take a seat." The nun's expression was unreadable, her eyes hidden by the reflection that bounced off the glass in her spectacles.

Brigid did as she was asked. The door opened again, and Sister Agatha came into the room and took the chair to Brigid's left. "We should both like to speak to you about what is to happen next," she said. "We have a special couple on our list, and they are very keen to meet their new baby…"

Mother Mary Frances made a shushing sound and Sister Agatha stopped midsentence. "Let's start with you first, shall we?" She pushed her spectacles up on the bridge of her nose and looked down at the papers in front of her. "I understand you had a bright future ahead of you, before this trouble."

"I'm not exactly sure what you mean."

"Come now, this is not the time for modesty. I see from Father Anthony's letter that you were top of your class."

Brigid looked at her mutely. She knew what the nun was getting at now.

"Wouldn't you like to go back to your family? I'm certain they all miss you very much, and you must want to see them. You'll be able to return to school, and I'm sure a smart girl like yourself will have no problem catching up on what you've missed. This time next week, you could be at home again, and you'll be able to put these difficult months behind you. Make a fresh start. As if it never happened." Mother Mary Frances looked at her encouragingly.

Brigid bit her lip as the image of her daughter at her breast swam before her, the whorls of hair, the tiny fingers stretching, exploring. She was sure she'd seen her smile for the first time that morning. As she thought about it, her breasts began to tingle, and she felt a rush of warmth. Embarrassed, she folded her arms in an attempt to cover up the two dark spots that had appeared on her blouse.

"The family is a fine one." Sister Agatha appeared not to have noticed. She thrust a photograph under Brigid's nose. "Well educated, cultured." As if these qualities might make handing her baby over any less heartbreaking.

It showed two people, posed for a studio portrait, a blonde woman sitting on a chair and a man—her husband, Brigid supposed—standing behind her, tall and broad, his hand resting protectively on the woman's shoulder. They looked like the definition of a perfect couple and Brigid would have laid bets that they'd once been homecoming king and queen, high-school sweethearts, the whole wretched shebang.

"They especially requested a daughter," Sister Agatha added. "They are wonderful people, who can't wait to give a child a happy upbringing. The baby would be so fortunate to call these fine people her parents."

Who was Brigid to deny her daughter the chance at such a life? To have two parents; to want for nothing? There was no doubt that she could easily pass as theirs—she shared her dark hair with the man in the photograph, his wide forehead too.

A growing suspicion snaked its way into her thoughts.

Did they show this same photograph, or one just like it, to all the reluctant girls? Brigid's lip began to tremble, and she reminded herself that these nuns definitely did not have her best interests at heart, despite what they were telling her.

"I have the necessary forms here," said Mother Mary Frances, picking up the paper on the top of the pile and pushing it across her desk toward Brigid. She held out a pen. "All you need do is sign where I've marked, and we'll take care of the rest. You won't have to worry about a thing."

Brigid gazed steadily at Mother Mary Frances. Could she really add her signature, the one she'd only ever practiced on her exercise books, to the form? It seemed unthinkable to give her daughter away with the mere stroke of a pen. "May I have some time to make a decision?"

Sister Agatha's face darkened, but Mother Mary Frances remained serene. The nun knew she had no other option. "Of course, my dear. You may have until the end of the week. But do be aware that this family might find another little girl if you take too long to decide."

Brigid was nearly overwhelmed by despair. Everything was against her. She felt her earlier certainty waver; every sensible thought in her head was telling her to do this, for her daughter's sake.

"You can keep the photograph if you like," said Mother Mary France, holding it out to her. "While you decide."

Brigid had no choice but to take it.

"We know you'll make the right decision for your baby, Brigid."

THAT AFTERNOON, her chores completed—she'd been put on light duties since the birth—Brigid slipped out of the house unnoticed. She didn't want the company of another girl, the mindless chatter, for she needed time to think about the nuns' proposal, and her baby's future.

As she made her way to the water's edge, out of sight of the house, wind-driven spray from the Sound froze on her face. She barely felt it, consumed by the choice she was about to make. She pulled the photograph from her pocket, examined the bland faces for signs of a future, but could see none. Even if they *were* real, the nicest people in the entire world, they weren't her baby's parents. She was her mother, and that surely had to count for something? Didn't it?

Almost without realizing what she was doing, Brigid began to tear at the edge of the picture. Moments later it was nothing but a collection of tiny scraps, a mouth here, a finger, a brooch, a lock of hair…she raised her hands and let the wind carry the scraps away. No one else was going to be her baby's mother. The baby was hers: her flesh and blood; she belonged by her side.

She turned away from the water, skirting the edge of the forest until she reached the chapel, walking around to the back of the building, where she would be out of sight of prying eyes. She stopped short as she reached a low dirt mound. It was lightly covered with fresh snow, a barely noticeable rounded hump in the ground. "What the hell…?" she said out loud.

A bird called in reply, a mournful sound.

An involuntary shudder ran through her as she realized what she was looking at. Had she nearly walked over a grave? If so, whose was it? An oversize glove had been dropped nearby—tan leather with red stitching—and she knew where she'd seen it before, and who it must belong to.

By the time Brigid returned to the house, frozen but electrified, she knew she had to get away, and it had to be soon.

There were only three days left until Mother Mary Frances's deadline, and Brigid had little opportunity to put her plan into action. She was counting on Sister Clare being assigned nursery duty, for she often let Brigid keep the baby with her after the last feed for the night. It was probably as much out of laziness as kindness, for Sister Clare liked her sleep, often grumbling to Brigid how tired she was, kept up by babies crying to be cuddled and fed.

Brigid had been keeping a note of the days and times that the supply boat called, waking before dawn to watch for the approaching lights down by the jetty.

The first night, Brigid's face fell when Sister Jude brought the baby to her at midnight and waited there until she had fed her. She forced herself to be patient, told herself there was still time.

The night before Brigid was due to sign the adoption forms, Sister Clare came in for the last feed. The baby was uncharacteristically grizzly and took a while to settle in Brigid's arms. "May I keep her here?" Brigid asked, willing the nun to agree.

Sister Clare looked at her, squinting from lack of sleep.

"She'll be absolutely fine, just as she was last time. I'll bring her down after the first morning feed and no one will be the wiser." Brigid tried to keep the pleading tone out of her voice.

"I suppose," Sister Clare sighed. "Our secret, okay?"

"Of course, Sister," Brigid promised solemnly.

After the nun had closed the door behind her, Brigid fed her daughter and then settled her on the bed. Since Sara's disappearance, Brigid been in the room on her own, something she was now very grateful for. Had a new roommate been assigned, her plan might not have been possible.

Moving quietly, she slid her suitcase from under the bed and began to pack her scant belongings, putting on her warmest clothes and taking a sheet from Sara's bed in which to wrap the baby. Adrenaline at what she was about to do kept her alert to the slightest sound.

Her daughter slept.

At around five-thirty in the morning, Brigid judged it time to leave. She gathered her sleeping baby and placed the only thing she'd managed to knit—a misshapen, too large cap with several holes where she'd dropped a stitch or two—over her head. She still hadn't decided what to call her daughter, part of her hadn't wanted to jinx her plans by naming her little girl and then having her taken away. She bound the baby to her chest with a torn-up length of cloth taken from the sewing supplies, before putting on the coat her mother had loaned her. She bent down awkwardly, trying not to jostle her daughter, and picked up her suitcase. Getting everything down to the jetty wouldn't be easy, but harder still would be escaping the house unnoticed.

The doors—back and front—were locked at night and Mother Mary Frances always made a performance of it, turning the key on its clanking chain before hanging it high on a hook in the study.

Brigid eased open her door, checking left and right

to make sure the hallway was empty, before tiptoeing as soundlessly as she could manage toward the stairs. She paused at the top, thinking she had seen a movement in the shadows below. She waited, listening over the thump of her heartbeat for a noise, anything that would indicate that someone else was up and about.

Eventually, having convinced herself that she was alone, she lowered herself and her luggage down each step until she reached the ground floor, praying that the baby wouldn't wake and give her away. The hall here was dark, but she knew the way by heart. She paused outside the study, then turned the handle and pushed the door open a few inches. Feeling her way along the wall, she ran her fingers over its rough plastered surface. There was a clank—too loud in the sleeping house—as her hand encountered the keys and she stilled their chimes in her fist.

She nearly leapt a foot off the ground when a hand came down on her arm and then another over her mouth, stifling a squeal.

"Shh. It's only me."

"Catherine?" Brigid's heart thundered in her chest.

"It's okay. Come on, we need to hurry." Catherine pulled Brigid toward the mudroom, relieving her of her suitcase.

"I don't understand." Brigid spoke in a whisper as she pulled on her boots.

"Understand what?"

"Why would you help me?"

"You have a plan. That's more than the rest of us."

Brigid didn't have the heart to tell her that it might be a foolish one. "How did you know?"

"I saw you hanging around the jetty. Watching for

the boat. You never talked about going home, not like everyone else."

Once out of the back door, they hurried down to the jetty. Brigid could not risk tripping and waking, or worse, hurting the baby, and was thankful that Catherine was there to help. The snow of previous weeks still lingered in patches, but not enough to leave footprints that might betray them. A heavy mist hung above the ground, rolling in from the water. That was good, for if someone were to look out of the window from the house they wouldn't be likely to spot the two girls standing at the end of the jetty.

Dawn would soon crack the sky, but for now the world was poised on the cusp of night and day, neither one nor the other, and there was little to make out amid the dark and the drifting fog. The girls stood on the end of the jetty and peered into the gloom, clutching their coats tight around themselves, for an icy wind tugged at their clothing.

As the air began to lighten, Brigid saw the boat slipping through the water, her hull causing only the slightest ripple on its glassy surface. The captain stood at the wheel, and he drew close enough that she could see him scratch his head, nearly dislodging the fisherman's cap that covered it.

"What's that Ted?"

His voice carried easily across the water. Brigid willed him to be silent, for any untoward noise might wake someone in the house. A little dog, a light shape in the dark, tripped along the deck to the bow, his claws tapping on the varnished timber.

As the boat came alongside, her timbers creaking like an old woman rousing herself from sleep, Brigid saw the name *May Queen* painted on the hull. It wasn't the vessel she'd been expecting, for a vessel called the *Martha-Ann* usually delivered supplies. She hoped it wouldn't matter.

"I didn't think I'd come across another living being, let alone two, at this hour of the morning. For a second I thought I was seeing things." The man's voice was gravelly, as though he rarely had cause to use it.

The sky had lightened a little more now and Brigid could see the stubble on his chin, his eyes reddened by salt spray. It gave him an unwashed, wild look and she began to worry she had made a huge mistake.

It was too late for second thoughts.

He slung a rope toward them and Catherine caught it easily, looping it around a post at the end of the jetty.

They both stood back as he hopped ashore and began unloading his cargo, grunting with the effort of it. Brigid saw crates of apples, burlap bags of potatoes, dark green cabbages, two sacks of flour, and one of mail, a box stamped with the name of a city bookstore.

"Can you take me?" Brigid asked.

"Quiet, Ted," he grunted as the dog let out a high-pitched yip. "You'll be wanting a passenger ferry." His voice was curt as he lined up the boxes.

She hadn't wanted to risk the ferry; certain she'd be spotted straight away. "But they don't call here." Brigid hoped she sounded more confident than she felt. "If it helps, can you pretend I'm cargo?"

"Strange kind of cargo." He finished unloading.

"What about the other one?" he asked, gesturing to Catherine. "I've no room for two."

"Oh no, I'm not coming," Catherine said, shaking her head.

The sky had lightened some more, with a faint blush on the horizon. Brigid shifted the suitcase in her hand, silently pleading with him.

"Please? I can pay." She still had some of her baby-sitting money left.

His eyes softened.

"Come aboard then," he said eventually, untying the line and preparing to leave. "Before I change my mind. I wouldn't leave my sister out here on her own, stands to reason I shouldn't turn you down. I'd say there's a damn good reason you're out here at this hour of the morning, though I'd prefer it to be none of my business."

"We have to hurry." Brigid glanced over her shoulder, seeing the hazy outline of Fairmile behind her, almost swallowed by dark pines. A light glowed from a downstairs window.

"Makes no difference to me."

She turned and gave Catherine a brief hug, her arms barely reaching around the girl's belly as she whispered words of thanks in her ear. "My real name is Ingrid," she said, suddenly desperate for Catherine to know it, to know who she really was.

She saw the white of Catherine's teeth in the moon-light.

"Diana," Catherine replied. "Mine is Diana. Now, go on, quick," she squeezed her friend in return. "Be safe."

They both stilled as a shout came from the house. It sounded like Sister Agatha's voice.

"Go," her friend urged. "I'll tell her I couldn't sleep. That I came out on my own for some air."

Brigid hesitated.

"Go!" her friend hissed. "Before it's too late."

The captain extended a hand and Brigid grasped it,

climbing aboard and settling herself low in the boat so that she couldn't be seen. She crouched among the remaining crates, her daughter still bound to her chest, as the dog lay at her feet, and she gave him a scratch. The motor kicked throatily into life, and they chugged away from the jetty.

Ahead lay the vast estuarine bay of Puget Sound—flooded glacial inlets, if Brigid remembered her geography correctly. She didn't dare look back. "A person could lose themselves out here," she said, staring blindly into the fog.

"I've been lost myself, on more occasions than I care to admit, though I eventually found my way back." The captain scratched his chin and squinted at the lightening horizon. "Where to?" he asked.

"That depends on where you're headed."

"I'd imagine somewhere as far away from that place, am I right?" he asked, coming toward her. For a moment, Brigid was frightened. He had complete control over her future. "Here, have this," he said.

She looked up to find that he was holding out an apple.

"Thank you." She rubbed it on her sleeve, bit into the cold, sweet-tart flesh and tasted freedom.

FORTY

Puget Sound, 2013

"LIAM!" FRANKIE DIDN'T bother hiding her shock.

Of course, she remembered now, he had said he had a house in Crane Bay.

"Sorry to disturb you so late," Molly said. "But we're looking for Isabella Gray." She held out the photograph. "She's been missing since around noon yesterday."

"My daughter," Frankie interrupted. "Izzy. You've met her before."

"Of course, I remember," he said, his gaze darting between the two of them. He licked his lips and seemed nervous. "But why would you think she'd be here?"

"We're conducting house-to-house enquiries, that's all," said Molly, her voice even. "Trying to find out if anyone knows her whereabouts or might have seen her in the past twenty-four hours," Frankie added.

"I've only been on the island since this morning, but I'm afraid I haven't. Seen her that is."

His smile didn't reach his eyes.

"That's a nasty cut you've got there," said Frankie. He had a graze on his cheek, dark with dried blood.

"Blunt razors." He shrugged. "What can you do?"

Frankie caught sight of several objects on the hall table behind him. Tiny origami cranes, like the one he'd made at the café. Fashioned from brightly colored paper.

"Do please let us know if you see or hear anything," said Molly, her voice still pleasant. "Anything at all."

They said a brief goodbye and he closed the door, leaving the two women standing on the porch for a moment.

"Something's not right," Molly whispered. "Did he seem odd to you?"

"The origami, on the table behind him. They were made from the same paper as the notes left on my truck."

"Right." Molly thought for a second. "Perhaps I heard the word *shed*. In Izzy's message."

"You did?"

"Possibly. Let's take a look down the back, shall we?"

They skirted the area, keeping to the shadowy pines that surrounded the house. Frankie could smell the salt water, feel the chill air rising from it. Over the drumming of the rain, came the sound of halyards rattling against a mast.

Frankie risked turning on the flashlight on her phone and saw a narrow path that led to the shoreline. She quickly flicked it off again, not wanting to be seen. Scruff wriggled in her arms until she couldn't keep hold of him. He dropped to the ground with a thud and a yelp, racing off into the darkness. Exasperated, she hissed to him to return.

Being careful not to stumble in the dark, she began to jog along the path, Molly following a few steps behind.

Several hundred yards below the house, Frankie found the dog at the end of a jetty, in front of a narrow boatshed, his tail wagging furiously. He let out a short yip, then a bark, and Frankie only hoped they were far enough away from the house, the noise swallowed by the rain, for it not to be heard. She tried the handle, but it was locked.

"We should get a warrant," said Molly, who was right behind her now.

"Charge me with breaking and entering if it comes to it. Scruff knows there's something in there." Frankie backed up a few paces, then launched herself at the door, crashing shoulder-first into the old wood. It splintered but held. "Izzy!" she called, but there was no response. She backed up and ran at it again.

"Around here," Molly hissed, and Frankie turned to see that she'd gone to the side of the boatshed, where there was a small window.

"It's set too high," said Frankie, assessing the distance.

"I'll give you a boost," said Molly, bending over and resting her hands on her thighs.

With Molly's help, Frankie was able to reach the window. It had an aluminum frame, with a sliding section, and so she scrabbled at it with her fingers to see if it would open. She pulled at one end with all her might, nearly overbalancing the pair of them, before giving up and sliding to the ground again.

Scruff was running laps around the building, yipping constantly now.

"It's no good, I can't shift it. It must be locked from the inside, or corroded shut."

They cast around for something that might help.

"I'll have to break it," said Frankie.

"I'll get fired if you're wrong," said Molly, handing her a fallen pine branch.

Frankie smashed the glass, and it was a matter of seconds before she was able to slide it open. Shining

Molly's flashlight into the pitch-black space, she could see a pile of folded sailcloth directly beneath.

"I'll be able to get in, I think," she said, before hauling herself through the window. She landed heavily, feeling a searing jolt through her right leg, but the worst of her fall was cushioned by the sails.

The boatshed smelled dank and briny. She raced to the door to let Molly in, but it was wedged shut. Methodically directing the flashlight around the space, she located a switch and soon the place was flooded with light.

Her eyes snagged on a blue shape in the corner, and she bent down to retrieve it. "Izzy's backpack," she called out.

"I'm radioing for back up," Molly shouted over the sound of the rain.

Frankie was about to reply, when she heard a crash come from outside the boatshed, followed by sounds of a scuffle. "Molly? Are you okay? Scruff?"

There was a scream, a grunt, and then nothing but the sound of the rain.

FORTY-ONE

Seattle, 1950

A HIGH EVERGREEN hedge hid the house from the street. Brigid checked the number posted on the gate. It was the right place. She'd found it. The first part of the plan had worked. But instead of easing, the jitters that had accompanied her the entire journey only grew worse. She had no clue as to the reception she would receive.

The *May Queen*'s captain had deposited her at a wharf near Pioneer Square and waved her off with her directions to Capitol Hill. "It's not that far. You'll find it easy enough. Look after yourself now, d'ya hear?"

Brigid nodded and returned his breezy wave, pretending far more confidence than she felt. "Thank you."

The walk had taken more than an hour, and at one point she rounded a corner and came face-to-face with a pair of nuns, making their way toward a church that she'd passed at the end of the street. She felt sure she had "Fairmile girl" branded on her forehead and her heart pounded so loudly that she worried it would wake her daughter. She gathered her coat around her, hiding the baby, put her head down, and prayed that she wouldn't arouse their suspicions. It wasn't until she'd turned into the next street that she allowed herself to breathe normally again.

The weather had turned warmer, but this meant that

instead of snow, rain fell, softly at first, but gradually becoming steadier, until her coat was sodden with it. Her hands were blistered from the handle of her suitcase, and her boots soaked through from trudging through the dirty slush that lined the streets. She couldn't wait to sit down and unwrap the cloth around herself; the weight of her daughter dragged at her lower back and made it ache as though she was in labor again.

Capitol Hill seemed like a nice neighborhood, certainly fancier than the town Brigid came from. Neat grids of tree-lined streets featured tall houses with a wealth of windows. As she walked, she caught occasional glimpses of well-groomed front yards, mostly hidden behind high fences or hedges.

She reached the address she sought and craned her neck upward, seeing a slate roof, dark brick, and smartly painted window frames. Peering through a crack in the gate, she saw twin planter boxes sitting neatly on either side of a front door, though nothing bloomed there. It was such a beautiful house that, despite everything that had brought her to that point, Brigid's spirits lifted just looking at it. It had to be a sign that everything would be okay.

It was, however, impossible to tell whether there was anyone at home.

She prayed that someone—her Aunt Helen specifically—would be.

Her daughter shifted against her, and Brigid gathered her remaining courage, reaching for the handle of the gate, walking purposefully up the path and pushing the bell, her wet fingers slipping on the polished brass.

Almost immediately, the door swung open.

"No peddlers, thank you. Didn't you see the sign?"

A woman with a voice like the rasp of a rusty saw, fashionably dressed in a gabardine skirt cinched at the waist with a belt, and a fine wool twinset in the same red as her expertly applied lipstick, stood in the doorway. She was regarding Brigid as if she was a street urchin, or worse.

"Please…?" Brigid put out a hand to stop her shutting the door. "Please, I'm looking for my Aunt Helen. Helen Lindholm. She…she lives here. Or at least I thought she did."

The expression on the woman's face relaxed a fraction. "I'm afraid you've had a wasted journey, wherever you've come from. Miss Lindholm hasn't lived here for several years."

Brigid slumped against the doorframe. A tear slid down her cheek and she dashed it away. She'd pinned all of her hopes on getting here, on pleading with her aunt for help. She was fresh out of ideas of what to do next. "I've been traveling for a while, and I've no place else to go."

The woman eyes her suspiciously, then appeared to relent. "It's not fit for man nor dog out there and you're wetter than an otter. I suppose you can come in for a minute. The coffee pot's on; I'll fix you a hot drink, if you'd like."

Brigid sniffed, wiped her eyes with the back of her hand, and picked up her suitcase. "You're very kind."

"I'm not so sure about that," said the woman, leading her into the entrance hall lined from floor to ceiling with books. "You can put your coat there," she said, indicating a set of hooks. A fire must have been lit in one of the rooms, for there was the faint smell of woodsmoke in the air. Brigid unbuttoned her mother's coat and placed it on the hook, where it dripped steadily onto the tiled floor. She hurried after the woman. "But it would be unchristian of me to turn away a body in need. What did you say your name was?"

Brigid hesitated. The last thing she wanted was for this woman to report her to the nuns and have her sent straight back to Fairmile. "Ingrid," she said, chancing that she could risk using her own name.

"And the baby?" The woman missed nothing.

She didn't want to admit that her nearly month-old daughter didn't have a name. "Diana," she said impulsively. For the girl who had helped her escape. "Diana Lauren."

"Well, Ingrid, I'm Virginia. Now where did you say you'd come from?"

She hadn't.

"Uh, California," she said, quickly improvising. "Santa Barbara." It was the first place that came to mind.

"Never been there myself. Long ways away. You must have had quite a journey." Virginia turned and gave Ingrid a suspicious glance. "No wonder you look tired out." She led them into a large kitchen. "Have a seat and I'll fix you a cup of coffee. You look like you could use something to eat too, am I right?"

She nodded. "Thank you."

"There's some biscuits and gravy leftover from last night's dinner. I'll warm those."

As Ingrid pulled out a chair, the baby began to grizzle, which escalated to a thin, high-pitched bleat and then worked up to a full-blown scream. Her cheeks turned the color of cherry juice, and her mouth was a wide howl of protest.

Ingrid jiggled her daughter up and down, but if anything, the screams only intensified in volume.

"Would you mind if I fed her?" She had to speak up to be heard.

"Be my guest."

She began to unwind the cloth that had bound her daughter to her all morning. "Do you have children?" she asked.

"Nope. Never married neither." Virginia sounded pleased at that state of affairs.

"Oh."

"I'm an English professor. At the university."

That explained the books in the hallway.

"I'd like to go to college someday." Ingrid's voice was wistful.

"But now you're a mother," Virginia said bluntly.

"Yes."

"And I'm guessing there's no father."

Too late, Ingrid hid her left hand. "No," she said in a small voice. "There's not."

"And your parents have kicked you out and you were hoping that dear Aunt Helen, wherever she is, would take you in?"

"Something like that," Ingrid admitted, surprised at the accuracy of Virginia's assessment. "Do you have a forwarding address for her?"

Virginia pursed her lips. "Can't say I do. The sale was handled by my lawyer. I moved here from the East Coast last year."

Ingrid had unwrapped Diana—she was still getting used to the name—and wrinkled her nose as a foul stench reached her. "I'm sorry," she said, reddening. "I think she needs changing."

"I'll say. There's a bathroom down the hall. I take it you have diapers?"

Ingrid nodded. "In my case. Would you...?" she held the baby out to the woman who looked horrified.

"Why don't I get them from the suitcase?" Virginia suggested.

"They're right on the top. Thank you."

Virginia left the kitchen, giving Ingrid plenty of time to look around. She held Diana against her, and stood up, jiggling her daughter to stop her grizzling. It was a welcoming place, with a big stove and refrigerator, cheerful yellow curtains at the window framing a view out to a long lawn spotted with patches of snow. Such a lot of space for one person.

"Here you are." Virginia had returned, holding out the cloths in one hand, keeping herself at arm's length from the baby.

"Thank you."

When Ingrid returned, there was a cup of coffee steaming gently on the kitchen table and next to it, a plate of golden biscuits.

"I don't suppose you have something I might wrap this in?" She held up the soiled diaper.

"Middle drawer, over there." Virginia pointed across the kitchen. "Actually, why don't you put it in the laundry. You can soak it in there."

"Oh, okay." It seemed that Virginia had changed her mind about letting her into the house for "a minute."

The coffee was hot and strong, and the biscuits light and buttery—"oh, no I didn't make them," Virginia said with a throaty laugh when Ingrid commented. "My neighbor brought them around yesterday. She can't understand how a woman living on her own, one with a vocation anyway, can possibly manage to look after herself. I indulge her." A smile flickered across her face. "In any case, she's a far better cook than I will ever be."

Ingrid drew out her coffee as long as she dared. When she had drained the last drop, she discovered Virginia staring at her.

"How old are you?"

"Seventeen next month."

Virginia sighed and lit a cigarette, drawing deeply. "Tell me, before all this…" she exhaled and indicated the baby. "What kind of a student were you?"

That was an easy question to answer. "Straight *A*s, ma'am."

"I thought as much. Someone plucky enough to travel so far must have something about them." She pulled out a chair next to Ingrid and fixed her with a no-nonsense gaze. "So, tell me. What's your plan, Straight-*A* Ingrid?"

FORTY-TWO

Puget Sound, 2013

"I KNOW YOU'VE got her," Frankie yelled, swallowing her concern for Molly. She went to the boatshed door and hammered on it, biting down on her lip to stop herself from crying out at the pain that shot down her leg. "Stop being a coward and come for me too." It might not have been the smartest thing to say, but all she could think of was keeping Liam from leaving, at least until she could confront him face to face. She needed to get him inside, or at least to open the door; then she might have half a chance to overpower him. She waited, hands clenched into fists, barely able to breathe, listening for anything that might tell her where he was. All she could hear was the barking of the dog and then a whimper. "Open the door!" She hoped to God he hadn't hurt any of them: Molly, Scruff, Izzy...

Seconds ticked by but there was only the sound of the rain on the roof and the lapping of the water. Then, she heard a different sound, somewhere at the back of the boatshed. She turned around, seeing a lumpy-looking sail that she'd missed before.

Frankie raced toward it, hauling back the stiff fabric. Dammit, there was yards of the stuff. She was breathing heavily now, adrenaline spiking through her body and her hands trembled as she grabbed at the fabric. It crackled beneath her fingers, and she was alarmed to see smears of blood, red against the white. She must have cut her hands when she smashed the glass in the window.

She stopped as she heard the grate of a bolt, and turned, half crouched, to see Liam silhouetted in the doorway.

"Move away from there," he shouted.

Frankie straightened up slowly, very slowly, not wanting to spook him. "Is she okay? Tell me she's okay. Where is she? Where is Molly?"

His eyes flicked behind her. "You wouldn't stop. You just wouldn't stop." He sounded less sure of himself now.

"Wouldn't stop what?"

"Trying to find out what happened to that woman."

"Bernadette you mean? Is that what this is all about?"

"You were going to ruin it."

Frankie trained her gaze on his, not betraying the slight movement she'd seen, Molly looming out of the darkness behind him. He must have thought he'd taken her out of action, but he'd clearly underestimated the woman.

"Put your hands in the air, right where I can see them," Molly yelled so loudly that Frankie nearly over-balanced.

As Liam turned in surprise, Molly stepped forward, wincing as she did so. But she managed a well-executed grip on his wrist and wasted no time in twisting it be-hind his back. She staggered as she cuffed him and Liam began to struggle, but she held him firmly, giving him no chance to escape.

Frankie turned back and found the end of the sail,

using all her strength to heave it away, terrified of what it might reveal.

She gasped as she saw her daughter's hands, that they had been bound with thin rope. As she pulled harder on the sail, Frankie uncovered Izzy's face and for an agonizing second, she felt her heart almost give way. Her daughter was pale as marble, her eyes rolled to the back of her head.

She heard a roaring sound in her ears as her knees buckled and she collapsed on the floor.

"Check her vitals," Molly shouted as Liam struggled to free himself. "For Chrissake."

Frankie blinked, coming to. Of course. She'd assumed the worst.

She felt for a pulse, leaned in to see if she could feel her daughter's breath, holding her own. Seconds ticked by. Then, she found it. Faint, thready, but there. Izzy was breathing, but shallowly, and as Frankie ran her fingers gently over her face, she felt the swell of a bruise on her temple. "Oh, thank God," she breathed, fumbling to untie the rope that bound her daughter's wrists. Relief flooded through her like a drug. "Call an ambulance," she yelled.

"Already on its way," said Molly as Frankie heard barking coming from somewhere outside.

She cradled her daughter's head in her lap, then turned to Liam.

"I didn't mean to hurt her," he stammered. "I swear. At first, I wanted you to stop digging at Fairmile, and to stop asking about the nun. I couldn't have you find out the truth." He inched forward and Molly screamed at him to keep still.

"I get that, really I do," said Frankie, in an attempt to mollify him.

Liam's face crumpled, as if the fight had gone out of him. "No…you don't."

"The notes. That was you, wasn't it?" Frankie asked. "You're the one who slashed my tire after the funeral. Why?"

"I only did it to protect Rosalie," he pleaded. "She's suffered her whole life, losing me, and then finding out that her daughter hadn't survived." He raised his hand to the cut on his cheek. "She told me she had a breakdown because of what happened to her at Fairmile. And then seeing that woman again, every day, living in the same facility, brought it all back. When Ingrid told her she thought that woman had buried her little girl, my sister—that she'd seen the mound of earth—all that time ago, well, how would you feel, in her shoes? She asked me to get some pills and I couldn't refuse…"

So he had known about his twin. Frankie then realized what else he had implied. It was *Rosalie* who had given Sister Agatha the overdose. Her mother had never been in any way involved.

The sound of barking drifted toward them. "What did you do with Scruff?" she asked. "If you've…"

"He's tied up, for God's sake, do you think I'd harm a dog?"

"I wouldn't be at all surprised," said Frankie.

"I did it for her," Liam's voice broke. "I only did it for Rosalie. I was trying to protect her. You have to understand. She's all I've got. I can't lose her now."

"And what exactly were you going to do with Izzy?"

"You were so superior, so sure of yourself in the café. You don't know how lucky you've got it. I wanted you to see what it feels like to lose the person you care about most in the world. To have your family torn apart, even for a little while. I would have let her go, of course I would, you have to believe that. But she fought me." He put a hand to his cheek. "And I panicked. I just wanted to scare you both. I never meant to hurt her."

FORTY-THREE

Puget Sound, 2013

"SHE'S DOING OKAY." The nurse looking after Izzy checked her vital signs, the third time since Frankie had pulled up at the one-room emergency department of the island's small hospital an hour earlier. "Might have a nasty head-ache, but other than that she'll be fine."

"Any idea what he might have given her…?" Frankie asked. The nurse had taken a blood sample when Izzy first arrived.

"We won't know for sure until tomorrow—the test has to go to the mainland, but from what I can tell I don't think it's anything more serious than a sedative."

Frankie smoothed the hair from her daughter's fore-head. She still looked desperately pale.

"How is she?" Diana swept aside the curtain and bustled into the cubicle, handing Frankie a paper cup of coffee.

"Oh, Mom." Frankie was almost lost for words. She sipped her coffee, grateful that it was at least hot, if somewhat lacking in caffeine. "Mom. I thought you…" She was about to confess her darkest imaginings, the ones she had barely even been able to admit to herself, but Diana shook her head and reached for Frankie's hand, giving it a reassuring squeeze.

"Hush now."

"Hey." Izzy had opened her eyes.

"Sweet pea," said Diana, dropping Frankie's hand and taking Izzy's.

"Where am I?"

"The emergency room, but you're just fine."

"Love you Mom, Granny."

"You too, darling," Frankie whispered back, blinking away sudden tears. Her emotions were far too close to the surface, particularly when they involved her daughter. Frankie's earlier adrenaline had worn off, exhaustion taking its place.

"How're you doing?"

"Never better." She gave a weak thumbs up. "I'm sorry. I messed up."

"No, you didn't darling."

"I thought it was okay; I'd seen him with GG, and Rosalie. He seemed nice when he was around them, and he was nice to me, at least at first. He told me we were all going to go sailing—that you were meeting us at his place. I wanted to make Zac jealous."

Frankie stroked her daughter's forehead. "You're safe now. And it was my fault. If I hadn't been so intent on finding the truth, none of this would have happened."

"Don't be ridiculous, Mom." Izzy gave a weak laugh. "That's what you do."

The effort of talking must have exhausted Izzy and her eyes fluttered shut again.

"How's Grandma?" Frankie asked Diana in a whisper.

Her mom raised her eyes skyward. "It appears that she and Rosalie got into some sort of a disagreement.

That's why I went to Pacifica and why I was already here when you arrived with Izzy."

"A disagreement?"

"I've no idea what about, she couldn't tell me, neither could any of the staff, which—let me say—I am not at all impressed by. Anyway, it was enough for her to fall and knock her head on the sideboard. She was out cold for more than a minute. They're pretty sure she's broken her hip too, though the radiographer doesn't come in until the morning."

"Oh no." Frankie had seen how strong Rosalie was when she hadn't wanted Liam to leave, could imagine her easily overpowering her frail grandmother. "Can I go and see her?"

"She's pretty heavily sedated. She's in the women's ward, first left down the hall. Why don't we tag-team it? I'll stay with Iz if you go to Ingrid."

GRAY. THAT'S ALL Frankie could see when she found her grandmother. Gray walls, gray blankets, and gray skin that seemed to have had all the life sucked out of it. Ingrid's cheeks were sunken and there were dark shadows beneath her eyes. She was hooked up to oxygen, with a bag of IV fluid going into her veins for good measure.

Tears pricked Frankie's eyes and she blinked rapidly lest they spill over. She still had so much to learn about her grandmother's life, she needed more time to just *be* with her. It *couldn't* all be over so soon. "Hey there," she said softly, pulling up a chair at the head of Ingrid's bed. "Got yourself in a bit of trouble, huh?" She pressed a hand to her grandmother's cheek and she stirred, mumbled something. "Don't try to speak," Frankie soothed. "Rest now."

"I'm not in trouble. That was years ago."

The words were perfectly clear.

"It's all okay now. You're being taken good care of."

"No care. No." Ingrid began to thrash her head from side to side and a machine started to beep.

"Shh…" Frankie patted her hand. "Grandma, it's Frankie here, Diana's daughter. Your granddaughter."

"I had a daughter. She was the most beautiful baby."

"You did, you had Diana. And she grew up to be a wonderful woman, and a mom, and a grandmother."

Ingrid seemed to calm at these words, and her breathing steadied as Frankie sat with her, in silence now.

"WE NEED TO talk to the management," said Frankie later that week, patting Scruff. She was in the dining room with her mother, who was sifting through a pile of bills, totalling them up with a calculator and a frown. Izzy was resting upstairs. "Don't you want to know exactly what happened to Grandma? I'm not sure she should even go back to Pacifica Gardens." Ingrid was still in the hospital, though her hip turned out to have only been badly bruised, not broken as they had feared.

"Of course I do." Diana was indignant. "The director rang me, but he didn't exactly say very much."

"Why don't I go over tomorrow? Speak to him in person?"

"Are you sure you can handle it?"

"Mom." Frankie was firm.

"Okay, okay, then yes, that would be good. Thank you—I'm still so angry that this happened to Ingrid under their care, I think I'd only lose my temper with them." Diana returned to the paperwork in front of her, pecking angrily at the calculator.

Frankie's phone beeped with a message. It was Molly wanting to know if they could catch up, suggesting a beer at The Cabbage Shed if she had time. She texted back, wishing there was a cocktail glass emoji, agreeing to meet her that evening.

Molly would see that justice was done in regard to Liam, but getting to the bottom of what exactly had happened between Ingrid and Rosalie was now Frankie's main concern. She hadn't pressed her grandmother for details of the incident: Frankie hadn't wanted to upset her by pressing her to remember while she was still in the hospital.

WHEN FRANKIE PULLED up at Pacifica Gardens after lunch, many of the residents were enjoying the fresh air, sitting in the shade in groups of two or three and watched over by the nurses. Frankie waved to one of them, a young blonde care assistant who was wheeling an elderly man onto the grass.

As Frankie strode into the reception area, the director, who must have seen her approach, came out to meet her.

"Why don't we convene in my office?" he suggested, after shaking her hand. "June, perhaps some ice water for our visitor? It's a warm day." He bestowed an oily smile on Frankie as he ushered her into a room that led off the reception area.

Frankie took an instant dislike to the man. She'd only ever seen him once before, that was on the morning that Sister Agatha's—Bernadette's—body had been discovered. She guessed he wasn't based at the nursing home, and that he must have come especially for their meeting, probably brought in for damage control.

"Now, Ms. Gray, I understand this is in relation to your grandmother, Ingrid Abrahams. How is she?" He folded his hands on the table in front of him, leaning forward in an apparent expression of sincerity. Frankie decided he must have had training in how to appear sympathetic to relatives; she didn't believe for a second that he was genuine.

"She's very shaken."

"But happily, no serious damage done?" he asked, reviewing a folder of notes.

"You clearly don't have the latest information on my grandmother's condition." Frankie sat back in her chair. "She has a badly bruised hip—damned lucky she didn't break it."

"We care very deeply about the welfare of all of our guests," he replied blandly. "Now, in light of what happened at the end of last week, you will be reassured to know that we have stepped up our monitoring, with increased staffing levels in the common areas." He droned on about the specifics of their changes until Frankie interrupted.

"No one has been able to tell me exactly what caused the altercation between my grandmother and another resident, Rosalie Shanahan. I should like to know."

"I'm afraid that won't be possible. We did—gently mind you, given her age—question Ms. Shanahan regarding what might have occurred, but she was unable to tell us very much at all."

"Unable or unwilling?" Frankie fixed him with a gaze made of flint.

He smiled his oily smile again and Frankie shuddered inwardly. She didn't know what she'd been hoping for, but she wasn't going to get anywhere with him.

"You have our utmost assurance that your grand-mother will not be in any danger when she is well enough to return to all her friends at Pacifica Gardens."

Some friends.

"And exactly how can you guarantee that?" Frankie asked.

The director assumed an expression of saccharine concern. "In addition to the measures I have outlined, I am afraid to say that Ms. Shanahan—Rosalie—will be leaving us next week."

"Hang on, if you don't know precisely what happened, why is she leaving?"

"Unfortunately, Ms. Shanahan is a very unwell woman. Liver cancer." He gave her an undertaker's somber look. "It's been very sudden. The doctor treating her for abrasions ordered some tests and that's when it was discovered. She will be transferred to a hospice in the city."

"Oh no." Frankie's hand flew to her mouth. She had wanted Rosalie to be held accountable for what she had done to Ingrid, and more importantly to Bernadette, but not like this.

The director folded his hands again. "It will be the best place for her at this point in her journey."

Journey. He sounded so unemotional that it made Frankie want to spit. "May I see her?" she asked.

The director looked about to object, but Frankie continued. "Her most recent actions aside, I have gotten to know her a little, in recent weeks."

"I really don't think that would be appropriate."

Frankie fixed him with a steely glare. "Do you want me to lodge an official complaint?"

"She's heavily sedated, but I suppose it is acceptable. For a very brief visit." He pressed an intercom on his desk. "June, would you please escort Ms. Gray to see Ms. Shanahan?"

Rosalie appeared to be asleep as Frankie and June entered the room, her thin white hair brushed back from her forehead, her hands loosely curled on the sheets, her mouth slightly open.

She looked hardly capable of harming a fly.

As Frankie drew a few steps closer, her attention was snagged by a flash of silver on the nightstand. It took a moment before she realized what it was.

Square. Flat. Designed to hold half a dozen cigarettes.

Not a swan on this one though. Instead, a crane, picked out in mother-of-pearl and jet inlay in an Art Nouveau design.

FORTY-FOUR

Seattle, 1950

INGRID SWALLOWED THE lump that was threatening to choke her. "I… I'm not exactly sure," she replied to Virginia's question. She thought hard, feeling the baby squirm in her arms. "Perhaps the local library?"

"Whyever there?"

"Won't they have telephone directories? I can try and find out where my aunt moved to."

Virginia laughed, a dry, crisp sound that Ingrid decided she liked. It wasn't a mean laugh, not like the one that Sister Agatha used so often. "Oh, my dear, you'd be searching for months, even if they have a complete collection. It would be like trying to find a needle in a haystack." She stood up abruptly, gathering their coffee cups and rinsing them in the sink. "However, I like your initiative."

Ingrid slumped in her chair. "I can't go back. Not home. My mother told me that I was never to return if I had my baby with me." There seemed no point in hiding the fact anymore.

Outside, the rain began to fall in sheets again and she shivered at the prospect of having to go back out in it.

"I can well understand that." Virginia dried the cups and placed them precisely back in the cupboard, before pausing at the window. "I can't send you on your way, not in that."

She appeared to come to a decision. "I have a proposal." She turned back to Ingrid and lit another cigarette. "You can stay for a few days, until you figure out what to do next. I'm rattling around in this huge house; there's a whole floor I never even venture to. I've been wondering what I might do to put it to better use."

"That's…that's very generous of you." Ingrid was almost lost for words. It wasn't merely generous; it was a lifeline.

"Charity begins at home, dear." She frowned. "But I'll warn you, I'm none too fond of children—babies especially—so you'll have to keep the little one quiet. I will not be disturbed when I am working."

FORTY-FIVE

Puget Sound, 2013

THE CABBAGE SHED was cool, the air-conditioned interior making goosebumps rise on Frankie's skin. She spotted Molly straightaway, the bright copper of her hair glowing like a new penny as the evening light slanted through the windows.

"How's things?"

Molly inclined her head. "Overworked and understaffed, same-old, same-old."

"You okay?" Molly had twisted an ankle in the tussle with Liam. She'd told Frankie afterward that she'd also pretended to be knocked out so that he would leave her alone, that Frankie's hammering on the door had helped distract him.

"Trying to keep off my feet." She lifted a leg to show Frankie a bandaged ankle.

"Good. What are you drinking?" Frankie indicated Molly's nearly empty glass.

"Coke, thanks."

"Coming up." Frankie went to order, scanning the bar for a sign of Joe, but there was only a young barman, idly polishing glasses.

"Your brother not here?" Frankie said as she set down the drinks at the table a few minutes later.

"He's been known to take the occasional day off—

something I should perhaps try." She gave a dry bark of a laugh. "Actually, I think he headed out of town for a few days." Molly took a sip of her drink and leaned back in her seat. "He didn't tell you? I thought you guys…"

Frankie shrugged. "I've had a lot going on." She felt bad that she still hadn't thanked Joe properly for helping in the search for Izzy. She'd been so worried about her daughter, and her grandmother, and then it had taken a considerable amount of persuasion to stop Lucas from jumping on a flight and coming to see them when she told him what had happened.

"I know, it's none of my damn business," said Molly, trying but failing to look disinterested.

"I don't want anything to get in the way of us being friends, as well as colleagues," Frankie insisted.

"Just to be clear, I'd have no problem with it…if you guys, you know, do get together…you're both good people. You're also more alike than you probably realize."

"What, we're both woefully bad at pub quizzes?" The tension in Frankie's shoulders eased a fraction.

"Well there is that," Molly said, returning Frankie's grin. "Oh, Liam Gardener's been charged, in case you hadn't heard. Kidnapping and assault of a police officer." Molly took a sip of her Coke. "The irony is that we would never have suspected Rosalie if Liam hadn't gone and kidnapped Izzy."

"Will you press charges in regard to the homicide?"

Molly sighed. "Rosalie has suffered her whole life— we don't need to add to that, not in the short time she's likely got left. She might not even be alive by the time we were ready to proceed, certainly not well enough to stand trial. I—and the higher-ups are in agreement—

have recommended that it's not in the public's interest for us to prosecute her. Insufficient evidence."

"I can understand Rosalie wanting revenge. She spent *sixty-three* years, almost her whole life, wondering what had happened to her twin babies. Imagine getting to her age and still not knowing if the babies you gave birth to were even alive." She shook her head slowly. It would eat you up. "But it doesn't make what Liam did right. After all, he supplied the sedatives."

"If we charge him, then we have to charge Rosalie. At the moment, we're concentrating on what we can make stick. We'll reassess further down the track." *Give Rosalie time to die in peace* was what she really meant.

Frankie considered Molly's words. It went against everything she believed in—those who committed crimes should be brought to justice and punished. She had always seen things in terms of right and wrong, black and white, but in this case, there didn't seem to be a clear-cut answer. Her grandmother's story had had a far happier ending than Rosalie's, but would she have behaved any differently had she been in Liam's shoes? She liked to think she would, but then she also knew she would do anything for her mother, as well as for her daughter. Anyway, perhaps the truth didn't always need to be held up for everyone to gape at, to pick over as if at a yard sale?

"By the way, I contacted an adoption reunion agency—there's a state-based organization—and made arrangements to hand over the ledgers I found. You never know, they could help somebody find their child or their birth parents."

"Good idea," said Molly. "It breaks my heart to think of the pain those girls went through, Ingrid included."

"And their children."

"Now how's Izzy?" Molly asked, changing the subject.

"Doing better than me I think." Frankie smiled wryly. "She's a good kid," she added. "Better than I probably gave her credit for. And I'm not saying that because she's my daughter."

"And you're a good mom."

"That's a first, but thank you for saying so."

EARLY THE NEXT WEEK, Ingrid was given the okay to be discharged. Frankie thought she should go back to Pacifica, to minimize the disruption to her life. She had checked with June: Rosalie had been moved to a hospice in the city the Friday before, "So there's no reason why not," she argued to her mom.

Diana wanted her to stay at Fairmile for a couple nights. "I'd really like her to see the place now that it's ready." The builders had finished, the furniture had all arrived, turf was laid, garden beds weeded, and every one of the more than fifty fruit trees planted in the orchard. "Before we get too busy with paying guests. She could give it a trial run for us."

"Don't you think that might be upsetting for her?"

"I hope it might be healing actually," she dismissed Frankie's concerns. "Besides, the place looks completely different. She'll hardly recognize it."

It was true—where the facade had once been a grimy mustard-yellow with olive trim, it was now a crisp white, with pale blue shutters and a clean path leading to the portico. New drapes and carpets had been installed and Frankie, Diana, and Izzy had cleaned the place until it gleamed. "I think she'll be happy with what we've done," Diana added.

"Come on, Mom," Izzy urged as they discussed it over a plate of sticky ribs and potato salad. "It will be so nice to have her here for the weekend—we can all make dinner, hang out together…"

And so, against her better judgment, Frankie agreed, arranging to go and collect Ingrid in the morning.

"THIS ISN'T PACIFICA GARDENS." Ingrid's voice wavered as they entered the long drive that led to Fairmile.

"I know, Grandma; remember, I told you that Mom—Diana—and Izzy were waiting for us at the house. We thought it would be nice to spend the weekend together—all four generations." Frankie sighed. She'd known this would be a bad idea. As she was contemplating overruling her mother and taking her back to the nursing home, Ingrid spoke up again.

"Fairmile."

Frankie caught a tremble in her grandmother's voice.

"Oh my, the trees sure have gotten tall."

Frankie gripped the wheel but drove on, slowing as the house came into view. She parked in the driveway and sat for a while, assessing Ingrid's reaction.

Apprehension and then something that looked like fear flitted across the old woman's face.

"Are you okay, Grandma? We don't have to go in if you don't want. I can take you straight to Pacifica Gardens if you would prefer."

Ingrid, who still sported a Band-Aid above one eye, squared her shoulders, sat up a little straighter. "No, dear, but you could help me out of this jalopy."

"Of course." Frankie got out of the truck and hastened to the passenger door. "The step is a little high," she said, offering Ingrid her arm.

By the time they reached the portico, Diana and Izzy had come out to greet them, enveloping Ingrid in hugs before leading her into the house.

"So many girls. So many babies taken away." Ingrid's voice was heavy with regret.

Her memory seemed clearer the further back in time she went.

"If it's too much…" Frankie rested a hand on her grandmother's shoulder to reassure her.

"This was where the laundry was," said Ingrid, indicating a door that led to the pantry. She shook off Frankie's hand and took careful steps along the hallway.

"We made this room into a library—the windows look out onto the water." Diana opened the door to a room featuring a large stone fireplace and furnished with low couches, armchairs, and window seats, with cashmere throws and plump down-filled cushions in shades of moss, sage, and oatmeal linen, as well as thoughtfully placed lamps. There were shelves featuring books on sailing, local history, interior design, the geography of the area, wildflowers, and a selection of the latest bestsellers. "Anything someone on vacation might like to pick up and leaf through," Diana had explained to Frankie when the shipment arrived. It looked like a place where one could linger on a rainy day, sipping tea and reading, perhaps calling for afternoon scones or a glass of red wine as the fire warmed your toes. A world apart from its former life.

"I had one book the entire time I was here," said Ingrid, looking at the bookshelves wistfully. "A math textbook."

They moved farther into the house.

"And here was Mother Mary Frances's office." It was the room where Frankie had found the ledgers. "And this, this was where Sister Jude examined us." Ingrid stopped abruptly in front of another room. "It feels like only yesterday," she shivered. "I should like to see upstairs. One of those rooms is where you were born, Diana."

"And what about your parents? Did they ever meet Diana? Did you have any brothers and sisters?" Frankie asked gently, as they ascended the stairs.

Ingrid stopped again. "Twin sisters. A brother." Her voice broke on the words, and she shook her head as though to rid herself of the memory. "It was so long ago. I didn't ever go --back. They wouldn't remember me now. That's if they're even still alive."

Frankie had never heard a sadder voice.

"I'm sure they would." Izzy put an arm around her great-grandmother's shoulders. "We can help you look for them if you like. Can't we, Mom?"

"We can certainly try."

They continued along the hallway.

"GG," Izzy said, a thoughtful expression on her face. "You said that most of the girls who came here had to give their babies away. How come you didn't?"

Ingrid's eyes glistened as she looked across at each of them. "I ran away. Escaped. Got a ferryman to take me and my baby to the city." She blinked. "It all sounds rather unbelievable now." Ingrid stopped at a door second from the end. "This. This was it."

Frankie and Diana exchanged glances. This was the room that Diana had decided was to be set aside for honeymooners. It was the nicest bedroom in the house, with a pair of dormer windows that looked out toward the water. They'd decorated it in shades of smoky blue and gray, and converted the room next door into a private en suite, with an enormous bathtub. Izzy, who had been walking slightly ahead of them, turned the handle and threw the door open. "Take a look. We made it beautiful."

Ingrid stepped into the room and turned in a slow circle before sitting down on the edge of the bed. Tears began to trickle from her eyes and Frankie went to comfort her, but Izzy got there first.

"I wanted you to be proud of what we've done," said Diana, putting her hand to her mouth. "But I shouldn't have brought you here. I'm sorry, Mom; it's too much."

"No, no, I'm glad you did." Ingrid gave them a tremulous smile. "I never could have imagined this day. That I'd be here with my daughter, my granddaughter, and great-granddaughter. My family."

Frankie took a breath. Her grandmother was right: These three women, no matter what, were her family. They were what was important; everything else was just noise.

AFTER THEY HAD given Ingrid the full guided tour, Diana and Izzy went to make coffee and Frankie took Ingrid outside. "Izzy will bring it down to the jetty," Diana suggested. "It's not too hot down there yet."

Frankie took her grandmother's arm and led her down toward the water. She saw a tear still glittering in the corner of her eye but didn't comment on it. Ingrid was showing more resilience than she'd imagined possible, and her mind, too, seemed clearer than it had been since Frankie had arrived on the island.

When they had each taken a seat, she risked the question that had been burning in her mind ever since her grandmother had been admitted to hospital. "Grandma, are you able to tell me what happened with Rosalie?" she asked. "Only if you want to though," she added.

Ingrid folded her hands in her lap. "Her daughter— Rosalie called her Jenny—was a very sick baby. She only lived for a few weeks, and the nuns wouldn't tell us what happened to her. It sent Rosalie into a state of complete despair. Depression or a nervous breakdown, I suppose you'd call it. And then her father came to take her home. Just her, not her little boy—Marty. Rosalie talked to me about it all the time when she came to Pacifica." Ingrid wrung her hands, twisting them around and around, making Frankie want to reach out and calm her. "She was fixated on it. I shouldn't have told her."

"Shouldn't have told her what?"

"That Sister Agatha buried something in the gardens, where the nettles grew in summer. I remember nearly tripping over a small mound; Sister Agatha's gardening glove had been left there. It was the same time that Rosalie left Fairmile." She shivered as she spoke. "It was so bitterly cold, there was no reason for anyone to be digging there, unless…unless…"

"Rosalie stopped talking to me about Fairmile, and the baby, after that." A shadow passed across Ingrid's face. "At least I think she did."

"And the nettles—the ones in the nun's room?" Frankie asked.

Ingrid looked suddenly guilty. "Rosalie asked if Diana could bring some when she brought flowers for me."

So Diana had been the one to bring them to the

nursing home. Frankie wished she'd simply asked her
mom directly, it would have saved a lot of time and
needless worry.

"It was an odd request, but Rosalie often behaved
strangely. I thought perhaps it might be a small comfort to have something that had grown there... But
after what happened to the nun, I became frightened.
I couldn't believe she would have done such a thing,
though; I kept telling myself it must have been someone else."

Ingrid put a shaking hand to smooth back a wisp
of hair from her face and Frankie resisted the urge to
step in and help her.

"Then, just last week, I saw Rosalie with Sister Agatha's cigarette case. We argued, I think. It's all a bit
hazy now." Ingrid slumped against the chair, the effort
of telling, of remembering, exhausting her.

"What did this case look like, do you remember?"

She sighed, and then continued. "Sister Jude had a tin
with a swan on it and Sister Agatha's was a crane. They
were quite fancy, such strange things for nuns to own,
though of course nearly everyone smoked in those days."

"I didn't think nuns were allowed possessions,"
Frankie said.

"Well, the ones at Fairmile were."

"Are you sure Sister Agatha's was a crane, not a
swan?" Frankie held up the case with the swan design. It had been returned to them once the police had
finished with it.

"Absolutely. The swan case belonged to Sister Jude.
Where did you get that?"

"It's okay, Grandma," Frankie reassured her. "Sister Jude lent it to me," she lied.

There was absolutely no point in telling Ingrid that this was the case that had been found with the remains, that Ingrid had been mistaken in thinking it was Sister Agatha who buried the tiny body all those years ago.

FORTY-SIX

Seattle, 1955

THE APPLAUSE GREW until it filled the auditorium, bouncing off the walls and roof and the little girl sitting in the third row put her hands over her ears, dislodging the bright blue ribbons in her hair, and scrunched up her face until her button nose almost disappeared between her cheeks.

"Diana." Virginia leaned over and pointed to the stage in front of them. "There's Momma."

"Where? I can't see." The little girl dropped her hands and sat up in her seat, peering over the heads of the people in the row ahead. "I still can't see."

Virginia lifted her to her feet, standing her on the chair and keeping both hands around her waist to hold her steady. "Is that better?"

Diana nodded and began to wave. "Why's she dressed so funny?"

"Remember—your momma's graduating today. She's going to be a teacher."

Ingrid had stayed that first month, and then another. Then one day, Virginia told her about a night school for women run by the university, organizing the necessary documentation without a question. "If there's one thing I can't bear, it's seeing a good female mind go to waste," she had said, holding out the enrollment paperwork.

It hadn't been easy and there had been many times when Ingrid thought she might quit, when she mourned for her former life and missed her family until it hurt, but now, as she looked out on the assembled crowd and saw her daughter and the woman who had been there exactly when she needed it the most, she began to believe in her good fortune. A bright future beckoned.

FORTY-SEVEN

Puget Sound, 2013

FRANKIE DECIDED ON the path that led to the highest point on the island, which was at least a four-hour round trip. It had finally stopped raining, the air was newly rinsed, and a blue sky was appearing from among the clouds. Izzy had surprised her by agreeing to come along. "Though I'm not sure about being seen with you wearing those socks, Mom," she said before they set out.

"But they're cool—Molly wears them." Frankie looked down at her legs.

"They're so *not cool*, Mom." Izzy rolled her eyes, amused.

"Well, I don't care. They're practical anyway."

Outwardly at least, Izzy seemed to have bounced back from her ordeal, though she did seem to want to stick closer to Diana and Frankie these days.

It was only as they reached the top, thighs burning from the steep climb, both dusty and sweating, that Frankie remembered the last time she'd been there— with Joe. Who had helped her look for Izzy even when he had a busy bar to run. And whom she really should get in touch with.

She stood at the summit, hands on her hips, and caught her breath. She'd been so focused on finding

Izzy that she'd barely taken in the view the last time she was here. Below them was a carpet of dark green pines and then the deep, unfathomably blue water. Tiny whitecaps told her that there was an ocean breeze, but where they stood, the air was still. Somewhere to the west was Fairmile, to the east was Pacifica Gardens, and she could just make out the marina at Huntley's Point, the masts of the yachts berthed there like tiny white needles.

"It's beautiful, isn't it Mom?" Izzy had retrieved her camera from her backpack and was clicking away, pausing every now and then to check the shots she'd taken.

Perspective. That's what had brought Frankie to this place.

"The island feels tiny. And we're nothing but dots on it. Like sugar sprinkles on a cupcake."

Izzy's voice returned Frankie to the present. "It's not a bad thing to feel like that," she replied with a smile. "Sometimes it helps you work out what's important, and what can be let go of."

"Yeah, I guess. But it can make you feel so insignificant; that you don't matter."

Frankie turned to her daughter. "Oh God, Izzy, you matter—to so many people." She was horrified to think that her daughter felt like this. "Would you like to speak to anyone about what happened? A counselor?"

"Chill, Mom, I'm fine." She reached into her backpack. "Water?" she asked, holding out her bottle.

"Thanks. I already finished mine." Frankie took it from her, touched that she had noticed. Izzy's comment about insignificance had set off the spark of an idea. She would need to speak to Diana about it first though.

Izzy inclined her head. "Can we go out for pizza tonight, do you think?" she asked.

"Granny has her book club," said Frankie.

"That's okay. I'd like it if it was just the two of us."

"It's a date." Frankie grinned at her red-faced daughter. "Now should we head home before we fry to a crisp?" She made to walk back down the trail.

"Mom?"

"Yes?" Frankie turned to see Izzy holding out a tube of sunscreen.

"PEPPERONI?" FRANKIE LOOKED up from the menu at her daughter. Izzy had dyed her hair fully purple that afternoon, and Frankie still hadn't got used to it.

"Is there any other kind?"

The girlish grin was still there, a brief flash that Frankie caught as Izzy bent down to stroke Scruff, whom she had insisted on bringing with them.

They'd snagged the last outside table at a heaving Cabbage Shed. Frankie had been on edge ever since they had arrived, wondering what she might say to Joe when she saw him. So far, however, there hadn't been any sign of him. Molly had said he'd left town for a few days, so she told herself he was probably still away. She tried not to wonder where he might have gone. It seemed unusual that he should be away on one of the island's busiest weekends.

Izzy took a sip of her drink. "What about if we made a garden?"

"You mean for the baby that was buried?" The exact same thing had been on Frankie's mind since their hike that morning.

"Yeah. That would be cool, don't you think?" Izzy twirled her straw. "But we don't have a name. A garden that is *for* someone should have a name."

"It turns out that the baby did have a name," Frankie said. "Her mother called her Jenny."

Frankie's eyes followed a couple as they made their way to a table, and as she recognized Emma, the carer from the nursing home, something surfaced from her memory, clicking into place.

"Oh hey!" Izzy brightened and Frankie looked up to see Joe. Here, in front of her, large as life. It was like finding the surprise toy in the Cracker Jack box when you were least expecting it.

"Nice to see you," Frankie managed.

"You too." His smile was the same, but Frankie sensed that he was holding something back. "How've you been?"

Frankie shrugged. "Oh, you know…" She was lost for words. "Busy." It was no excuse for not calling him and she knew it, but he had the grace not to remind her. "I didn't get the chance to thank you," she said. "For all you did…"

"Anyone would have done the same." He picked up an empty glass. "Fairmile must be nearly ready, right?"

"Soft opening in two weeks, according to Mom. Staff training is next week, the website's live, and we're already fielding inquiries."

"Sounds promising."

"I hope so."

"Okay then, see you around."

"Yeah, see you, Joe."

"Stay out of trouble there, Izzy," he said with a wink.

"Oh, Mom, he *likes* you," said Izzy when Joe had ambled out of earshot.

"Oh stop it."

"And you *like* him," said Izzy, grinning.

"That's what I'm worried about."

FORTY-EIGHT

Puget Sound, 2013

IT WAS THE worst possible time to break down. Rain, which had been a faint drizzle when Frankie left Fairmile, now poured from above, thrown at her windshield by the bucketful and making visibility almost impossible. The truck had sputtered to a stop on a narrow back road about a mile or so from Huntley's Point and she'd managed to steer it partially off the road before it died on her. She was supposed to be collecting a few last-minute things for Fairmile, including a plaque that Diana had ordered, which was waiting for her at the post office in town, and she was wearing thin-strapped sandals that definitely weren't up to the walk into town in such conditions. She pulled out her phone and called the auto shop, asking if they could send a tow truck. The guy on the end of the line said they'd try to get someone out to her in an hour, but he couldn't make any promises. Frankie said—in the sweetest voice she could muster—that she hoped they'd be there soon.

She hung up with a sigh and turned on her four-way flashers, riffling in the glove compartment where she found a tube of cherry Life Savers. She popped one in her mouth and settled back to wait, cocooned by the falling rain, not as agitated by the delay as she might once have been. Perhaps she was finally learning to chill out.

After an hour and a half, she had finished the entire pack of Life Savers and was on the point of calling the auto shop again in order to put a rocket up their asses, when a truck came swishing past, sending dirty water in an arc across the side of her vehicle. She watched as it braked, stopped, and then reversed back toward her.

"Oh Christ," she swore, recognizing Joe's truck. Frankie hated feeling helpless, and it was becoming far too common an occurrence where he was concerned.

He stopped next to her and wound down his window. She did the same.

"Need a hand?" he asked, regarding her with amusement.

"I don't need rescuing."

"You think?"

She explained that the auto shop's towing trailer was on its way. "It was only in there last month, a spark plug on the fritz. They were supposed to have fixed it."

"Hope you're not in a hurry," he said. "They're not exactly the most reliable; it's not like they have much competition on the island."

"So I'm learning."

"Why don't you hop in, and I'll drop you in town— I'm on my way there."

"Okay," she said grudgingly, pulling her jacket over her head as she made the dash to the passenger seat of his truck.

"Anyone ever tell you that you smell like cherries?" he asked, as she fastened her seat belt.

"Life Savers. Sorry, I was waiting so long, I ate

them all. Would've kept some if I'd known a knight on a white charger was on his way," she grinned.

"Well now I might need to reconsider," he teased, starting the engine.

The radio was playing a soulful tune and as they drove along the air felt suddenly electric. Frankie indulged herself in a small fantasy that they were on their way to remote cabin in the woods, one with a king-size bed and a fire already lit…a smile tilted her lips.

"Thinking about something good?" He shot her a look that was a mix of wry amusement and something deeper, something unsettling.

It was just as well he wasn't a mind reader.

She turned to face him. The time for being coy was over. "I'm sorry, Joe. I meant to get back to you, about the date, then everything with Izzy…"

"Your daughter was kidnapped; I'd say that lets you off the hook." There was a smile in his voice.

"And then you were away…" She was trying so hard not to be curious.

"Portland."

That was where his ex-wife and son lived.

"Nat's birthday."

"Nat?"

He gave her a look that said he knew what she was trying to figure out. "My son."

"Of course. Any chance of a rain check?" She grimaced. "Terrible pun."

They reached a flooded stretch of road and he pulled over.

"Is there another way into town?" she asked, despite knowing full well that there wasn't.

"Apology accepted." He reached toward her and

lifted a loose strand of hair from her face, tucked it behind her ear, cupped her chin in his hand.

"Okay," she said, feeling suddenly breathless.

He leaned in and touched his lips to hers, slowly, gently, feather-light, with none of the desperate urgency of the first time. It was even better than she remembered, and she let herself sink into the feeling, becoming oblivious to anything but the softness of his mouth on hers.

"Is this such a good idea?" she asked eventually, pulling away. "I should warn you that it might go horribly wrong. I don't exactly have a great track record when it comes to relationships."

"Well, I'd say that's up to you, Frankie," he said taking her hand and threading his fingers through hers. "We can take it minute by minute if you like."

He was right. It was a decision, or a series of decisions. To decide to be happy, to take the leap and trust that she would be caught. It really wasn't that complicated. "Sounds like a plan." She gave him a smile that cost no effort at all, a grin that made her feel light and free.

"Now, about that date...?" His eyes shone.

"Oh yeah?"

"I happen to know a cozy little bar, not too far away."

"I hear the beer's cold, and the owner is somewhat hot," she said.

He laughed, a loud sound in the cabin of the truck. Reluctantly, he released her hand and swung the truck back onto the road.

"Are you sure?" Frankie asked, looking doubtfully at the flooded way ahead.

"Yeah. It never gets that deep here," he said, plowing through the water with practiced ease.

"THANK GOD IT'S finally stopped," Diana said, peering out through the kitchen window. Raindrops glittered from the leaves of the newly planted shrubs, and everything had begun to gently steam in the rising heat. She fanned herself with a tea towel. "I can't believe I'm at the age where I appreciate a cooling breeze."

"Would you like me to cut up these sandwiches?" Izzy offered, as Frankie laid thin slices of ham across slices bread that had been buttered and spread out on the counter. Pitchers garnished with mint and lemon slices stood waiting to be filled, and Diana had made shortcakes that she was about to fill with whipped cream and raspberries.

"Thank you, Iz." Frankie paused in what she was doing and watched her mother dither by the window. "Isn't it time to go and fetch Grandma?" she asked.

"We won't be late," Diana replied.

"I know, but…"

"Everyone is arriving at three. There's plenty of time."

Ingrid was coming, Molly and Scott, Joe, a handful of Diana's friends, the president of the island's chamber of commerce, a reporter from the island radio station, the town's self-appointed PR busybody…

It was a small gathering, to launch The Fairmile Inn and declare it open for business, and to celebrate a historic house that had been brought back to life.

But there was another reason that Frankie and Diana had wanted everyone to gather near the white-painted gazebo that stood beyond the boatsheds. Only they (and Molly and the plumbers) knew that it was the spot where the tiny skeleton had been found.

The bones had been released by the medical examiner a week before, and Molly, Scott, Frankie, and Diana had been the only mourners at a brief committal service on the island's church. Liam had been released on bail, but remained in the city, and Rosalie was, most unfortunately, too sick to travel.

Over the previous week, Izzy and Frankie had worked to make the garden that surrounded it appear as though it had been there for years. It would be called Jenny's Garden, and they would offer afternoon picnics on the lawns and in the gazebo. Tucked a short distance away, in a stand of pines that bordered the garden, a small brass plaque had been fixed to the trunk of one of the trees as a remembrance of a pitifully short life.

People began to arrive on the dot of three, and Frankie was relieved to see her mother pull up with Ingrid beside her. She went to the bathroom and straightened her shirt, checking her hair in the mirror. "Come *on*, Mom," Izzy called from downstairs. "Everyone's here."

"Okay," she said, and went out into the sunshine.

Later, as people had started to drift back to their vehicles, she caught up with Molly.

"I've got a name for you," said Frankie.

"A name?"

"Emma Riley. A young care assistant at Pacifica Gardens. I think you'll find that she was in league with Alan Bloom, passing on pills to him. That could also be how the local kids got their highs." She thought of the memorial by the bridge.

"Okay." Molly blinked in surprise.

"I didn't figure it out for a while, but the first time I met her, the morning that Sister Agatha's body was found, there was something odd about her."

"What?"

"She was terrified. Not upset, not worried, not sad… all emotions I would expect, but no, she was scared out of her wits. There was no reason for her to be like that, unless she somehow knew more than she was letting on. I found photos of the two of them together on her Instagram feed. They looked much closer than you'd expect former colleagues to be."

"Got it. And Frankie? Thank you."

"You're welcome. Nice to know I haven't completely lost my touch."

"No one ever said you had."

* * * * *

ACKNOWLEDGMENTS

BETWEEN 1945 AND 1973 one-and-a-half million babies were given up for adoption in the United States.

After the Second World War, young men and women had greater freedom than ever before, and, for the first time, access to private spaces in the form of automobiles. Many girls were kept in the dark about the basics of reproduction; sex education was almost nonexistent. Abortion was illegal, expensive, and dangerous. Contraception, for unmarried females, was almost impossible to obtain.

Girls—especially white girls—who became pregnant were shamed by their families and society, were sent away under a false pretext, given almost no support, and many were coerced into giving up their babies within a few weeks of birthing them. Their names were often left off birth certificates or removed and replaced with the name of the adoptive parents.

These babies were not generally, as is so often assumed, unwanted. These young mothers had no way of being able to keep them, no way of earning a living while looking after a baby, and no way of repaying the bills that would be charged to them if they did not relinquish their babies.

The psychological damage they suffered was immense and lasted the rest of their lives.

Much has been written about the effect of adoption

on adopted children, but less about the women who had to give away their babies, along with all hope of ever seeing them again.

Women's reproductive rights are under greater threat than ever, and it's important to look back to a time (not so very long ago) when sex education, access to birth control and safe abortion was extremely limited, when homes for "fallen women" existed in almost every major US city (and in the United Kingdom, Ireland, and Australia too), and to remember the devastating effect and lasting trauma of such restrictions.

When I first began to research this book, I came across Ann Fessler's moving documentary, and her book *The Girls Who Went Away*, published in 2006. Hearing of the young women's experiences and the trauma they suffered informed the writing of this story.

Orcades Island is an imagined place in Puget Sound, as is the home at Fairmile, but it is based on real-life mother and baby homes that operated at the time. What the girls experience in this story, right down to having to take assumed names, is also faithful to the times. Fiction is about what is possible, not what is actual; my imagining of the events is exactly that—an imagining and not based on an actual event. All incidents and dialogue and all characters are products of my imagination and are not to be construed as real. Any resemblance to persons living or dead is entirely coincidental.

A big thank you to my Australian editor, Rebecca Saunders, who is so understanding and supportive of my writing and who always pushes me to be a better writer, and to my agent, Jill Marsal, who among other helpful things, helped me strengthen the contemporary sleuthing storyline until it was far better than I originally imagined it. To Charlotte Mursell at Orion in the UK, for her continued enthusiasm for my writing, and also to Luisa Cruz Smith at Scarlet in the US for her love of this story, and for making sure that in writing something set in the USA I did not commit too many cultural and social crimes in regard to the narrative. I am incredibly fortunate to have four such smart and savvy women in my corner, and live in fear of disappointing them.

Thank you also to Bronwyn, Helen, Jesse, Lisa, Michelle, and Siboney, the most delightful, kind, hilarious, and cheering group of writer friends I could hope to have.

And thanks, always, to Andy, for your careful first reading and calm reassurance that it really will be okay in the end.

Finally, to every reader who's picked up a copy of one of my books, who has messaged me, recommended it to their book clubs, joined me at events, and told their friends how much they've enjoyed my work, and to every book blogger and reviewer who shares their love of books and reading, thank you for making it possible for me to continue to dream up more stories and create new characters. It is the greatest privilege.